ALSO BY ZANE KOTKER

Bodies in Motion

A Certain Man

A
Certain
Man

ZANE KOTKER

Alfred A. Knopf   New York   1976

THIS IS A BORZOI BOOK
PUBLISHED BY ALFRED A. KNOPF, INC.

*Parts of this novel were written with the support of a grant
from the National Endowment for the Arts.*

Library of Congress Cataloging in Publication Data

Kotker, Zane.
A certain man.

I.   Title.
PZ4.K869ce   [PS3561.0845]   813'.5'4   76–26162
ISBN 0–394–40262–6

Manufactured in the United States of America

FIRST EDITION

For Edward,
who lies among the generations,
and for Jean

Speak to me, dead man! That I may speak for you.

CONTENTS

A Certain Man

I

Thanksgiving, 1909

THEIR VOICES circled above him like a whirlwind, faster and faster until the gathered sound broke through him and into the empty space that belonged to God. He heard them telling their stories in snatches at holiday time, when the words were interrupted by laughter and uncles slapping their thighs, when aunts risked choking on chicken bones to get out the story of how Papa had dug the tunnel to the barn in the blizzard of '88.

"To feed the horses?" Justine his sister asked, concerned.

"No, to get to the outhouse!" Papa replied, laughing, the pumpkin pie splotching his chin like stuffing coming out of a turkey.

"To feed the horses, Justine said. Oh no, Papa said, to get to the outhouse!" By next year the story had grown and when his Great-uncle Win told it to his Grandma Percy they laughed while the coffee steamed up out of their cups and life went on, yes on: *Brightly beams our Father's mercy from His lighthouse evermore.*

Then, hunched over the oak table, the whole house of them, fat and thin but mostly fat, would lean on their elbows and stretch forth their pudgy hands to hold out delicate green glass plates for more apple pie, peach pie, pumpkin pie and someone would tell "How We Killed the Pig," usually his oldest brother, Fred, already grown to be a man. Fred didn't like to kill things so he told the story with a lot of up and down in his voice, as if to get it over with and into the open, out of the dark where maggots grew. It began in the orchard with a big cauldron of scalding

3

water and it went on a day and a night. It went on while Mama simmered lard, while Fred and his red-haired brother and sister, Sam and Maud, stuffed sausage meat into what looked like old stockings 'til past the time when hunks of meat were hung down the well to cool or up on hooks in the cold room. It ended when Mama cooked bacon the next morning and by the smell of it. Except usually somebody, when Fred forgot to, would digress with the story of long ago "Somebody Else's Pig." You see, somebody else's neighbor boy wanted to find what was at the end of a long plank his pig would walk, so he followed the plank to the trap, which hurled him two-legged into a scalding pool. Fred would finish off "Pig" fast, amid shrieks and laughter, even then; and they would crook their arms and hold out their coffee cups for more coffee and the steam misted up the silver coffee pot and the music came, not real music, not the kind of music other people knew, but Arley's own music, knowing, remembering, being.

Fred never told the other story "Birds" there in the dining room with the oak table that stood on the oak floor laid down by Mama's papa on granite foundations stingier than those their own papa would have laid. So wide, so strong were their papa's cellar walls that Mama always said, "You keep laying foundations like that and we'll be poor forever." At least, that is the way it was told at church socials, where considerable talk was spent on what a good Christian his papa, Joseph Minor, was, who built on solid rock. No, Fred never told "Birds" here within the bunch of them with their elbows and plates; he saved that for private walks with Arley. Then he would say, once, *Once*, and Arley would repeat the story inside himself, word for word, watching it as it came out of Fred's memory and into the open between them—for what is the world but spirit? And so it would begin, *Once*.

"Once when I was fourteen I set out to Grandma's in the wagon to pick up Mama and when I was unhitching the horses up by the back wall, around comes the hired man and he hands me a gun and he says, 'Got too many birds here, Fred. You shoot some, I'm too busy.' " So Fred had taken the gun, standing almost in the very spot he got it, at the corner of the stone wall, the northwest corner—because Fred was very exact; exactness saved Fred from something which Arley did not yet know. Fred had stood there spreading his feet for a good stand, had leaned back and aimed up at the willow tree full of blackbirds, had shot with scatter until birds began to fall out of the tree, hunks of birds, black lumps falling already dead, no longer birds by the time they reached his feet.

Is that when you said it, Fred?

"I said then I'll never shoot anything again." And he never shot anything again.

Sometimes his second brother, Sam the red-haired one, would tell his story "The Bird" at the oak table but that was a public story of speed flying, talons at a forehead, a boy falling.

"Knocked off his feet by a bird!" The whoops of laughter then, as they trimmed the Christmas tree in the cold living room where Mama's papa had stored the gear for the stables, the gear that was in the cellar now. Everything, you see, was lodged somewhere in the house, and the great glass eye of it was his eye, Arley's eye. He was a boy who, as the last and smallest child, had named himself. His every utterance, or any heard above the melee, was preserved in one form or another, to be used, in mockery if nothing else, even his mispronunciation of his own name, Charles.

It was always amidst plenty that Joseph, his father, told his stories of "I Was Poor," usually when the fat of his favorite fatback-and-meat drippings was popping its spit on the stove, or after the mortgage checks had been lifted carefully from envelopes, or sometimes when Arley was staring at a roasted chicken with a crust so thick a person really had to use his front teeth to get it apart. Then the fat man with the gold chain that crossed his round belly low in summer after the planting and reaping and high in spring after a winter of sitting would tell how as a boy he.

As a boy I.

"The first year after my pa died, we didn't ever get the wood cut," Joseph the father would begin, spooning fatback into his fluted plate. "Pa hadn't cut enough—too sick, it came on too fast. Sometimes he just kept on doing the same task—not knowing it was done, saying to Ma."

Ma. This was long ago, beyond the memory of the boy Arley, having taken place in the quiet around the kitchen table of an old farmhouse out in Southlee. But such was the power of their stories that things not seen could be known and never lost.

Joseph Minor the Christian gentleman repeating scenes did not bother to describe that kitchen table to his children at his own more ample board, assuming that they shared his memories; that they, too, had lain with him among his brothers in a low room off the kitchen where they listened to the breathing of the stove and of their parents, who sat within the glow of a lamp. His father's voice a sharp sound that matched a bony face, a thin sound not yet small enough to enter the ground, but growing smaller.

"It shifts when I look at things: the boys' faces—themselves one minute, and the next, ever so slightly changed. As if they are not themselves anymore. What do you think, Ma?" But her reply the boys could never hear from their bedroom; a plump woman's voice, soft, lost in rotundity and kindness.

"Before the year rounds out of winter," the sharp voice said, "by the time the land softens and rain presses in the seeds, I will be there, too, planted in the ground. Who am I to outlive the Lord? Choose someone else, I am a modest man." Had his pa really said those words? Whitehaired in his forty-sixth year, Joseph Minor examining the fatback on his plate could not remember for sure but knew the memory to be like a dream, very true, and, like a dream, not true at all. Then the headaches and the anger. The old fear coming back to his pa, they had said, but what had the old fear been? "I'm not sure," Ma had replied. "He would say that when he looked at the eyes of the cows in the barn, he was not sure which of them owned the eyes, him or the cows, not sure where each began and ended and then it was as if his own body had soaked into the walls of the barn and the barn into himself. . . ."

"Get out! Get down out of there!" His pa's dark beard moving on the narrow jawbone and Joseph Minor the boy in the barn's forbidden hayloft, shrinking as the shadow of his father with its screaming voice fell toward him on the wall and became silent.

"It was not your fault," his mother had reminded him, gently, in the evenings after they had pushed the box into the earth. The face of his pa in the woolen gown in the long box in the parlor had turned darker and darker while they waited for the relatives to come. They were quite a while coming and Joseph began to wonder if his own dear pa had been a colored man. When all the uncles had finally arrived, they carried the box out through the special wide door of the farmhouse parlor to put it on the wagon. So that was why the door was so wide! They had walked to the cemetery behind the wagon with some of the brethren from the church who had joined them saying how young and unexpectedly he died, how like Mr. Lincoln, the two of them dying in the same year. And Joseph vowed to grow up fat.

"Papa?"

"Joseph? You were talking about being poor?"

"Ah, yes, Polly, yes, so I was." The fatback was gone from his plate and Joseph examined his listeners and took another helping. "I had no shoes that year, and so I stood in the warm places where the cow had lain when I milked her." He had expected the relatives to bring wings for the man in the box. Did they hook in under the sockets of bone? In the picture at the front of their Bible, our Lord walked on air surrounded by angels that flew above the gravestones, flapping wings. Wings seemed essential.

Thirty three years, six months, and fifteen days, his ma had inked slowly into the line in the Bible beside his pa's name. As a boy he had waited trustfully for the stone to roll away, had appeared in the cemetery on the afternoon of the third and appropriate day to wait and watch, but had left full of suspicion at dusk beneath a light snow. Perhaps the rising must be done in the spring when the earth is soft and the air warm?

Or perhaps it is not done in the spring when the earth? It was Ma read to them now every night from the Bible: "CALL NO MAN YOUR FATHER UPON THE EARTH; FOR ONE IS YOUR FATHER, WHICH IS IN HEAVEN." For the second time Joseph had finished feeding himself the fatback from the fluted plate and for the second time there was a silence around him.

Papa was telling the story "No Shoes" over again—to himself, perhaps? Arley could not be sure. Could it be that Papa was remembering a story that had never been told? Was there such a story? And where does a story stay when no one tells it? The shadow of the fear touched Arley's hands.

ARLEY RAN HOME FROM SCHOOL, worried lest he be separated from the household activity that produced the Great Holiday. Last year and in the years before, he had lived at the core of such preparations, but this year, finally gone to school, he felt separated from it. It was essential that he see all the acts take place, so that he might seize them from their time of happening at stove or table and press them flat behind his eyes among the flickering shapes that could be brought to life whenever he wished, forever, never lost. That was the power stronger than the sword of kings, invisible, unrusting.

He ran down the street from school, away from the direction in which the cemetery lay, toward the four corners at the center of town, where his house stood. Past the lilac bush whose season lay secretly within, down the lawn, up the steps of the back porch and into the house.

"Charles!" Only his mother called him by his Christian name. She was pouring him a glass of milk.

"I didn't fight today." He came home. He told the world to her.

"Good," she said.

He deserved the milk, he was good after all.

"Drink your milk slowly now, then you may help me get the nuts." He climbed into the chair and rested; it was all falling into place, the holiday; he felt at ease.

"You may go down into the cellar for some Baldwins," she said.

"I can't carry the bag!" He sipped his milk.

"There's a half bag there. You can carry a half bag."

He was afraid of the darkness in the cellar.

"You may leave the door open," she said. "And you may call up to me if you have to."

He opened the door and lit the cellar candle that stood in wax on the little shelf at the top of the stairs. He could not carry the candle down, it would be too hard coming back up with the bag. Besides, it was better to go in total darkness; moving shadows on the earthen walls of the cellar were more terrifying than nothing at all.

"Mama?" he called from the bottom. "Did you say Baldwins or Macs?" He knew it was Baldwins; she made a point of using only their own produce for Thanksgiving and he knew the Macs had come from Grandma Percy's orchard.

"The Baldwins," she called down, her voice a thread to the world upstairs. "You'll find a half-empty bag right in front."

He felt for it, found it, and hoisted it over his shoulders, turning toward what he hoped would be a friendly glow. And it was there, marking the stairway but little else. He did not turn to look behind him; there was evil in the world, its shape changed as quick as water.

Hah. He rose up out of the pit, blowing out the candle as he passed it, and was back in the familiar daylight of the kitchen where she stood.

"Those should fill the barrel in the pantry," she said. "Should bring them right to the top."

In the pantry he noticed with relief that she had already brought up the jars of corn and tomatoes. That part of the cellar was the worst, a storeroom full of jars, cobwebs; and fear of the shutting door.

"Now," she said, "we'll go upstairs for the nuts." She led the way up the back stairs and past his small bedroom and through the large bedroom they still called Fred and Sam's though Sam had left it. When she opened the door to the attic stairway and they started up, the smell from above enveloped him in age, as if the nuts lying scattered on the floorboards had opened and wrapped him in their secret processes poised at the exact point between ripening and decay. His mother knelt and began to collect the driest walnuts in her apron while Arley stooped and stuffed others into his pockets. The warmth from the chimney, to his left, had dried the pumpkin seeds in their baskets. He would plant them for her next spring behind the house and pick pumpkins next fall to store in the cold room, where sausages hung. He could stay here forever. When her apron was full, they walked downstairs single file and dumped their walnuts into a box in the pantry.

"You want to get the potatoes?" she asked as she prepared to bake.

"I'd better do the wood." He excused himself, happy to see the woodbox by the stove half empty. If he took long enough with the wood, Justine would be home from school and could help with the potatoes. Even if she bossed him around or called him stupid, it would be worth it. The dark bins were under the barn and he could hold the bin door open while she foraged below. Or maybe she would make him forage while she held. You had to keep the door open because the Minor barn was so different from other barns.

"I'll do the wood," he repeated. Now that Mama was starting to make the pumpkin pie she might even forget the potatoes. He could taste the pie finished, sitting on the table, luscious with steam. He watched her a while, sitting by the woodbox. He must know exactly how the pie got there tomorrow when they sat together with the harvest gathered in. They would all joke with him and try to tickle him. Sam would come back from being married these last three weeks and bring Catherine. Maud would come back from living down past Southlee with the husband she had had all summer. Fred would bring his girl friend Georgia and that would make how many? Arley counted first the left hand's fingers, then the right's: ten. Every one of them was bigger than he. His far-off parents stood the highest and the farthest; then came Fred and Sam and Maud, who looked down at him from midway points; then came Justine and finally himself. There was, of course, the hole that separated the two younger children from the older three. That was Elizabeth, the dead, the hole through which both he and Justine must pass on their way up. Taller yet than his parents stood Jesus and, so high he was out of sight, God, whose everlasting arms circled the sky and the green earth and all of the Minor family. Arley felt pretty safe, after all; if only Papa. He drew in a long breath.

"Here comes Justine, now," his mother said. "Don't forget about the potatoes."

You cannot touch the fear, it touches you.

Before he'd gone to school it had been Justine and Mama laughing by the stove, Justine and Mama climbing up the stairs together, Mama kissing Justine good-bye before school. But after Justine had gone out the door with her brown curls bouncing on her shoulders, each curl having been wrapped around Mama's finger with the pearl-handled brush, or sometimes while Justine was still walking up the path, Mama would turn to him and everything would be fine. And on Wednesdays, he had always had Mama completely to himself on the ride to Grandma Percy's.

Up at daybreak, out of the house right after breakfast, Mama knowing he was afraid of Prince; but telling him anyway how to handle a horse. In case he should ever lose his fear, should ever grow up out of her domain into the world of giants and of presidents, where men were alone with each other.

"If I want him to come into the homestretch fast," she would point out, not forgetting she had said the same thing the week before, but telling him each week, like prayers, "if I want him to come into the homestretch fast, I let him out slow."

He held on to the side of the wagon, shutting his eyes and seeing again the time when no one was in the wagon with him and the horses began to trot, hearing again the scream, his own. The power sometimes worked against you.

"I hold him back," she repeated, sitting straight in the wagon, her slender hands grasping the reins with the same authority they imposed upon lima beans served from a casserole. "I keep him in." Prince's hooves thudded on the dirt of the road, up the hill, onto the main road; once out on level ground, the horse strained to go faster, but she held him. She held and Prince accepted it, settling into a pace that matched the delicate control of her fingers. Arley found he had been holding his breath but he let go now. They passed the town hall where Papa was writing up wills, passed the street where Justine sat in school at her lessons, the drug store where he took his penny Monday mornings and Rhodes Academy where Fred and Sam had learned their Latin and their Greek.

"Then I let him out a little," Mama explained as they pulled beyond Rhodes toward the open stretch, where the houses grew farther apart. They talked little but enjoyed the ride through reddening leaves; the gait of the horse was soothing now and Mama held the reins more loosely. She would not dare race here on the road as she had done in "Didn't We Have Fun?" With her first three babies crouching low in back, she had stayed late at the trotters' and raced the circle of track despite her promise to Papa. "I'll get scolded tonight, but Didn't We, Didn't We?" Since Mama kept things from Papa, Arley could tell her anything. Soon now he would begin to look for the house of Grandma Minor on the right of the road, small, white, rambling backward into a hollow.

"There it is," he would call, breaking the silence and pointing to his dead grandmother's house. It was the house where Papa had lived when he was Arley's age.

"Half an hour," Mama would announce, reporting on the progress of the journey to his living grandmother's house. She kept the horse steady.

How could he already be hungry? It didn't seem fair. He let go of the side of the wagon and jounced when it jounced, feeling settled into his seat by the half-hour of motion. Now came farmland between the towns, orchards with the smell of the apples so strong he feared Prince might bolt for them. But that had never happened, not with Mama. "Hold on!" Sam had shouted from the barn door that other time, but Arley had let go, his fingers undoing in a slow roll-out against the pressure of the reins he had been holding.

Over Percy Brook, named for someone in Mama's family. And into the next town, where the pace picked up. It was here in

Shiloh that people began to wave to Mama as she rode through at a pace faster than most women drove. She was the daughter and the only child of a man who sold horses. He had built the stables that had once stood on the great lawn in front of their house, adjacent to both churches. He, of course, had been a Congregationalist and would not have sat in the Methodist church, but it was fine for the horses of the Methodists and Congregationalists to stand together under cover during the winter services.

"Mornin'!" Mostly men waved to Mama and she returned a salute of the hand and sometimes called out and sometimes smiled. Arley would wave back, "Mornin'!" When the houses grew closer together they would pass the schoolhouse where his sister Maud taught before she married Ted. Both Arley and Mama would peer through the doorway to see if they could catch a glimpse of Maud but, if not, they would be seeing her at Grandma's in the afternoon. Next came the First Methodist Church of Shiloh, which Maud attended so often. Arley had not understood why they questioned her about it. "Been to church today?" Sam would ask four or five times whenever Maud came home. "Anything new on sin?"

"An hour," Mama would say and they kept on through Shiloh with the sun rising higher in the sky and the sky growing bluer and Arley feeling warmer and warmer. They didn't stop at the store in Shiloh for candy.

"Too many sweets," his mother said. "When we get home you can have a ginger cookie." You did not disobey Mama, she would think less of you.

Finally, at the white house with the green-roofed well, they turned left onto the Chester Turnpike. Now they were trailing dust on a road running through trees. Arley could hear the sound of the brook to the left, and birds. Here there was no one to wave, except occasional children, to whom Arley would call from the wagon. Sometimes, standing but hanging on, he rested himself from sitting: Mama stood up in the wagon on this road, too, to get the cricks out of her legs, and they sailed up the slow hill with the horse breathing steadily before them.

"An hour and a half," Mama would point out when they came

to the place in the road where a hill and a sharp path angled off. On then to Percyville, a section of Shiloh, and when they finally emerged through the archway of trees into another open plateau, people would start to wave again, sometimes relatives of Grandma Percy's, and Arley's hand would automatically seek the edge of the wagon.

"And then I give him his head," Mama would pronounce and Prince would gallop through what Mama called the homestretch, his head held high and his mane flying, and they would pull to a splendid stop by the stone wall that squared off Grandma Percy's farm from other farms.

"It's Phoebe." Grandma Percy would call from the door, where she had been standing, weakened by the walk down the long stairs from her bedroom. "Morning!"

"Two hours, I'd say," Mama would conclude as she unhitched Prince from the wagon and patted him. Arley hated the ride to end, for then Mama would belong to Grandma Percy. But he would have her to himself again on the ride home and on Thursday and Friday after Justine had gone to school, and, in a way, on Sunday.

On Sundays, he leaned against Mama in the pew, sleepy. The Reverend Mr. Tiding finished shouting, red-faced; he was the only man Arley had ever known to shout at Papa. Then an even older man stood up. The piano began to play. Arley shut his eyes.

"*I come to the gar-den a-lo-o-one,*" began Mr. Hershey with a high, thin voice sinking in air too heavy to hold it up without damage.

"*When the dew*" . . . fading out . . . "*the ro-ses,*

"*And the voice . . . hear . . . falling . . . my ear*

"*The son of God dis-clo-o-ses.*"

Mr. Hershey was picking up steam. Arley opened his eyes to watch him sway in the choir loft.

"*And,*" a high note set in the air as a separate and triumphant entity.

"*He walks with me and he talks with me*

"*And he tells me I am his own.*"

A reedy quality held, despite all the attempts of the strong tenor that still resided somewhere within the withering Mr. Hershey.

"*And the voi-ce I hear*

"*Fall-ing on my ear*"

He was almost deaf, people said.

"*None o-ther,*

"*Has ev-er*

"*Kno-own-nnn.*"

Arley shut his eyes. He felt strangely comforted.

WHENEVER HE WENT OUT RIDING with Papa, there were always sights to be pointed out. Just around the corner we will come to.

I know! But Arley never shouted. Not at Papa. Not at Mama. At school only, fighting. Whenever he stood in the farmyard of his dead grandma's place, where his father seldom went because it was owned now by an Italian, Arley felt he belonged to the hollow of that land and had a right to the stories there, but he knew he would not hear the ones he wanted. When no one tells a story the parts of it lie waiting at scattered points. By the rock, perhaps?

"This rock." Joseph slapped it. "A giant used to scrape his boots on it, my father told me." No, that was not the kind of story Arley meant. But Joseph Minor had no intention of recalling to his boy how the purple evening had enclosed him here, himself a boy milking in a barn warmed by the bodies and the breath of cows and hoping. If you climb to the center of the birches on the hill, you can look over rolling land that is like the waves of the sea in the engraving of the flood of Noah. From that solitude you can know snakes gliding, insects in their buntings, birds returning, the heartbeat in the ducts of trees. Water seeps beneath you to the lowland, where in summer you can stand unseen in corn above your head and hear it say: I and I have made you; we have made you. The train whistle sears the edge of the field and cars pass with cargo: ice in the ice car; granite, marble and iron in the flat cars; rich men on blue upholstered seats under lamps of colored glass in the dining car. They are riding home to New York after depositing their well-dressed sons at boarding schools. Will Joseph of the needy brothers become Pharaoh of Egypt? Rich enough to ride the train with a signet ring? If so, he vows to show his gratitude to fortune by returning soon to set himself down near the waxy pod that had once split and deposited him. He was born of this land, fatherless.

Except it belonged now to an Italian.

"Come on," Joseph called. Arley followed him back into the wagon, quickly. When your Papa is never wrong, you move fast.

Out walking, too, there were places, times. "This is the kind of day," Papa would say every March as the two of them walked past the pond on the road to the cemetery; "this is the very day," feeling air with his fingertips, testing, "the men would come to cut the ice.

"A few days before Christmas it starts to skim over, and you can cast a stone, see, like this"—Joseph paused to skip a stone on the ice—"to see if it holds or breaks. When it's a foot and a half, the men would come and I helped them saw off the top of the pond in fifty-pound blocks and wheel the blocks into the ice shack where we packed them in sawdust. When the shack was full, we would load the rest into wagons to sell off on the way to town. We saved some for the inn and some for the undertaker, of course."

"Of course!" Arley responded quickly with the expected laugh. He had to get there as soon as they did, not be caught unawares.

"We had, each of us, one new thing for Easter," Papa said every April, usually at the tailor's in Chester in the middle of a long afternoon shopping trip. "One new thing. I would get the shirt and Thaddeus the hat because he was the oldest and Orlando the pants and William the shoes. Next year, though"—Joseph would gesture to the clerk to shorten further the already short pants of Arley's Easter suit and he would take a good breath so he could speed up the sentence beyond recognition—"I would have Thaddeus's hat because I was the second and Orlando would have my shirt and William Orlando's pants and Thaddeus would get the new shoes. You got that, boy?" Joseph turned out of the three-way mirror in which he had found himself well-dressed, red-cheeked and handsome yet, if a bit plump. His town's continually re-elected judge of probate, solid. His boys called him stern. They ought to have known the sternness of the lesson he had had from his father. Standing by the grave on Easter Sunday morning, the boy Joseph had no longer waited for his pa to rise. The possibilities of reaching heaven from a coffin trapped under several feet of earth were smaller than those of sinking through its rotting bottom into the fissures between the rocks and falling to the roaring flames so long, so possessively rehearsed from the Methodist pulpit.

"Papa was much stricter with us than he ever is with you," Fred and Sam would point out to their little brother Arley on the front porch as the nights of summer brought them the disguise of friendly darkness. "He's nothing to be afraid of now." When Arley heard his brothers talk of how Papa used to be, he half wished him that way still, for his brothers had grown strong.

"He said, 'Don't go skating 'til I get back,' but we did and he found out. 'Take your choice,' he said, 'a whipping in the barn or no fall clothes or no Christmas presents.' Three choices!" Fred on the glider still impressed; Sam still laughing.

"I don't believe that story!" Justine would interrupt at the door. She was his favorite.

"You don't know what he was like then!" Maud the older daughter sat by herself on a wicker chair.

Bending closer over the porch furniture so Joseph at his devilish catalogues could not overhear, Fred would continue. "School began, so we said we would take the school clothes and get no Christmas presents. Then Christmas came and we said we would take the whipping. So on Christmas morning he took us out to the barn and whipped us with his leather belt."

"He was a man of his word," Sam would add, like a benediction.

"He had to work, he didn't get to go to school." Fred would
try to explain. Like Mr. Lincoln, Joseph had begun to read law
on his own until his older brother went off to relatives to learn
butchering and left Joseph home as the provider. He stopped
reading and took to the ice trade.

"Remember how Papa got from the ice trade into the funeral
business?" That was always a good one; Arley kept it in reserve
for when the stories slowed down. Joseph had used it to break in
his sons—for one of them must be groomed to take over the
family business that was bringing them into prosperity. How
then did Papa get out of the ice trade?

The fourteen-year-old Joseph drove the horses rapidly, smartly,
hauling ice off at the inn, carrying it in bags on his shoulder into
the big kitchen where he smelled vegetable soup in the pots.
Next, he swung open the big back door of the creamery and
dropped the steaming bags in its ice room. Then he took his
smaller chunks to the cellar door of Willie Peach's house and
down his cellar steps.

"You can put it right in here," the undertaker said, indicating a
large metallic container. Joseph saw that one side of the container
was open and was advancing toward it with his bag when his eyes
registered the presence of a doll-like object the size of a man
within it.

"Here," the undertaker said, raising the lid of the other side of
the compartment so that it blocked the view of the dead body.
"You can dump it right in here," he explained. "New box I got,"
he went on. "First time I've used it."

"Oh," said Joseph, looking toward a corner where old brass ice
containers had been pushed aside.

Waves of nausea registered far below in Joseph's stomach, but
he dumped his ice into the empty compartment, making a hollow, echoing noise until it filled up a bit. There was not enough
ice to reach the top, and Joseph turned, indicating wordlessly
that he would be back with more and hurried up the cellar stairs.
Once outside, he took quick deep breaths of air, feeling his lungs
expand and contract within his chest. He fumbled in the sawdust

and extracted ice to fill his sack, delayed, but finally dragged the sack along the ground. Sixty pounds?

"Come from New York just last night." Mr. Peach was excited and laid a proud hand on his new, improved ice compartment. "Ordered it in June," he explained, "something they started using during the war. . . ."

Swinging the sack up by the slow spiral rise he had perfected, Joseph managed to press its opening against the bin with his hip, and the ice in the free top half of the bag began to spill out wildly. A few chunks fell over the side of the compartment and scattered on the cellar floor. Joseph kept his eye on the peak of ice rising in the center of the bin. With the empty bag in one hand, he spread the ice out evenly with the other.

"I'll show you how to close it," the undertaker offered generously. "You take hold of this brace, and fold it back like this, and down she goes!" The lid came down and Joseph found himself only a few inches from the corpse which lay on the other half of the cooler at about waist level. Stomach level.

"That's handy, Mr. Peach," he said to the undertaker. "Mighty handy gadget." This was no more a man but part of the known, not knowing world. He could know no more than stones know, or rain. He had been an old man. A fringe of fine white hair outlined his head and one of his legs had successfully been guided through a black woolen trouser leg, but only one. Joseph felt the nausea again but far away, very far away. His dead father had been a young man, with full beard and well-developed muscles, though equally emaciated. A fine down of white hair covered the old man's chest; hair grows longer in the grave, they said.

"I was just dressing this remains," the undertaker said. "But it looks like I'm going to have to cut these trousers to get them on!" Joseph saw the jacket of the black suit hanging from the back of one of the cellar steps that must lead to the Peach's kitchen.

"I dropped a little ice," Joseph apologized, trying to look at the floor but noticing a piece of ice on the cooler an inch from the corpse's ear.

"Never mind," the undertaker said. "It'll melt and I wear boots anyway." He indicated his legs in rubber boots. "Cold down here," he said, "damp."

Holding his empty bag, Joseph reached over and carefully picked the ice off the cooler. Mr. Peach smiled at him.

"I'll show you up," he said, and put his arm on Joseph's shoulder.

"Aren't you one of the Minor boys?" he asked as they walked toward the cellar opening.

"Yes," Joseph said. "I'm the second one."

"I hired out to your pa one summer haying," he said. "He treated me good. I thought when I saw you, you looked familiar. It's not that you look like your pa, you take after your mother more."

"We all look like her, she says." Joseph wondered for the first time whether or not it was true.

They reached the base of the stairway to the outdoors and Mr. Peach gave his shoulder a squeeze. "All done with your school?" he asked, as Joseph started up the stairs, holding the empty bag in two hands now.

"Got done in June." He took the stairs sideways, to be polite.

"I could use a fellow like you in my business," Mr. Peach said. "It's a growing field! Come around tomorrow night, if you're interested. Three times the pay for hauling ice, and steady work." Mr. Peach smiled and Joseph found himself, to his surprise, smiling back. It was years, though, before he took up the invitation.

Some stories were not even privately recalled in the big house where Hathaway Street crossed Main; so they waited, as innocent and full of longing as the others. Joseph simply refused to call up the story of the night William Peach had shown him how to embalm. Sitting at the table where his mother-in-law held the baby—as if to say, This is my house you're living in, Joseph Minor—he tried to chew an apple but found himself distinguishing too much between the outer skin and the inner meaty body of the fruit; he spit the half-masticated bite into his napkin. Later, he made Polly sit up in bed, fearful of seeing her horizontal. It culminated the next day at church before the service as he grasped the hand of the deacon in the vestibule only to see him in his mind's eye, horizontally frozen and himself pulling the skin around the deacon's eye halfway to the nose to reveal the red tissue beneath, making the small incision like a puncture in the corner of the eye with his free hand. Inserting the needle-point of the hollow trokar that was connected to the tubing and to a syringe and a raised bag. Pushing the trokar in until it settled. Making an incision at the navel and inserting more tubing. Resting the tubing on the stiff body and pouring the poisonous formaldehyde into the bag that fed the tube that entered the eye. It would push out the blood that would otherwise rot in the veins. Egyptian Supreme—the lifegiver—had flowed into the arteries, making the body harder and loglike. It would keep the exterior white for a few days and prevent smell.

"Keep it going in steady," Willie Peach had advised him. "Hold the bag higher. Better than ice, eh?"

"Good morning." The upright deacon smiled at Joseph, revealing yellowed teeth and reddened gums. "Good to see you here, the two of you."

Sweating, he ushered Polly into his ailing mother's pew, which they used to save money. Looking around the sanctuary he saw everyone lying flat, trokars inserted, having reached the end and goal of life. Jesus in the tomb had been cool and white. Had someone sneaked in to embalm him in the style of Egyptian nobles? To wrap him in white both inside and out? Did only his embalmer know the truth of his death? And by what name was that embalmer called? Joseph? A certain Joseph of Arimathea? The bloody carcass of the preceding hours on the cross had been turned into something quiet and white. Even the Father in Heaven need not have looked upon the broken body of his son as it descended the cross. Only the undertaker need view death, a business arrangement.

Music for the hymn; the congregation that rose toppled one by one as Joseph with his trokar struck them: for all of them the death, for none the resurrection. The Reverend Mr. Tiding, he must see the face of the dead, too, must he not? Another business arrangement. Somewhere between the people and the paid hands of their minister and undertaker stood the deacons. To pass money to the minister for his stories and to the undertaker for his plugging, washing, pumping and stitching. "No, no, Joseph, from the bottom lip up to behind the nose, that's right. That's right, now knot the thread around the front tooth and tuck it in. No pucker in the lips, see?" It was only Joseph of Hathaway and Main who waited at the end of the long road, to meet the dead and escort them to the eternal life.

After the service, once more in the vestibule, he grabbed Polly's hand and said, "Let's run home."

"I can't," she motioned to her swollen body. "The new baby!"

Of course, that's why he was taking the job in the first place: not enough to eat from the farm, not enough money in ice to support his small family, no time to read for law. And what about the unborn baby? He could not strike this one dead; it wasn't even born, it was still safe from him.

IF I SHOULD DIE BEFORE I WAKE, Arley whispered from under the bed covers, pulled tight around his head, I pray the Lord my soul to take. The distant, giant ear was always listening, the fingertips above the clouds were always clutching the millions of threads necessary to reach each soul in the world. Two eyes as brilliant as the sun and moon shone day and night in the face of God that arched the sky, but Arley still pressed his fingers to his right knee. He tightened them three times against the scar where he had as a baby crawled over a burning sparkler. The spirit he had just committed to the Lord must not leak out of him unbidden, must not begin its dark solitary flight into a darker sky unwelcomed. And he must try not to dream about the. It was best not to think about the. He turned in the bed toward the window through which no light came. It was not, however, the dream of the bodiless hand he dreaded that met him as he fell toward sleep. It was something peaceful, for his other self rose in it slightly above the grass and hovered, twisting, full of the power to go wherever he wanted to go just by wanting to go there.

He woke up while it was still dark. What noise? A dog barking? A horse trotting by? No, a pan in the kitchen below his bedroom. Old Simon must be getting things ready for the Thanksgiving meal. Probably he had moved Papa's pot of oatmeal that cooked all night on the rearmost of the black iron circles. Next came a creak of the closet door in the hallway near Mama and Papa's room. Was she getting dressed to go downstairs and boss Old Simon around? Mr. Lincoln had freed the slaves and Papa paid Old Simon, so it was all right. Wasn't it? Were the other colored people in town awake? Young Simon, the boy he had known forever, seldom played now in the kitchen while his father worked. He must be home in bed.

He was the reason for the first fight at school, when the tall, black-haired boy had called Simon names. "Our judge's boy?" the principal had said, pulling Arley off. "You ought to know who to have for a friend!" Brown-haired Stanton Goode had never called Simon names but he would not walk home with Arley when Simon was along. In Stanton's home a few doors down Hathaway, the rugs lay flatly on floors polished by Simon's aunts. When Arley had sat at the table the night he'd stayed there for supper, Mrs. Goode had pressed the tip of her shoe against a bell and Simon's mother had come out carrying a silver tray and only Arley had said hello. "One slice is proper, doesn't he know?" Stanton's sister had laughed when Arley took two. Well, he would learn the manners of the rich and they could learn that both Abraham Lincoln and Jesus had said all men were free. He would tell them, as he had at school. And equal, though in the library after supper, when he and Stanton had twirled the globe to race in finding ancient Palestine, Stanton had won. He always did. He was smarter than Arley, even though Arley was older than Stanton and the others, and ought to be smarter. Stanton was the smartest boy in the class.

The sky outside Arley's window was lightening from gray to white. He moved his left foot along cold sheets. Though the chimney from the kitchen fireplace carried the stove flue up

through Arley's room and brought him the heat of the oatmeal
fire, the cold of the countryside seeped just as steadily through
his shut window. By morning the bed was warm only in the
patch that ran like a noontime shadow beneath his body. Was it
his shadow that took him where he went in dreams?

More creaking in the hallway, on the stairs. Mama going down
to Old Simon? "Yes," Mama had answered his sister Maud that
summer while they sat on the kitchen steps shelling peas.
"Whenever I look at Old Simon with those black cheeks shining
and those fat lips spreading to show me that pink tongue, I
wonder."

"That's not what I meant!" Maud said sharply, her diamond
ring bright among the peapods.

"No, I do wonder what's wrong about it. That's when I get the
fog. Whenever things don't quite make sense but there's nothing
you can do about it. I get it at your Papa's Methodist church so I
just work out my menus, a little ham, some scalloped potatoes. I
got it from my father; I always had to look like I was obeying,
even though I wasn't. It's the same when I don't quite tell the
truth to Papa because I can't get what's due me otherwise. Some
things are so big you have to go around them. You find a way to
turn an insult into victory. You'll learn it too, Maud. Married
women have to. So does Old Simon."

"I'd rather stand up straight and fight!" Maud shelled peas
almost as fast as Mama. Arley quieted in the bushes by the house
so they would forget him.

"Old Simon needs the work. What would the Browns do without the Percys and the Hathaways and the Goodes? And now the
Minors? And what would I do without Old Simon? The Swedes
don't come anymore and I certainly don't want the Irish around
my children, do I?"

"Mama!" Maud tossed a handful of unshelled peas back into
the basket.

"You keep on with those peas." Mama stared Maud down.
"Who fixed it so you could marry the Reverend Ted, anyway?
You won't have to sneak off to Chester like I did!"

That was the story "Wedding Invitations." Arley knew where

he was. Mama ordering the invitations printed in Grandma Percy's name and sending them out. "Now, if you still won't let me marry Joseph Minor, you'll have to tell your friends it's off."

"You do things for the boys, Mama, but not for me." Maud's head was down.

Would Maud tell "Pennies"? How Papa offered her a penny for each day in the year she didn't cry? How she had only earned fifty-seven pennies, the boys had worked so hard to make her cry? Or "College"? How Fred could go and Sam, if he had wanted, but not Maud, a girl?

No, Maud stood and carried the pail of peapods inside while Mama followed with the peas. Arley had been left alone in the bushes, listening to his favorite, the secret "Eaten Beef." He had heard it only once, when Mama had told it, laughing to Uncle Earl out at Grandma Percy's. It came from before the time that Arley was born and yet he knew it and could hear it when he wanted.

How long ago is long? It is all here, resifting, seeping about us; she plans a dinner. Building the fire in the stove early in the day and increasing its heat, his mother had packed the beef with dried prunes and apricots and placed it in the oven. She had set on the Indian pudding and waited. Light faded from the windows, his father came in to wash his hands of Egyptian Supreme and to sit in the carved rocker in his alcove off the dining room, with its black-painted safe displaying its brass combination lock. His mother did not think of asking his father then. She fed Justine and made Maud stop studying at the dining table and lay the forks and knives. She greeted Fred and Sam as they came through the kitchen door smelling of cows and she gave a private nod to Fred, but she did not begin it. Later, when the meal was ended and the dishes piled in unstable stacks near the sink, the table wiped with a damp cloth so the older children could study there, she knew it was time. His father returned to his seat in the rocker near his catalogues from the Chester Coffin Company and she went to him quietly and put her hand on his neck to tell him that his son, his firstborn, the smart, careful boy who worked and played so hard and who had grown taller than either of them, did not want to follow in his father's business and dress the dead. "He says it saddens him, and yes, he's afraid." It took a long time. She had begun with the remembrance of eaten beef.

"A happy Thanksgiving to you, Simon." Arley heard his Mama's muffled voice in the kitchen rise through the chimney.

"The same to you, Miss," Old Simon answered, "and to the Mister." A heavy sound then. Was Simon smiling, wetting his lips to show his pink tongue as he dropped onto red flames that shot up from the belly of the stove the heavy iron circle that fitted so neatly into the black iron hole?

Would Mama save him as she had Fred? Or did she do that only for Fred, her favorite? Perhaps if he were very good?

He chastens and hastens His will to make known. They pushed back their chairs and sat down to the feast. It was Justine who caused a silence in the noise of forks and jaws and conversations shouted between swallows and gasps for air and new forkfuls. Knowing there was suspicion and mystery about her sister's husband, Ted, she twisted her linen napkin and looked up to inquire of that dark-eyed, dark-haired man how he had voted three weeks earlier. Arley stopped eating.

"I voted for the best man," Ted replied, and then there was the silence.

"And who might that have been?" Justine would not stop.

"Young lady, it isn't . . ." But Polly was interrupted by her new son-in-law.

"Bryan," he replied, cutting a bite of turkey from the thigh upon his plate, but slowly, as all eyes were directed to how he managed his knife and fork.

"Why is that?" Justine continued, speaking out of all their secret desires, as family scout.

"Because I don't like monopolies and I don't like high tariffs." Ted sawed doggedly at his meat, but that did not seem to be enough. "And because I'm a Democrat."

That was it! The word!

"There are seconds on turkey, everybody," Polly spoke hurriedly. "Joseph, will you carve?"

Joseph stood to carve.

"Well, I voted for Taft," Joseph began, "because he's for the businessman."

"Joseph," Polly continued, "tell us how you voted for Blaine."

"Blaine?" Something darkened in Joseph's voice. He picked up the knife and put it down. He turned the turkey over and picked up the knife again. "Dark meat?" He looked suggestively around the table. Polly lowered her eyes.

"Blaine? I voted for Blaine to keep out the Catholics, the Irish, the Italians, and all kinds of Southern people. People who like a drink. There's places in Europe, you know, where they don't even have a pump in the kitchen. So you have to be careful who you put in down to Washington. White meat?" He had spoken calmly, however, and conclusively; his forehead and cheeks did not go scarlet. He was not going to explode, no thunder above the table.

"No, no, I meant the part about how I was sick and Grandma Percy was sick and you had to take the baby—it was you, Fred, and now you're getting married!—with you and you'd never voted? Here you were a man and had to go in to vote the first time like a woman?" Polly laughed, anticipating the end of the story.

"Yes," Joseph replied, slicing. "I know you meant that."

Mama did not say anything else.

"Tell what Grandma Percy said when you got married, Mama," Arley tried to help. Usually everyone laughed when Mama told that story and so maybe it would help the troubled feeling at the table.

"Not now, dear," Mama replied. "It's time for me to get the pumpkin pie."

The pie was coming! Talk picked up again round the table. Things were better. She had told what Grandma Percy said after they got the new set of dishes from England and she had told it the evening they laid the Persian rug down in the living room. Why not now? "He's poor, your Joseph Minor," Grandma Percy had said to Mama, snapping beans the way she did, rapidly and without mistakes. "A farm boy; you'll never have any money. You'll work from dawn to dark and you'll never have anything." But things had worked out very nicely, after all, hadn't they? Arley told the story to himself then, and set it out over the table, letting it go silently to spread like twigs that land so peacefully on water.

After the feast, they were sleeping. Mama in the chair in the living room; Papa on the couch, half his body covered by newspapers; Justine upstairs on her bed with the bedspread pulled down. Fred had gone over to Georgia's house and Sam and Catherine had returned to the new house down Hathaway Street that Sam and Papa had laid the cellar for last spring.

"Want to come along?" Maud asked Arley. She and Ted were going out for a walk around town. They didn't often get up from Shiloh.

"No, thanks," Arley replied. Somehow he did not want to leave the house in the company of Maud and Ted; that would separate him from the family proper.

"Good-bye, then!" Maud called with a wave, and the door shut.

Arley waited for them to disappear around the side of the house. Then, pulling on his sweater and cap, he went out to the yard alone. It would probably snow soon, turning white the long lawn whose immensity was the first thing he could remember. You had to repeat the stored scenes if you meant to keep them. You see, everything began on this lawn: once the blue-white of the sky and the green of the grass had been twirling as he flung himself down the slope like a rug unrolling. When he stood, the sky had pitched and swung until he staggered to the ground into the smell of cut grass. Flopping onto his back, he stared upward at the sky, whose blue darkened to a throbbing black. He was blind! He squeezed his eyes shut to heal them. When he opened them there was the same green grass and palely distant sky, the same white porch with pillars, the same quiet summer spread about him. Thank you, thank you, God. *This is my Father's world: I rest me in the thought.*

All the time running, though she did not let him go beyond the boundaries of the lawn. In summer the hooves of horses sent the dust rising on the road at the top of the lawn but in winter he could not tell where his white lawn ended or the white road began and the hooves of the horses were muffled in the snow, the runners of their sleighs soundless. Summer again and the dust, until finally, he had dared climb beyond the boundary and start across the road.

"Come back!" she had yelled.

But he had not gone back.

"Charles Minor, I'm surprised at you." He had kept going, with his heart pounding and his legs grown heavy with the weight of disobedience until he was gasping through the dust. When she finally caught him from behind, the back of his knees stung numb as she struck them with the lilac switch.

That switch or another stood peeled year round by the back door in the kitchen. He had been staring at the switch on the morning of his birthday several years ago when the short red-haired man came through the door.

"Are you coming to my party?"

"I guess so!" The red-haired man rubbed Arley's red hair and the scalp beneath too hard. "Are you ten today, Arley?"

Sam was funny. He was four.

His mother had not been fixing the cake but was bent over the sink; some of the reddish-gray hair she tied back had gotten loose.

Footsteps on the stairs. He waited by the stove, finishing his toast. It was Maud with her red hair fixed in a braid; he had often seen her separate the hair into thinner bunches, then bring them together and fix them on top with a long shiny pin. All of the ones with red hair were in the room together.

"Are you coming, Maud?" he asked, chewing.

"Coming where, Arley?" She picked up her oatmeal from the stove and crouched down so she was not a great deal taller than he.

"To my party," he said. "It's my birthday. I'm four."

"Oh, yes!" she said, putting an arm around him. "I'll have your present when I come home from school and then, at suppertime, you'll have your cake."

"Does it have candles? Is it chocolate?"

"Oh, yes," his mother answered from the sink. "And four

candles with one to grow on." He waited. He would grow as big as the rest of them. But not old enough to die. There was a way: if you were very, very good and never got mad, God might take you by the hand and walk beside you. You couldn't die then. You couldn't even get sick.

So far it wasn't working too well. During the summer after his sixth birthday he had lain in bed with a bad cold and then gotten the infection in his eyes that made the doctor say he should wait a year to begin school. On the lawn Arley pulled his cap down around his ears and walked toward the barn. Once, long before the sickness, he had been looking everywhere for the small window and finally found it again at the back of the barn. Jumping and taking a glimpse. Jumping again for another. Trying to fit the glimpses together. A woman stiff upon a table, her loose hair spread around her head in a brown halo. Was it The Dead?

The dead came to his barn. The dead were brought in to his father. Sometimes his father went to get them. So, it was true?

"Charles!" Mama picked him up in her arms and showed him to a visitor plucking strawberries at the kitchen table. "This is my baby!"

He brushed aside her hair and whispered in her ear. "Is Papa God?"

"Oh heavens, no," she answered, too loud near his ear. "Why did you think that?"

"When you die you go to God," he answered, repeating the words of his Sunday School teacher who coughed so much.

"Yes?" Mama said, appearing to be waiting.

"The people in the barn," he explained. "They died and they came to Papa."

"Oh," she said, putting her hand upon his head and letting him rest his cheek upon her breast.

"So, isn't he?" he repeated, his voice smothered. "God?"

"No," she said, drawing back where he could see her face. "No, he just helps people on their way to God," she said more quietly.

He felt relieved.

It would not be into Papa's arms that he would go in heaven.

That was not the bosom of Abraham. It was good to know things. Knowing things is what separated grown-ups from children, even more than growing tall. The dwarf from Elmsy, for instance, was a grown-up. He was even a father.

"How does he get them up there?" he continued. But she had turned back to her visitor.

When Maud and Ted returned and Maud took off her coat, Arley thought he could see that her stomach was growing bigger. Not her stomach, she kept telling him, her abdomen. The baby would be born in Africa.

"Africa!" Papa had said to Mama. "A good place for him!" Ted and Maud didn't stay for Thanksgiving supper and when Arley stood with Sam and Fred in the cool pantry, eating left-over pumpkin pie, his brothers were still talking about them.

"Papa says he won't be sure until he sees that baby." Sam paused to take a bite of pie.

"He's just teasing," Fred said. "He's no Negro. He's just a Democrat."

Arley did not understand; it was clear that Ted was not a Negro. Negroes did not marry people. Even though they were equal.

"Sam, Mama wants us to come in and decide what to wear at Fred's wedding." Catherine the bride found her husband in the pantry and Sam put his arm around her narrow waist. Her face was broad with bright red cheeks, her black hair parted in the middle. "Our English rose!" Papa called her.

They finished up their pie and Arley trailed after them, wanting to linger over his but not wanting to be left alone in the distant pantry. Ring-bearer again. The same blue velvet suit as at Sam's wedding in October and at Maud's in June? The same burst of white pellets like hail, arms reaching out, wet lips pressed to his cheeks? What would happen if Justine left home? Would he ever have to leave? He must fill himself with their stories, like layers of nuts piled in a box, until he was made of them and could take them with him always.

II

Midsummer, 1911

"WHY DON'T YOU walk up to the town hall and fetch Papa for lunch?" Polly broke up Arley's play with young Simon, and the boys parted. Arley walked up the path that cut through the lawn he would have to mow again soon and across to the town hall. The door was heavy, but he managed. He walked with appropriate slow grandness under the high-ceilinged corridor and turned into the probate office, where a long oak table stood beneath a tall oak clock that was ticking loudly. Shucking dignity, Arley ducked quickly into the alcove where his father wrote in the big books.

"Hey, boy," Papa said, never surprised. He bent over a paper on which he was writing and he spelled out loud for Arley the letters: "E-l-i-z-a-b-e-t-h."

"Elizabeth," Arley answered. Didn't Papa know he could read? "What's it for?" he asked. Papa spread out the will he was inscribing and showed him where he had written in a strong, clear script the words *My Daughter Elizabeth.*

"Who's it for?" Arley asked, knowing his own father had named a daughter Elizabeth. Everyone in the family had known her, except Arley. But only Justine would tell him about her.

"Junior Goode," Joseph answered. "Uncle of your friend Stanton." He finished writing and signed the document handsomely, without flourish.

"They're an old family," Joseph went on as he gathered up the papers. "Been handing down the same cherry table, the same six cherry chairs with carved slats and two cherry armchairs, matching, and the same French silverware made in Paris for over two hundred years." Joseph wrapped a ribbon around the will of Samuel Goode, Jr., and filed it next to the will of Samuel Goode, Sr., which lay next to that of Sara Goode, which backed up on that of Adino Goode. The whole package he wrapped together with a ribbon.

"Of course, they have been known to take a drink and they are Congregationalists," Joseph explained by way of moderating the glory of their history. But it didn't seem to Arley that either charge quite invalidated the Goodes.

"What about us?" Arley asked, running a finger along the oak shelf where the red folders stood, thinking of the shelves in the library at Stanton's, where there were so many real books.

"The Minors are an old family, too," Papa said, getting into the suit jacket he wore winter and summer to the town hall. "But we don't have so much silverware. And we tend to oak instead of cherry," he added. Indeed, his own property list would read a bit like one drawn up for repairs: one oak table with bad burn; two oak chairs with backs of pine; one oak rocker carved with lion emblem, left rocker broken. Joseph shoved the Goode family between the Gardners and the Haggertys, who were known to do worse than to take a drink.

"Lots of new families coming into town now." Joseph ushered Arley out of the alcove, stopping to pull his watch from his vest pocket and check it against the clock in the office; he took his hat from the coat-tree, settled it on his head, straightened his cuffs, and they walked out.

"Good day, Judge," the town clerk called from his office.

"You can't judge a man by his ancestors," Joseph informed Arley as they walked across the road. "The sons of kings often accomplish nothing. And vice versa," he added at the top of the lawn. "Look at me."

"I never saw the inside of school during plowing or planting," Joseph began as they hitched Prince and Marjorie to the plow.

Arley did not listen. He had sometimes ridden the plow on Joseph's lap as a child, but now he was learning to manage it alone. He could break only a few rows of soil before his muscles tired but he never plowed long before Sam or Papa would hail him down.

"Hey, Prince, keep it straight there." Arley talked to horses as calmly now as Papa and Sam. "You're wavering on it, Marjorie." The horses paid little attention to his voice and Arley kept on behind them as they pulled, the plow turning over a layer of earth and setting it on one side. When the blade caught on a stone and Marjorie turned, he held her straight. Plowing was all right. Then they changed the big blade of the plow for the small discs of the harrow and ran aslant of the furrows they had made, breaking up the clots and clumps of earth and leveling the soil. Then they planted.

Working with a seed bag over his shoulder, Arley walked and watched Sam ahead of him. He saw Sam under the bright sun, outlined with a kind of sun-blackness at the edges, crossing and recrossing the plowed field, scattering. Arley followed him. Plowing was all right, harrowing was harder, planting was the best. And pinching the worst.

He crawled along the rows of potato plants, looking among white flowers and green leaves for yellow-and-black-striped bugs. Finding one, he would pinch it between his fingers, lift it gently off and drop it in the half-filled pail of water he carried beside him. He would crawl and pick, crawl and pick, his straw hat hugging his heat-swelling head tighter and tighter, until, looking into the pail, he saw bugs crawling up its side, out of the water, bound for life; then he would have to shake the pail as Papa had taught him and make the bugs fall back into the water. Soon they would cut hay.

"Hey, boy, steady now. Keep it smooth." Sam gave Arley an encouraging smile in the dimness of the cellar; they worked by the open stairwell. Sam pressed the first of the mowing blades against the stone. He bore down hard, without mercy.

Arley held steady, turning the handle that rolled the stone upward out of its tub of water, while Sam stood in front of the

wheel, bearing his full weight against the passing stone, first
side of the blade and then the other—oh lightning whil
switched, the stone speeding in Arley's hands. At least Arley
not required to run along the turning stone like the caged squirrel
that ran the wheel in Stanton Goode's library. Still, his was not
the smooth rhythmic style needed to keep the wheel turning fast
when Sam put on the pressure and slow when he took it off. The
ache that developed in Arley's right shoulder after an hour or so
at the grindstone was beginning.

"We going to hay today?" Arley asked Sam.

"No, tomorrow."

Arley hated to hay. Better than the grindstone or pinching, but
it was still harder than planting or plowing. Surely, he could not
grow up to be a farmer. He was beginning to sweat, a bad sign. It
meant he would soon get itchy on his hands and, after that, the
blisters.

Sam breathed heavily; he was half done with the mower blades.
Arley could see that Sam was sweating through the rag around
his forehead and that his red hair was streaked dark with dampness. Sam's baby boy had black hair like Catherine's; Maud's baby
girl had red hair like Maud's and did not look at all Negro in the
picture that had come from the Methodist Mission in Rhodesia.
Sam never stopped to rest. They both looked forward to the
scythes, which were larger and gave more of a feeling of accomplishment. And they meant the end was near. Sam was the best
sharpener in the family, knowing exactly when to bear down and
when to give the light touch that brought out a razor's edge; his
knives could be trusted to cut the thickest stubble. Sam had red
hair and had grown up to work for Papa in the barn. Arley had
red hair, did that mean he could not escape working for Papa
either?

Tomorrow they would mow the hay. They usually took in
three or four loads a day, though Arley didn't work straight
through with the men. He had his own responsibilities. Tending
the biggest lawn in Connecticut, keeping a small garden of
tomatoes, cucumbers, radishes and green beans for Mama. Tonight we would watch the Home Guard drill. In a week or

two, they would cut the first corn with the sharpened scythes: ten stalks—cut, swish, dump. Ten at a time; not him, he could only do three or four at a time. Then after that, digging potatoes, and after that, the trip to Lighthouse Point. Yes, tomorrow they would mow, if today ever ended.

Joseph buttoned up his fly and walked around the front of the barn to check on the boys. Fred had agreed to help out on Saturdays and Joseph saw that his oldest son had driven the wagon around the way Joseph hated it. It was faster, Fred explained, for right-handed people to throw the bales up from that direction. That was so like Fred, precise and probably right, but annoying.

"You see that one?" Sam called out, as he tossed a bale that slid down a slope from the loft and came to rest against an upright two-by-four. Sam pitched the way Joseph did, with a pause over the shoulder and a heave. Sam was in his image, jollier than his older brother, as Joseph had been, and marrying younger. Sam's baby boy, Joe, would hay like that one day; Joseph would see to it.

It was the strongest tie, Joseph's love for his children. He pitied Fred, who had none after two years of marriage. "You seem to hate them!" Polly used to whisper when he whipped the boys. True, when he whipped them something slacked between his brain and hand. "You whip them like horses." No, he whipped his horses smartly and well, while he whipped his boys wildly. It's what a father was supposed to do and his own had done it, a bony arm raised high with belt or switch. Hands and arms, they went with children. He had always found, with the dead children he collected, a sense of manual transmission from one adult to another. With their hands still on the child, parents would look suspiciously at him and at his outstretched arms, as if measuring his fatherhood and finding him wanting. "How could you?" their eyes said. Or, "Do you really expect me to let you?" Indeed, he had not worked on Elizabeth. Could he work on Fred? Or Sam? Or Maud, the odd one?

"Why not burn the bodies in the woods, Papa?" Maud alone had dared challenge him, her gray eyes lingering on him, keeping him always in her gaze. "They will mold in the ground, it's damp." Maud had gone away, out of his reach. Farther than Elizabeth, who had only died. Justine alone of his daughters stood by, and daughters do not stay for long.

Joseph smiled as he watched his sons pitch hay. The same ritual movements he had taught each of them separately. Both his boys were sturdy. Fred was all right, even if he had always favored Polly. He must call them men, now, Polly told him. Sam he could because Sam was a father. Boys or men, they were young with young veins and arteries. They had life. He used to love to touch the tops of their heads, laying his palm where he could feel the force of their growing.

"Good work, boys," he called out as he approached them. Fred turned to him, surprised at the rare praise.

So what.

"And you, boy." He saw that, on his approach, Arley had gone guiltily back to harvesting. Always a surprise, his last son. After Elizabeth had died, he had no longer expected much from any of them. Especially when the new baby had turned out frail. But the boy had strengthened and Joseph would turn him into a man, like Sam. Like Fred.

The land was his sons' only competitor for Joseph's commitment: the way he fitted into and rose up out of the land that was his, no matter what Italian owned it. There was no longer any mystery. He would go back into the land here in Judea, where he would be sucked at by the roots of trees and carried upward in long liquid filaments. He would be spit from the stomachs of bees, beaked at by birds, engulfed and eliminated by earthworms. And somewhere under the Judea cemetery underground water seeped to the hollow in Southlee, where his father had plowed and his mother harvested their own fields. He would be back with them. There was nothing at all wrong with moldering.

"Watch it!" Sam swayed, laughing. Joseph loved to hear his boys laugh. Their laughs came from another world. Joseph was always sitting children on counters or barrels at the trolley station where he could tickle them and hear them laugh.

With Polly it was different. She was not connected to him in the long sifting of time that the Reverend Mr. Tiding preached so testily against. Or rather, she was connected but too late, in the next generation, where the blood and bones of their bodies mixed in the children. Their own link was not for the time before birth, nor for the time after death, but for their lifetimes only and so it was wavering and frail, the bond that kept him to her breast. With his seed he had made her fruitful but they were always to pull apart, to be separated into male and female. And he had hardly had Polly with him all his life. Nor the other woman he had loved, his mother. Since she had died, there was no continuity that ran the length of his. Except that of the earth, which was both before and after him.

"Are the scythes sharp, boy?" Joseph asked of any of his sons who might be listening. "We'll get to Lighthouse Point before the week's out." He had forgotten that the older boys no longer went.

"KEEP YOUR ARM INSIDE THE TROLLEY!" Justine still liked to give Arley orders even though she would hardly play with him these days. They sat in front of Mama and Papa as they rode beside a green field where the men were cutting corn under a blue sky. Arley leaned his chin on the window ledge and looked out. God's domain was that of the mysterious air that added and multiplied itself into sky, into heaven. You don't ask how the three fish became three hundred. By faith. Once you had the power, you could move mountains. At Chester they changed to the New Haven line.

"That's where the trolley pole comes in," Justine said, climbing on first. "Touch it and it's sudden death." She still had information beyond his. But he would know it all one day. If he could pierce the soil of the fields with his eyes, he would see exactly how the seed he tossed and covered grew into corn and died and became part of next year's soil. That was no mystery. It could be pierced with a microscope. But no instrument could show how God had unbound the living from the dying and set men free. That would always take faith.

In New Haven, they changed at Church and Chapel for the

open yellow car to Lighthouse Point. "I can smell the sea!" Justine sat but Arley stood holding a pole. Justine was too old. They never rolled on the floor. They never hid under the lilac bush while she turned her hand into a claw to show him how Elizabeth's had looked while she was dying in the downstairs bedroom. She never played the piano for him while he stood at Papa's catalogue rack making his voice as loud as the Reverend Mr. Tiding's and telling them all what for. "The God of Moses is not enough! To lay the Egyptians in a watery grave, that's easy! But Our Father Who Art in Heaven, He made the dead to live! He brought Our Lord Jesus Christ out of the darkness of the grave! Now, how did He do that, my people?" Justine would swell up the music and Mama would come from the kitchen to hear him unravel the greatest of the mysteries and the one in which Papa, he suspected, did not believe.

"There's the water!" Justine stood up but Arley pushed ahead of her and jumped from the steps of the trolley before she could, running toward the blue water and domed buildings as bright as Jerusalem's.

"This way," Papa pointed. But who had forgotten the boardwalk? The shore dinner? The water lapping the pier as the living crabs were killed before your eyes? The green tide and the black undertow? Unwise to have eaten so much before the merry-go-round.

His stomach moved up and down on the camel. He waved to Mama and Justine. This year she was even too old to ride the rhinoceros, as she had done last year. He had chosen the horse then. He held a rag of carpeting underneath himself on the shoot-the-shoot and he was slipping, falling, whooshing down the long, twisting chute, whose high sides protected him, eyes shut, plummeting too fast to think about his stomach. If he didn't work for Papa, would he ever be a man?

When they walked around the old mill, Justine looked almost like a lady, holding Papa's arm beneath the armband that circled the striped sleeves of his shirt. Mama was holding Papa's other arm; the light that entered the holes of her hat was casting tiny spinning flecks of light on her cheeks. Arley didn't walk on the other side of Mama, as he usually did, but—now that he wanted to—he couldn't get to Papa, who had both arms taken. So he walked ahead, kicking stones and not kicking stones, thinking, Why kick stones today? What was Simon doing? What was Stanton doing?

They waited in line for the steamboat.

"Tickets!"

Papa unfolded the strip of four, their last tickets, and they boarded for a slow ride across the bay to the point. White, tall, upright, the lighthouse. They would walk inside it.

"Something to think about next year when you're pinching bugs, hey, boy?" Papa knuckled him in the shoulder.

It was for children that Papa appeared happy and, knowing this above all, Arley feared to grow into the world of men where such patronage would end.

III

Christmas Day, 1913

THE SUN SPARKLED reassuringly off the metal buckles Arley was fastening onto Prince and Marjorie. Arley looked away from the barn and up to the town's oldest intersection which lay directly below God's vision at the apex of the sky. Sun must be lighting up the names of the boys on the stone obelisk there. Their blood at Charlottesville and Bull Run had made the nation one. Each time he passed the monument, Arley read out loud at least one of those boys' names, rolling it long out of his mouth where the breath of life could warm it. The spirit lived.

Lots of spirits were bad but the One was good. He had finished hitching the horses and now had to bring a small coffin from the barn's new annex. He pressed his palms to his heavy jacket and went in for it. The sunshine must be streaming through the shallow basement windows of the town hall onto the floors of the two jail cells and lighting up the lidless toilets, including the yellow stains within. "Mornin', Judge," the chief of police had always said, nodding. "So you're our judge's boy? Guess you'll stay out of trouble." Arley picked up the empty coffin and went back outside.

The sun could not yet have reached inside the drug store to the candy jars. "I'd give ten thousand dollars for a boy like that!" the pharmacist said. For a boy with freckles and a scrawny neck? The coffin was so light he did not even need to situate it on the rollers in the floor of the funeral wagon. The smallest coffins bothered him the most. How could that baby have sinned? What kind of Father sends his children out knowing they will die? The

sun must be curving and tingeing as it passed through colored glass
into the Methodist gloom. Why didn't Jesus tell God he would
not go down there and die? Because God was the father and he
had to obey? He shut the doors of the wagon. The sunlight
entered straight and clear through the untinted glass of the windows of the clear-minded, upper-class Congregational church
where Arley sometimes went with his Grandma Percy and where
he had once thought he felt God touch his shoulder. Or did
Jesus accept the job of going down to die because he knew
from the Trinity that God and he were one, so everything should
work out all right? Arley himself had a lot of trouble remembering the Trinity and how it worked. He climbed up to the driver's
seat and clucked the horses up the drive to the intersection and
was soon hitching them to the post outside the town hall.

"Who were they?" Arley asked as a group of middle-aged
people left the probate office.

"Survivors of Felicia Goode," Joseph told him. "And just as
the old girl described them, too. Tricky." The judge picked up
scattered papers.

"Who got the money?"

"*Per Stirpes* to the grandchildren," Joseph explained. "The
middle son is angry, of course, since he's childless." Joseph came
to a sudden halt. It was simple. A boy without a father is always a
man. A man without children is always a child.

"He'll sue, but even if it goes to court, my decision will be
upheld," Joseph assured his youngest son, a boy who worried.
"Only been contested once, remember? And the court fell all
over itself backing me up." Lately, Judge Minor ran on both
Republican and Democratic tickets. Not that he lost any love on
the Democrats.

"Put this back on my shelf, will you, boy?" Joseph handed
Arley a tied sheaf of papers. "The open file." The judge made his
way to the coat-tree for the suit jacket he wore on all but the
coldest days, and his hat.

In the alcove, Arley pushed the thick folder into the open
cardboard file and tied its string: Goode. His eye picked out a
new folder: Minor.

"What's the Minors doing here?" he asked, as Joseph came back into the alcove to close his desk.

"I made some copies of our papers in Southlee," Joseph said, and rolled the oak desk shut abruptly. "I'm making a file."

"Oh," Arley said, feeling calm at his father's unease.

"I'll show you sometime," Joseph offered, "but not now. We've got to get on over to the Ewings. Sam went by to do the work, but we've got to pick her up." A man does not stand upright at the center of things forever, holding the dead in his hands, closing their bodies, laying them in the earth, smoothing them out. No. A man's children grow to reach his knees, his waist, his shoulders, grow taller than himself. Joseph the judge, father of six, husband of Polly *nee* Phoebe, is no longer at center stage. He becomes a twig on a family tree, written down, but never to be erased; the firm, middle-sized handwriting—why, people said it would last three hundred years. Though a man's children do not always outlive him. Of that he had been apprised. It is the worst thing.

"Any trouble with the horses?" Joseph asked, as he climbed into the seat and squeezed himself beside his son, who drove for him now, although there was scarcely room for the two of them on the driver's seat. "Runners okay?"

"Yes," Arley answered. "But I wish you'd get an auto, like Stanton's."

"I ever tell you about the World's Fair?" Joseph asked, with a chuckle.

"Yes," Arley answered. "You said a funny machine like that that ran on gas would never replace the horse."

"Well, I was wrong," Joseph admitted.

"Yes," Arley pointed out, unnecessarily, "you were wrong."

They rode in silence.

Nearing the Ewing home, Arley started to give the horses their head.

"Keep 'em in!" Joseph rebuked him. "You're not at the races!"

Smarting, Arley held the horses down.

"Tie them up," Joseph commanded; and while Arley threw the

reins around the post outside the Ewings' house, Joseph selected a small white satin rosette from the box below the seat.

"Wait here," he said, walking around back to open the door of the wagon's low, windowed compartment. He never took the basket in for children. He removed the coffin lid in readiness, picked the brass hammer out of its niche on the wagon wall and swung open the two back doors. Then he walked up the flagstones to the doorway. He stood at the doorpost and held the infant's rosette high while he hammered it in. *Tock, tock, tock*: the hammer produced a delicate sound.

"*Were you there when they crucified my Lord?*" The voice of the darky bass engulfing, blaming the assembled ladies and gentlemen at last year's Methodist Open Invitational Good Friday Evening Service. A darky's Lord.

"*Were you there when they nailed Him to the tree?*" Old Simon was all right, he was loyal. He never accused.

"*Tock, tock, tock. Sometimes it causes me to wonder, wonder, wonder.*"

"*Were you there when they hammered in the nails?*" But the others? You could not trust them.

Joseph straightened the rosette on Ewing's post. Wittenberg. I hold these truths to be self-evident. I hold these truths. By these truths am I held. He opened the door.

It was an old house. He stood in the small hallway, looking at the steep staircase that rose in a diagonal across the wall.

"Hello?" he called. Sam must have left about an hour ago. Babies didn't take long but it was awkward working if the family wanted to watch. And with babies they usually did.

"It's Joseph," he called again. "Joseph Minor." Come for your firstborn.

He stepped over the threshold into the living room and saw them on either side of the fireplace. Ellen Ewing on the left, her mother on the right, each sitting stiffly in a chair, and the chairs facing each other.

Between them, in a high cradle, lay the baby, dressed in a pink bunting, wrapped in a blanket. For warmth? Sam would have put on whatever they wanted. Joseph's already quiet step muffled completely when he stepped from the wide floorboards onto the Persian rug.

"Ellen," he said, not nodding, not approaching her, trying to reach her with his voice.

"Mrs. Pearson," he said to her mother. It was not a question, not a demand, just something you said to calm a dog before you stole the bone.

Then he was beside the cradle. He reached down slowly. He did not want to make sudden movements. Slowly he picked up the tiny corpse, as if it were living, and cradled it in his arms. Fifteen pounds. Sam had done a good job, diluted the fluid just enough to set the jaw but not to pinch the nose.

"I will be back," he said. Ellen had not moved but Mrs. Pearson was nodding at him slowly.

He crossed the carpet, the wide-boarded floor that squeaked, the hallway to the door, which he opened with his right hand. He carried the small bundle back to the hearse and, with one leg up on the wagon, settled it in the box, lowered the lid and swung the two doors shut.

"I'll be a minute more," he called to Arley, and went back inside.

The door, the floor, the carpet. He put his hand on Ellen's shoulder.

"Come at six," he said, squeezing slightly. She did not move, but he saw the tears gathering.

"She'll be all right," he said, placing his hand on the top of Ellen's head, her hair. With these hands. Ellen should feel the hands first, for her daughter.

"I promise." Then he took away his hand and reached over to shake the hand of Mrs. Pearson, who had stood up. She walked him back to the door and leaned against it.

"It's almost the Christmas season," she said, in a normal tone.

"Yes," Joseph answered, starting down the steps. "It won't be long now." He had promised Ewing to have the grave dug in the frozen ground, had hired the diggers for twice their usual price. The poor, of course, had to wait in the cold vault, even their babies.

"Make sure she comes this evening," Joseph added. "After six. It's the best thing for her."

Mrs. Pearson nodded.

Joseph turned and, walking toward the hearse, motioned Arley to untie the horses and be ready. He swung up onto the seat.

"Get going," he said to Arley.

He turned to wave. Mrs. Pearson still stood at the door beside the post that bore his rosette. AND I WILL MARK THEIR DOORPOSTS WITH A SIGN.

"How old?" Arley asked.

"Eight months." Joseph shut his eyes and saw himself leading the horse to Willie Peach's, the body of his eleven-year-old Elizabeth stretched upon the open floor of the wagon hearse. Thin, braided hair that did not cover the scores of lumps ringing her neck. He had not been able to put her in a box. He had covered her with the afghan that had been on her bed for so long.

"Sorry to hear it, Joseph," Willie had said, his eyes bright in the light from the open door.

"Simon will be down for the horses later," he had explained. "You carry her in, Willie. Will you?" He had walked home crosslots on the snow without turning back.

"Runners are going good," he said to Arley. Eleven, this boy was the same age now.

"That's because the snow out here is packed," Arley said. "In town the autos heat it up."

"We'll have ten inches by Sunday, enough for all the runners in town. And it'll last over Christmas."

There was ice crust on everything. Each single twig and branch of every bush and tree was encased in a shining ice that seemed at once brittle and soft because the feel of it underneath was hard and would clack against his fingernail but the sliding wetness of it on the surface was soft and liquid. There was a layer of ice on top of the snow that covered the lawn and there were icicles hanging from the roof of the porch and from the roof of the annex to the barn where Mr. Justus Cobb lay in a state cold enough to preserve his contours throughout the Sabbath if need be. The sun did not so much shine as glint across the roof of the barn that sheltered the black-haired corpse and over the roof of the adjoining house where Polly washed breakfast dishes in the steamed-up kitchen and Arley parted his red hair straight down the middle of his head, drawing the comb right across his forehead and along the center of his nose. He had once believed the image in the mirror could look back at him, and see him. Out of the kitchen window he could see the clattering, clicking bushes that the wind blew against the side of the house. Lilac bushes. Sleep well.

Arley had been waiting for just such ice. He had been by the pond twice this week and the ice was deep, a foot perhaps, but very rough and gray: it needed only a slick freeze to coat it into perfection. And last night that freeze had come. But it was Sunday. You don't play hockey on Sunday.

He thought about how to ask. Beg; he thought about how to beg. He put the comb back on the wooden shelf. He ought to have gotten to Mama sooner; the early bells were already off and running on *For all the saints who from their labors rest.* Their sound was brittle like the ice. Thin, cold little notes. Church should be on days when there was nothing else to do.

"Do you think," he began, when his mother came into the kitchen with her hat on, "that Papa would let me go skating today?"

"Sunday?" His mother wrung out a dishcloth. "I'm surprised at you."

"But the ice is perfect, probably the best of the year."

"You know what Papa would say." She hung the damp cloth on the pump.

"Will you ask him anyway?"

"No." She turned from the sink.

"Please," he said. He heard the shouts of his friends and saw the bonfire burning, the flakes of chipped ice running behind his ankles as he cut a quick groove in the cold skin of the pond.

"Charles," she said, putting her hand on his shoulder, "if I ask when there's no hope, it will weaken my asking when there is. Get into your boots now."

"I get firsts on the footwarmer," Justine said, coming into the kitchen.

Minutes later they were crossing the crusty yard. His father carried the footwarmer, around which waves of heat emanated as he led what was left of his family across the wilderness of snow, his booted footsteps firm and wide, all of their steps fitting neatly inside his. A footprint is not a shadow, it is of the world, worldly. The air was so cold Arley felt it like a wall against his nose. At the road he stepped out of his father's footprints into the mush that auto wheels had made of the snow and stood level with his father, whose nose was red and almost translucent. He hated it, it was ugly. Next thing you knew a drop of the stuff that comes out of noses would hang from it.

"You'll never get to go," Justine said breathily into his ear as they sat down.

Bernie Necomber, the goalie, sat a few pews off to his right, and Simon, the forward, over his left shoulder. Arley put his right hand around his mother's furred arm and ran the fur along the sensitive places inside his fingers. He raised his left elbow slightly and brought it into brief contact with Justine's left hip. He followed her gaze to the back of Paul Hathaway's neck.

"It's mine when the hymn starts," he whispered, nudging the footwarmer under Justine's boots. Subtle changes in pitch and drone indicated that Mr. Tiding was sliding to a close. The piano pattered into action: *Once to every man and nation.* Arley waited for the pick-up on the last verse, when the congregation would rise as one. But in a shattering veer from form his father stood up alone. The man who did all things correctly rose up out of his seat on *For the good or evil side.* With the rest of the congregation seated, the great judge looked splendidly if inaccurately tall. Arley forgot the footwarmer. He glanced up to see if Tiding would say anything about the big mistake. Joseph was just beginning to bend his knees to sit when he was rescued by *twixt that darkness and that light* which brought the rest of the world onto its feet. Joseph was blushing! Some Sunday!

"The ice is perfect today, Papa," Arley said at the dinner table. "The boys are planning a hockey game this afternoon and they're expecting me to play right guard because I'm the fastest."

"On Sunday?" Joseph chewed a forkful of roast chicken.

"It's an unusual day, sir. The ice is perfect."

"You know better than that, boy," Joseph said, picking up his knife to cut off another bit of chicken. "More peas, Justine, if you please, my girl."

The peas came between Arley and his request. Like a punctuation mark. It was over.

"Jesus picked corn on the Sabbath." Arley sucked in his breath, waiting for the blow by making himself big. "And not everybody does everything properly all the time."

His father's voice grew rough. "That will be quite enough." He handed Arley the bowl of peas but Arley hated winter peas, mushed up over the months and grown too sweet. The wind blew the iced bushes against the window in his father's alcove and against the barn where Justus Cobb lay, making its way through cracks and riffling the black hair that fell across the forehead of the corpse. Arley would have to sit home reading his *American Boy*.

"You can always walk up to the cemetery," Papa suggested as he prepared for his Sunday afternoon nap, "and think God's thoughts after him."

"Or hike over to the falls at Southlee if you bundle up," his mother added, folding her napkin. "Your cousin Sam Percy's probably going."

"Or could just *watch* the boys playing hockey," Justine offered in her soft-voiced way.

"The way you watch Paul Hathaway?" But she didn't answer him, only climbed the stairs with her skirt raised, so that from below he could see almost to her knees.

It was too cold to take a walk. Arley sat in a patch of sun in the window seat with an *American Boy* he soon discovered he had already finished. There was too much time on Sunday afternoons. Like a hole, you could fall into it. Come evening and the grownups would get up from their naps and round up the leftovers, and before he knew it, he would be off to the Methodist League, where he and Bernie Necomber would joke about the woman with the issue of blood. But how could he live through the empty hours? It seemed blasphemous to think God's thoughts. But if

you were going to try, you had better start with time: IN THE
BEGINNING, God had. Arley looked out the window to the town
hall. Time ran through the files of the probate office and spurted
with each swing of the pendulum within the great oak case of the
clock. It ran like electricity through the stone monument to the
Union dead and sparkled through their bodies en route to seep
into the cellars of houses. There it billowed upward from coal
furnaces to ripen the fetuses in the bellies of the wives. It frag-
mented into a million moments and encountered ups and downs
of gravity, which was a small wavering force compared with the
great dull presence of time. Time was bigger than anything else;
it could not be contained at the center of the planet by the axis
that held fast against the turning and was the one incorruptible
pivot. There, was that the kind of thought God would have?

It didn't seem to have God in it at all. Arley shifted his knees
to catch up with the moving sun and tried again. You could chase
time backward by catching hold of it in your parents. From there
you had to take all the stories on hearsay. No, there was
Grandma Percy, but she rushed children at anagrams and could
not be trusted. Backward from her, the story-tellers were all dead
and it was a long gap through to the Crusades. The gap again 'til
you reached Jesus. But once there, you were plugged in again
and could spin down through the begats to the birth of the
world. To God hovering in the waters, calling out for light.
Until the light burst upon him and the waters drew back and he
stepped out upon dry land. And his eyes were dazzled by the
light and he opened his mouth and cried out: "It is good." Then
he dimmed the light into sun and moon and made all the rest of
the world. But before that? You weren't supposed to go backward from there. It had to be the Spirit which filled every crev-
ice, was sufficient unto itself, existed before the world and made
it.

And Arley didn't want to go forward. He had seen the bodies
himself, seen Papa and Sam measure out Egyptian Supreme and
put the good black jackets on. Neither forward nor backward
then, but standing still, holding onto each minute. He found himself staring at his hand, a child's hand, but the veins were begin-

ning to show on it the way they did on grown-up hands. Half-grown he was; he memorized the lines of his tendons and of the fleshy elipses at the knuckles. He shut his eyes. It would always be now.

"IT WAS BULLY," Arley said. "My favorite part was when they..." The train swerved and threw him against Justine, who was clutching the new fur neckpiece they had gone to Hartford to get.

"I would have preferred a lighter fur." Joseph stroked the tip of the dark neckpiece lying in his daughter's lap. "More becoming for a young girl." Through knowledge of pelts of another sort, he realized, he had grown well-to-do and could clothe his little girl in furs. And himself in sealskin, especially reserved for the graveside and for trips to Hartford. Polly had owned a fur coat as a girl. When Polly's father had died young, he, at least, had left some money.

"And I loved it when they . . ." Arley continued describing the afternoon's moving picture, *Uncle Tom's Cabin*. Nobody listened to him. Had no one in his family any gaiety?

Polly talked to her daughter. "Grandma Percy always told me how much warmer fur is. Of course I never believed her. But when I pushed my fingers through the sleeve of my first fur coat and out through the end of the satin lining, I knew she was right. I wore it right outdoors and up by the horse trough which was by the birdbath. The water in both of them was frozen over but I was perfectly warm."

Arley stopped talking. Better ice than the limp reddish water that lay in the birdbath throughout the summer. A green slime collected under it.

"I like the neckpiece all right, Mama," Justine said. "It's just that I thought we might get a coat."

"You're only fifteen!" Polly said. "I was eighteen." She was fifty now, old enough to shut her eyes on the train, but Joseph wouldn't have liked it. "Your papa didn't come to the top of the lawn that night, out of the blue, as he often did. But, I had my coat."

"Paul is coming over tonight." Justine leaned against the darkened window out of the train. "I forgot to tell you."

Believe me, he would kid the life out of them. Arley watched Mama run her fingers along the string from the fur box. Justine would sit on the blue velvet sofa, so close to Paul that her dress would cover part of his trousered leg. With her curls gathered up in back, she would sit staring straight ahead. She would be wearing the soft blouse through which he could see the curve of her bosoms. Her breasts. There were two of them; of bosoms there was only one. Paul would sit staring straight ahead too, forever, while members of the family came by from time to time. Namely Arley.

"Remember that, Joseph?" Polly in the seat across from him looked to Joseph like his own mother. She had grown stocky about the waist, and the fingers which fondled the string from the fur box were plump between knuckle and palm. Polly would never be as big as his mother, though. His mother's hands on a soup lid were larger, and her ankles had always been thick.

"Hi, Ma," he said, coming in from the cows to wash his hands at the sink. "I got to eat early." The dirty water foamed in the slate sink. "Got to be back to town by half past seven."

"Polly?" she asked, moving toward the sink lightly. Her feet remained slender; the heavy fleshing began directly above them.

"Methodist League," he replied to her question.

"That doesn't start 'til eight." She set soup in a bowl before Joseph.

"I might stop by and see Polly first. Can't have her waiting for me and I don't show up, can I, Ma?" He started the soup and his mother laughed with him. They did not have so many secrets.

"You and your town girl, have you taught her how to milk a cow yet?"

He shrugged and reddened, remembering Polly's breasts, which he had only that week reached, though not seen. Did his mother know?

"Sleepy?" Joseph inquired of everyone as the train bumped lullingly over the tracks to Christmas.

"It's a diary," Justine explained excitedly, before Arley had finished unwrapping the white tissue paper.

"Mama suggested it," Justine said, when Arley showed no enthusiasm at reaching the red-bound book.

"You'll like it." Polly had watched the unwrapping. "I kept one once. You'll always have your childhood if you make sure to write in it every day."

"Thanks a lot, Justine," Arley said. He had wanted a new subscription to *American Boy*. But after the walnuts and the oranges, the squeals of Sam and Catherine's two boys and the voluminous dinner, he opened the diary and inscribed with no hesitation: *Diary of Charles P. Minor of Judea, Connecticut, age 11. Go to Hathaway School in 5 grade. Father, name: Joseph S. Minor, Mother, name P. Percy, sisters, Justine, Maud, Elizabeth, brothers Samuel, Frederick. Elizabeth died.* Perhaps this was the perfect place to stop and save time, a diary. How had Mama known he wanted it, when he had not known it himself? Words would hold time forever. But since written words belonged to God, he would have to be careful. Nothing selfish could be put down, nothing angry. The diary would have to be like an Indian's knotted string, tied to remind only him of what unspoken things were meant. He longed for the New Year, so that he might begin his recorded life.

Wednesday, played checkers with Papa. Papa won. He had been very annoyed to lose. *Thursday. Shot two baskets and won the game for our team.* Proud. *Friday. Sliding at Mrs. O'Neil's,* he wrote by the lamp in his small bedroom. They had paused with runners hushed at the ends of ropes.

"I've told you boys before! No sliding on this property!" Mrs. O'Neil's voice was loud but pinched. She slammed the back door and they saw her bulky shape appear in the kitchen window to watch whether they obeyed.

"Let's go around back!" Simon said; and they turned up the

hill to approach Mrs. O'Neil's sloping field from another angle. The sun was orange and only a few inches above the horizon as they pressed upward, rapid breaths condensing.

"Don't tire yourself," Mama said so often. What was wrong with him? "You were frail, as a baby."

"Beat you to the top!" Arley started to run, his sled clattering on icy ruts. He threw back his head and the two triangles of red hair that fell over his forehead from Papa's barbering blew back. Still Simon was beginning to overtake him and when they reached the top of the hill and ran wavering into the deep snow, Simon flung himself down to win by a body length. They lay in the snow, chests heaving. After all, Simon was taller.

Smoke lifted out of Mrs. O'Neil's chimney, and the orange sun glinted off the granite in the brook to the left below. To keep off her property they would have to follow the bank of the brook without sliding into it.

Snow blew into Arley's face and filmed his new glasses, but he would need them to make out the crevices in the dimming hillside. "Come on!" he shouted, throwing himself onto his sled, digging off, leading Simon into action. At the top of a rise, he threw his weight into his left shoulder and yanked back on the right but Simon was too close behind him, too fast.

"Get over!" Simon screamed on his left and when Arley swerved he jumped the crest and began a rapid descent straight to Mrs. O'Neil's door. Snow packing his cuffs, he finally tunneled into it, while Simon shot the same crest and rolled to a stop beside him. They laughed in bursts that were like shouts. The door opened.

"No trespassing, I said!" The lamp from her kitchen glowed behind Mrs. O'Neil, who stood in the doorway with a broom.

"Arley Minor, you still hanging around with that nigger? The whole town's talking about it!"

Arley brushed snow from his wrists.

"A spook on my property? A coon?" She advanced toward them, her long skirt dragging with snow, the glow from the kitchen making her look holy, somehow, right, though she was wrong.

Simon stood as she lurched toward him, pushing the broom into his face and grabbing for the rope of his sled. Simon let go and was running.

"Hey!" Arley stumbled uphill after him with his own sled still responding at the end of its rope. He never caught up.

"That sled was Simon's property," he said at the supper table.

"That field was Mrs. O'Neil's," Papa replied.

Arley shut the red diary and pushed it under the bed; he pushed his glasses after it. He said his prayers and pulled the blanket over his head, but he could not sleep. God should strike Mrs. O'Neil. If only he himself had enough faith to get the power. Maybe if he studied the miracles more carefully and didn't just joke about them with Bernie Necomber, he would get some hints. Now all he could do was go over the names Mrs. O'Neil had called Simon and erase each one from the air. He was still awake when the horses came back with the funeral wagon, and he heard his father and Sam stifle a laugh as they lifted the creaking ambulance basket out. Mr. Hubbard of Hillsboro, who had died after a supper of duck and apple pie, was being brought to the judge at last. In all the world there was no power stronger than the judge's; the world itself ended in his barn. Where else could he look?

"And a hockey stick, and a diary. What did you get?" Arley walked through the kitchen with his second cousin.

"I got a diary, too!" Sam Percy said. "And I'm not going to let my dad see it. I'd get it then!"

Arley wondered what sins Sam Percy had committed. He probably would not understand why Arley kept a diary. If only Sam Percy were smarter or Stanton Goode heartier.

"Let's go look for butternuts," he suggested; but as they passed through the pantry, Sam Percy picked up an apple and, once out the back door, flung it at Arley. Then they were jumping each other and Sam Percy downed Arley, turning his face into the hard crust of snow, where his glasses came off. Squinting, Arley managed to get out from under and pin Sam Percy to the barn door by the neck until he surrendered. Of course, he was almost two years older than Sam Percy, though scarcely bigger. **He** could not find the glasses. Neither could Joseph, who searched an hour for them. *Papa is mad as sin*, Arley recorded. Eight dollars thrown into the snow. It was all right to record anger so long as it was somebody else who got mad. That night it *snowed like time*, but by the arrival of his new glasses, it was *raining like the old Harry*.

Two loads of kindling. Shame at what he'd said. Simon and he took turns pushing each other on the sled up the road to the farm, where they tucked the sled upright on its runners at the edge of the woods. Light showed among the young growth there, gray birch, white pine, a few maples no higher than Simon. Snow covered the rocks and roots along the path and they could hear the brook far ahead.

"Follow me." Simon ran long-legged and steady over the treacherous path. "My old man caught your cousin Sam Percy smoking in here last week," he called, his voice producing the slightest echo.

Arley struggled to keep up; his boot buckles had come undone again.

"And that's not all," Simon pointed to the right. "That's the pine he caught Catherine and your brother Sam under, the spring before they were married."

Arley's galoshes had been Sam's, saved seventeen years for the winter they would fit. This, apparently, was not it.

"Lying down," Simon, now twenty feet ahead, added. "Did you hear me?"

"Yes," Arley replied. Had Catherine slipped on the root-filled path?

"You know what they were doing, don't you?" Simon continued, coming to a halt in a small clearing, panting slightly as he waited for Arley.

"What's that?" Arley inquired. It registered on him that Simon was using the tone that Arley and Bernie Necomber adopted for talk about the woman with the issue of blood.

"Knowing each other." Simon stood tall over the finally **halted**

Arley. "Like in the Bible," he grinned, his brown face white at teeth and eyes.

"Oh, sure," Arley answered. "My brother Sam knows all about it." It had not actually occurred to Arley that the mating of men and women could take place outdoors. Wasn't it always late at night in a heap of nightgowns and bedclothes? And never before marriage? Only what Papa called the poorer element did that.

Simon laughed. "Before they got married he knew all about it? So what about her?" Simon restated his accusation. "My old man shooed them out!"

"Oh, did he?" Arley answered. He stooped to rebuckle his boots.

"Your sister-in-law Catherine, she sure was mad." Simon reached for a fallen birch branch. "She tried to make Pa promise not to tell. But he wouldn't promise." Simon began to strip the branch.

Arley stood up and started to pick for kindling. "He shouldn't have shooed them out," he finally said with deliberation.

"Why not?" Simon sounded surprised, as he turned for kindling.

"These are my father's woods," Arley explained carefully. "They aren't your father's."

One morning Arley and Sam Percy stood the tall, black-haired Starkweather in a snowball fight with what was to be the last of the spring's snow. Later, in the locker room, by a vote of five to two, Arley outplaced Starkweather and became captain of the fifth-grade baseball team. To you who have made all things possible, my friends, I promise. Yes, it was clear now, he had always been a success in the world, away from home. It was okay with the boys and God if he breathed. In fact, God even wanted him to, perhaps smiled when Arley breathed, and took his great hands and clapped them together in a great albeit little gesture of applause.

As captain, he was not only suddenly automatically equal to the other boys, but better. Hold it. Five to two. Two had voted for Starkweather? Had they no loyalty to Arley? He would see that they developed it. What was it they didn't like about him, anyway? His shortness? His glasses? His former frailness?

"I'll buy you a soda," Starkweather said. At the drug store on the way home from school, Arley joked with the former captain so graceful in defeat, but could not finish his chocolate soda.

"Well, captain, we'll have to fatten you up!" Polly stroked his hair at breakfast.

"In front of Sporting Goods, quarter of five." On his morning stop-by to see Polly, Fred told Arley where to wait for him that afternoon.

"Quarter of five," Arley repeated, swallowing oatmeal in gulps.

"We've got to get a suit for our captain, don't we, Mama?" Fred went off to catch the trolley for Chester.

"You come home from school first, Charles," Mama reminded him. "And get home early enough to rest."

"I'll try," Arley promised; but he barely got home in time to leave his books before running out to catch the trolley. It was his fifth trip to Chester alone and he leaned out the window looking for landmarks. There were more autos on the road than last time. He began to count. Yes, about two thirds horses, one third autos.

He got off at the city's center and walked with no trouble to Sporting Goods. Inside he cast an eye about for a tall figure and listened for a voice engaged in conversation with a clerk. A man of character whose hands were clean of both manure and embalming fluid. Fred would be eliciting interesting facts about the sporting business. But Fred wasn't there. He must have been detained making an important decision on the manufacture of umbrellas, perhaps planning the sale of umbrellas to the entire state of Illinois. Abraham Lincoln's state; the people's choice.

Arley stood outside, leaning in a casual pose against the doorway. Simon had always been their star pitcher. Simon must have voted for him, and Bernie Necomber? They must think of him as a leader, not just as a skilled player. When Joseph Minor walked into a room, people turned to laugh at his jokes, to pull at their lips and lean toward him expectantly. Fred, too. Even Sam, who knew what to do in the woods. Now Arley would be like that.

He would be a captain in life—famous, perhaps historic. Children would be taught his name at holiday celebrations. He would never die.

Had the umbrella machines jammed and reversed directions in a sinister misapplication of the laws of order? Was the factory a mass of twisted handles and wrenched canopies? Or had Fred simply forgotten? Arley checked the clock in the store: 5:15. He went back inside. He would put Simon on the mound. He would put Starkweather on second base. Who needed a baseball suit? He walked up to the clerk behind the counter.

"If Mister Frederick Minor should come looking for his brother Charles," he said in a reedy voice and blinking only once, "please tell him that his brother Charles has returned home on the trolley."

Fred had, indeed, forgotten. Unusual for him, but within a few days he delivered the suit. He added an expensive glove, a dollar thirty-five: wonderful. The days twisted and turned toward baseball.

"Pupils who have scored one hundred percent on their grammar quizzes," began Miss Bolton in her daily litany, "may move among the lesser pupils to correct mistakes."

Arley rose, the only boy among the handful of correctors. His feet were hot in his high galoshes, but it seemed needless to take them off so near to lunch.

"Caesar gave the order to Brutus and me," he read aloud for Rowena Peterson, a pretty yellow-haired girl who sat at some distance from him. "Not to I." The lunch bell.

Waving good-byes, sharing thumps upon the shoulders, Arley left the school yard and ran home, with his galoshes generating more heat. He raced through the back stairs and let the door slam shut behind him.

"The athlete!" his father said, swinging around in his swivel chair. "Mother! The athlete has returned for lunch." Joseph stood up, rebuttoning his black vest and checked the time on his gold watch: "Twelve-oh-seven. You're a minute late, aren't you, boy?"

"Sixty seconds," Arley said, as he peeled off his spring jacket.

Mama came around the corner with a covered pot of something. Lamb stew? Smelled like it. "Sit down," she ordered.

Joseph returned the gold watch to one vest pocket and settled the gold chain that hung in an arc to the other pocket. He sat and began to serve the stew.

"Thirty-one bouquets," he announced.

"So many!" Mama apparently knew what he was talking about. "Gertrude won't like that one bit."

"She'll love it," Joseph said. Everybody wants to get a lot of flowers.

"Gertrude's old-fashioned." Polly passed the mustard relish that Joseph liked to eat with all his meals. "She doesn't like fuss."

"Think she wants to see Walter in a shroud?" He piled the relish onto his own plate, where it ran together with the stew.

"What's a shroud?" Arley asked, forgetting to suppress questions about the business, as he was usually careful to do.

"A sheet," his father explained, taking a spoonful of stew. "Wrap it around the body, tuck it under." He was speaking with his mouth full.

"What for?" Arley inquired. He might as well appear completely unknowing. Had he made it sufficiently clear lately that he had no intention of joining the family business?

"So they could leave their good suits to their sons." He smiled as he chewed. "Believe me, shrouds must have been a whole lot easier to get on!"

"Joseph!" Polly interrupted her husband. "It makes a family feel better, Charles, to see the person who's gone looking nice in his own clothes. And with all the work your father does on them, it would be a pity to cover their faces." She helped herself to some cucumber pickles with a slightly tarnished silver fork. "Thirty-three," she added. "That's a waste!"

"Thirty-one," Joseph corrected her. "Now, Polly, remember, you're to pick the next-to-cheapest mahogany and bury me in that stained morning suit." Joseph continued in an amused tone. "Save the snappy green tweed for Charles here, if he ever grows into it."

"I'm playing baseball this afternoon and tomorrow afternoon," Arley put in. With thirty-one bouquets it would be a busy day.

"Then you go down to Willie Peach's tonight with Sam. He's got to pick up a hundred folding chairs for Gertrude. Make sure you get his Herkimer Noiseless."

"Yes, sir," Arley said.

Polly began to clear the table. On the buffet, behind where she had been sitting, Arley saw what looked like a pair of handcuffs.

"What's that?" he asked, eager to change the subject.

"It's handcuffs." Joseph wiped his lips with a white napkin.

"What for?" Arley stood up and walked over to the buffet.

"Criminals." His father was not going to give him a straight answer.

"They're for a joke at the social Wednesday," his mother began, going into the kitchen with a second load of dishes.

"Some folks are planning to hitch themselves up to some other folks in the dark." His father finished the explanation and laughed. "It was my idea. Here." Joseph stood and took the cuffs from Arley. "Stick out your wrists." He snapped the cuffs around them.

"You've got me, Judge," Arley said, pulling the chain taut.

"You promising the truth, the whole truth and nothing but?" Joseph fingered his watch chain.

"Sure am!"

"How much apple pie you eat last night?" The judge indicated the half-eaten pie Polly was bringing to the table.

"All of it, Judge, I'm guilty, yes, I'm guilty." If you made the accusation against yourself before the judge did, you were as powerful. And perhaps more innocent.

"You're free then!" Joseph reached to open the cuffs. "So long as you can admit you were bad."

Papa knew the same trick. But the cuffs did not open.

"Put your hands on the table." Joseph squinted and pushed the knob again. "Must be a combination lock," he considered aloud.

Polly sliced. "Dessert at jail today will be apple pie."

"We'll be a minute," Joseph said.

"I'll serve it up," Polly answered.

"No, you won't," he said quietly, but rather too evenly.

"But he has to get back to school," she said, knife stopped in midair.

"You won't serve!" Joseph flushed red, the color flooding from the edge of his white mustache up to his hairline.

"Hold still!" he shouted at Arley, who had not moved.

Arley could not look at his mother for fear he would laugh. He thought of his brothers' stories about Papa's rages, while laughter, mixed with fear, bubbled in his stomach. Remember the time Papa and Justine had got to laughing at a prayer meeting?

His father fumbled with the lock; it was so quiet Arley thought he could hear his mother buttering a leftover piece of bread.

Slamming Arley's hands to the table, Joseph strode to the telephone on the wall near his desk. He gave the operator the number. Arley did not dare to move.

He was breathing heavily. "Tommy, what's the combination of that lock? It's Joseph."

"Okay, I've got it. Good-bye. Never mind about that, Tommy, I said good-bye." He hung up and with pursed lips undid the lock.

Mama handed Arley a piece of warmed pie and he bolted it down, standing by the table, still in his hot galoshes.

Ha ha ha, he would write in his diary. *A good one on Pa.*

Then he was off running back to school, where he was older and free and people liked him. "Hey, Minor!" Mama was plenty clear on right and wrong, her systems were the right way to do things. But Papa just liked bossing people around. Arithmetic, spelling and then the closing bell that freed him further to the locker room and to spring that lay on the ball field. Across the road, on a broader, greener field, the Rhodes boys played in their blue sweatsuits. Fred and Sam had never played sports at Rhodes. They had been due at the farm every afternoon for milking. Two for the price of one, Joseph had bargained with a headmaster desirous of seasoning his city boys with some old-fashioned locals. Tossing the ball on the grammar-school side, Arley knew that one day he would grow big enough to cross the street and toss it at Rhodes. Sam had joined Papa. But Fred had risen free.

It didn't matter how. Everything he wanted would come to pass. Baseball gave Arley that feeling through its inexorable slowness. The desperate grabs and truncated slides into bases took place within timeless afternoons that neither began nor ended. Lazy, the ball spun toward the batter, suspended idly, reversed and spun out to soar above the uplifted hands of the outfielder. Then it dropped, predetermined, through all of April into those waiting hands. *The score 10 to 8, the score 14 to 15, the score 7 to 12;* Arley recorded sacred numbers each night. The winning itself was never predetermined. You fought your hardest to win, and if you won often enough, you would grow up to be a man.

LIVING FOR JESUS *a life that is tru-ue, striving to please Him in all that I do-oo.* The blue of the shepherd's coat in the stained glass over Arley's shoulder suddenly dulled, as small drops of rain were blown in chilling drafts over the Methodist church. Was it raining over the Congregational church as well? Or had the wind pushed a single cloud above the Methodist steeple, smack over the wooden cross and over the soul which now and evermore was struggling to rise out of the vertical body nailed there? Straight out of the top of the body's head it blossomed, flowering with the white wings of transubstantiation that unfolded from the shoulders, which straightened as they rose? Not dead. Never to die. Born again. Well, not really this week, wait until next Sunday, Easter.

Willing to suffer affliction and loss, Arley sang with the others. Before Easter, on Thursday evening, he was supposed to join the church. But Jesus had not called to him, nor God. He wanted assurance. It was hard work the dying Jesus did, but at least Jesus had known when doing the miracles, when waking fellows from the dead, and when carrying the cross that he was Jesus. If you knew you were full of glory as the son of God, you could afford a few nails.

The song drained to an end. When the congregation had sat down the new Reverend Mr. Albee was standing alone. Had Jesus really known who he was? Mr. Albee wanted the boys and girls preparing to join the church to think it over. What if he had been taking a chance? Arley felt sweat on his forehead.

Mr. Albee leaned over the pulpit: "In those days the prophets of the Hebrews went about preaching in brown robes tied with belts of hemp or rope." A graduate of Yale Divinity School, Mr. Albee was not to be messed with on matters of historical detail. "Jesus, too, no doubt wore that same brown robe when he entered Jerusalem on Palm Sunday. . . ."

Next to the sheep in the stained glass, the shepherd Jesus was brightening; the sun shower must have stopped. His seamless robe glowed its usual luminescent blue. Had the robe really been brown?

What if Jesus had not been sure if the Father would save him on the cross? And had God really come to the rescue? Or had Jesus risked it all and lost? Jesus either was or was not the son of God; Arley had to stake his life on which was true. An unimportant prophet carelessly murdered? Now the sweat began to prickle along Arley's neck.

"The same people who acclaimed him that Sunday were to abandon him on Thursday. . . ." Arley shut out Mr. Albee's voice. If he were going to give his life to Jesus Thursday, and make him his captain, didn't he have to know that he was going to rise and win?

His mother pressed pages in her hymn book from the fat to the thin side as the congregation stood. *Jesus calls us . . . saying, "Christian, follow me."* The minister and choir strode out, singing their way home to chicken dinners. In the Minor pew, Arley bowed his head. If you won in the world, you lost in heaven; if you lost in the world, you won in heaven. Which should he choose?

The benediction came to him from the back of the church, where Mr. Albee stood with outstretched arms calling out: "THE LORD MAKE HIS FACE TO SHINE UPON YOU." Arley felt the blessing coming from God's hands. "THE LORD LIFT UP HIS COUNTENANCE BEFORE YOU." Benediction hitched the upper arc of heaven, where the spirit was, to the lower arc of earth, which bodies occupied. In that giant shell, Arley might curl himself; he could have both heaven and earth. If only he could hear God calling him. Down the aisle and into the vestibule, Arley followed his mother. Her body was shapeless in the gray and white spring suit, her shoulders rounded and her forward-bending head was totally gray.

That afternoon he dared not nap for fear of waking in the dark room wondering if he were his shadow from the dream or from the mirror, imagining himself again. So when Papa suggested that the Minor men take the new Reo out for a spin, Arley jumped at the chance. Justine refused to go; she had wanted a Buick. Out on the road, Sam steered while Papa gave the orders. Fred and Arley hung onto the running boards, ready to push on the gentle rises. For the steeper hills, Papa got out and helped. "Let 'er roll!" Papa and Fred jumped back in while Arley hung off the running board, stretching for branches during the sweep downhill. The Minor men worked together. He felt much better; the world was good. Thursday would never come.

But the fear that had licked at his heels all day and followed beneath them as he climbed the back stairway to his bedroom finally planted itself firmly against the soles of his extended feet, in perfect match. With his inner eye he saw Jesus twisted on the cross: his eyes held Arley's, his lips moved: "Follow me." He had always suspected it would be Jesus, rather than God, who called. "All right," he said in a whisper, "I won't leave you there alone." Besides, Jesus could not have lost, he assured himself as he curled up his legs and pressed his fingers against his knee. This is the nineteen hundred and fourteenth year of Our Lord Jesus Christ and that proves it. God did come to rescue his Son. The fear separated from the soles of Arley's feet, and he slept.

"Let's take the auto, Mama," Arley urged, but no. As she had for years, Polly drove the horse to her mother's on Wednesday, and now that summer was here Arley went along to play tennis with the Cobb girls on their court.

"So Maud has three daughters." Polly spoke of the new letter from Rhodesia. "I wish I could see them."

Those daughters must be to Mama like the perpetuation of her

line. Arley held his tennis racquet between his knees. Sam had
two sons, but a line of women descending from women was
something entirely different from a line of men descending from
men. It was a shadow, but the shadow of something invisible,
hidden, about to be. Who knew the Virgin Mary's great-great-
grandmother? But it was essential to all of history that she had
lived. Even though you didn't have to believe Mary had remained
a virgin after Jesus, as Mr. Albee had allowed to the newest
members of his church.

"So long," Arley called the minute they stopped in front of the
hitching post. He avoided Grandma Percy and her two fanciful
brothers whenever he could. But at the Cobbs' large house, he
was told that the girls had gone to Chester with their mother.
The taste of tennis in his mouth all morning gone, and the private
tournament he played against Doris Cobb halted with the score in
her favor. Disappointed, Arley walked past the large rock his
mother used to point out to him. A seedling had grown right
through and split the rock: "shows you how you can win if you
keep on trying." He headed over the high land of his grandmother's farm. Turning into a new angle of a rising slope, he noticed a
figure slumped against a tree at the top of the rise.

Was it his Great-uncle Earl, who was becoming daffy? Or his
Great-uncle Win, who always had been? Something about the
old man's posture made him look strange.

"Hey!"

Arley froze in his tracks with a stare boring through his neck.

"You, there!" Uncle Win motioned him to the tree.

"Uncle Win," Arley said, walking toward the sour-breathed
man, "I didn't know that was you."

"Humm?" Uncle Win's ninety-year-old eyelids squinted
against sunshine.

"It's Charles," he identified himself. "Polly's boy."

"Of course it is!" Uncle Win's voice was hoarse. "You are the
one I was expecting. I have a message for you." His eyes were
such a pale blue that the light did not seem to go into them, just
as it did not enter a cow's flesh-like eyeballs.

"From Grandma?" Arley asked, sitting cross-legged by the
tree. She was sick and might come to live with them in Judea.

"Oh, no." The old man's voice lowered and rounded into a secret. "It's from the spirits." He swung his arm to encompass the slanting fields around them. "This is when most of them come round to talk to me, you know."

Summer was in the field, the noon light wavered under the tree and the buzzing of insects became sinister.

"You may not hear them, of course, but I do." Spit came from a corner of the old man's lips and he looked away, widening his eyes and giving a slight nod toward the middle distance.

A bee buzzed near Arley and landed on his wrist. He held still. That's what you did for bees. What did you do when crazy old men lit on you?

"Polly's boy?" The lips covered the gums and vanished inward when he smiled. "It was for you, the message. Death before the summer ends." He spoke in an offhand manner and his gaze wandered out. "I'm glad you came by."

The light dimmed and brightened as clouds passed overhead. The bee flew away.

"I got to go." Arley stood up. "Good-bye now," he called in a last attempt at normal behavior. Then he started slowly on a long traverse that would take him to the lower road without having to turn his back on Uncle Win. There were snakes in this field and Arley let his gaze dart from the grass to Uncle Win's tree, his slow escape becoming faster and faster as he began to run in wide criss-crossing sweeps down the sloping field. Straight through the boggiest ground he ran, his eyes continually off the ground now and his feet almost off, too. He pumped so fast that if he should step on snakes he'd hardly know it. When he finally flung himself onto the dust of the road, his mouth was dry from panting and his whole body damp from sweat. Looking back, he could make out a dark figure the size of a silver dollar leaning against the tree. Dotty as birds, everybody said. His father joked about Uncle Earl and Uncle Win. Ought to hire them to dig graves. That's what dimwits were good for; sometimes Joseph did hire dimwits from the state farm—when Old Simon couldn't come.

Spring deepened toward summer and its danger. From the spirit? Or from the flesh? By daylight Arley was fine. *Blest bee-ee the tie-ee that binds our har-erts in Chri-is-tian love:* Old Simon hummed as he troweled grass near where Arley was mowing. Yesterday Old Simon and Arley had laid cement on top of the dirt path through the Minor lawn.

Today they worked apart. Arley mowed at home without pay. At the cemetery he got twelve and a half cents an hour from Papa; he already had eleven dollars and twenty cents in the bank, and eighty cents of it he hadn't even worked for. Interest; wonderful! Sun shimmered off the grass with a dazzling that must be like radiance; did Jesus feel that way when he rose? Arley turned the mower away from Old Simon. Saturday night he was going to the Winchester Revival.

By mid-afternoon the whole lawn was in shadow and the trees no longer offered local shade. A few big drops of rain began to fall and Arley ran the half mile to the farm to help get in the last few bales of early hay. The storm held over the roofs of town until darkness came, with thunder. It was lucky there were no finished bodies in the barn's annex; they usually went bad during electrical storms.

Arley said goodnight and hurried into his checkered pajamas. It would be fun to watch the storm from the newly glassed-in porch upstairs, where Mama was letting him sleep this summer. Watching the storm, he needn't worry about the death Uncle Win had promised him. He wrapped himself in a bedsheet and sat in the middle of town, eye-level with the top of the long lawn and the base of the Congregational steeple. Thunder was God's voice and Arley liked to listen; he was not afraid of it anymore. The town shrank closer to ground under the clouds and Arley watched a quick fork of lightning lick out of the sky. FEAR NOT, the big voice said, FOR I AM WITH YOU; the voice rumbled and amused itself.

The lightning became louder and more frequent, cracking nearer and nearer to the thunder as the storm moved over from Chester. Arley watched the sky near the Congregational steeple warily. A crack right over his head made him flinch and it was joined immediately by thunder. When he opened his eyes he saw a round glow at the top of the lawn. Uncle Win's spirits? A round glowing eye? Whatever it was it knew Arley and was rushing down the lawn directly at him in his glassed-in porch. Why him? He would be seared! Consumed!

The dazzling was gone and rain beat steadily on the porch roof. He heard loud voices and laughter downstairs.

Wrapped in the sheet, he ran down.

"Ball lightning!" his father said, jovial and impressed as he pulled on his waterproof.

"We'll have two swaths across the lawn, now." Polly was laughing. "One of cement and one of fire."

"I bet not!" Joseph said, but he went to check. Ball lightning could leave a wake of burnt grass or a path of charred wood along a fence.

Justine and Paul Hathaway were sitting on the sofa. They had not even gotten up to look out the window.

"Scare you?" his mother asked, putting an arm around Arley's back.

"Oh, no," he said, shivering. He was almost her height now.

"My Uncle Winslow was always terrified of ball lightning," she said. "He called it God's eyeball."

At Winchester Methodist Camp Ground the four hundred candles burned as separated parts of one flame in the grove under the pine trees. *Are ye able, said the Master, to be crucified with Me?* Mosquitoes buzzed around him and Simon and all at once everything was changed and the world was good, and clothed in its own resurrection. Arley knew for sure that nothing dies. Except, was he crazy? Was this something new sent from Uncle Win?

"How different everything seems," Simon said to him as they filed out with the others, their candles all thrown into the campfire. "How can we be anything but cheerful and good?" Simon caught a firefly and showed it to Arley, cupped in his hands. When two of you had the same idea, you couldn't be crazy. The one Spirit would protect him from the many of Uncle Win.

Death by the flesh was coming from across the water. Ticking over the wire from London came stories of the Hun, who cut off babies' hands. In Chester, Connecticut, the press would not have to work overtime to impress these truths upon the Judea hinterland or upon the mind of Joseph Minor. Indeed, with the continual whisper of a few key words, Joseph would come to realize that he had always known the Huns to be evil brutes stabbing their swords into the chests of good Englishmen, the broad chests of the barons of Runnymede, proud fathers of the Bloodless Revolution, sole heirs of Christ and all the rest of ancient history. But first, he had to get the news.

"Good morning." Joseph spoke and nodded stiffly to the Italian police sergeant newly stationed at the intersection. In southern Europe people had hair in their noses. What did they know of the glory that was Greece, the grandeur that was Rome? There was something wrong with that, what . . . ?

"Mornin'." He interrupted his thought to greet the Irish police chief coming out of the town hall. A cut upward from Italian, though barely American. There was their pope, the loudness of their talk and the softness of their singing. And though they could save money, they spent it on all the wrong things: drink.

A smile for the man sweeping the floor of the probate office. Not a black boy—too few in Judea to go around. A Polack from Elmsy. He was, at least, white, but God knew what went on in his head. Poland was a part of the world that had no history: where was Poland when the Romans were out conquering? Not even on the field! And the British hadn't even tried to get them into the empire! Their little summer cottages out at the lake were filled with litter and the floors unswept. And so cold in winter. They would never work their way up; their women kept their hair in curling papers.

But the Germans? He had always respected the Germans: they kept a good store and ran a good farm. Though he did not understand their heavier music, the band from Chester was the best around; it always made him feel like marching, and that's what a band was for.

"What do you think of the news?" The first selectman poked his head into Joseph's cubby-hole.

"Depends on what it is," replied Joseph in the manner for which he had gained local renown.

"The Archduke, the shots—in Bosnia." The selectman looked puzzled at the judge's ignorance.

Bosnia, where was that? Joseph stared blankly and expectantly ahead. It was June, 1914.

IV

Armistice Day, 1918

"Gᴏᴛ ɪᴛ!" Arley spoke as much to himself as to Bernie or Stark-weather.

"Mine!" Bernie caught the ball as it fell through the hoop and he dribbled his way back for a long shot.

"Okay," Starkweather the captain said, reaching from his height to palm the unsuccessful shot off the backboard.

A door opened in the back of the gym.

"Here's Conley," Bernie said, passing a long shot across the court. Conley connected with the ball as if it were part of him, the combination a modern centaur.

Conley tossed it easily toward Arley, moving in his loose, swaggering way as if he never thought ahead but as if each move-ment came up out of the balls of his feet, right up out of the floor and the earth beneath it.

Arley flubbed the shot from Conley, but quickly recovered the ball and tossed it in a sharp jerk to Starkweather. A short man has trouble swaggering, Arley told himself; it requires leg-length. Still, here he was, an elected vice-president of the sophomore class, throwing a few with the president and with two members of last year's team. He was the only one of the four who had not made Judea High's first squad last year, and this was the year he hoped to become one of that quick-moving bunch. Not the captain. Not yet. In imitating Conley off the court, Arley had come to stand a lot with hands in his pockets or with a leg up on a chair. He had learned to turn the upper half of his body around without moving the lower half. The thing he did not understand was why a boy like himself had to work at popularity while a boy like Conley just moved with it among crowds. The girls leaned a little away on the balls of their feet and then pressed forward toward Conley when he passed. And when Conley ringed a ball, the crowds of the Valley League cheered with a hard love that swelled up and out of the bleachers to fill the gymnasium with satisfaction and longing.

"Minor, old man." Conley tossed him one slowly and Arley caught it. In a deliberately long movement he arced it up, but it fell short at the edge of the hoop. He tried not to show he cared. Conley came around corners with the ease of people who did not struggle with God. Well, Conley was a Catholic, things were thought out for him. He would not stoop so low as his father and call Conley the "wretched refuse of our teeming shore." But Catholics did have it easier, didn't they?

"Nice shot!" Starkweather complimented Bernie. Those two and Conley and Simon and Melko had formed the first string last year. With Schless and Riccio as the substitutes. This year Simon had dropped out of practice and gone to work for Arley's father at the cemetery in the afternoons. Arley hoped to replace him by playing better than either Riccio or Schless. If only school hadn't shut for the flu and cut his practice time.

"We open tomorrow," Starkweather the class president reminded his charges.

Conley slipped one over the hoop and suddenly bells began to ring.

"It's it!" Arley shouted. "It's the armistice!" Scooping up the ball as he ran toward the door, Arley led the other boys in a burst out the back door of the high school.

"They signed! They signed!" The fat man from the fire department was out on the road, running with his arms up in the air.

"Hey!" The boys gave a cheer with him and Arley heard the notes of the bells of the two churches mingling above the green on which the suddenly old war monument stood.

"Let's go ring them!" Arley shouted and was off to the Methodist belfry with Bernie behind him. Later, he realized that

Starkweather must have broken for the Congo church, and that maybe Conley had joined him. Running fast and breathing heavily, Arley passed through the arched doorway and up the tower stairway to the steeple belfry, where he heard men's voices. Reaching for the rungs of the ladder, he realized he still held the basketball, and he tucked it in a niche. He climbed up hand over hand, with someone clambering behind him.

On a narrow balcony that gave onto a deep drop filled with hanging ropes Arley stood and watched hands reach out and grab for a rope, shoulders lean onto them and let go. There was no tune beyond clamor, and Arley was just stretching for his first rope when he heard the sound of Mr. Albee's voice on the ladder.

"False alarm, boys!"

Arley hesitated and his rope swung away, its looping tip thumping against the wall far below.

Mr. Albee came dustily into the cramped space, the only man there in a suit jacket. "It's a fake telegram," he explained, a little out of breath. "The war isn't even over."

The last bell sounded above them and then they heard only the swish of settling ropes. Bell tones were still in the air from the Congo church and then those, too, vanished.

"Fake?"

"Yes," Mr. Albee said, leading the exit from the belfry. "One at a time now; these stairs are rickety. When the war is really over, you come on back and we'll ring them again."

On the way down, Arley picked up the basketball.

THE SONS OF LIGHT had still to beat the sons of darkness; would the war drag on until March, when he would be seventeen? A few men were still volunteering.

"Brown from River Road, Chester." Papa read their names out loud from the Chester *Star* after supper that night. "Someone for the colored unit, Polly." He raised his voice so Polly could hear. "Hope he knows how to cook fatback!"

Studying at the dining table, Arley tried to shut out Joseph's voice.

"Caplan, a Jew in the army? Taking a chance, wouldn't you say, Polly?"

She didn't answer him. "Turn around," she said through pins to Justine, who was modeling yet another dress for her trousseau while Polly hung the hem.

"I'm going to bed," Arley announced and gathered up his books. He did not want to hear Justine laugh. Or see Polly stick her head out of the sewing room and nod toward Joseph. Polly's power came from the backs of chairs and perhaps she was already thinking up a way to prove Joseph wrong. Sometimes you didn't know Mama had won until days later.

"Goodnight!" Arley called into the sewing room. Nobody called it the dying room this year. It was waiting for someone young like his sister Elizabeth or someone old like Grandma Percy, who had lain there last year.

He climbed up the kitchen stairs to his room and got into his pajamas. Justine had begun preparing for her wedding the day they brought her back from Boston last June after she finished finishing school. Justine was both beautiful and proud, and he was neither. But she was the nearest to him, the only Minor to have seen him naked. Long ago, of course. Mama had, too, perhaps. Justine was the only Minor he had seen, a glimpse in the bathroom.

He picked up his diary. *False alarm*, he wrote. *The clash of the sword, the sound of the shell continues.* He flipped to the back to measure himself against his life's plan. *Physical perfection by 19.* Dr. Frank had already told him he possessed the best physique of any Minor man. And if he could sleep on the porch through Christmas, that should further harden him. *Mental perfection by 29. Spiritual perfection by 39.* After that, he could not imagine himself and had simply drawn an arrow into the future. He picked up the Bible to begin his spiritual exercise.

In the four years since the Winchester Revival, when he had vowed to read the Bible daily, he had gotten through from the Old Testament to the New. Had gotten from where flesh was given for flesh and careful justice reigned to where spirit overcame flesh and what you did didn't matter so much as what you thought. And all because God had given his son away. You were not supposed to think of a girl like Laura naked and Arley opened quickly to where he was in the gospel of John. I GIVE UNTO THEM ETERNAL LIFE; AND THEY SHALL NEVER PERISH, NEITHER SHALL ANY MAN PLUCK THEM OUT OF MY HAND. Arley readjusted his pajama bottoms where they pulled too tight. MY FATHER, WHICH GAVE THEM ME, IS GREATER THAN ALL; AND NO MAN IS ABLE TO PLUCK THEM OUT OF MY FATHER'S HAND. A car backfired up to the intersection. I AND MY FATHER ARE ONE. Arley's eyes hurt and he blinked. THEN THE JEWS TOOK UP STONES TO STONE HIM. It was a pretty good story with lots of action, but this was not one of those nights he felt like more of the Bible than would fulfill his vow. He shut out his light and walked past the guest room where his brothers had slept long ago, past Justine's, where she would lie thinking of Paul, and into his parents' room, from which one door opened onto his sleeping porch. The other entrance was from Justine's room, but he never used that door. He stubbed his toe against the cot, but, having found it, stretched out his winning physique and silently moved his lips: "Please don't let any American boys die tonight. It wouldn't be fair."

Not smoking was important, too; maybe if he never took it up he would keep on growing. He crossed his hands under his head and was back in Boston. After the long drive in the Reo, they had found Justine taller and with her hair piled up. He had stared at her white dress with flowers over the breasts until she introduced him to Laura. Then there was no one but Laura. All the next day he had thought of Laura's small body while his father pushed him along on a tour of Boston. Joseph stomped up and down the grassy aisles of Boston's cemeteries to test the condition of the turf or laughed his short bark at inscriptions: "Mother Maisie dead at thirty, my but she was sweet and pretty." Laura was twenty or so, older than he. But wasn't everyone in his family? He had kept his head down, watching where he stepped. His father's first formal lesson: never walk on the dead. What? Samuel Adams? Arley had edged his toe to the line where the shovels had once dug. So it happened even when you were famous?

On the dormitory porch after supper Laura had jokingly put her arm around him and he had taken that opportunity to lay his head close to her breasts. Brother! "I wish I had a brother like you," Laura had said and laughed at him with Justine. They showed him he was younger by giving him such privileges. Rubbed his face in it, so to speak. Well, what did he care! *It was some trip!*

The church bells struck eleven times each, the Methodists' bell beginning early, while the Congregationalists' started fashionably late. Looking uphill from his bed, Arley spotted a distant light crossing the playing lawn at Rhodes. Probably a school car bringing the rich boys from Chicago and St. Louis home from their sports; he was glad not to be among them. He loved Judea's high school because there were all kinds of people attending it. Conley and Schless and Goldsmith. He didn't hate Schless, and knowing Schless had made him feel a bit hesitant about hating the entire German army. He didn't think Goldsmith was odd or foreign or dangerous, though he couldn't understand why he never went out for sports. And he loved Conley as much as the next person. His class, the Class of 1921, was only the second class to be graduated by the new school but it would show the world how. If only Stanton hadn't moved away, he could have learned it, too. The letters Arley sent him were probably not doing the trick.

He woke suddenly with a picture in his mind of Laura leaning over him and smiling, of her reaching down to bring his head to her breasts. He heard a noise. The whistle at the umbrella factory? The war was over again! He was out of bed before the light in Mama's room went on.

"Where are you going?" Mama opened her door.

"To ring the bell! Mr. Albee said we should come back!"

"Charles, it's probably just another false alarm." She pulled her bathrobe around her.

They heard a noise on the lawn.

"Hello up there?" The voice was tentative, Mr. Albee.

Arley swung open a window. "Hello! I'm coming."

"Come back for breakfast, then!" Polly called as he ran down the stairs. "And don't forget your coat!"

But Arley was gone in jeans and a sweater, running across the yard after a vanishing Mr. Albee. He saw the lights going on in the church, first on the lower level, then gradually mounting higher and higher. As he pushed through the door the first bell reached him from above, clear and pure on the cold air, announcing victory. There would never be a war again, Arley knew as he swallowed against the tears that were mounting into his eyes as fast as he climbed the wooden stairs and then the rungs of the ladder. Never another war; now men would finally learn to love each other as the Lord urged them, yes. Up, up, he climbed, as mankind would climb; oh, it was fine, fine!

Mr. Albee and he alternated ropes in a steady pattern. Willie Peach's son came up and Bernie Necomber's father. The clatter of bells outside doubled.

"The Congregationalists are up!" Arley saluted them in his own belfry. Men and boys kept on coming off the ladder and grabbing for the ropes. It was getting crowded. Mr. Albee gave him a nod and Arley let go his rope. Someone else should celebrate, should spread joy in the town! Running down the lower stairs into the churchyard, Arley heard voices all about and then the Catholic bell from Elmsy began. He wiped at tears. Boys don't cry; they grow up to be soldiers. Well, not anymore; it's over! God was seeing to that.

He skirted the war monument and mouthed five or six names. Those dead boys should hear the bells most, shouldn't they? The obelisk looked like a dark shadow against the Congregational steeple; both carried names, stories, into the sky. He dashed off a short one as he ran in the darkness under the bell: "We thank Thee, Heavenly Father, that this morning people are no longer rushing at other people's chests to stab them." He ran toward the town hall, where there were lights.

"Ar-ley! Ar-ley!" A Ford car slid up beside him with Simon driving. Men piled out of the town hall and cars drove up in front of it. Boxes of flags appeared on the darkened lawn—from where, Arley never knew. A stack of horns. "I'm coming!" he called, and grabbed flags and horns for himself and Simon and the two dark shapes he counted in the back of the car, and climbed into the front. The hoots of horns and shouts of men formed a hovering sound along the ground while the bells above them kept on ringing. It was Simon's cousins in the back and Arley gave them their horns and flags. Before they knew it, the Ford was in the middle of a parade of honking cars which was making its way toward Chester.

"Peace! Peace!" Arley and Simon screamed, in alternating syncopation with the rest of the shouters in the shut and open cars that moved, bumper to bumper, through town. The swell and push of it reminded Arley of the commotion at the Chester station last year when the boys had come back from the Mexican border. Now those soldiers seemed to belong to another time, as did the boys from the Civil War, who had aged almost into knights.

"Peace! Peace!" Arley shrieked. Suddenly he saw the shape of Jesus waiting on the cross; for him there was no victory celebration. Jesus was still up there, trying, losing. So what. Maybe this was his celebration, at last! Arley was hoarse by the time they got to Chester, where the cars thickened to such a jam that motors were turned off. Arley waved to people from Judea whom he saw hanging out the windows of Fords or standing on the open seats of Reos. People in the distance were banging pots and pans. "They're burning Kaiser Willy!" a man shouted, but they were too far from the corner to see the effigy in flames. By the time Simon got his cousins' car back to Judea and turned the wheel over to them, at the school where he and Arley got out, it was daylight. They joined a group of some fifty schoolmates who were standing about in the front yard or strewn on the steps singing songs. Someone tapped on a megaphone: the town's big parade would begin at 1:00 p.m. and marching groups were announced. Should he march with his church or his school or with the Masons and their sons? Arley chose the Boy Scouts, because he was the patrol leader, and stopped off at home to pick up a doughnut and change into his uniform before running off to the rooms of the Bison Patrol.

When the parade started Arley was in the front column carrying the American flag and Joseph was several units behind with the Volunteer Fire Department. The pocketed leather belt into which the flagpole fit already pulled against Arley's kidneys, but he was relieved to be carrying the flag in cold weather. Last summer he had lugged it for several hours in the high heat of Memorial Day after having been up at dawn to lay the wreaths on the veterans' graves and stick in the little flags his father ordered from advertisements in *Sunnyside*, the undertakers' periodical. Had Papa expected him to put up the flags today?

There's a long long trail a-winding, into the land of our dreams. The German band from Elmsy was doing its best to include all the groups, and this one was surely for the Scouts. Good thing the Germans had not been disbanded, as some people had wanted. *The greatest of all years in the history of the human race:* he could see it in his diary tonight. *The insane breed of Prussians has been brought to its knees. Prussians* was the magic word he had used as a Methodist Cadet last summer, when he had lunged with a bayonet at an imaginary enemy. *Germans* did not do the trick; it only brought Herman Schless to mind.

He had the flag-tip level with the front steps of the town hall, where the governor had made his Liberty Bond speech by candlelight as the Chester Home Guard stood at attention and Arley pledged to sell bonds all week. His father had stood on these steps twirling the cage from which the thirteen names of Judea's draftees were called. Down those steps Arley and his father had accidentally dropped the five hundred ballots for the town election they had brought from Hartford. Papa had gotten lost up there in the city, but it had been all right as soon as they had begun to follow the golden dome of the capitol. The sun shone off that dome as it must have off the tips of the gold-topped pyramids. The same light that fell on the capitol at Hartford had fallen on the Parthenon and on the helmets of the Roman soldiers. The light of men was a public light: it shone on the hairs in Joseph Minor's mustache and curved under his chin, which was a strong one. Sometimes it was too bright and seared the grain right in the fields. The light that shone on Galilee was different; like moonlight, it could drive you crazy. His father running on both ballots had gotten elected again, while Arley on the school slate against Starkweather for presidency of the sophomore class had lost.

They turned a corner and Arley had the flag pointed **right** down the path toward yellow-haired Rowena Peterson's house. He had walked her up it last year. One icy night after Young People's he was making his way down the slippery church steps and had come up beside her and taken her arm. Talking constantly about the rehearsal for the Christmas pageant so he wouldn't have to take his arm away, he had led her up the path onto the verandah. But the next week, Rowena was arm in arm with her girl friend. Since then, he'd kissed five girls at spin the bottle and walked three more home. If you counted Doris Cobb. *Believe me, it was fun,* playing games with the other sex. If you counted Agnes Necomber.

Onward Christian soldiers, marching as to war: they continued to the gates of the cemetery. Arley saw with relief that the flags were up. The long column curved inside and Arley passed the first grave he had dug.

"Yeah," Simon had said when Arley came over to confirm the report that Simon was working afternoons at the cemetery. "I got to help my pa out." They had stood by while a short ceremony took place over a windy grave. There were bent heads, curved shoulders and handkerchiefs to faces. For the flu? When the mourners were gone, Joseph Minor had given Simon a sign and he had picked up the shovel and the spade and headed for the grave, where he removed the burlaping that covered the mound of dirt at its edge. The dirt was partly frozen and landed sharply on the metal vault that shielded the casket. After standing by for a minute, Arley took off his mittens and picked up the spade. He turned the dirt carefully at an angle above the hole. "If we get done faster," he said, eventually beginning to toss it in, "maybe you can come over to shoot a few before supper?"

The column formed into a big U and speeches began from a platform at its apex. Standing still was the hardest part and Arley spread his feet wide to balance the increasingly painful flag. There had been two funerals a day for two weeks in the second half of October, after school shut abruptly following the kissing party in the gym. Arley had worked almost full-time for Joseph. His job was to drive the Sayers and Scovill combination car while Joseph and Sam went in for the bodies. When there were too many bodies, Old Simon was brought over to work with Fred, who came home from the factory. The Minor men had to stick together. In November people had stopped shaking hands and Joseph and Sam wore gauze over their mouths at work. Would they catch it? The ringing of the telephone meant only that someone had died; Joseph grew tired but strangely patient.

"Winonah Goode dead?" he had asked one night at the table, and Fred, who had stayed for supper, exchanged a look with Polly.

"You worked on her yourself, Papa," Fred said. "Remember, we didn't have any ladies' burial shoes left?"

"Oh, yes," Joseph said, shaking out his napkin. "Oh, yes."

Then the bells had rung, yesterday for a false alarm. Today for victory. It had not come in time for everyone. To his left was the fresh grave of Mrs. Rutherford. One hundred and twenty miles in the Sayers car with Papa, to carry his first body. The lighter-weight baskets were in use at home, so they took an empty pine box to the front porch.

"She . . . it was this morning." A slender young man greeted them apologetically and motioned them upstairs. Joseph stooped to pick up one end of the box and Arley's fingers curved under the other. It felt suddenly light. When Joseph started up the stairs, Arley began to wonder how they would make it down. He had heard years of jokes about that very situation, and never laughed. Clumsily his feet found the steps hidden by the box and up they went into a hallway and up to a door where Joseph came to a stop. Arley walked his end out in a semi-circle and they sailed straight through. They set the box down at right angles to the bed. Joseph took two squares of gauze from his suit pocket and handed one to Arley, who tied it on hurriedly.

Joseph pulled the sheet back and Arley saw a face more blotched than any he could recall from glimpses into the barn. A brown froth oozed from her nose and mouth.

"Go for the smaller bag in the car, Arley," Joseph said. When Arley returned, the brown liquid was gone and Joseph had rolled the top sheet into a wad.

Joseph hung his jacket on a bedpost and tied an apron from the bag around himself. With scissors from the bag he trimmed a small piece of paper. "Fill that bowl with water." He raised an elbow to indicate which. He laid the circle of paper on one of the open eyes and pulled at the lid.

When Arley returned, both eyes were shut but the mouth was still open. Joseph was threading a needle. "See that stack of forms? Go ask the young man all the questions, look as if you've done it plenty before. Take off your gauze." Joseph pulled on a pair of rubber gloves and picked up something like a hypodermic syringe. "Get going."

Was he embalming? Arley found the young man by the window in fading light. "Time of death?" he began, realizing he had not heard his own voice for some time.

Back in the room he found Mrs. Rutherford's mouth closed. Joseph was washing her, had already reached the knees. "I'll embalm her at home," Joseph said through his gauze. "I'm just cleaning her up a little so the boy can take a look. Go tell him to come. Make it clear you expect him to."

Arley could barely make the young man out, it had grown so dark. He didn't want to go upstairs. "She looks a lot neater," Arley finally thought of saying, and they went up together. Professional; perhaps he could be a Minor man, after all? Joseph stood with his gauze off and his suit jacket back on.

"Son," Joseph said after the young man had glanced at his mother. "Do you have a place to stay the night?"

"Down the road," he replied. "My uncle's."

"Good," Joseph nodded, dismissing him. "You all be at Judea by one tomorrow afternoon."

"Down the road!" Joseph said when he had left. "Everybody's so afraid they'll catch it, they wouldn't even wait with him!" He opened the coffin and moved to the head of the bed. "You take the feet."

Arley took hold of the ankles, professionally. Joseph lifted his end under the armpits.

"Together now," Joseph said, and Arley bent to let the feet sink into the box as his father settled the shoulders and head. She wasn't as stiff as he had expected. Joseph tucked the black bag in at one side and swung up the lid.

"Now," he said. "I'll go down first. You come exactly at my

pace, not faster, not slower. Stay near the wall." Arley nodded. His father stooped to grasp the box and rose and Arley followed, stepping too rapidly at first. At the top of the stairs, Arley saw Joseph feel for the wall with his right elbow and start down. He copied him, feeling with his right shoulder and sensing his father's pace. He felt the weight in the coffin shift and heard the body slide forward a few inches. Her head must be pressing against the end of the box now, matting her hair like sheep's wool. They were reaching the bottom of the stairs, his father's advance leveled out. The young man appeared to open the door.

"Up," his father urged at the car and, stepping sideways, heaved his end until it caught on the rollers. They pushed it in and shut the doors.

"Well, that's done," his father said as Arley started the Sayers engine. "You should have been with us the day we went for Ben Humphrey!" his father began, and laughed. Arley knew that story. Two hundred and seventy pounds. His father and Sam and Fred, not all the Minor men together could get Ben Humphrey off his bed! Old Simon had arrived in his butler's jacket. For the first time, Arley wanted to laugh.

"I knew that wasn't embalming," he said, instead, pulling onto the main road. He must be very careful now, or the Minor men would have caught him.

"I'll have trouble with her later," Joseph waved to the back. "I put in a little fluid through the mouth so she wouldn't purge anymore on the way home. But that'll freeze her up!"

In Lenox, they pulled in at the Red Lion Inn and parked out of sight in back.

"Next time, don't use your shoulder on the wall," Joseph said confidentially as they washed their hands in the men's room. "It doesn't look so good to the family, but the elbow, they can hardly see that."

"Okay," Arley promised, forgetting to be careful. He foamed the soap up to his wrists.

"The lobsters are very good here," his father recommended at the table. "Come all the way from Maine on the refrigerator car."

"I'd rather have roast beef," Arley said, remembering. He could not eat a whole animal tonight.

"Come on!" Joseph thumped Arley on the shoulder. "You run the flag back and meet me by the town hall in about fifteen minutes."

You don't run with flags, but Arley made it as quickly as anyone could to the Scout rooms and back to the wagonful of men in front of the town hall and climbed in. Immediately they started off toward Southlee. He sat among them happily. Judea's Civil War obelisk was of dressed stone. At the suggestion that afternoon of their judge Mr. Minor, a half-dozen townsmen had decided not to wait and vote a lot of money for the great war's stone. Instead, they would ride after a huge rock the judge described lying in a hillside near his childhood home.

It was dusk by the time the wagonload of men returned, shouting and laughing. Six of them together with horses and the boy had struggled for two hours to haul the rock out of its bed and up the ramp. Now with a whoop they shoved the rock down the ramp and cheered it as it rolled across the grass outside the town hall and came to rest.

"That's a decent distance, boys!" The judge selected a final location discreetly removed from the polished obelisk. The world war had been rough and so its memorial ought to be rough, he would tell the town at its next meeting. The American stone against the Goliath of Europe. And so cheap. There were not so many dead that they would have to dress more than one surface of the rock. And he had moved it, a rock put in a field by giants, as his father had always told him.

Arley's head pounded as he helped settle the rock. It was so tempting, traveling among his father's friends. He must remember what the price would be. "Belaski," he recited prematurely. When this soldier's name was graven on the rock, his wife and children would finally be Americans.

"You're late for service!" Mama said as they entered the dining room. "Justine's already gone over with Paul."

"We'll have a bite," Joseph informed her, acknowledging the small supper of sandwiches and cake laid out on the table. Arley's back ached as he ate.

A few minutes later they were entering their pew across the road and, instead of going first, Arley motioned his parents in and sat beside his father.

"Let us pray in silence," Mr. Albee began in the candlelit church. Arley could not listen to a word of Mr. Albee's prayers. He saw only the minister's dark shape on the dark lawn calling, "Hello up there." He checked the congregation, which had swelled beyond capacity to the balconies. Bernie Necomber, Simon and all his family. Melko and Conley and Riccio—had he not just left them?—would be down in Elmsy with the Catholics while Starkweather and Stanton Goode—no, Stanton had gone to Arizona, hadn't he?—would be up on the hill with the Congregationalists. All of the boys would be thanking the Father for the soft peace that enveloped them. There were even a few Methodist boys from Rhodes sitting in their special pew. Let them have their hockey rink and their gigantic playing fields. Let them smile at him and the other townies in the drug store. The seed of the flower was already planted at the high school *where cross the crowded ways of life*. Wasn't it? The new Athens was beginning to bloom in home-room number seven; the great world of international brotherhood that was born tonight—now that the Prussians had ceased to crawl—had been known to him for a year. He knew more than his father. Sitting in his long gray jeans, he had recited *amo, amas, amat*. I love, you love, He loves everybody.

The world was one tonight, all on the same great team, all victors, even his father and himself. Mr. Albee sounded tired as he announced the hymn but Arley felt too excited to be tired, though his hands hurt when he took hold of his father's hymnal. He stood with the others: *Are ye able, said the Master, to be crucified with Me?* The words were those he had sung that night at the Winchester Revival four years ago during the summer of the ball lightning. That was the summer after the spring when he had turned twelve and finally passed the hole in the sky that was his dead sister Elizabeth, leaving her behind forever, as if he had killed her with one thrust from a Cadet's bayonet. Yes, it had all been so clear at Winchester, God's mind larger than the earth and time and there no reason not to rejoice. You couldn't lose with God! He had gone back to the Methodist campground year after year. But they should never have given him that bayonet last summer. He could see that now. He would not fight again. The strength of nations was nothing. The light that shone on Galilee was the true light. I am coming, Jesus, do not despair.

Lord we are able, Arley sang mechanically above his own thoughts. It would be simpler now that the war was over. The need to win could be laid aside. O Prussians, I forgive you! O 1918, I will remember your date not only because of the peace but because one boy prays God he will grow in bigness of soul—forget about physical perfection. *Are ye able, when the shadows close around you with the sod, to believe that spirit triumphs, to commend your soul to God?* Thank you, God, for making me a Methodist, and a town boy, and a son, and a brother. Pictures flooded his mind then and the candlelight blurred in the tears that came to his eyes but which he did not let run over the edges. His sister Maud would be home from Rhodesia soon. In two days' time—he had almost forgotten. Home for Thanksgiving with Ted and the four children he had never seen. His whole family would be together soon in a world of peace. I am able! I will come!

"No, Charles, you can't go to the movies, for heaven's sake; you've been up since before dawn, ringing bells and the Lord knows what else." Polly had moved his comforter in from the porch and made up his bed in the back room.

The longest day I have been in, Arley noted in sprawling pencil. By morning his temperature was up to 102° and he showed the classic signs of influenza. Polly brought him what food he could eat up the back stairs. The fever leveled at 104° and by Thanksgiving he was well enough to sit briefly at the table with the reunited family, wrapped in a blanket and eating from special dishes that would later have to be boiled.

V

New Year's Eve, the Early Twenties

Judea Reds 27, Elmsy 10; Judea Reds 19, Rhodes Second Team, 9; Judea Reds 25, Chester 18; She was waving at me again. His own name, Arley Minor, reverberated against the cheeks of girls cheering him on in the bleachers of neighboring towns, and his own father was among the crowds that rose to their feet in gymnasiums along the valley. "You see, you're the favorite. Papa would never have come to watch us play!" Sam said. "When did we have time?" Fred asked. The first team's center, Conley, and its forwards, captain Starkweather and Melko, flapped him, the right guard, with towels. Necomber was left guard. Both of them small, quick and Methodist. The slow giants Schless and Riccio had remained on reserve call throughout their sophomore and into their junior years. Even Mama said he played bully.

Then, prompt as the Chester trolley, the mighty falling.

The phlegmatic, early-blooming Starkweather had overmatured. Once the automatic captain and president of everything, he began to shed his offices like snakeskins, providing hopes of glory to others along the corridors of Judea High. Who, for instance, would be the new basketball captain? The centaur Conley? Or quick-footed, quick-witted Minor?

Three to two.

Conley.

The world was lost. If only Simon had been on the team. Simon, who wasn't even in town anymore. He would have voted for Arley and Arley would have won. Except, of course, if Simon were on the team, Arley would not be; it was Simon's place Arley had taken not long after Simon quit practicing in order to work in the cemetery.

They slap you in the face but you find a way to turn the pig's ear into solid gold, that was one way. Or you could blame it on them. Or on yourself. You could call it the sin of pride. If you were God, wouldn't you strike pride down? *Though I feel I have not been treated right, still I will not forsake a minute the task allotted me, whether it be a captain or a private in life's works. C. P. M. May 27, 1920. Thursday.*

Thursday. The days were hard throughout the year, passing one by one to evening when he heaved each of the three hundred and eight newspapers on his route at their verandahs, missing forsythia by inches. When summer came, he stopped writing in his diaries. Why save such moments? He heaved newspapers over roses until they withered and fell and Justine was finally standing behind their parents' door in a corset and stockings and a swirl of white underthings. He knocked to alert her and her maidens of honor to his presence. But when he pressed open the door with the corner of the tray of sandwiches, they paid no attention to him. They were all looking out the front window at Paul in the gray Chrysler that was pulling into hiding behind the Methodist parsonage.

The fallen rice left Arley at home as his parents' only child. Polly moved his things out of the back bedroom into Justine's. "This way you'll have your own door onto the sleeping porch," she explained. And he would be closer to them in the big house at night. Had he perhaps always been their only child? The other brothers and the sisters but a clever ruse to distract him from the fact that Polly and Joseph most wanted him to stay a child? The smell of Justine's room was far too flowery, and so as soon as he had changed into the pajamas he kept under her pillow and opened his Bible to flash a line or two before his eyes, he hurried onto the glassed-in porch. Once away from Justine's brass bed, he could pretend she still lay on it anticipating Paul. Justine and Paul had known each other now, had eaten from the tree in the middle of the garden, had touched the fruit, become wise and left him here alone.

School began and things got better. He was very busy. Busier and busier, stretched tighter and tighter, running. President of the senior class, they made him. Consolation prize for a failed captain. He stomped through crusted snow to retrieve newspapers he had accidentally hurled under shrunken vines. He kicked his snowshoes to turn himself back at the run-down house on Red Rock Road where the new girl lived. She was the prettiest girl in town, his cousin Sam Percy insisted. Her house meant the end of Arley's territory and he shoed home through darkness in rhythm with the evening bells that rang out *O Jesus Thou art standing outside the fast-closed door.* If he had lost in the world, all the easier to win with Jesus, who wanted you just as mocked, scorned and abandoned as he had been. A close shave, he could have won the captaincy and lost God! Herod was a captain, wasn't he? When Arley got home Joseph was reading aloud from the medical column of the Chester *Star*: "The influenza can produce years of subsequent melancholia."

"Not in our boy," Polly laughed. "He's too busy!"

He began to feel better. *Took a girl home*, he wrote in his diary. It didn't matter, her name. The blond girl who cheered for Chester wrote him a note, but they lost the next game there and he never introduced himself to her. "A girl in every port," it said under the picture of himself in the yearbook. As editor, he had chosen his own opening quotation. It did not seem to match his variation of the Minor face, thinner, more earnest and with a determined gaze he recognized as reflecting his conviction that the photographer was recording Charles Minor for all time and could see into his heart and find him worthy or not of being preserved.

Most Popular Boy they voted him, Most Likely. Things were picking up, but he had grown wary of the heights. For his last speech to the class, Arley compared Napoleon Bonaparte with Abraham Lincoln and found the former not to be recommended. For his valedictory, he urged Judea's red-blooded boys and girls filling the gymnasium with perspiration to turn their passion for war toward winning peace. It was no great feat, being the best scholar—if you were also the oldest. "Your voice still needs a good oiling," Joseph commented. "And you talked so fast you stumbled over your words."

"I thought it was pretty good, Charles," Polly said. "You should do all right at college. But the other boys will be smarter there."

He drove the Reo full of classmates through a tunnel of ripening foliage with all that was the past pushed somewhere behind the exhaust pipe. The Reo's nose cut through the future: ominous, hazy. What would he become if not a Minor man? Would God be watching him as he went out into the world? Arley felt enveloped in strangeness. He saw himself as if he stood apart, though he sat on Red Rock like the others and ate the same ham sandwich and piece of crumbling cake the Class of '21, in a mood of self-congratulation, had baked itself. Raucous and tender, their voices bounced off cliffs and seemed layered with hollowness from the quarry pool, into whose water dark snakes slid from the sun. He would remember their voices this way years from now, he promised himself. By then they would sound even more husky, more confident. Rowena Peterson would rest a yellow-haired infant's head against her own soft neck and whisper, "I was Judea High, Class of 'Twenty-one." The new girl was Class of '23, lucky for her! She didn't have to leave yet.

"Come on, Minor!" The boys were hoisting Conley with a can of paint onto their shoulders. Vandalism? Arley stuffed the last of the cake into his mouth and wiped his hands on the seat of his gray jeans.

"Okay, here I come, Schless!" He climbed up onto the sizable neck of Herman Schless. He locked arms with Necomber, who was standing on Riccio's neck.

"The Jay!" Conley moved his foot to Arley's collarbone as he announced the first letter from above, and a splattering of red fell onto Arley's shirt.

"The You!" Conley shouted.

Arley squinted up at dribbles of red paint running down the

granite. The town would forgive Herman Schless, who would work out his debt for public defacement at the needle factory until fifty years had passed and he had forgotten all of the town's gift to him: Cicero and Cato, algebraic equations and the Peloponnesian War. Remembering only needles, all sizes. But would the town forgive Arley Minor, the class president, the judge's son. who would be far away by then, succeeding?

"The Dee!" Conley was screaming now.

"The Eee!"

"The Ay-ay-ay!" The letter was blurred in a premature waver of the pyramid and Arley, who had opened his mouth to join, closed it just in time. It was not right to be swayed by mass emotions. Crucify him! A crowd's response.

"The Two!" The pyramid screamed, giggled and spattered itself with red.

"The One!" Arley's mouth opened again and before he knew it he had joined in the last hoarse peal that loudened as the pyramid tumbled into a bunch of boys pounding each other's shoulders, not seeing, blinded with joy. In the melee, the team that had been this year's boys wheeled and ran back to this year's girls scattered on the sun-baked rocks, to Rowena in her snug bathing suit, to plainer girls who continually pulled their wrinkling suits into place. Arley flung himself against Conley, who lost his balance, falling, shouting into the quarry pool. Then Arley was pushed from behind, by whom he never knew, his legs suddenly not on solid ground, his body hovering above the water, a true spirit at last. Happiness buoyed him up and he knew he would never sink, never fall, that he would fly timeless and forever. The water was cold, sudden and all-consuming.

POLLY'S FACE WAS DRY and lined over the deviled eggs she seemed determined to make too many of. She still missed Justine. The flesh on her upper arm swung shockingly as she spooned custard from a cut-glass bowl. Joseph's face shrank above what had become permanent fatness. "Justine'll be over after supper," he promised Polly and himself and Arley.

Ought he be leaving his parents to sink into their dining room chairs? Would they grow smaller and smaller when he went off and left them? Should he stay home and care for them instead? It would only be a month more, a month of mornings on the tennis courts and afternoons at the cemetery.

"Hey, Minor! What're you up to?" On the road, Conley raised a hand to slow him as Arley drove the Reo past a road crew. Conley emerged from the handful of men wearing the cotton hats of the road crew, hats just like that of Mr. Conley who had worked the Elmsy crew for years.

"Hanging around, mostly." Arley's hand relaxed on the brake. "Waiting for college."

"When do you go?" Everybody knew where, Wesleyan— Fred's college, the best in America, better than Yale.

"Early," Arley explained. "Frosh hazing, you know how it is."

"Sure," Conley smiled, leaning on his spade, his tanned skin dark against his white teeth. He'd put on a few pounds since June and looked grown, but oddly smaller, a finished product.

"Staying on with the crew?" Arley inquired.

"Hope so." Conley resettled his cotton cap. "I'll know in September."

Arley palmed the brake lever.

"Working for your dad?" Conley asked as he took his muscled arm off the side of the Reo.

"Just for the summer," Arley asserted, and they waved to each other as he pulled stylishly past the crew and on to the cemetery's graveled road, but not so fast as to splay out pebbles.

There is a green hill far away. Arley hummed as he oiled the mower and dragged it into the newly opened section of hillside. It was much easier to mow here than over in the old cemetery, where it was hard to push the bulky machine among the tall, closely-spaced monuments he had once believed encased the dead. The low stones had babies inside them? No, Joseph had laughed. "The whole thing's hard to understand," he had conceded. "Nothing's left in fifty years anyway. But it's a good business for you and your brothers." There were black snakes on the old side, too. Arley pushed the heavy mower, good for the triceps. He no longer feared he might have to follow in his father's footsteps. He had escaped the little man who cut other men down to size, who parceled out their belongings coat by chair, who joined the reaper in the final felling, cutting into the flesh itself. No, whatever his business would be, it was not going to be that of his earthly father's. He was going to college. And from there, into the world. The ground shook as Arley accidentally jammed the mower against one of the new headstones. Getting crowded on this side, too.

"Hi." Arley brought the Reo to a stop in front of the gray house and got out. "Heard you were back."

"What you been doing?" Simon stood at the edge of his family's small yard.

"We won county." Arley leaned on the front of the Reo and started from where Simon had left off in the spring of their junior year.

"Oh, yeah?" Simon seemed to move less than he used to. The gray house formed an assenting background for his immobility.

"Conley got captain." Arley could not stop himself.

"Not Starkweather?" Something registered on Simon's face, something near the lips.

"No."

"Not Minor?"

Was it a smile?

"Nope," Arley grinned. "But I was . . ." He stopped. "That is," he said, "I took over your old job of basketball manager." Yearbook editor? Band founder? Athletic Association president?

"And you ran the school besides?"

How like a shadow of himself Simon was, knowing his heart. Arley shrugged and hoped he did not blush.

"How was it after I saw you?" Arley asked Simon and hushed his own recital. In response to Judge Minor's request, the police chief had gladly unlocked the barred door to admit Arley as a visitor the spring evening over a year ago when Simon had been caught.

"Not bad," Simon said. A few days later he had been sent off to a distant Republic for Boys. "Attempted car theft," the judge had read from the *Star*. "He had no business doing that, Arley! But his father says he's a good boy."

"What're you going to work at this year?" Arley stood up to separate himself from the auto.

"Didn't he tell you, your father?" Simon answered. "In September I start full time at the cemetery."

So Simon was going to do it for him.

"There's the ATS house," Fred called out, as he had every chance Saturday the family had driven this long street of white mansions on their way to Wesleyan football games.

"Looking good," Arley called from the rumble seat. Fred had been president of that fraternity. Arley pushed his glasses up on his nose. He rode in fine style, protected by his new tennis sweater and ready to learn Greek, how to smoke a pipe but never cigarettes, and dancing. The roommate Wesleyan had assigned him was delayed on a Scandinavian cruise, and Arley had to enter the world alone.

He should not have worried about his parents; within a week it was Arley who had grown very small. "Mr. Minor?" The professors expected complicated stretches of reasoning from him, obscure points of fact. Nobody shouted, "Hey, Minor!" as he crisscrossed the paths of the quadrangle. And he could not believe that they would. Serving on a hundred committees, reading the Bible every night, always saying hello first—none of these stratagems would ever give him the tilt of body and the tone of voice all Wesleyan men seemed to possess. It was not only as if he walked among a thousand Conleys. These men were simultaneously a thousand Stanton Goodes in their smartness, a thousand Simon Browns in their steady standing, a thousand Starkweathers in the early stages of superiority. Where had they come from, these Vikings whose jackets hung just right and whose words flew in elegant circles? From Rhodes Academy a thousand times across the country?

It could not be so simple. The less people recognized him, the more he shrank into himself. It was as if the crowd of witnesses that had always surrounded him in Judea had become, by his removal here, imaginary. These Wesleyan people did not know Arley Minor. Only the Judea witnesses knew, and God. Only the world of the spirit comforted him. He stayed up later and later to study, emerging groggy in the morning at lectures he could not follow. "You're not sick, son," the campus doctor assured him, "just tired and worried. It's perfectly natural." But it was not natural. Indeed, nothing seemed quite natural anymore. The spirit world swelled up to occupy odd pockets of air about him; the real people grew more and more artificial in their movements, like puppets on wires. In a dream he saw his Greek professor trip on a staircase and his pushed-up trouser leg reveal one wooden, wired knee. After that, he dared not look at people closely. "Is there a God?" he asked one day, exhausted on his bed. "Yes." An answer lower than the human voice collected around him from the corners of his narrow room. After that, he dared not pray. It was not at all natural. The lamp spilled palpable yellow light onto black letters that refused to form into words and fell out of his vision through the unread bulk of the book, dropping silently onto the floor. That is not the way light looks, that is not the way letters are supposed to be. Only he existed. When he looked over his left shoulder at the drizzle outside his window, he wondered whether there really was a three-dimensional, physical world. Was it only an outdoor scene painted on the glass?

Or was he thinking up the glass? Was he creating the world out of his own mind? Was all outdoors only a thin layer of paint upon his gigantic eyeballs? The supper bell a minuscule scratch upon his eardrum?

Uncle Win had been right.

He was crazy, after all.

"But we're worried about you, Arley." Fred's tall frame did not step over the threshold. "Come home with me, it's no shame."

"I can do college work," Arley said dumbly from the chair, wearing the tennis sweater he had expected to be so happy in. Its cuffs were dirty.

"Of course you can," Fred assured him. "But everybody thinks you should come home for a while, even Maud and Ted. They wrote to Papa from Seattle. Ted says lots of boys feel very taxed when they first go out into the world. He thinks you ought to take an extra year at a prep school and try again."

To go out into the world? Did Fred still believe there was one? Arley did not say good-bye to anyone. For the first time on that grand street of white mansions, Fred did not point out the ATS house. That hurt the most.

Arley's throat closed as Fred turned the car down the long driveway he had meant to leave forever. Up the back steps, through the back porch door, into the dining room, stiffly back from his mother's outstretched arms: "It's Charles! Charles is home!" It did not mean he was a man. She had never called him Arley anyway.

HE WAS NO LONGER FIT to do, or even to refuse to do, his father's business. "No funeral work," he heard Joseph tell Sam. And Simon was already installed as the cemetery caretaker. There was nothing left but yard work and farm work for little Arley. "I want you up at seven every morning." Joseph gave him his instructions. "More outdoor work and fewer thoughts, please." Joseph seemed to expect recovery.

"They're sending me to work in the umbrella factory later," he explained to Annah Trevellack, the new girl from Red Rock Road. He had met her the day he wandered lost in the halls of Judea High looking for trophies of himself. "Is it really Arley Minor? Back at school?" She had invited him to a class party. Since then he had met her every afternoon.

"That's good," she said. "It will be better for you to be with people." The brown of her eyes was very dark and the white very white. Sam Percy had confessed to Arley that in September he had taken to following Annah Trevellack home from school. Or preceding her, jumping out from behind trees to startle her. But she would have nothing to do with him, he had grown fat.

"You're sure I'm not crazy?" Arley had told only Annah of his

fear. Though you could never be a man without the admiration
of other men, you might begin with women and their comforts.

"Yes," she assured him, holding his arm around her waist.
"You're just high-strung. You're very sensitive."

"You're really sure?" The grayness of November dislodged
him easily. Was Uncle Win laughing at him from the other
world?

"I'm really sure."

"I hope you're right," he said, as they turned with the road to
her house that needed paint worse than last year. Here her
mother argued every day but Christmas with her father, a salesman who read Shakespeare every night until the tissue-weight
pages were too heavy for him to turn. He drank; though you
could never tell it. No one had known in Cleveland or Culver
City, in Louisville or Charleston.

"I know I'm right," Annah responded. "Your nerves were . . .
well, you did too much, you ran the school. You wore out your
nerves. They're still recovering."

Her phrase presented a funny picture of him, but he appreci-
ated her conviction.

"How was school today?" He had forgotten to ask.

"All right," she said. "We had glee club try-outs. I've got to
help my sister with her piano lesson this afternoon."

Her younger sister, Hope, sat evenings in the living room with
Arley and Annah. Sometimes her older brother, George, played
the harmonica while Hope outlined black manuscript letters with
a thin line of gold, careful not to lick the brush. Arley sat next to
Annah and looked through the Trevellack photograph album.
There were pictures of Annah wearing a stiff satin bow and
standing beside her seated papa, her hand raised progressively to
his knee, to the arm of his chair, to his shoulder.

Arley did not listen to Annah as they walked home, only
floated gratefully on the sound of her voice until they reached
the tree outside her house, where he backed her against it and
kissed her.

"Arley?" she asked him, questioning, smiling. "Did you read
the paper this morning?"

"The *Announcer*? No, I always read the *Star*." He put his hand through her open coat and around her waist.

"Well," she said, smiling, moving closer to him. "Please don't look at the *Star* this afternoon, all right?"

"All right," he said. That was one of the nice things about Annah, she smiled a lot. If only he could spend all his time with her, but Papa set out daily tasks for him.

Arley drove the horses into the barn up at the farm and got them unhitched and into their stalls before the rain. Purple was a son of Prince but nothing like his father. A mild, earnest horse. He shoveled oats for Purple and for Marjorie and then went out to look for the break in the wall Papa had sent him to fix. "Boys," the judge had concluded, not really knowing why the stones had fallen.

Walking uphill past the potato fields through the drizzle, Arley tied the string on his father's waterproof. At least he had his own boots this year. His feet hadn't grown for several seasons and now he knew what size feet he would always have. Small to medium. What size feet had Jesus had? Standing, waiting outside the door? Irrelevant! Jesus' powers were hidden, he didn't kick with his feet or fight with his fists. He used the power he'd gotten by harnessing himself to God.

Arley's booted feet moved one by one, crushing grass into mud. Did those feet down there really belong to him? His watching of them was more real than their being feet. Next his hands; he felt himself moving out of his hands. Was he going to leave his body now? He pulled his hands quickly from the waterproof's pockets, where their pressure against his thighs alarmed him. Hanging down out of the sleeves, they were worse. Like wooden logs, inanimate. Was he a puppet, too? He walked faster into the upper pasture and hurriedly scanned the broken wall for fallen stones.

Rain misted his waterproof as he knelt to pick up stones. The sky was not exactly gray but rather white with a too knowing light behind it. Arley worked quickly, his alien wet fingers nudging slippery rocks into place, wedging larger ones, supplying tiny stones for close fit and finishing with the slate spikes for bracing that were part of his father's wall-repairing litany. Then he felt the *me* that had left his feet and hands rise up and leave him entirely. From above he watched the lifeless waterproof-covered automaton mending the wall.

It was too late.

He was running, his heart beating in his throat as he turned into the hollow darkness of the barn, screaming, "Come on, Purple!" He pulled the horse outdoors into the rain and, squinting, ran inside again and groped for Marjorie's reins: "Get going!" He strained against her and got her out. He got the wagon hitched. He got the body of himself seated. He got the batch of them, all bodies, under way, over the softening ruts. Only when an auto passed them did he begin to feel a bit like himself.

"Did you have a nice morning?" Polly asked as he hung Joseph's waterproof in the kitchen. "You got up so early! Sleep late tomorrow. It's good for you."

What a relief to have her speak naturally. As if she lived her own life and did not exist solely in his mind. Last night when he lay in bed she had tiptoed in to spread an extra blanket over him. Over him, a college man. Or *old* enough to be one.

"I think maybe I'll start work in the umbrella factory, tomorrow, if Fred can fit me in," he heard a voice almost his own say, as he pulled off his boots.

"Arley Minor, always one of our town's most popular young men, has returned from college." Polly read the Judea column from last night's *Star* to Justine, who had stopped by early from her house on Field Street to go over Christmas plans with Polly. "He is presently employed at Judson Umbrella."

"So long," he called and set off to work. Umbrellas. Umbrella boxes. No umbrella had a history, each umbrella had a future. The fear let loose its grip in the routine of the factory. He must never try to flourish in the world again, to be acclaimed. From now on, humility. Arley sometimes met Simon for a half-hour's skating after supper. Or he walked out to Annah's to play cards and games. If her father was feeling jovial, they would all sing and eat one of the chocolate cakes her mother continually baked. The Trevellacks fought, but they had fun. On the first peal of the ten o'clock bell, he would grab his jacket and start home, running to make his own yard by the tenth peal. Mama wanted him in bed by 10:30; Papa wanted him out of bed by seven. After the Christmas season he would be off to the Hanley School to prepare again for college. "I couldn't go to college myself," Papa told everyone, "so I sent my son twice." Shame made Arley's hand shake under the table where he sat at "his" place to his father's left in full view of the entire family gathered for Christmas Eve. Mama must be proud to have produced all these people. His father and mother had brought forth upon the earth but their last son had only ventured forth to come home defeated.

"Nope, wouldn't do it, if I were you." Papa was talking to Fred over the heads of the children.

"You know him, then?" Fred had been approached for money by someone who had mortgage payments backing up.

"Trevellack? Haven't I seen his name in the papers a few weeks back?" Papa raised a goblet of ice water, significantly. "Never lend money to a man who drinks. Isn't that right, Joe?" he inquired of his oldest grandson, on whom he had begun the lessons.

"When does Hanley start?" Fred asked Arley, who was having trouble getting his goblet to his mouth. Not because of Trevellack; he had heard all about that from Sam Percy.

"Middle of January," Arley replied, setting the glass down.

"Say," Fred leaned toward him, "Judea Reds are playing Saturday night at the Rhodes gym, you want to go?"

"No."

"No more basketball!" Mama insisted. "That's what put him under, all that practicing and those late nights playing."

Everybody had a theory.

"Eat up your ham, boy," Sam told his son Joe. "Your uncle Arley was a big basketball star and he got his strength from eating ham, right, Arley?"

The tomato aspic was quite beyond him. Its wobbling returned as he sat in the flickering candlelight and sank into the smell of pines that rose right and left from the darkness under the Methodist balconies. Annah was nowhere in sight; perhaps the one happy day between her parents had begun on Red Rock Road and nobody wanted to leave. He would never mention the loan. The opening of the hymn books was unusually quiet: *Round yon Virgin Mother and Child*. Arley swayed as he sang; Mary and her baby, nobody else's. The congregation swayed together as they sang about the baby in its mother's arms. Slowly Arley rocked with the congregation, careful not to touch his mother.

A weakened, aged Mr. Tiding had been brought back to share the service with a flourishing Mr. Albee. The old man read in a faltering voice of the decree from Caesar Augustus concerning the fullness of time. Arley stopped listening and cupped his cold hands to breathe into them. The piano wheezed out something unfamiliar and they sang again *O come, O come, E-ma-aa-aan-u-el and ransom captive Ih-ih-ih-is-ra-el*. His eyes filled and he was afraid he might blink and further disgrace himself with wet cheeks. He swallowed instead, and found the saltiness pleasant in his throat.

Until the son of Gaw-aw-od ap-pear. God had loved the world, after all. He had sent it his son. Some gift! And sent him as a baby. Now, that was really taking a chance! They could have killed him right there in the straw. He could have got German measles. Appendicitis. Spanish influenza. But God had chosen to take that chance, had trusted him, Arley Minor, to receive that gift! Pride came swelling up from his knees. "Thank you, thank you, God!" he prayed, for the first time since Wesleyan. He would take that baby into his heart, where it would grow inside him, reaching all the way to his fingers and toes, to replace the gray sack of shadow that acted out his dreams. He would be safe then, the baby would grow into the Lord Jesus Christ! How God continually amazed him; the fruited plain, the mighty rivers were nothing to his greatest gift, for whosoever should receive it should have everlasting life!

When the last verse ended, and Joseph and Polly stood round-bellied to let Arley out of the pew first, he took his new-found pride to Simon, who sat several pews behind him.

"Simon," he said, reaching for his hand. But then he could think of nothing else to say.

"Merry Christmas," he finished, his first formal words to Simon Brown.

"Sure thing," Simon replied, eyeing him slowly. Then Simon took his hand away and clapped Arley on the shoulder.

"Say, Esther and I are skating tomorrow afternoon, Stoughton's pond," he said. "Come on down!"

"Okay," Arley said, feeling good again. "After dinner."

You don't build it in a day.

CARRYING THE LORD WITHIN, Arley was free to travel. In January he was deposited two towns off across the tops of hills and he unpacked his trunk at Hanley with assurance. With Jesus inside, he had roots set right down into the lap of God. He would get to the power that could heal. And kill? No, Arley did not want to kill. He wanted to be good. With Jesus inside, he could rise safe each morning from his dormitory bed having someone to talk to, something to hold him into himself, a portable companion closer than the proper suit about which Papa had nagged the tailor. "He needs the pants shortened, and tighten up the shoulders of the jacket; he'll be traveling in high society."

On Sunday mornings in the white church on the town's green, he stared at the girls from MacKenzie Hall and thought of Annah cutting across his long snowy lawn on her way to school. He had given her permission to do that. Sunday afternoons he would open his yearbook, skipping the pages he knew by heart: "Who is that yellow-haired cheerleader waving at Minor during every game at Chester, hmmmm?" He hadn't even written that. After selecting opening quotations for himself and his classmates, he had turned the rest of the work over to an assistant. "Seventeen umbrellas open on Minor's verandah, he's had a few friends in for tea." Not Annah Trevellack, though. She had yet to set foot in the Minor house, afraid. He opened to the picture of the sophomore class and found Annah's face rounder, her eyes both darker and more bright than those of the other girls. It was the only picture of her; she did not belong to things.

On Sunday evenings he tried to explain his new feeling of strength in the triune Lord at the weekly prayer meeting he had started in his room. "God the Father sent the flood to punish men when they weren't good," he told Wilson, who had acne, and Peters, who had a cold. "But God the Son was never angry like that. Jesus kept his faith in men even when they were killing him. I like to think of him daring God to take a chance and send him down to prove that love beats anger any day. Now God the Holy Ghost lives within us." Wilson was strong in the Lord, Peters turned to alcohol and cigarettes.

He did wear his tea suit once, on the spring weekend Annah came to visit. They walked together past a high fly-buzzing cemetery full of malice: *As you are now, so once was I; as I am now so you shall be*. It wasn't so bad with Annah there.

"The woods between here and Judea are the most beautiful in all of New England," Arley quoted his father; but Annah would not be distracted.

"Why not a coach?"

"You can't play all your life." He put his arm around her.

"A judge?" she inquired. "Judge Minor is never wrong!"

"Never wrong? You know what the good judge had to say about the auto exhibit at the Eighteen Ninety-eight World's Fair? 'Never replace the horse!'"

But she didn't laugh. Odd, at home everyone laughed. Screams of laughter.

"You see, the auto . . ."

"I got it," she explained. "A doctor?"

"Oh, I want to heal," he said. "But not broken bones and stuff like that." Mr. Albee said he could. And Dr. Hanley urged him to try. Not with his brains, but with ordinary industry, a step at a time. You could get too melancholy sitting in one place like a stone. You could sink into the ground of your own weight. When you had wanted to rise like a bird. Not the crazy way. How? Don't ask me. Ask Jesus. He did it. He had the strength to rise up and join the Father. Dear Lord, give me the strength.

Please pass the strength. No, it wasn't funny. God could take a joke, but not Jesus: he had the cross to carry.

"I am going to speak for Jesus," he explained to Annah. "Come on! Let's run back to tea!" He dropped his arm from her shoulder and took her hand. Girls didn't like you to be a Christian, and a preacher was worse. "Faster," he called forward into the air, afraid to turn and face her disappointment.

WHAT WAS IT ABOUT FOLLOWING JESUS that made everyone joke about girls as if you didn't like them? He loved girls. He loved Annah in the brown sweater she wore when she stepped into the Minor house. "Anyone would like you, Annah." Was one foot more nervous than the other, as Joseph always put it, recalling his first entry into what to him had been the Percy house? He loved kissing Annah good-bye in the cold pantry while Fred packed the car to drive him and Sam Percy up to Wilby College in New Hampshire. "You'll lose your faith at college," his brother Sam promised him when Annah moved out of earshot. "Then you'll have to watch out for those freshman girls."

"It's okay, Sam, if I keep my faith," Arley said in a flash of inspiration. "You'll bury them, and I'll marry them. It's a way of expanding the family business."

When Annah came closer, Sam Percy swept off his cap: "Miss Trevellack, let me recommend this man or shall I say boy bound off for college, as one who stimulates alarm and fear, a wild, reckless ladykiller known to have overstepped the laws of our land. In oratory he is notorious, unlike myself."

"Into the car, please, boys!" Fred said. "It's time to get under way."

"Words, my dear mademoiselle, spring from his lips at the sight of a crowd. . . ."

"Come along, boys!"

"His special aptitude is at rephrasing the Ten Commandments: 'Sam Percy, thou shalt not drink during vacation!'" He climbed into the car after Arley.

Fred started the motor and Arley and Annah exchanged a last look through the open window.

"She is the prettiest girl in town," Sam Percy said when they were driving past the house. It was a good send-off.

At Wilby Arley found no threats to his religion in modern science. The glacier that covered the earth melted in orchestration with the tides that swept the shore and broke the rocks into stone and cracked the stone to sand—it was all a marvel of forethought. Monkeys that swung on long skinny arms from tree to tree and shared with him a common ball-and-socket joint gave him a pleasant sense of companionship. And it was child's play to fit Ur's epic flood into Noah's and to compress the star cluster with its thirty million suns into the mind of God. The many-parted structure of the world was dazzling, but only man could pierce it; only man could think God's thoughts after him. As one man had done so perfectly, he had never died.

He and Sam Percy made it into the same fraternity and Arley moved into a small room there that led onto a tiny balcony. He slept outdoors and found that whatever terror ordinarily radiated from him to the walls of a bedroom and bounced back to the bed to drown him there, only sped outward on the balcony so far it finally became absorbed into God, who stood at the edges of the sky and bade him sleep. He might recover, after all.

"Hey, Minor!" He would not be carried home this time. He led his fraternity in marks and won his athletic letter in tennis. So long as the boys were neither too close nor too distant, he made friends. One day he filled his shirt pocket with the cigarettes he himself would not smoke and handed them out to those who did. They voted him house president for the coming year and he decided it would be a good idea to stay in New Hampshire over the summer, moving into the Wilby Inn, where he got a job waiting tables.

Standing on the high serving verandah of the inn, Charles watched farm folk move in and out of stores on the street below. Multitudes were moving on streets like this the world around and they had done it in Ur after the damage from the flood had been repaired and in Athens beneath the statues of the gods; the strangeness of life surfaced and he caught a glimpse of himself watching the scene. But, filled with Jesus, he stayed steady. Why do we toil and eat, sleeping here today and tomorrow in the cemetery? To glorify and enjoy God!

"Watch it, boy!" A New Yorker expounding on the perfect marvelousness of the rural sunset snapped at him as his tray wavered. The man's high-heeled companion nibbled on a Nabisco wafer and Arley apologized immediately. He was always wrong.

"Don't you feel just a bit guilty lying on this green lawn in the mountains, while off in China and Russia and Germany people are dying just to eat bread?" She was a slender girl on a striped blanket.

"My sister was in Africa," Arley replied, moving his red and white towel closer to her. They exchanged names: Jessica, Charles. She was from New Jersey; all the most sophisticated girls at the inn were from New Jersey; why had he never set foot in that state? "She says you can't run a country for other people. That's why she and her husband finally left Rhodesia. The Rhodesians have to do it themselves."

"Well, that's just what I mean," Jessica answered. "They do have to and that means bolshevism. Are you for or against?"

"I'm for food for the soul. Christian food." She would laugh, but could he compromise on basic issues?

"Jesus?" she asked, her voice rising somewhat shrilly. "In this day and age?"

Perhaps he could convert her?

"For any age," he answered, trying to keep his voice lower and fuller. "And for all ages."

She didn't answer.

He liked her better when she didn't talk. He looked at her lying in the sun. Jessica gave off a light that was not only the reflection of the sun against her pale hair. It was more a burning, a wavy radiation. Her slender hands were pointed like stars. She ought to ride on trains with her chin resting, mouth shut, on one of those hands, her head reflecting flatly in a window that moved past prairies.

"No ideology can be trusted that does not rest on bread," she finally replied. She ought to smile and nod and never speak.

The workers' dormitory, atop a hill, seemed dangerously near the sky at noon. By night, the whole hill had been consumed. *The night sky here is like a woman with stars for eyelashes,* he wrote in his notebook and summoned Annah. She might not know what Moscow was up to, but she was smart enough to beat him at cards. Seldom at tennis. "Remember to bring your racquet," he wrote to her in Pennsylvania, where her parents had relocated. In a college town a salesman like Trevellack could hope to educate his children. Had Trevellack found a loan there? He had forgotten that Annah had no racquet.

"I love you, Annah," he whispered on a blanket by a lake where small waves lapped.

"I love you, Arley," she answered, and her words riffled within him. His quick arousal was such a surprise. He hoped she did not notice. But she did and he apologized. Though their souls be one, their bodies must not yet unite.

"Is everything all right?" she asked in darkness, where he could see little but her eyes.

"Yes," he said. "It's wonderful." He lay beside her and stared at what he could see of her. But when the crickets of August had deepened to an unbearable calling, her letters from Pennsylvania cooled. He opened the Judea '23 yearbook she had brought him as a present; her yearbook contained more references to him than it did to her. He turned to her page and read the words stamped beneath her curly hair, beneath her smile promising to smile back. "Annah Trevellack. *Annah was queen of Red Rock Way / and the prettiest girl that we knew. / What better man should we lose her to / than Minor, the king of the day?* Occupational Goal: Nurse. Activities: Glee Club, 4. Quotation: She runs hot and she runs cold." But surely, she had not wanted him to carry through the physical act? And defile them by the flesh, corrupt and doom them? *Lay it not up to rust.*

He broke the silence of four diaryless years when as a junior at Wilby he hurriedly bought a notebook in a drug store and wrote on its front cover: *Thou art the Potter, I am the clay.* The wind blew cold at the outside of the church as he stood in a pulpit to practice preach at twenty-odd farmers. Yet God's wind warmed, yes, burned his neck. He must try to keep humble, but he was full of hope when he rose from the faded chair. Some day he would preach his last sermon, why not be joyful at his first?

"Scripture tells us that if a man sue us at law to take away our coat, we should give him our cloak also. If ever someone compels us to go a mile, we should volunteer a second. Now let's talk about purity." He cleared his throat to make his voice louder. "The law says we cannot have more than one wife at a time. But compelling . . . complying with law does not satisfy you and me. No, we go the second mile to God's law of purity. For Jesus said even to look upon a woman with lust in your heart is sin." Afterward he opened the notebook: *May my life glow and burn with God! I have no more doubts about his existence!*

Back at the fraternity he wrote nightly in the new notebook before he scraped the icicles off the balcony railing and lay down in his sleeping bag. He set his goals for the morrow and, like a mole, gobbled time to get to them.

November 6. A warmer letter than usual from Annah, she loves her sophomore classes but she wishes she could live in a dormitory this year instead of home.

November 8. The Harvard–Wilby game at Boston with Ellen, from my Classics Seminar. It isn't fair to a girl to go all the way. It undermines her dignity.

November 23. Dance at Smith. I told Jessica I'd managed to stay at college for almost two and a half years. She looked as if that were to be expected.

December 6. Annah writes she'll miss Judea this Christmas but that she can't come to visit. They're going to rent out rooms next semester and she has to help her mother. She invited me to come down next summer.

December 21. I'm coming, God, get terribly selfish sometimes, but have bright hopes.

Christmas was lonely without Annah. The day after, Arley walked around to deliver leftover things. Catherine's oranges were bulky and he carried the box out Hathaway Street on his shoulder. He swung it down before a plump Catherine standing at a sink. Was she pregnant again? After six children, you could hardly tell. Her eyes were still bright and her cheeks red, but that was all that was left of the slender girl who had once lived in that body.

"Would you take them down cellar, Arley?" she asked, and she switched on an electric light in the cellarway, revealing below the foundation bricks Sam and Papa had laid fifteen years before. The house seemed older than that, and crowded with children.

"A regular baby factory," Fred called his sister-in-law. Arley walked along a short side-street to Fred's. Like Papa, Fred had a long lawn with a birdbath. It was iced over. He pulled the tiny bottle of Georgia's forgotten French perfume from his coat pocket and raised the brass knocker.

"Arley, come in!" Georgia was pert and final, identical to the bride who had come to her brand-new house fourteen years ago. There were no children here to alter either flesh or property.

He walked to Justine's in the new part of town which had sprouted out of Field Street, past the cemetery.

In her living room, which, like Mama's, was fitted out in blue velvet, Justine lay on the sofa with her feet up. Justine was supposed to rest a lot now that she was pregnant again. Her first baby had been born early and dead.

"I'm feeling better," Justine said. "Now that I'm under way again. Did you see Maud's pictures?" Her sapphire sparkled as she held out the snapshots from Seattle. Ted looked the same, though he had become a college professor of religion, instead of a preacher. Maud's hair was wound around her head in a long braid; her oldest daughter looked as grown-up as Annah when Arley had first met her in the high school corridor. He longed for his small room at college and for his snowy balcony, for his own story—whatever it might be. *December 31, 1924: Home in Justine's room. The clock is striking 12, it's 1925. Someday I'll be writing 1950, and, oh, may the spirit be more in possession of my soul at that time.*

. . .

GOALS FOR 1925: *1. To stay in college with credible marks. 2. To win my Wilby W in track as well as tennis. 3. To strive to be the number one tennis player at Wilby. 4. To be more respectful to my parents. 5. To do a good turn daily. 6. To strive to live by Christ's principles. 7. To win over self. To one reading this—if any ever do—these words may sound senseless, but to me they have a meaning. It is not only the sins of the body, the desires of the flesh, but also the sins of the soul.*

January 10. Jessica sent my letters back with one sentence: "I have made other plans for the February dance."

January 21. Annah has not written in a while.

January 30. Fair, but did what I should and didn't what I shouldn't.

February 1. About the best day in my life, snowshoe hike with Ellen from my Classics Seminar. She is a healthy girl, if stocky, but some hiker!

February 2. Jessica wrote with an apology and her usual position paper on her feelings toward me.

February 4. Annah wrote, the boarders are fun. They'll be gone by summer and I'll stay in their room.

February 10. Nothing special, a little tired, lowered my conduct.

February 12. Used head, slept when I wanted to do something else. Life is Great.

February 15. Fair, but sometimes my mind is small.

February 18. How happy one is when one is not selfish.

March 8. I wonder if a man can love a woman until he has felt her slipping from his grasp? Mailed a letter to Annah.

March 13. Little girl, where are you?

March 14. Depressed in spirit, but never defeated.

March 15. A quiet day, but peaceful obeisance to duty brings happiness.

March 16. Some days go and some are lived with God.

March 17. My soul fluctuates! But I believe I will get the light.

March 20. Things of the flesh die. Christian things are of the spirit and only by spiritual growth can we loose the Bonds of Death. But there is so much to give up!

One afternoon in a semicircular amphitheater, Professor Gottlieb pushed a magnet through a coil of electric wire that charged more and more as the magnet passed through. He exaggerated his movements to show the assembled juniors the resistance he was meeting. "So it is, ladies and gentlemen," he addressed them full face, "in life. The more energy you expend for an ideal, the more opposition you will meet."

"Thank you, sir." Charles shook his professor's hand gratefully as he left the classroom.

April 1. Fine walk with Ellen. She really likes me.

April 7. Run for the ball, every ball, no matter. That gives you muscle power. Trying against all odds, that gives you character. And never giving up, that gives you life.

April 18. Ellen's sorority dance, soft color, low lights, an enchanting girl. Dreamland with airy, fleeting bodies, but we must never forget those not privileged to be among us.

May 10. "Mother." How that word endears / thy sacred form to me / and sets about thy hallowed head / visions of eternity.

May 11. One of the very best days of my life. I lost the consulship of the fraternity, but have felt no feelings of bitter jealousy like I did five years ago when I lost the captaincy of the basketball team. To be free from jealousy is to be like green grass in the midst of parched dirt. Won in tennis.

June 5. I lost the tennis championship in semi-finals. But hope to regain it in the fall. God gives me knocks so I can learn to stand.

June 10. An average of 89.5, not bad for a little guy from the country. Annah still wants me to visit this summer.

August 2. A minister is a doctor of the mind whose medicine is Christ.

August 10. On my way to Annah's in Pennsylvania. Is there hope?

"Well, Arley Minor you look just the same in this part of the world!" Mr. Trevellack opened the door. He was carefully dressed, as usual, but looked thinner.

"It's all the same to me," Arley replied, trying for the right note. Trevellack's tone had changed toward him since Fred had refused him the loan. Did he suspect Arley knew about it? Did Annah suspect? Did she know herself?

"Hello, Arley!" Annah ran down the stairs. She was wearing a red and yellow dress, her sorority colors, as it turned out. Her face was a bit thinner, grown-up. The outer curve of her eyebrows, Arley realized, was exactly that of his Grandma Percy's in the photograph of her as a young mother.

"Annah!" She hugged him and it was wonderful. He was whole. At rest with her.

"And so he's making me drop nursing," she explained to him later in the kitchen as they sat at the table. "Bedpans, mopping—too menial, he says."

He watched her hands, so familiar. The plump place between thumb and forefinger was the same; she moved with the same proper grace, a bit more proper. Incongruously he remembered the night they had bumped into the cow on the dark road: she had jumped then! Every movement, every word, the inflection of each word, the rise and fall within each inflection, the miniature movements of her lips as she prepared to speak: they all added up to the one irreplaceable thing in the world. The most recognizable. If he were sitting in a dark movie house in London or Paris and if she were ten rows behind him and should happen to clear her throat, he would stand and search for her face: Annah! She was herself. He couldn't speak.

"My father expects more from me, he says." Annah talked on while Charles stared and smiled. We all do, he said to himself.

August 15: We had fun like we used to. The night in her kitchen.

September 28. Ellen loves me more than she should.

October 29. Regained tennis championship.

December 10. Annah will visit me at Wilby here on New Year's Eve for the Tennis Team's party. Still remember every moment of my visit this summer. And of hers two summers before.

I know she is the little girl I dreamed of and she belongs to me body and soul.

With his freshly packed laundry case thumping against his knee, Arley hurried from the Wilby railroad station to the fraternity house and ran up the stairs to his room, where he quickly opened the brown notebook and wrote down the momentous sentence that had tailed him over the train tracks from Hartford northward: *How hard it is in this modern day to be a Christian and a man.* But when he read it over, it didn't seem to say anything! He pushed the pencil aside and unwrapped his long scarf. Here was a young red-haired man, round glasses, discreet freckles, the best athletic build, blue eyes, wide mouth, narrow nose and strong chin. Democrats had weak chins, the judge said every fourth November. But did he look like a man or a Christian? There it was, their oppositeness, in a nutshell.

He stood to examine himself in the mirror and impulsively combed his hair from a middle to a side part. Why were parsons always presented as fools in the movies? Surely there was no more courageous stand than that at Golgotha? Daring not to fight, risking all?

"Minor?" He was being paged from below. "You eating supper here tonight?"

"No," he called through the stairwell's smell of roast beef. "I'm taking my girl to dinner at the inn." Annah's mother must have put her on the train before noon, admonishing her not to go into any hotel rooms alone with Charles. He wouldn't ask that of her! Something more, marriage? He leaned over his desk and wrote: *Jesus does not want followers who are not true men, so I must be a man first, then a Christian!* He shut the notebook and pushed it between the bookends, grabbed up his heavy sweater and scarf and ran lightly downstairs. Noticing a corner of white in his foyer mailbox, he reached for Annah's envelope before he realized it was hers.

"Dear Arley, It may come as a surprise to you that I will not be joining you at Wilby on New Year's Eve, despite all our plans. I have met a man whom I must admit interests me a great deal.

He is a friend of one of our boarders. Although I can't say yet if I love him, it doesn't seem fair to continue with you if I could be this easily interested in somebody else, does it? Please forgive me. Ever your friend and admirer since long ago in high school, Annah."

He opened the fraternity door and turned out onto the street, north, toward the Arctic, in a sweater. He would not feel the cold, withdrawn into his fortress, its moat filled with water and its bridge closed while the world *flowed and glittered* about him. A phrase from where? One of the greats. The greats were always so reassuring. Having them there, like God. He wrapped his scarf around his neck.

He walked.

Jejune. He reminded himself of his new vocabulary. The godless life is dry, barren, jejune. *Jejunum.* The name given the middle part of the small intestine which after death is emptied. By whom?

Without Annah, there was still God: *Let me hide myself in Thee.* But without God? The gutter of the road was glazed dark like ice on a skating pond. Saturn was covered with ice. What if God had not created the universe? If it were all an accident? Look, he doesn't have to have a white beard. He can be thought of as a force. Like a river's force, you don't see it, but it's there. Arley sank into the river. You don't have to take the world literally as an aging Methodist would. Had he told Annah that? She had reservations about dogma. Well, Christianity had not been the only religion, he could admit that. Arley let himself sink into the more ancient and saltier river that had circled Ur.

His walk was taking him on a slight grade downhill; behind him the college gradually raised itself. You did not have to lose your faith at college, you could accept parallels. He noticed a farm road he had never taken and turned west to follow it. The sun was inches from dropping over the western edge of the world. You could, for instance, understand how the men of Ur had imagined the sun, as Lord Shamash, slipping beneath the western mountains to his underground tunnel. It was just a story. Into that same tunnel their hero, who was half man and half god, one day walked. Gilgamesh has gone there on his search for everlasting life. Walking, walking. There is silence and darkness and the tunnel enclosing him. He cannot get out. His body fails him and he falls, kicking. His mind fails him, and he hears voices whisper and babble into laughter. They are his. There is no hope. He is mad. A breeze touches his face. Is he near the opening? He presses against hands and knees to rise. Sighing and weeping, he pushes and pushes himself until he pops out and plunges into a blaze of sunlight in the Eastern Garden of Lord Shamash: "I am!" he shouts. "Hello!"

What could be frightening about that? Arley walked faster toward the low sun, looking cautiously around before unbuttoning his fly to urinate. Guiltily revoking claim to the yellow pool, he proceeded. This field, too, lowered and he walked farther down toward netherland. Would he hear the boom of Persephone's kettledrum as the door to Hades slowly appeared before him, slowly opened? The sun's bottom rim passed out of sight. The earth's curve was lit by an orange glow and he was alone in the snow-covered field. The world could not be simply rock and barren matter. God must have created it. Must watch over it, be watching him now. He dared not walk another step toward the sun. He turned on the ball of one foot and began to retrace his steps. *Jesus Savior, pilot me*, he recited to himself; if only he could sing on tune. He whistled the rest of it until that solitary noise raised goosebumps on his neck. What was behind him now? He should not turn. He couldn't help himself: a winking sun and black twisted limbs of trees that would fall, become carbon; he stood at the bottom of a future sea. Quicker, but don't run; he had done so well at college, had come so far. He must not fall into panic now; *over life's tempestuous sea*. What exactly did *tempestuous* mean? A college man learned words, a thousand separate storehouses of knowledge in which lay the way to truth.

But *I am the way and the truth.*

It's okay; Arley slowed as he reached the main road. I believe you.

He turned uphill. The field of darkened terror on his right looked almost peaceful, though he worried at having abandoned part of himself, yellow in the snow. The sky approached full black on his left. Lord Sky, the Sumerians had called it. They had never gotten to one single God. Been stuck forever at Lord Earth, Lord Storm and Lady Springtime. Lady Springtime, that is what he wanted for himself. Will it not be you, Annah? Would there ever be anyone else? Oh lady, lady, lady, lady spring!

Take it easy.

You know I'm yours, Jesus.

VI

Palm Sunday,
the Middle Twenties

CHARLES PERCY MINOR, divinity student loose in New York, grasped a handrail and peered out the front of the subway that rocked like a horse. Lights blinked red and green and a narrow future rushed at him through the echoing tunnel. At 116th Street students from Columbia University came through the rubber-lipped doors. They looked as smart as his fellow classmates at Union Seminary on 120th, or at Wesleyan, but Charles no longer envied them their articulateness. In fact, he suspected they knew too little of the valley of the shadow. "Avoid clichés," his prophets professor had written on Charles's first paper. But life was clichés: birth, growth, death.

Union Theological Seminary stood like a walled fortress against the city beyond. While outside the poor of New York . . . and so forth. Since coming to the city Charles had frequently essayed but never completed a sentence about the poor. "Only at Union," his brother-in-law Ted had written from Seattle, "can you best prepare yourself for the coming disintegration of the Christian church as we know it." Ted resembled an old-fashioned social prophet, blaming politics for everything. Like Amos, he had a point. But was it enough? Stepping down from the northern limit of the Broadway bus, Charles had been shocked to see the squalor in which *hordes, whole armies of colored people* lived. And the white people sleeping under newspapers were worse off than any of Judea's.

"Got a dime for coffee and a doughnut?" an unshaven man had asked of Charles and his roommate, Barclay, as they walked one night on Broadway.

"Don't give it," Barclay whispered. "He's just going to buy a drink." Barclay was an Episcopalian, he knew the world.

"Here you are, sir." Charles gave a coin. Methodists knew the heart.

"Let's trail him!" Barclay whispered when the man had passed Liggett's. Almost immediately they saw him con another student. Perhaps the Methodists did not know everything, as was so often implied at Union. Ted would lay it all up to capitalism. We must have the wisdom of snakes to know the world without becoming cynical.

Charles would get off the subway at Chambers Street today and try again. The prophet Hosea had pierced through social justice to God's love. Just let the people know the loving Father, he said, and they'll run into each other's arms as brothers. Just set their hearts on fire. Last week he had ridden straight through the waters to Brooklyn to hear Uldine Utley, the girl evangelist, and to study her technique. Waiting in the crowd in the gold-encrusted lobby, why had he not opened his mouth and prophesied? "Your voice needs oil." The subway braked into Chambers, and Charles strode through the tiled tunnel to be spewed forth. Out of the maw of the whale, Jonah from the belly of. "That's not the belly, Arley, that's the abdomen." Charles emerged at the top of the stairs.

Where shall I be led? Lead me, Lord, and I shall follow. Charles turned west; had Jerusalem been so cold? The late sun cast a shadow behind him. Two chubby girls came out of an office building. Had they a soul? Was that paint on their cheeks? And were their eyelids colored blue? Well, they didn't look wicked. If not pious, certainly kind. If he could show them God was love, would they still need their paint?

As the sun began to set, it grew chillier and he buttoned his top button and stuffed his hands in his pockets. He stood in a warm doorway where heat from many cups of coffee might reach him as the door opened and shut. He would not go in and give pleasure to the body, not yet. He had work to do.

Now the people came in droves. He concentrated on the girls. What messages did he have for them? The one with the almond eyes, her eyelids greased in a blue-green pigment such as the Egyptian women used, dead and alive, what could he tell her? I am the servant of the Lord, let me give you rest. She didn't want rest. She wanted to go to a party. I am the servant of Jesus, let me give you peace. She wanted excitement. I am the servant of God, let me strengthen your heart. She could already dance beyond midnight. She smiled as she spoke to the girl beside her. Plans, no doubt, for a holiday. Charles himself had no weekend plans. What message had he for them? Out of a whale I have come to you, to prophesy, to promise, to give my life for others that I may live. And ye? Some words were better for certain feelings. Oh, will ye not help me? God loves you, will you not love him?

Why did he not speak now, simply open his mouth, extend his arm in an oracular arc and begin? He wasn't crazy, he wasn't dumb and he did want to pull in the world. Here I am! I will show you the ways of the Lord and we will sing his praise!

It was hard to be a prophet, and cold. He turned into the shop and ordered a hot chocolate. He burned his tongue by drinking it too soon. The city could be dangerous. Perhaps it would be easier to start prophesying with Isaiah. With anti-ritualism, people seemed to know what you were talking about. Episcopalians. They were the ritualists of the Reformation. He asked directions to St. Paul's Church and soon entered its quiet yard. A graveyard. He felt at home here. He was about his father's business. In more ways than one. You can say that again! No kidding! Voices of his school friends called from the basketball court, though their bodies were frozen in movement, stopped dead like the marble headstones and crumbling limestones sticking up here to guard the living. Watchmen from the past generation standing near to ward off evil: SEEING WE ARE ENCOMPASSED ABOUT BY SO GREAT A CLOUD OF WITNESSES—Charles struggled to remember the rest while his eyes picked out details. Mehitabel. Sara. There was running in it—toward the face of Jesus, wasn't it? Radiant, encouraging, as he looked down from the right hand of God? No good, lost. Paul's sentence to the Hebrews was not stored among the others Charles had collected in his hat as they fell about him at seminary like rain.

"There is one God and he has not just been discovered; don't fall in love with the religion of nineteen twenty-six!"

"Keep the cross before you: don't be vulgar but have the rich color of dignity."

"Stay seven years in the first parish, stay alone and meditate, remembering you have earth as your mother and heaven as your father."

"Contrast our former President Roosevelt, who shouldered his way through a crowd, with the gentle Prince of Wales, who begged a disfigured soldier to unwrap his face so the prince might kiss it."

Charles entered the lighted church and walked smack into George Washington's pew. Now there was a man of the world! The sanctuary was decorated with flags: Episcopalians neither refuted the body nor disdained success. They simply became governors and presidents. Isaiah would be lugged out of here and his parents notified. The candles carried by acolytes chilled Charles. The Gospel came out resonantly from the cavern of a middle-aged minister's mouth. Even if Charles worked daily on his high, stumbling voice, would he ever have such a polished delivery? Maybe he should keep on being a Methodist, despite his recent leanings toward Congregationalism. In Methodism the heart counted, but in Congregationalism you had to think and speak clearly. Those were hard-headed men who had boarded the *Mayflower*. "They're not any smarter," his father had always said, "just uppitier." "They have," his mother would defend her family's sect, "a certain restraint. And they've been here longer." Hello pilgrims! I may be coming, too. *Land where our fathers died*—whoops: mother's fathers—*of thee we sing*. Maybe he was no more cut out to be a Congregationalist than a prophet. His Four-Year Confidential Rating Sheet from Wilby had been graphed by his professors to display a general decline from Exceptional in Industry and Cooperation, to Good in Personality and Intellectual Ability and on down to Average in Initiative. You had to work with what God gave you.

In his Father's house were many mansions. The room of the Methodists was upstairs in back and well-heated. The room of the Congregationalists was upstairs in front and well-lighted. The main living room was gorgeously furnished by the Episcopalians, while the Baptists occupied an upstairs maid's room. The cellar steps served as a temporary camp for Hebrew prophets who made forays up there to speak to their people below. Women of all reform denominations shared the kitchen. Except for pretty girls who roved the hallways in caroling choirs. Charles's heart was soothed. There was room for him in God's house, though he stood yet at the doorway, hesitant.

"THERE'S NO SUCH THING AS SIN," the acned soda clerk at Liggett's insisted. "There's a little good and a little bad in each of us."

"No," Charles explained. "To sin is to disobey the Father's will. We get a choice."

"Why would he take a chance like that?" The clerk settled the chocolate soda in front of Charles and left.

So he could rejoice with his children for choosing right. Or strike his nations with the whip of bondage for doing wrong. Charles paid for his soda and crossed over to Union.

"Hard work?" he inquired of the Negro porter washing the floor. "I'll watch where I step."

In his and Barclay's room, he dropped his books onto his desk, being careful not to knock over the delicate ivory box Maud had brought him from Rhodesia. The lawyers of Deuteronomy said the masters must give the servant his rest on the Sabbath and his freedom after six years of labor. They even suggested you cancel all debts after six years. He could see his father chuckling at that one. "Old Simon's dying," Joseph had written him, "but your young friend is doing twice the job his father did. He's a good boy."

"Hard work?" Charles inquired of the cleaning woman who was at work in his room. Was she the regular one? He wasn't sure.

She dusted. "Not too bad."

"You like the work?" A dumb question. Do you love the Lord? Are you circumcised of the heart?

"It's all right," she answered. "You like yours?"

"Studying? Yes, I do!" Charles felt a need to continue. "My father was a farmer, I hated farm work."

"What is it you boys are all studying?" she inquired, reaching down to pick up the wastebasket by his desk.

"Oh," he said, "we're studying to be ministers." She should have been around the night they rolled the garbage cans down the stairs.

"Ministers?" she looked inquiringly at him.

"Preachers."

"Ah, preachers." She smiled and left the room to dump his trash.

It was all his fault, he knew. But how, exactly?

Green traffic lights in the dusk along Riverside Park, green leaves unfolding on the trees and everyone walking in couples. Charles walked alone. Would he ever have a woman on his arm? The branches of the trees bent over him reassuringly. He raised his face to them.

"You see that man?" A fellow in a plaid lumberjacket picked a cigarette from above his ear. "Why, he looked at me as if I were a murderer. The city does that to you. But people are good. Adam and Eve, we're all descended from them. The Chinaman, the Negro, you and me."

"We're all brothers." Charles shifted weight on his feet. It was not unlike a late bull session with Barclay and the boys across the hall.

"Now, don't misunderstand me." The man dropped the match on the spring grass. "Who made a king of bluer blood than you or I?"

False prophets could be dangerous. Back at his desk, Charles wrote to Stanton Goode, who was getting a Ph.D. at Palo Alto.

"I begin to see things more as my father sees them, though I haven't given up my inward longings. What I once thought un-Christian seems to have some wisdom, especially as I grow close to providing for myself. Looking out my window toward 125th Street and trying to imagine the salary of a soda clerk, I wonder what I would have done if my parents had not had the money to send me to college and to seminary." He finished the letter, licked the envelope and set it aside. Umbrellas?

"There is a joke," he wrote to his mother, "that a poll-taker looking for people at Union who believe in Jesus' divinity was sent down to the basement to interview the janitor. By the way, I may go up to New Hampshire at the beginning of the spring vacation." He set that letter aside. With spring he must stop mourning for Annah, a year of that was enough. He wrote to Ellen at Wilby and asked her if she had snowshoed much that winter and whether he might visit her Saturday. Holding the letter, he stood by the open window and looked out toward the barely-lighted area beyond 125th Street. "I wish I . . ." he began, but still had no idea how to finish. That night he dreamt of doors shutting and opening in a corridor, girls running naked down the hall; one turning to stand before him, surprisingly small-breasted, a look of shock gradually freezing on her face as she examined him.

Ellen wrote back: by all means, yes. He had to save for the train fare and bought only tangerines and cookies for lunch. At suppertime he filled up in a dirty restaurant for forty cents and, much later, boarded the 2:00 a.m. train. Ellen looked pasty in the early morning light outside the restaurant in Wilby center where she met him. And she had not gotten any thinner.

"English muffins." She looked across the booth at him too happily. "Whatever you do is all right with me," she had said a year ago at Christmas, when he had turned down her invitation to Albany since Annah was coming, "because I love you."

"Two English muffins," he told the waitress. "Two marmalades."

Being loved was not so important as loving.

"As I wrote to you," he began, busying himself with marmalade, "as I wrote, Annah and I are no longer together and . . ." His throat constricted. "And," he continued, "life goes on." He smiled wanly. Avoid clichés.

"He got here at twelve fifty-eight, just when I told you," Joseph said to Polly as Charles came in late from saying hello to friends after the Easter morning service. "So, I was only two minutes off." The three of them sat at the table with Fred and Georgia.

The kitchen door swung open and Charles saw a familiar pair of shoulders moving in a familiar way through the opening. It was not the sure gyre of Simon on the ballfield, but the remembered solidity of Old Simon's roundness under a white butler's jacket. Why hadn't he known? Simon carried a platter of roasted lamb.

"Hello there . . ."

"Hello there . . ."

They each began, but Simon paused.

"Simon," Charles finished.

"Well, Arley," his father interrupted, motioning Simon out of the dining room, "since you are to be a preacher, at the cost of some several hundred per annum to me, why don't you ask the blessing?"

"Our Father," Charles shut his eyes, "Which Art in Heaven, grant us this day"—he heard the kitchen door swinging shut— "that we will open our hearts to Thy Son. . . ."

"WHAT EVIDENCE EXISTS, Mr. Minor, for the exaggeration of the miracles?" His New Testament professor's voice reached him from near a dim blackboard, curving in and out among leather chairs and over a blue Persian rug. Divinity students were to be gentlemen.

"In Mark, sir, there is the case of a raised child and you don't know if she was ever dead. In Luke, there is a man being taken out for burial. By the time it gets to John, it is a man who is four days dead." The Good News at Union in the year of Our Lord nineteen hundred twenty-six / twenty-seven was that Jesus had been the most highly developed human to date. Charles feared he

was being corrupted and rehearsed his own story continually to
find out how.

After the trip to Caesarea Philippi, Charles now knew, Jesus no
longer called himself the Way, but the Son. Not a king who kills.
But a servant who will be killed. And he walked toward that
death. Fording at Jericho, he climbed rocks piled on top of each
other that leaned together closer at the top and seemed to form
the city of Jerusalem. Where would it be coming from? The
opposition without which there is no power. They had been
watching him in Galilee. Would he be noticed in Jerusalem?
Could he collect a crowd quickly enough to keep himself from
being knifed by hired assassins before he made his announcement?

Get them shouting now. Shout! He heard himself whispering.
He must not die a fool's death. The carpenter's son rides into a
hole. How far to the temple? He tried to remember from other
springs. The women's voices carried well, but they weren't quite
loud enough. He could still be knifed by a shadow inside the
wall. His brother James would begin a cheer from somewhere
within the city, if they made it that far. And if they did, on to
Bethany for the night, where they would be safe. The women
had relatives there.

On Monday the eleventh of Nisan, he spoke quietly in the
temple precincts.

On Tuesday the twelfth, he climbed the steps amidst doves.
Would the words come out?

"Wicked, it is wicked to profit from changing money in the
temple!" Not loud enough. He tried again. People silenced each
other then. Two men came toward him.

"What'll it be today?" The Liggett's soda clerk's acne had
worsened. From private or public sins? Charles wondered, and
ordered his standard grilled cheese sandwich.

He had to get the pilgrims on his side before he made his
announcement: "I am the Messiah!" Not yet, not before the
crowd tripled. At supper the woman gave him the rites of the
dead. He shut his nostrils against the smell of ointment from

Egypt. Ointment for him? Whom the world would watch rise? The smell frightened him.

By Wednesday the thirteenth of Nisan, the Greeks were calling him clever but saying he had gone to Egypt to learn his medicine. A slur from a Greek. A carpenter's son does not study medicine, anyway. What he knew he had taught himself from a child. Those were the only things worth knowing. The birds, for instance, flying.

Thursday the fourteenth. The women seemed at times to have their own plans for him, seemed to nod after his announcements as if he'd said exactly what they planned. The men must eat together away from the household of women. He would take them into Jerusalem and speak to them there.

He could not eat. Food was too heavy. He needed lightness. He gave the men his bread and portioned out his wine.

They would be lost without him, sons, all of them. But you have me forever, this is my body. The Greeks did it like that—strange, so physical.

Leaning on the rock, he tried to reach the power, to stay with it, but something was missing. A torch. Judas walking toward him. Of course! The jail was underground. Into this dark hole comes, falls Jeshua the carpenter's son, whose mother cannot now rescue him nor call to him in the deep. Whose father is dead. So laugh, laugh, Joseph, I am in stocks. He felt the anger rise, not now! Not yet.

The law was strong and old, for blasphemy you needed three witnesses. They did not materialize.

So, who is your father?

Do you not hear your accuser?

Will you not speak?

Are you the son of Joseph?

Or the son of God?

Oh I am I am and I shall rise to the sky and sit at his right hand, by which happening you shall know for sure, for surely, that is to be my proof of who my father is and it is not Joseph.

This is no death by ordinary stones! This is messiahship! This is for Rome: we have him, bound!

Had he made a mistake? Wait! My Kingdom is not of the world!

The crowd.

Who is this Barabbas?

Clever.

Stones he knew but not the nails of soldiers paid by Rome. The hardening not just of skin but of breath itself.

You said you could come down!

He could not do it all by himself, he could only wait for larger hands. They would lift him, free him.

But the light was no longer his light, this was not Galilee. He had been wrong? *Why don't you come?* The voice was loud, hard to hear, it did not sound like his own; he could not wait more. A sponge was stuck in his face. No: he must be awake for it. He cried out again.

Three o'clock.

Hands came then and gathered him.

Up.

Joseph, a rich man, went to Pilate to beg the body and at half past six the soldiers took it down. Mary of Magdala and Mary of Galilee began to perform the laying out, but it was too late toward Sabbath. They lay the folded winding sheet over him and pressed the heavy spices to hold it there until they should return to this room cut out of rock. In Galilee there was no such glory for the dead. They walked back to Bethany for the paschal meal, which their law required yearly. Bread without leaven, no time leaving Egypt to let it rise. The lamb was well-spiced but nobody ate the meat. The women told the men what they had seen. The men were mute. How could they now become men, who had fled? Who had feared? There must be a way. He had shown them. They broke the bread. They drank the wine.

"Telephone for Minor!"

It was a nice house in New Jersey but not so elegant as Charles had imagined for Jessica.

"Arley," she said. In a drab knot, her yellow hair no longer gave off light. "Thanks for coming." She took him to her sister's room, where a pale girl with braids lay sleeping. Her narrow hands had not yet turned to claws.

Downstairs, Jessica fixed dishes of strawberries and sugar and they went outdoors to the chairs in the back yard.

"I don't believe in any of it, Arley. But I know you do." She ignored the tears that came into her eyes and she ate her strawberries. "So I called you."

He stood up and put his hand on her soft hair. "He will be with her," he said. "Always."

It rained the whole day of the funeral, an April rain as virginal as the dead girl. They had used the best raffia grave liner and a sterile earth cover, but you could still see the Jersey mud if you knew where to look. Charles sat up with Jessica until dawn and then took the train into the city for his last final exam. On the walk to school he rescued a ball for a little girl and tossed it to her lightly and well. Jesus had risen. Because he could not possibly be held by the bonds of death, he was not held by the bonds of death. It was as simple as that.

"THANKS VERY MUCH and have a good day." Charles sounded like his mother. He paid the taxi driver and then he was alone, standing in the churchyard with his suitcase and bag of books. Canada? Wisconsin? Wyoming? "Dear Son in Christ," the summer pulpit advisor had replied in May. "Nothing left but Connecticut, its smallest parish, East Meadow." He left his bags on the grass and walked into the church, where white walls and windows of pale lavender sealed a quiet space. His church. No, the church of Jesus. His coming here was not a unique venture in the life of Christ, Arley reassured himself. It hardly mattered how well he did. Still, he meant to win back the two members lost since fifty years ago, when the church had been started by eleven Methodists. "I'll get them back," he promised. Then he was ready to meet his people. Were they ready for their healer?

"The man that invented daylight saving time ought to be hanged." The old fellow rocking on the porch sounded as if he already relished the dangling feet and fallen hat. "Good day," Charles said, and walked farther along the street, introducing himself to strays. He passed the gas station and the hardware store and a couple of houses where he thought he could smell the mud from boots and the scorched yellow scent of ironing. "I'm Charles Minor, the summer pastor."

Praise God from Whom all blessings flow, the Renfrews sang in the kitchen of his summer's home. They pulled chairs back over flowered linoleum and sat to an evening meal of ham and scalloped potatoes.

"You ought to stop in on Mrs. Martin tomorrow." Mrs. Renfrew continued to fill him in on parishioners.

He had come home. When the late meal was over, he walked to his room at the end of the long upstairs hall and lay down. Here he was, on the long green strip of Riverside Park magically stretched north and drawn into a ribbon that curved through Connecticut to run up this particular hillside. He knew just where he was. Later, he got up in the dark to go to the bathroom. The hall was pitch-black, nothing in front of him, nothing behind. He spread his arms until the knuckles of each hand touched the walls on either side of him. "I am with you," the small voice whispered within him. He radiated warmth outward, felt himself enlarging and expanding as he progressed through the narrow hallway. His own presence was sufficient and assuring. The physician had healed himself. Hello! Hello! He had not been so happy since the day he had packed his trunk to go to Wesleyan. He whispered back, "O God, be Thou close!"

He wrote careful letters to Jessica. She would have called these people cute and he would not feed that mockery in her. When he smiled at Mr. Cady rocking on his porch across from the church he had not entered since 1875, that being the year they had accidentally left his name off the founders' plaque, it was not the same as Jessica's laughing.

"Nope," Mr. Cady said when Charles stopped by to invite him.

"Hope you'll change your mind, sir." Charles raised his straw hat and walked down the porch steps.

So far only Miss Sigerist at the library—eighty if a day—had promised to attend Charles's first service on Sunday. She had topped it off with a library card pressed into his hand; when she nodded good-bye, he had seen the pink flesh of her head through the sparse white hairs.

"The man who said we all got to think about God together at ten a.m. on Sunday wasn't using any brains," Mr. Brewster at the store replied, eyeing a young girl at his penny-candy jars.

Candy. Not a bad idea. Charles ordered two pounds of butterscotch and licorice.

"Why, you're a grown man!" red-faced Mr. Brewster objected as he scooped and weighed. All the while he looked not at Charles but at the bare legs of the girl. "Say hi there to your Ma for me, Frances." Even his requests sounded like reprimands.

He could think of nothing to startle Mr. Brewster into generosity.

"It's for the children," Charles explained. "And where do you live, Frances?" he inquired politely of the girl, who was no younger than Joan when she had first heard the voices shimmering and sliding over high Burgundian meadows.

"Down to Poortown," she replied with a grin.

"Out toward the lake," Mr. Brewster interpreted, pointing eastward. "Next to Petey Wilson and his Ma."

Petey Wilson, the forty-five-year-old man who had amused and startled the seventy-, seventy-five- and eighty-year-old parents of the town by firing a supposedly defunct cannon on the tiny green last Fourth of July. A whole town of old people, and a little child shall lead them: Charles P. Minor by name.

Charles set out toward Poortown with candy in his pockets. Petrucci, the first house, was Catholic, but he went in anyway. Why shouldn't he bring the name of Jesus here, in passing?

"Some coffee, Reverend, and a little cake?" Mrs. Petrucci was kind. Her two babies were in and out of the house one after another and her older children called outdoors, but she smiled with a serenity that made Charles feel peaceful.

At the next house Mr. Turnby asked Charles to repeat himself.

"I'd like to extend to you a special invitation to attend church

this Sunday morning at ten a.m." Charles spoke as loud as he
dared and still remain on social terms.

"What's that?" Mr. Turnby was not deaf, only timid and
without hope.

"Shall I stop by to walk over with you?"

"Nope."

"Why not?"

"I'm busy," the frail man replied, looking vacantly at his spare
but immaculate living room in which nothing could be imagined
happening.

Like dawn on execution day, the first Sunday came. Charles took
his brown notebook over to the church. In the unfinished corridor behind the sanctuary his black morning coat hung on a
hanger stuck into the pull of a window shade. He put the notebook down on the window sill and took the robe off the hanger.
Carefully he pushed his right fist into the sleeve and pulled the
coat on. Then, leaning over the notebook, standing up so as not
to get wrinkled, he wrote: *June 5, 1927. Just getting ready for
my first sermon in my first parish. Long black coat and all. May
my God be the nearest possible.* At 9:55 the piano keys were
struck by Mrs. Renfrew's determined hands, and he walked into
the sanctuary and up the stairs to the pulpit. There were a handful of people in the pews, fewer than when he had practice
preached in New Hampshire. Two handfuls?

"Welcome, Holy Morning." He opened the Bible after the few
voices and the piano had made their separate ways to an ending.
"CALEB STILLED THE PEOPLE BEFORE MOSES, AND SAID, 'LET US GO
UP AT ONCE, AND POSSESS IT, THE LAND.'" He paused to look at the
congregation as Fosdick had suggested in practice preaching at
the seminary: Miss Sigerist was there, holding a hymn book on
her lap. "NOW THE MEN THAT WENT UP TO CANAAN WITH CANA . . .
WITH CALEB BROUGHT BACK THIS REPORT: 'WE BE NOT ABLE TO GO UP
AGAINST THE PEOPLE; FOR THEY ARE STRONGER THAN WE. ALL THE
PEOPLE THAT WE SAW IN IT ARE MEN OF A GREAT STATURE.' You
see," Charles explained to the girl Frances, sitting with a swarm of
brothers and sisters beside the worn woman whose complaints he

had endured only yesterday, "they were afraid to go and were trying to make the task look too hard. 'WE SAW THE GIANTS,' they said, 'THE SONS OF ANAK, WHICH COME OF THE GIANTS; AND WE WERE IN OUR OWN SIGHTS AS GRASSHOPPERS, AND SO WE WERE IN THEIR SIGHT.' You see," he added, speaking slowly so he wouldn't stumble, "if you feel small, you're apt to look small." A young man in a wheelchair was being pushed through the doors by a woman. Like the leper dropped through the ceiling? So soon? Charles shut the Holy Book.

The piano began again and he counted the congregation: the young couple wanting their baby baptized were not there, the rest of the Renfrews were properly dispersed, and that was it. Seventeen people, mostly children. As the hymn came to a close, he gripped the side of the pulpit. It was from above that the power came; through the windows that light converged on him and he was supposed to take its power in his hands and spread it over the docile parishioners below.

"We in America can march toward Canaan, too. But there are giants before us, and, indeed, within ourselves: the lust for money, the hate some people feel for people who are different and the thrill of war. The best in each of us must not feel small before those forces. Caleb was not afraid, nor was Columbus, nor was Peary at the Pole. The great war is ended, but the fight has scarcely begun. We need red-blooded men and women who are neither pacifists nor gushing club women. We need hard-minded thinkers who will study men's instincts and find the giant-strewn road to peace as our fathers before us could not." The actual peace of East Meadow, Charles realized, was this moment hovering about them, June-bright and eternal.

When Mrs. Renfrew picked up at the piano, Charles got down the stairs and out the aisle to the front doors, which he swung open to let in the glorious day. He heard the sounds of distant voices and the motors of cars.

The youth in the wheelchair came out first.

"Good morning," Charles said to him. "Where do you live?"

"Tumberlee."

"We'd love to have you come by," the woman replied. "Mrs. Renfrew knows where we live."

"I should love to come." Charles waved good-bye. The mother looked like a New Yorker, young for her age.

"Good morning and thank you for a lovely sermon." Miss Sigerist's hand produced more pressure in his than he expected.

"Good morning." The washed-out voice of Mrs. Martin.

"Good morning!" Her lively daughter Frances.

"A good job!" Mrs. Renfrew in her pianist's robe grasped his hand firmly. "Hurry along now, it's roast chicken."

Across the street Charles saw Mr. Cady rocking on his front porch. Reluctantly, he shut the front doors and walked back through the sanctuary. He picked up the collection plates that had earlier been borne through the pews by the Renfrews masculine and carried them to the corridor. He hung his coat on the window-shade pull and turned to the brown notebook. His hands were sweaty as he picked up the pen to write: *Think I did fairly well. Number out—17. Collection—$4.25.*

If the young couple wanted their baby baptized, would they join the church? Charles loaded his pockets with candy and set out on the long sloping road of farms. Whenever he spotted a few tow-headed youngsters hanging on pasture gates to stare down his passage, he reached into his pockets.

"Here comes the Reverend!" Some of the boys already knew him.

He reached the farmhouse where the young couple lived.

"Home?" he called through the screen door, over the top of a sleeping dog. Even the dogs were old here. Then Charles saw the baby carriage out under the apple trees. He rattled the screen door and opened it, leaning in so that his voice would circulate inside the house.

"Is anybody home?" No answer.

"It's Mr. Minor," he seconded, introducing himself to no one—a man, *Mister.*

He shut the screen door, stepped carefully around the dog and then around its leavings strewn on the scrawny lawn. He reached the old carriage. How many infants had slept in it? There was mosquito netting over it. He peered through, placing his glasses and nose against the net. Ah, yes, it's you, Elizabeth Caroline Emmons, the potential baptizee. THE LORD IS MY SHEPHERD and I, I am His. Soon, Elizabeth Caroline; but where is your mother?

A horse stood in the nearby pasture, a brown one rather like the Minors' Prince. Charles left the baby to run his hand along the horse's nose, quietly, slowly. Life was sweet, there were creatures in it. This yard was like all hollows and contained everything. In New York the only creatures were people, their fine differences so finely measured. Here rose a peace that seemed connected with the fact that the creatures were so grossly different in size they could not be compared: horse, butterfly, mosquito, the sleeping infant. Mrs. Emmons with a basket of clothes walked out of the meadow behind the garage. Ah, my lady, lady of the meadows. He must remember to send Annah a card congratulating her on graduating from college.

"Reverend." Mrs. Emmons acknowledged his presence in the ungrammatical vernacular Union urged undergraduates to ignore.

"Mrs. Emmons," he replied, "I have looked in on your fine baby, who is sleeping."

"Just hanging out the wash," she explained guiltily. She had a soul! He had better be careful.

"A cup of tea?" she inquired in country speech which reduced all things to things.

"Don't mind if I do," he replied, struggling for jollity, lightness. Why was he imitating the intonation of a Catholic priest?

He settled himself sternly in the kitchen rocker, a Protestant. He held his cup well, none of that spilling into the saucer that made women look at you as if you were hopelessly infantile. But what did one say to women?

"And how are things going for Mr. Emmons?"

"I read a great deal," Alan said, indicating a pile of books on the wicker table. The two sat on a wide verandah, where geraniums hanging from the rafters swayed ever so slightly.

"And whom do you like best?" Charles inquired. Who would

strike a five-year-old boy with polio? Couldn't God tell he was
innocent?

"Whitman," the youth said; "the poets. I like to keep one line
at a time and go over and over it."

TAKE UP YOUR BED AND WALK. In the presence of Alan, Charles
should not even have thought of trying to heal; it was an insult to
the boy.

Mrs. Winslow came out with a silvery tray and tea implements. Lumps of sugar in a bowl, rich people's sugar.

"We've been coming up here now for fifteen years," she said,
indicating the peaceful prospect of substantial summer houses and
small tobacco fields in the valley below.

Ever since the polio? You had to roll with the punches. Some
punch.

"One lump," he replied to the woman's question.

Charles walked down to the tobacco fields. He heard singing and
saw Negroes wearing red bandanas as they worked. It was not
the collected song he would have imagined; only snatches of song
and then silence under the white gauze nets that shielded the
tobacco. He tried to judge the expression on the Negro faces.
Cheerful? Could they take the heat better than he could?

"Oh, they don't knock themselves out working," the owner
told Charles a few minutes later as the two of them sipped lem-
onades from glasses with silver rims that had been dipped in
sugar. "And they can take the heat better."

The lemonade cleared a swath through the crystallized sugar
on Charles's glass. Somehow, when the owner said it, it rang less
true.

His seminary roommate replied to Charles's post card: "What to
do about Jessica? You know darn well what to do and go ahead
and do it! They all call me Reverend, too. It's better than Rev.
Seriously, in my first week here in Newark I made one hundred
and fifty calls and wondered if the Kingdom of God isn't an idle
fancy. These people need to know how to keep clean, how to
manage their incomes, and how to control the sizes of their families. I saw one girl of four soak a crust of bread in a mug of coffee

and that was her whole supper. See you in September, Barclay."
Charles sent another post card to Jessica.

"What about this week, Mr. Turnby?"

"Too busy." Mr. Turnby looked over his linoleum in fear.

"What about this week, Mr. Cady?"

"Not on your life!" Mr. Cady chewed up to spit and leaned
backward on his rockers.

"What about this Wednesday evening for a box supper and
card game?" Candy for the grown-ups, why not?

"Six-thirty?" they all inquired, breathlessly. "I'll be there!"
They needed fun, didn't they?

The second Sunday: forty-one in the pews, nine dollars and
fourteen cents in the collection plates.

"But you know we're Catholic," Mrs. Petrucci announced on his
second visit.

"Just thought I'd stop in again and pay my respects on the
way." Charles smiled and pulled back to leave. "I passed your fine-
looking children out there on the swing."

"Yes, my daughter goes to First Communion this year."

"Good to hear that." Charles nodded and put out his hand to
say good-bye.

"Stop in and visit a minute with Pa." The woman suddenly
turned and led Charles into a room off the kitchen.

It was an old man, thin and whiskered, on the bed; his eyes
were half shut.

"Hello there," Charles tried again to parley with Catholics,
extending a hand.

"He don't talk much," the woman said, fidgeting with a curtain
before she left the room.

Charles drew up a chair and sat beside the bed.

"I'm the pastor at the church on the hill," he explained, not
knowing whether to talk louder because the old man was deaf or
softer because he might actually be sleeping.

The man looked out of glazed eyes with an unmoving expression.

Charles decided to go on as if the man were perceiving.

"I'm out on a walk today, stopping in at every house I come to.

I give a little candy to the children as I pass by. They might think of the church as sweet that way, though some people tell me it's bribery."

Nothing.

"The laurel is out, covering the lanes, and your house, too. People tell me the berries will be out soon and everyone will be picking."

Charles decided to let him in on a few secrets of the trade. "You know, I call mostly on Friday and Saturday. That way if somebody promises me to come to church on Sunday, they're less likely to dare to forget in a day or two."

No response. Perhaps he liked flowers?

"The violets and honeysuckle are out now. I'm making a list as I walk along. Every once in a while I send my lists to a girl named Jessica. But, to tell you the truth, I'd rather be sending them to a girl named Annah. You know how it is, sometimes?"

It seemed to Charles that the blue of the man's eyes darkened the slightest bit.

"People ask me if I don't get tired of all this walking. Sure I do. I'm just starting out, but when I get through I want to be able to say I've worked as hard in my life as any Yankee farmer. And don't you think Paul must have worn himself out walking from village to village in Asia Minor and Greece?"

The eyelids seemed to be lowering a bit.

"St. Paul? I know you're Catholic, but I think we're all the same underneath. The human heart is one heart." Getting carried away, time to go.

"I'd better be off, then, sir," Charles said, and after patting the man on his shoulder, he walked toward the door. A noise from the bed. The man was clearing his throat of weeks of silence. Charles returned to the bedside and leaned toward the moving lips:

"You're a good boy," the old man pronounced in a croak. "Bless you."

"Come to my birthday party next week," Alan said from his wheelchair.

"How old will you be?" Charles poured more lemonade for the boy.

"Twenty-one," Alan answered. "I'm trying to finish Virgil before then. It's my birthday present to myself."

Was it Alan who could heal?

"Pork and beans," Mrs. Renfrew said. "Okay. Let's have that as a starter and some salads. Cakes are always nice. Now, you get the notice posted for six-thirty Wednesdays and I'll get the suppers on the table. I'd say thirty-five cents a head and all you can eat."

"Won't you need some help? What about the Ladies' Aid?" Charles asked.

"I'm it," she replied. "But when they start coming to the suppers, I'll pick off a few more."

The third Sunday dawned late, Children's Sunday. Rain poured down, would drench the children in their Sunday best.

"Take my car," Mrs. Renfrew said at breakfast. "Drive a circuit and pick up everybody on this list. I'll telephone them."

The children did well, and, while their captive parents sat in the pews, Charles announced the following Sunday as Go To Church Sunday. *Seventy-three, I was flabbergasted*, he wrote in his notebook. Then he crossed out *flabbergasted*. It lacked the seminary's rich color of pure dignity. He wrote in its place *astounded*.

His parents would be coming Sunday, and Charles set out Friday to add to his congregation. Four times as many people had once lived in the Meadows, but most had gone off in the 1790s when Ohio fever struck. They had driven their wagons down to Hartford and out the westbound road past Charles's own house. It must have rained on them, too. He carried Mrs. Renfrew's umbrella as he walked beside Mr. Turnby, who was showing him how to take a shortcut across the hilltops.

"And that one?" Charles had discovered that Mr. Turnby knew the names of flowers.

"Wild iris." The thin man carried a thin stick but walked with increasing vigor.

"And that?"

"Blue grass, I believe."

"And over there?"

"That's columbine." Mr. Turnby moved ever so slightly toward Charles, forsaking his usual head-averting gaze. "Shakespeare's columbine."

"Ah, of course!" Charles nodded. Trying desperately to remember from which play columbine had come.

"That's an odd sound!" Charles turned to birds.

"A bobolink," Mr. Turnby offered. "And over there"—the old man pointed and continued to talk, for the first time speaking other than to answer a question—"that's a chewink."

Was there hope for Mr. Turnby?

Silence. Walking.

"What's this?" Charles resumed his former questioning as they came to a stop before a foundation overgrown with grass.

"Worcester place," Mr. Turnby responded, cautious again.

"They go west?"

"Died."

They walked to the edge of the ruined house. There were the remains of a fireplace, foundation walls, and, exactly where it belonged, a wide stone doorstep.

"Nobody bought it?" Charles's own words telescoped to meet Mr. Turnby's halfway.

"Road didn't go through anymore," he explained. "Terrible farmland."

"Look at that!" Charles pointed to a white rose bush blooming on the far side of the stone step.

"Cultivated," Mr. Turnby added. "It was theirs."

"I see," Charles said, kneeling to touch the white curves of the petals. "The body goes, the spirit lives on," he said to Mr. Turnby, whose face registered a slight waver of alarm.

As they walked on, the drizzle started up again, deepening the color of the flowers.

"I'll turn back now." Mr. Turnby pointed him ahead to the Martins.

Had the woman with the issue of blood been a complainer like Mrs. Martin? Yet Jesus with one glance had dried the blood and the complaints. How? There did not seem to be one wife in East Meadow in love with her husband. Or one husband with his wife. The Renfrews scarcely looked at each other as they passed through their kitchen, a good thing for Charles. She was indispensable in the running of the church. After Mrs. Martin's, Charles had four miles to walk home in the rain. He was soaked through when he came upon a log cabin he had never seen lighted before. Wallace, the mail box said. Catholic? Protestant?

There was laughter in the cabin, four or five children, and the woman was serving the food. Put it all together; they were Catholic.

"Sit down! Sit down! You're drowned." They included him at the table. If he ate Mrs. Renfrew's supper, too, he need not feel guilty.

"I was just telling the folks what I saw at Wethersfield this morning," Dr. Wallace said after the introductions had been made and the Welsh rabbit put onto an extra plate. "We used the electric chair on a fellow just a bit older than you, I'd say. He had to crawl."

"What do you mean?" Charles did not pick up his fork.

"It's their last act, you know," the doctor went on. "They want to walk to the chair themselves, not be dragged. But they can't always make their legs go. So they crawl." The doctor's expression was jovial, though his big voice did not mock.

Charles picked up his fork and toyed with his cheese. Hadn't Jesus stumbled? Hadn't Jesus insisted on dragging the cross? But he was no common criminal!

"It's a problem," Dr. Wallace continued. "Because they go so slow that the warden and the witnesses get nervous and try to speed them up. So I always walk right behind the prisoner where I can keep the others down to his pace." He had finished his cheese, and stuffed tobacco in his pipe. "The governor's especially impatient; he stops in for the important ones and hasn't much time to spare. I carried a shot in my pocket all the way down today, but he didn't want it, poor fellow."

"Drugs? That's illegal!" How could they break the law right there in the state penitentiary? Charles had never cared for Welsh rabbit.

"Well, my dear young man, even the Lord Jesus Christ had an offer of a painkiller. Folks tend to look the other way, even the governor. Wouldn't you?"

"If you take the drugs, how can you even crawl?"

"More and more," the doctor replied, "we have to drag them."

"Cocoa?" Mrs. Wallace inquired, leaning solicitously over Charles's elbow with a steaming crockery cocoa-pot. Later, as he walked along the damp wooded road, Charles heard Joan screaming through the streets of Rouen and the cheers of the crowd in Florence, where limbs dropped from the blazing Savonarola. Why did being good have to get you killed? But it could not have been that way with Jesus; he wasn't fully human.

He should stop being so gruesome, get something good out of the experience. Dr. Wallace expected to be listened to. As Conley had expected to be looked at. Brewster the storekeeper had a touch of it. Timid Mr. Turnby not an iota. Did he have it himself? No, he expected to be interrupted and corrected. Could he give his people this power? Maybe if he stopped talking so much on his calls. Be a listener, make his people feel like men.

"Charles! You'll catch your death!" Mrs. Renfrew opened the kitchen door. "Supper's waiting for you on the stove!"

Charles was sweating under his robe; he could hear the crinkling of paper as women pleated their calendars and brought improvised fans into action. His parents, looking oddly citified, sat midway in the congregation of some seventy people. His mother had curled her hair for the occasion. His father's white mustache looked bushy and warm. Maybe Charles should grow a mustache in the autumn.

"Wherever we enter churches, we find row on row of empty pews." Charles could hear a motorcycle speed past on the road. "I want to kindle within these walls the blazing fire of a presence I felt years ago. I came out of a Methodist camp meeting where my heart had opened and the whole world was clothed in resurrection. 'How different everything seems,' a friend said to me. 'How can we be but cheerful and good?' You cannot worship alone. You must join with others. To bring in that presence we must open our doors to all men. Now, that means white, yellow, and black, Greek and Jew, the barbarian and the aristocratic New Englander. So long as I serve this meeting house, we shall worship the Father of All." His mother was fanning herself. Was she looking about at decoration?

"There was a boy given a suit by his father, but the boy's arms dangled out of the sleeves. Did that father cut off the boy's hands? No, he gave him a new suit. Our church is that boy, but it must have a new suit. Here in East Meadow we are weaving that new suit, we are sewing it, we are binding it by coming here every Sunday to worship."

During the final hymn, sweat ran between the blades of his back. He strode out the central aisle to the doorway.

"It was pretty good, Charles," his mother said.

Had she been composing menus?

"Lots of people out," his father said, shaking his hand in the customarily vigorous fashion that left Charles's fingers reddened and temporarily stuck together.

"Thank you." Charles separated his fingers slowly. "Thank you," Charles heard again and again as the congregation relieved itself of its morning remarks. His parents took him to dinner and then they went home so Mama could help Justine with the new baby.

Can't write a thing in you, Book, he inscribed that evening. *Why, I think I'm in love with Jessica.*

He signed Jessica's next post card "Yours, Arley." Would she understand the full implication? He waited.

Now that he had preached actual sermons for a month, he couldn't wait to get back to Union to practice preach. The attendance had risen steadily and the numbers burned themselves into

his memory: 17, 29, 73, 74. The Wednesday suppers were bringing them in, and his calls. At 74, the daisies and buttercups were
in the fields and blackberries grew along the roadside and the
edges of the meadows. "Blueberries be in soon!" the people were
beginning to greet each other, in a tone of combined delight and
dread. Charles went about his own business.

"This week, Mr. Cady?" It was a joke now.

"Nope." The old man chewed at his shot of tobacco.

"This week, Mr. Turnby?" Charles inquired.

"Too busy," he replied. "But come in." Charles followed him
to the window seat of his front room, where Mr. Turnby raised a
jelly glass. Inside it was a white blossom trailing roots into the
water.

"It's for you." He handed it to Charles.

"Why thank you, sir," Charles answered, looking up inquiringly.

"It's from a slip. Up the Worcester place?" The old man did
not know how to continue.

Charles clapped a hand on the arm of the man who had made
him a pastor.

The fifth Sunday broke hot and dry. As Charles picked up stray
bits of paper from the grass, he rehearsed his topic. "Once I
believed with False Patriotism and because of Propaganda that
the Germans had cut off the hands of babies." He looked up from
a cigarette package to see dust far down the road. Columns of
Girl Scouts were walking in parade formation: their green uni-
forms were dim in the dust raised by their phalanx. Twenty!
Forty! Sixty! Charles counted them as they marched straight past
him and into the church. The pulpit advisor had apprised him of
the Scout camp nearby, but he had forgotten.

There were to be eight weeks of Girl Scouts: 17, 29, 73, 74,
140, 124, 167, 148, 156, 198—with a collection of forty-six dollars
and thirty-five cents! Like a great dog, blueberrying stirred, rose,
shook itself, ran a few laps around the garden and settled into a
long sleep. Clara and George Emmons decided to join the church
when their baby was baptized but neither ritual could be per-

formed by Charles. The bishop would do it in September via his blessed hand. Charles had got his two new members though, and it was as good as beating the first team at Rhodes. Then the daisies and buttercups faded; astors and goldenrod moved in and the chirping at night grew louder still. Two more Sundays: 178, 167, falling off, falling off. The Girl Scouts crowded the road going home to Boston and New York. And Jessica came in their wake.

Sitting with her on the stone step of the abandoned Worcester house, Charles felt himself divide. Part of him longed to lie with her, to run his hand along her smooth knee, whose outline showed beneath the flowery dress. He imagined his hand reaching to remove her straw hat, to pull her close in a place so quiet he could probably hear her heart beat. He must think of something sober. Once entered into, the life of the flesh led only to rotting. She would be willing, he could tell that. After all, she was a socialist. Unfortunately, Jessica moved her leg and the skirt of her short dress folded a new way. He could see above her knee. He conjured the world's most sobering image, Jesus upon the cross. For once, it had not its power and Charles felt he might laugh.

"Let's get married," Jessica said.

Was she joking? Charles pulled back. Women did not propose!

"I'm twenty-five and so are you," she continued. She always had the facts.

"It isn't that I haven't thought about it," he began, apologetically.

"Oh, never mind," she said. She took off her straw hat and examined its weaving in the sunlight.

He reached for one of her star-shaped hands. "I'm not sure," he began, "what being in love is."

"Haven't you grown out of that yet?" Her light-blue eyes were angry.

"I hope not!" Everything about the actual Jessica alarmed him.

She laughed and reached up to stroke his face, his English nose. It was Jessica who had informed him that he possessed an English nose. "I like you, Charles, because you take me so seriously."

If she had only called him Arley; he wondered if he himself might then have suddenly proposed. He saw himself kneeling before her as boys do in yearbook cartoons. Was this the beginning of his married life? But Jessica let go of his hand and covered her knees with her skirt.

He was saved.

He let Jessica go too soon. A few days later the letter came from Annah. She was now in love with a visiting clarinetist she had met during graduation. Love was different from anything she and Arley had known. I'll bet; Charles stood stunned beside the mailbox. All along he had been hoping. Suspended, not taking life when it was offered to him. Just like a cynic, he lectured himself. No better than Jessica. Fooled himself. Fooled yourself again, did you, boy?

"Not this week!"

"Too busy!"

"Six-thirty!"

But he had been healed by his people and this time it was not so hard. *God Bless Her Richly*, he wrote in his notebook. Surely that was not self-deception, surely he wished her well? He gathered Annah's letters and, holding them close, so close, made his way through the dim hallway and out the back door of the Renfrews'. He crossed the shadowed yard to his own territory and let himself into the kitchen below the sanctuary. He built a small fire in the round black stove and as the croakers called into soggy overgrowth, he fed her letters to the iron mouth in the belly of the stove. Did he really wish her well? Yes; not to would be defeat.

On the last Sunday morning there was a wild turnout of a hundred and fifteen, even without the Scouts! Some were there for the baptism of Elizabeth Caroline Emmons, who wore her grandmother's baptismal dress. The bishop accepted both of her parents into the body of Christ.

And that evening, two hundred and sixty came to the farewell service. Charles did not preach because he was following a suggestion of his brother-in-law Ted who had a rabbi friend summering nearby whom Charles had invited to speak. So after the violin solo and the alto–soprano duet, the rabbi stood in Charles's pulpit. An inclusive religion is wrong, he pointed out. (Was his bald head the shape of Amos'? Hosea's? Second Isaiah's?) Nature has not two blades of grass alike, he reasoned; religions, too, can come in different species.

What an experience to have the church packed, including the galleries! Should he have called in a carpenter to make sure they held? It was not as if the galleries had not been sat in at all that summer. A handful of people had been up in the right balcony only a few Sundays ago, hadn't they? Stop it! This is a great experience, this is wonderful. People have come from almost every home. The wife of the Jewish doctor had been over that afternoon with her maid—who was a Seventh Day Adventist—to help set up for the coffee hour after the rabbi spoke. Mrs. Petrucci had brought over some homemade cakes. "Here I am a Catholic, coming to a Protestant church to hear a Jewish rabbi," Dr. Wallace had remarked, passing Charles that evening on the lawn. Surely this is how Jesus imagined it upon the Holy Mount? Catholics, Jews, Seventh Day Adventists?

"Surprise! For you, Mr. Minor!" The coffee hour had been a ruse. Charles opened the door and saw two hundred people seated at the paper-covered tables. His heart beat fast. People of all nationalities and beliefs gathered together and presenting him with a book of poems! With one hundred brand-new, spanking-clean, stiff and shiny paper dollar bills!

Applause!

Was he worthy?

And was it the Lord that leapt in his heart?

"AWFUL!" WITH THE ONE WORD Dr. Fosdick greeted the end of Charles's practice sermon in Union's chapel. It took two more words to explain: "rhetorical, sophomoric." Charles went back to his room to study. Maybe he wasn't a talker. It was as a walker that he had succeeded in East Meadow. The flesh of his feet had been stronger than the spirit of his words. He had wanted it the other way around. Barclay had grabbed the more comfortable chair, so Charles settled down at his desk.

Twenty-three years after the death of Jesus, he read, Paul was fighting to hold the body of Christ together. Peter had taken a bunch of James' people and gone out to preach a few towns behind Paul, refuting everything Paul had said. Look, they insisted, you do so have to get circumcised. You do so have to follow the law. And you do so have to be descended from Abraham. On hearing this, Paul sent a punitive letter to the scattered, bewildered towns. No, he said, you certainly do not. Don't listen to Peter. The law is a curse. God's better gift to Abraham was the promise of Christ. Listen, Abraham had a child by Sarah, who was free. He had a child by Hagar, who was a slave. Now the free child is the spirit and the slave child is the flesh and the law. You want to give up the flesh? You have to give up the law, too. Tears I have for you, Galatians, if you don't!

"Paul was rather severe," Charles remarked to Barclay. "Why, I had Jews and Catholics and Protestants in my church kitchen...."

"What?" Barclay looked up.

"Paul," Charles explained. "He sounds so angry."

"It wasn't easy." Barclay stopped reading to consider Charles's complaint about Paul in light of Union's particular preoccupations. "You want to be a Gnostic? You want to think Jesus didn't feel the pain?"

In November Charles met a fat girl from Barnard at the Congregational church on Broadway. He took her to Roseland dancing but she stumbled and he had trouble pulling her up. Annah's Christmas card crossed his in the mail: she was still in love with her clarinetist and she still disliked living at home; she had hated teaching and quit to take a job in a doctor's office; her father was sick; she had bought two silver bracelets with her first bit of salary. Judea Methodist wrote to invite its son to read the Gospel from its pulpit Christmas Eve.

The smell of pine engulfed Charles when he stood in the pulpit familiar from Children's Sundays and Youth Days. He was the boy gone forth, returned a man with full nets. Would they feel defrauded when they found out he was becoming a Congregationalist? "TO BE TAXED WITH MARY HIS ESPOUSED WIFE, BEING GREAT WITH CHILD. . . ." It was his own voice, not Tiding's or Albee's. "AND SHE BROUGHT FORTH HER FIRSTBORN SON, AND WRAPPED HIM IN SWADDLING. . . ."

Were Luke's words being heard in the prize pew? The one in which Mr. Reinhold Edgar had installed a hearing aid before he died? "BUT MARY KEPT ALL THESE THINGS, AND PONDERED THEM IN HER HEART. . . ." Directly below him sat Justine and Paul, renegade from the Congregational Church tonight, and each holding a daughter; two had lived since the first was stillborn.

"AND WHEN THE DAYS OF HER PURIFICATION ACCORDING TO THE LAW OF MOSES WERE ACCOMPLISHED, THEY BROUGHT HIM TO JERUSALEM, TO PRESENT HIM TO THE LORD; AS IT IS WRITTEN IN THE LAW OF THE LORD, EVERY MALE THAT OPENETH THE WOMB SHALL BE CALLED HOLY. . . ." Did a girl not qualify to open the womb? Even if it killed her? Jessica would be peeved. Old Mrs. Danielson in the prize pew adjusted the hearing aid. The virgin birth had not been claimed until Mary was upward of seventy. Speak up, madame, or do the klieg lights hurt your eyes? Barclay had done an elaborate imitation the night before Union's third-floor inmates had disbanded for vacation.

"Merry Christmas, Arley!" They squeezed his hand as they made their way out of the vestibule. "You've gone and grown into a fine young man." If I cannot heal, let me have the power to bless. It is greater than the power to mock.

"Blessings on thee, little man." One of Sam's boys gave a miniature recitation scarcely heard at the Christmas table.

"Someone who owns a barn," Fred's wife, Georgia, was saying, bringing down the story "Barn Burns." They were off and telling it then, interrupting each other: how Polly saw the barn in flames, called Joseph at the town hall. "Hold on," he said, walking out front to verify. "You're right," he called into the dangling receiver.

Would they never stop? Were there no people in the world but themselves?

"And that was my own barn! I owned it before I got married!" Polly handed Charles a serving spoon.

" 'Bout time you got yourself married, isn't it, Arley?" Sam carved for Joseph, who had been called to the telephone. In the silence that followed Sam's question, they all heard Joseph on the phone asking the first of his usual quiet questions: "Time of death?"

"Arley's taking his time," Justine put in, rescuing him as she settled the baby on her lap to feed her.

"Waiting for one of them rich Congregational girls, I bet," Sam concluded.

Nobody mentioned his sermon.

A week later he sat on the bed in Justine's room by the sleeping porch to write up the year, before somewhat reluctantly joining Doris Cobb's party at her big house in Percyville: *December 31, 1927. A fine summer at East Meadow with an average attendance of 144, but this fall at Union has been tremendously hard and I've been lonely and discouraged.* He looked out the window and realized that of the two churches his eye was flirting with, he could call neither his own. Come spring, however, and he would be a Congregationalist, where ministers had more freedom and where there was no hierarchical arrangement among the independent churches. But when his eye sought the Congregationalist steeple at the top of the hill, he found the window frame too low and he had to stoop to see it.

"Admirable," Dr. Fosdick said of his last practice sermon. Annah sent him a twenty-seventh birthday card: she was still living at home, where her father was sicker yet. He wrote her a long letter bidding her to fare well in life. She was so kind, so clever, so brave. She would surely flourish. Seven years he had waited for her, but he didn't mention that. He would step out alone. He was on his way to his first parish, if they hired him. It was the recently federated church at Shiloh where Ted had begun his ministry and met Maud. Would there be a girl there for him? Ted had already written them a letter recommending Charles. Soon he would go up there to preach and wait for the congregation to vote on him:

"God's universe startles me! Some hundred million stars and on our own pebble in the sky are untold cattle, smokestacks, Ford cars, plowed fields and millions of human beings with two mighty forces in their hearts. The first is greed, which in the last war sent ten million soldiers to their deaths. Now you folks here at Shiloh number about one thousand. Suppose you were all wiped out by nightfall, and tomorrow another thousand were killed. How long would it take to reach ten million dead? Twenty-eight years. And the second force is love. . . ." They hired him, a son in Christ, a walker sent out to witness Christ crucified in the provinces. Salary, two thousand dollars, and start in the middle of August; sleep quite solitary in an old empty house shown him by a deep-voiced deacon and his high-voiced wife.

Annah had not replied, had not blessed him, had not wished him well. Charles laid Maud's graduation wire on his desk, where it ruffled in the breeze from Harlem. He would leave the walled compound, go out through the gates of the city after twenty years of schooling and begin to preach brotherhood. . . .

"Charles!" Barclay's mother stuck her head through the door. "Will you join us for lunch? We're going to try the Chink's on Broadway."

"Barclay!" he called later, holding up the letter from Annah that turned darkness to light while he tried to keep the two boxed graduation robes from slipping out under his elbow. *Best day in all the universe*: the clarinetist, it turned out, had been married all the time. Annah was ready now, her only hesitation being that Arley was too good for her. He was glad Barclay was not in the room, after all. For the first time in three, yea seven, years, Charles was not alone. Annah's face settled into the third eye of his forehead, facing inward, as if placed into a locket of bone.

VII

Birthdays of the Thirties

You, you are me we are one: Annah's eyes at the hotel in the mountains pulled him by a force slower than time. I am Adam, man who knows woman; he knew for himself and simultaneously that the next and only remaining mystery to open its door to him would be death. He forgot about birth, having already done that, and soon enough found he had lived alone too long. The other forces that called him were more familiar: to be a father to Mr. Turnby, a son to Miss Sigerist, a brother to Alan—or to those like them among his new people—he understood. But to be a husband? A father? His own was dying, being called by the weighty earth of the long valley in which Judea, Southlee and Shiloh were neatly arranged. Annah had come into his life; if Joseph should go out, would he lose his balance? Be pulled apart?

When they got to the hotel in Times Square he left her at a dining table and telephoned long distance from the lobby. Papa had not died while Arley was out of reach. Mama asked if Annah meant it when she had requested yellow hand-stitched pillow-cases. He guessed things would hold together once they got to Shiloh. *What a honeymoon, and Annah, how like the dream which comes true!*

Things in Shiloh were held in place from below. The town's one thousand living residents had fallen from harsh snowlight into the bright green grass of their foggy valley, fallen so far into topsoil and English lawns that a few years back only some ten staunch black-coated, pale-eyed Congregationalists were left to sit weekly in their sturdy edifice while scarcely twenty-five

Methodists survived to sing out, as Wesley had urged neither too fast nor too slow, in their hundred-year-old barn of a place fit best for July humidity and berry suppers. The whole thousand walked with their heads down and it seemed to Charles that the great body of the earth, scarcely disguised by grass, pulled at whatever crawled above it in Shiloh, at whatever swam or flew, and called continually "Come back!" at whatever had popped out of it to sprout wings or legs. And when the one thousand raised their heads to see what newcomer walked beside them, it was not to Charles P. Minor but to his good-looking bride they raised their hats. As they once had to his handsome mother when she drove red-haired past them in her wagon with a boy clutching the siding. "Mornin', Missus," they said to Annah as she walked north from her house to the Congregational building of the Federated Church in winter and south to the Methodist building in summer, wearing skirts as short as they came and hats as broad. "Day," they nodded to Charles, who knew them well enough to hear them wonder: "What does a young fellow like that know?"

"I feel them staring at my neck in church," the bride complained.

"You're from Pennsylvania," the groom explained.

When Charles raised his voice from whichever pulpit the season dictated by order of the merger papers signed in 1925, he knew the people below heard the sharp voice of a compatriot speaking with the reassuringly resonated vowels existing in American speech only in that particular valley. *Home*: like them, Charles pronounced the *o* verging backward toward a *u* and so produced that welcoming hollowness found immediately inside the doors of aging, musty houses. Not everything sank into the earth, he promised them, adjusting the tails of his new gray morning suit. Why, right into their own balconies the spirits of the Christian dead had risen to take their seats, to lean over, to cheer them on in the great race ahead. Paul tells us to strip down and run toward Jesus. Charles did not mention the disputed authorship of the letter to the Hebrews. The Federateds folded their hands and crossed their legs and stared at the neck of his bride. We mustn't start out too fast, he warned them; we should save plenty for the homestretch. "Our young man," they would call him as they had called the other students fresh out of seminary, reserving "our dear friend Mister" for the tired old men who alternatingly came to their valley to lay themselves down upon the dewy grass and rest.

Charles had been at Federated a few months when the bottom fell out of the national economy, but it was a long time before the townspeople accepted the Depression as anything more than their usual state of mind. With the occasional luxuries gone, however, they did agree it was probably better they had an "our young man" this time. He and his wife might better counsel the year's unmarried pregnant daughter, whoever she might be. They might even forestall in town the generalized rolling boredom that foamed about the knees and thighs of its young, threatening to drive them off to Boston or New York. Charles settled in. "He comes from up Judea way," they said of him warily. "But," they added, "his grandmother was from hereabouts." A difference of four miles, but they relaxed. The edges of the world are dark and dangerous, you can fall off the earth at various unmarked town lines. When at dusk one October night, before the new street lamps had blazed into glory, the Reverend Charles P. Minor bumped into a lamppost and enthusiastically removed his hat to apologize, he was finally established as one of their own. The men thereafter waited for his enthusiasm to cool to irony and the women for his children to be born; on one of these scores they were never to be satisfied.

Into the white house with the green-roofed well Charles had brought Annah Trevellack Minor, a bride of one week who in that short time had found revealed to her the White Mountains, Times Square New York, and the long excited body of her husband. Weeks later he was still unsure of her response to any of these wonders, for she obliged him in words with whatever he wanted to hear. He was only just beginning to discover he must read her real feelings in small movements of the eyelids, in the position of the *v*'s at the corners of her lips, in the raising and lowering of hands. For in her attempt to escape her parents' angry home, Annah had zealously copied gentility as seen spread before her at Methodist picnics and long digested its basic ingredients: appear to lose and never state desires.

"I'm back!" Charles shut the door of the Model A his father had given him in June and opened the door to his own kitchen. Annah was talking on the telephone in the dining room.

"I will," she was saying courteously. "Good-bye." She smiled. Was she annoyed?

"Amanda Lamb!" Annah said as she hung up, her smile turning to a grimace. "She's always talking about that wedding and it's not even until spring!"

He put his arms around her, happy to be warmed by her warmth. Perhaps he had never known her, all those years he had loved her? Now he would. She kissed him lightly and led him toward the kitchen, where he leaned on the sink and watched her fork pickles out of their jar into a bowl. She forbade such vulgarities as pickle jars on the table; come to think of it, he had never seen a pickle jar on the table in the Trevellack dining room, where the old man, rest in peace, had always eaten his supper. His death had kept Annah from Charles's ordination in June.

He picked up some dishes and followed her into the dining room—a square in the quiet corner of a square house. "We don't have to eat in the dining room every night," he offered.

"Don't you like to?" She paused for affirmation before settling the pickles.

"Oh, yes," he said. "It reminds me of home."

She sat down with the pickles and smiled the smile that had won her the accolade Venus in her high-school yearbook.

"Well, I couldn't find a Sunday School superintendent or a Boy Scout leader," he began, "and I only made a couple of calls because I had to practice a lot of knots for tonight." He paused to chew.

"Oh, I forgot," she said. "Amanda can't give the lecture on Mark Twain tomorrow night. Can you do it?"

This was the ministry: nobody came through.

"I guess I'll have to," he said, chewing more slowly. Annah had a red scarf around her hair; she was very pretty. He relaxed. The empty old room reshaped itself around them, closer. They were not just playing house. They would be sitting here a year from now. Maybe a year after that. No more, though; he'd be on to bigger things. Hartford maybe, Boston. But by then, though he had no picture of himself as a father, he could easily see a baby in Annah's arms and her looking down at it, happy. Who could play the Madonna better in the Christmas pageant?

"You look so pretty," he said, interrupting her.

A look passed over her face that he could not read. The expression of her eyes drew inward, her lips flattened and her nostrils widened. Then she stood up to carry out an empty bowl.

It didn't matter. He remained sitting on the stiff chair that other young ministers had thought of as their own, too, as they sat waiting for a lifetime of wife-brought meals; those marriages had turned out fine. It would be even better if Maud and Ted had started here, but they had lived farther up the street in the Methodist parsonage.

"Annah!" he called, pushing back his chair.

In the kitchen he put his arms around her. "Are you lonely?" he asked. "Do you miss your father? Or your own home?"

"No," she said. "I just feel funny, sometimes, don't you?"

"Let's eat in the kitchen tomorrow night," he said. "It's better for two."

"The great Arley Minor brought so low?" She drew back in exaggerated horror. "Would your parents ever stop talking about it?"

They laughed.

Later Charles sat at the writing table in the living room, a second corner of the house. Annah dragged a straight-backed chair into the windowless hallway behind the large front door, where she smoked her day's single cigarette without fear of being spotted by a townswoman. Charles turned to his sporadically kept thought-book: *Chinese girl's confession of faith in Jesus, I knew him all my life and one day I learned his name.* Tonight study had lost its appeal and he felt peaceful just sitting in his new home.

"I think I'll cover some pillows for the fellowship kids to sit on Sunday nights," Annah said, the glow of her cigarette-tip red in the entryway.

"Good idea," Charles answered. In the room above, in the big mahogany bed, he would lie under the sloping eaves and love Annah as a man, sensing he was not quite pleasing her but unable to find out in what way he was inept. "Nothing," she would say, smiling slightly. "Everything is fine." But perhaps tonight peace would fill the bedroom, too, as it seemed to have come into the kitchen and now into the living room, warming and peopling the air. The air was indeed warming and he had forgotten to pay for the new load of coal. He reached for the checkbook and dipped his pen in the ink. *December 1*, he wrote on the dateline, *29. Shiloh Coal Corporation. One hundred dollars and 00/00 cents.* It was a lot of money and, unlike the house rent, it must come from his two thousand dollars of salary. He tore out the check and wrote on the one immediately under it. *December 1, 29. Annah Minor. One hundred kisses.* Maybe tonight Annah would turn her face toward him with the look she had given him in the White Mountains but not in Times Square. What had veiled her eyes? He would be patient and long-suffering; he would learn to please her. Tonight they had matured enough to people their downstairs; they would someday occupy their bedroom, too. He put both checks in envelopes and addressed and stamped them. Tomorrow he would mail them.

To the wrong people, he found out when Shiloh Coal telephoned.

"Hers go back to a boy John Percy from Taunton who set sail on the twentieth of March in the year sixteen thirty." The judge sat in a chair Charles had placed for him by the window in the downstairs bedroom where Polly no longer did her sewing. "He was a proprietor at the new Taunton over here, before he walked inland to Windsor village and got mixed up in the Indian war. Finally took himself upstream to Northampton where he died an elder at eighty-two. Who wouldn't be an elder after all that?" Joseph looked up for Charles to laugh.

"Excuse me now, Papa," Charles said and took his arm from the wall of the new bathroom that had been installed in a corner of the room. "But I've got to get back to my calls." He waved his way out. He stopped in the kitchen to tell Polly that the two girls he had spotted walking to school in open sandals through last week's snow had been given shoes and rubbers by his Ladies' Aid.

"That's good," she said. "They've been on my mind, but I wasn't sure you'd taken care of it."

Why did she never expect that he would do things right?

Charles shut the kitchen door. He had given the girls more than shoes, he had given them hope. In all of Shiloh's resignation, someone they didn't know was watching them and had seen their need. Given them shoes straight out of heaven. You couldn't live without hope. Or die. The judge was hoping to die on his birthday so he could have a nice round number on his gravestone. Or to find his ancestors. Both silly pastimes. Charles shut the door of the Ford.

The second of these pastimes filled the judge's days. In the downstairs bedroom he picked up his wife's family Bible from the window sill. The emigrant John Percy had known the death of his father at an early age, too. But lived to sire eighteen Percys. One of his sons had produced sixteen more. The last, Submit, born into the arms of a widow, had trekked south in 1700 to settle land opening along the western rivers of Connecticut, some of it becoming Percyville. Joseph counted the generations from Polly to the fatherless boy in England. Seven.

"Mama?" he called, but Polly was not yet home from Justine's, where the babies were sick.

The Minor history was not so well recorded. How far back could Joseph go in Minors? He closed the Percy Bible and placed it carefully on the window sill. Yesterday he had dropped it and been unable to pick it up. He leaned back in the chair and counted on his fingers: but suddenly his mother's father came to mind. Counting one's ancestors, how did one know where to veer off and which grandparents to ignore? How many ancestors did one have by seven generations back? Joseph dropped his hand. There were too many to count on fingers.

He leaned slowly toward the bookcase and reached for a piece of scrap paper that turned out to be the back of an envelope from the tailor in Chester. Let's see: he had four grandparents, they each had four, that was sixteen on step two. He had a pencil in his pocket. They each had four, that was sixty-four on step three. And they each had four; he wrote the numbers down: that was two hundred and fifty-six on step four. Hmmm. Didn't sound right. They each had four, that was one thousand and twenty-four. And their four, four thousand and ninety-six on step six. How could that be?

He had four thousand ninety-six great-great-great-great-great-grandparents? Who were they? And what difference could it make, with all that blood, if one of them had been the king of England? He must have done something wrong. He started over.

He had two parents and they each had two; by the seventh generation that was, he figured slowly, one hundred twenty-eight. Well, that was more like it. Relief, he felt better. He leaned his bulk slowly rightward and settled the pencil on the bookcase, where it wouldn't roll. And if you took away all the women, he thought, straightening himself and pushing the afghan off his knees in preparation for the walk back to the bed, you could get down to sixty-four. Sixty-four men coming directly behind you. No. That couldn't be it, either.

Sixty-four men in seven steps, almost nine men per step? Had he lost his reasoning faculty? Would he end up like Polly's uncles? Dotty in their dotage? The crazy sons of the eighth child of a man half of whose children never married? Had Joseph married bad blood? Had the good line of Elder John Percy thinned out, just as he, Joseph Minor, had merged his own blood with it? He raised himself in the easy chair, sure that both feet were flat on the floor before him. No, there was apparently only one way to manage genealogy, and that was the traditional way. You stuck with your father's father, and went up to his father and didn't veer. That way you couldn't get more than seven men in seven steps. Moving across the floor, he felt safe and faintly amused; he had battled the enigma and won out and if he himself did not understand why, so much the better.

But if he stuck only to men he would miss out on the comparatively illustrious and well-documented Bullman ancestry of his mother, who had raised him. He reached the bed and sat, swinging his legs up. Plump, a woman of a fat family. He pulled the blankets over himself, and poured a glass of ice water from the pitcher on the table. He lay back; he, too, was plump. So was his brother Orlando in Chester. But not his baby brother William. And not Thaddeus, his oldest brother, who had died a year ago, emaciated. Plumpness, that in itself was something of an accomplishment. He would grow very fat, as fat as possible. The fellows sent over from Peach and Sons for his occasion, they would have an awful time with him. Peach's son didn't even have a side-service funeral coach. He made a satisfying heap of himself beneath the covers and smiled.

AT THE FOOT OF LONG HILL, Charles turned into the fog of the valley, which seldom lifted before ten and which today in drizzle might never. "This is the foggiest part of the world," people said. His father had always carefully explained why. "The vapor comes up off the river into the air." Thank you, Judge, for the secret of ascension. Unfair, Charles knew, but he was angry. On the slickered road he saw Daisy Thompson and he slowed to let her in. "I seen Daisy this morning," the town said of her, "and she don't look a day older than she did twenty-five years ago." Daisy had been down to the store for tobacco, which she held in her brown hand—the fleshy fingertips on the underside so surprisingly pink. They rode sheltered together in the Ford past the town's high-linteled houses.

"I been in there working." Daisy pointed out the Lamb house, whose side lawn showed no signs of yesterday's gala tent.

"Me too," Charles said. "Yesterday." There on the sidewalk was where Amanda smiled, revealing her narrowed roots of teeth. There by the drive she handed me the fee envelope for my part in the wedding ceremony of her daughter. I did my part very smoothly and with all those New Yorkers there, too. About here on the road I said, "For you, Madame!" and handed Annah the envelope we figured must contain twenty-five dollars. Five! Five dollars.

"And there," Daisy nodded toward the Abbott place. "Bad floors."

"Hard work you do, Daisy?" He must get his mind off himself.

"Not here." She gave him the smile she gave the town. "In Carolina I used to plow. First they hitched me up, and while I waited in the harness, they hitched the steer beside me."

Hers was not a life of large hopes; perhaps that's how she managed.

"Where'll I let you off?" Charles turned onto the Hammerville Road. He had learned from his father that the whole section had been bought from the Indians for the price of a hammer. Broken, the judge had been happy to report.

"Past the brook." She indicated Percy Brook at the bend. "You let me off out here, it's muddy under the trees."

"See you Sunday, Daisy?"

"Guess so. Got to get my soul set for the week." She did not wave as she started under the dripping trees.

Charles turned the car back to town. His work was not that of leading men. Most of them stayed home Sundays. Those who came were trustees or deacons, who considered him their employee. The ministry in Shiloh was that of one man working among women. In his case there were four key women, like legs of a table that supported the rest of the parish. There was the widow Amanda Lamb, who spoke to him through a sherry-scented handkerchief and asked him to find England on her new radio when she couldn't get the gardener in to do it. Her yearly contribution paid his salary and that of the janitor. There was Daisy Thompson, who balanced Amanda by having nothing but spirit and who seemed to Charles to promise a hidden knowledge, a secret. At one end of the other diagonal was Mrs. Bowen, who ran the Ladies' Aid, which raised the rest of the money and produced the social life of the church. She was the only one of the four who had a man. That was Deacon Bowen, who snorted at Charles.

"Really working today!" Bowen always said when he found Charles raking leaves in front of the parsonage on Monday, his day off. Where was Bowen on the other days, when he was up at six to check on peeling steeples, leaky faucets, rain-soaked eaves? Did Bowen help him teach Sunday School classes when teachers were absent? Collect children for class? Run the Boy Scouts, direct the Book Club and feed the countryside's tramps? Once a month Bowen handed Charles a check in return for work well done, for hymn books all in their proper places. The Reverend Phillips Brooks had snorted back at his deacons when they caught him with his feet up reading. "What do you pay me for, gentlemen, my head or my feet?"

They paid Brooks for his head. They paid Minor for his feet, maybe his ears. Habits of calling and listening picked up in East Meadow had solidified into routines in Shiloh but there was so much more to be done here Charles worried he wouldn't learn anything new. He worked an eighty-hour week but not, as in East Meadow, for a short-term stretch and not as a gift sent free from headquarters but as a hired hand. He should look on the good side, as Daisy seemed to. He had his two stewards, Amanda Lamb and Mrs. Bowen. They could keep the earthly church going while he studied his two saints, who labored at the heavenly. Daisy would reveal the secret in her own time, he suspected. The fourth woman was Augusta Stiles. He pulled into her driveway, past forsythia glowing yellow in the drizzle.

"Arley, somehow I was expecting you." Augusta called him what everybody else in town did, perhaps for a different reason. Shiloh read the Chester *Star*, too, and had been following the deeds of Arley Minor for years. "What's the matter? You look awfully determined!"

She was the only woman he had found in Shiloh who meant it when she asked you how you were. "Don't you ever lose hope?" he asked.

"Out here on the road to Samaria?" She sat him at her kitchen table. "You put out your hand to help, it can take years before they take it." She poured him a glass of milk and brought out cookies.

"Just like my mother," he said, acknowledging the food. It was the best thing he could give her, coming as a son. "You Methodists," he continued. "You know the old stories so well."

"I'm no Methodist!" Augusta shook her head; the gray hair seemed wrong.

"Sure you are!" he said. She was the one who brought food to Shiloh's sick.

"Not on your life!" she said. "I'm Federated."

He laughed. She never joined the bickering between the former Congregationalists and Methodists.

"Augusta, I'm too angry to preach." She would tell him he could.

"The angrier they get, the less angry you have to be. Remember when Jesus started preaching? He came back to Nazareth to read prayers in the synagogue?"

"He read from Isaiah?"

"Yes, and they got angry he should announce himself a prophet like Isaiah and point out there were sick and poor and imprisoned and brokenhearted people in Nazareth, too. You're no prophet! they said. Well, Isaiah couldn't heal in his own country either, Jesus told them. They stood right up and walked him to the cliff to push him over. BUT HE PASSING THROUGH THE MIDST OF THEM WENT HIS WAY. That's what the Bible says, Arley. How do you think he did that?"

"I don't know," Charles said.

"He made anger his slave instead of his master."

"But I don't know how to do that," Charles confessed. "I never have known that."

"Do it by giving." She turned to examine her dark, polished floors. "Years pass and you may not be there to know when they take. But sometimes on the road"—she raised unaged blue eyes to his—"you run into others who are givers. That's all there is."

Why didn't the saints ever get married?

"All right, Papa, I'm off for church. You might smell the beef that's in the oven for Charles and Annah. I'll bring Fred and Georgia back, too, if they aren't driving off somewhere." Polly paused by Joseph's door with her summer hat already situated; an arc of her rimless glasses protruded satisfactorily through one of the spaces in her veil.

"I'll be fine, Mama," Joseph said, smiling a little to prove that insomnia mixed with pain did not keep him alert at night and irritable by day as he had heard her report to Fred. "Now that you've filled my water pitcher."

As soon as she was gone he reached for the atlas of England Justine had brought from the library and placed by his knees. He flipped past Polly's Somerset, with its vegetables, fruits, flowers, automobile machinery and oil refining situated atop hillsides that were doubtless as lush and green as those of western Connecticut and stopped at his own possible Warwickshire. He had traced the Minors back to one William Minor of Farmington, Connecticut, who may have been the William Minor who sailed from Stratford in Warwickshire in March of 1635, only five years after Polly's John Percy. He studied the Warwickshire key only to find that industry covered the land, and people had multiplied beyond reason. He was glad his ancestors had left Warwickshire —providing they *were* his ancestors. It sounded like Elmsy.

What kind of men leave a place? Not his kind. His seven male ancestors had farmed the land within a fifty-mile radius of the bed he lay on. His three brothers and he had done business within an even smaller radius of their mother's grave, as if they did not care to move beyond its pull. The grass grew smoothly there on the old side of the cemetery, and next to her was the small, impersonal grave of his father. Joseph had never been able to bring it together with the boy's sight of a large fresh November grave on which snow and hope fell forever. Six of the dead man's brothers and sisters lay in surrounding earth; the youngest sister had died at fourteen, on her birthday.

Now, that was art he admired. He had often stopped to study the child's perfect inscription. No doubt more people noticed her in death—"Hey, did you see this one?"—than had actually encountered her in life, and all she'd done was live fourteen years to the day in a quiet village.

He felt a bit better and decided he might sit up on the edge of the bed a minute. Then he'd walk to the kitchen for a bite to eat. He looked at an envelope he had addressed earlier that morning and noticed the ink stain where his hand had shaken, surprisingly, involuntarily. He placed his legs over the side of the bed and gradually eased his weight onto them; there was the prickling sensation in the feet: he hadn't been up much during the past two days. He walked unsteadily through the bedroom into the dining room where his six children had grown up, eating their way through meat and potatoes until they had obtained a decent height. Except Elizabeth, who had herself been consumed. If only her face would not look at him nights from a peculiar formation in the blue-patterned wallpaper of the room where Minors died.

Very slowly now. He reached the kitchen and then the icebox and opened its door. He saw some cold chicken, reached in for a legbone and stood by the icebox eating it: the skin, the muscle, and then he crushed through the bone for the marrow—had this chicken ancestors? From Warwickshire, perhaps? Dairy cattle, truck farming and all those industries, but nothing about poultry. He was so thirsty. Marrow was good for you. He sucked out all he could get. She had always told him that, a fat woman with a soft voice in a kitchen at an old farm.

Like Polly, his own mother went back to Somerset. Odd, wasn't it? His mother and his wife from the same soil thousands of miles away? But his father's people? Well, they must have come from England somewhere, even if it wasn't Warwickshire. It couldn't be all that hard to find William's town. The bells rang at the churches. Instead of walking over to the rubber garbage holder Polly kept in the corner of the sink, Joseph replaced the bone of the leg on the dish, pushing it under the bulk of the chicken, and made his way back to bed. He could get water from the table back there. Already his stomach hurt.

Charles's tea table wobbled. Not the real living-room table on which Annah had arranged the parsonage's silver service and their own china teacups and of which he had said, "It looks as good as if it had been arranged by the hand of Amanda Lamb herself." Not that real table, but the imaginary one supported by

Amanda, Daisy, Augusta and Mrs. Bowen. The fourth leg was resigning as president of the Ladies' Aid; the Bowens would begin to spend the winters in Florida.

"Here she comes!" Charles caught sight of the town's number-two Christian gentlewoman crossing his grass, in a flowing dress and a large straw hat. He hurried to open the two-hundred-year-old door, a task not always flawlessly accomplished. If Mrs. Abbott would not head the all-important Aid, who would? Amy Ferguson had refused. Resentment had come into Annah's eyes when he had asked her. "Of course I wouldn't let you down," she had replied, but then she had become speechless and twisted her handkerchief.

"Hello there!" He extended his hand and clasped Mrs. Abbott's, but not too strongly. She was such a lady.

"Good afternoon, Mrs. Abbott," Annah said, shaking the hand of her visitor, who had removed one glove for the purpose.

"This way, shall we, ladies?" Charles escorted Mrs. Abbott and Annah to the living room, where tea was laid. "How lovely it would be," he said, "if we could be outdoors on a day like this."

"Oh, shall we have it outdoors?" Annah inquired, her eyes indicating the elaborate indoor tea setting she had perfected over the last hour.

"Why, I hadn't thought of that," he replied, trying to gauge Mrs. Abbott's expression. "What would you say, Mrs. Abbott, to taking tea under the trees?"

"Why, I'm sure I don't know," the lady replied, faultlessly retaining the removed glove in her gloved hand in case the decision should fall toward the great outdoors.

"Why, me either; as you like," Annah replied in perfect kind, resting her hand upon the back of the small extra chair Charles had moved into the living room, resting her hand as if that were where she planned to keep it all afternoon, indoors or outdoors, rain or shine. It was not, you see, resting there because it was stopped midway in pulling out the chair for Mrs. Abbott. No.

Charles put both his hands behind his back and stood as firm as the ladies. So this was the ministry! He looked down at his black shoes that still possessed the high gloss he had given them that morning. The three of them waited by their chairs for a decision from elsewhere.

"The parsonage looks lovely, my dear," Mrs. Abbott said to Annah, to pass the time. They all stared at the expanse of yellow-flowered paper supplied to the parsonage by the Ladies' Aid and at the blue overstuffed chairs received so long ago following the death of Mr. Lamb.

"Why, thank you," Annah accepted, and gave in to Mrs. Abbott's superior manners. "Won't you sit down?" She pulled out the chair for Mrs. Abbott, who lowered herself expectantly into it and simultaneously withdrew her second glove.

"There," Charles said, "that should settle it. We'll take our tea indoors, shall we?"

They both watched Annah lift the heavy silver pot and pour a stream of tea into a flowered china cup.

"Lemon or cream?" she inquired of Mrs. Abbott.

"Either, my dear," Mrs. Abbott replied and sat back with her hands folded in her lap.

"Either?" Annah sounded just a touch too surprised.

"I'm sure she doesn't mean . . ." Charles began. But she did.

There was another silence.

"Well, would lemon be all right?" Annah asked of Mrs. Abbott, who masked a shade of disappointment at Annah's choice.

"Lovely, I'm sure. Anything, my dear. Anything." She pursed her lips and watched the administration of the lemon.

"One lump or two?" Annah inquired, on solid ground again.

"Whatever you say, my dear. I'm always pleased with what I get. How many lumps do *you* like?" Mrs. Abbott placed her hand upon her napkin but did not pick it up to unfold it.

"Oh, I vary," Annah said. "Sometimes two, sometimes one."

"I don't need much sugar," Mrs. Abbott replied at last, giving a hint.

"Oh, me either," Annah answered. "Half a lump, often I just take half a lump."

Annah poured her own and Charles's tea very slowly. Was she making her final divination of Mrs. Abbott's sugar desires?

Annah examined the three steaming cups. She added lemon to her own cup and cream to Charles's.

"Would you like half a lump, then, perhaps?" Annah inquired of Mrs. Abbott.

"Whatever you say, my dear!" the lady replied, beads of perspiration gathering at her hairline.

Annah picked up a lump of sugar with the silver-plated tongs. She rested it on the corner of her saucer and then laid the tongs back.

How can you split a sugar cube without touching it with human hands? Charles resisted the temptation to shut his eyes.

Annah stared at the single cube before picking it up in her fingers and breaking it in two. Half to Mrs. Abbott's cup, first. Half to her own cup, second. She picked up Mrs. Abbott's teacup and saucer and handed them across the table.

"This is yours," she said.

"And this is yours." Annah handed him the tea with cream. She was surpassing herself. Now for his part.

"Well, Mrs. Abbott," he began, stirring his tea. "Have you thought at all about my and Mrs. Bowen's suggestion and fond hope that you will take over the running of the Ladies' Aid this fall?" Was Annah ever going to pass the cookies?

"Why, yes, Mr. Minor," the visitor replied, thirty years his senior.

"Would you like a cookie?" Annah was passing them, but when the proffering and accepting was done Mrs. Abbott seemed to have lost the thread of the conversation.

"Well, Mrs. Abbott," Charles proceeded, "what exactly is it that you have thought about my and Mrs. Bowen's idea that you step into the breach?"

Annah began to cough.

Not now!

"Are there other ladies you have considered?" Mrs. Abbott inquired, biting off a tiny piece of her sugar wafer.

"Why, Mrs. Abbott," Charles said, stalling for time. Did one matron know that another—younger, more energetic Amy Ferguson—had refused? Could Annah have morning sickness in the afternoon? "As you know, Mrs. Bowen would like to step down from her thirty-year presidency of this so important an organization. Truly, the church could not go forward, the earthly church, that is, without the ladies of the Aid! And Mrs. Bowen so wanted to see you in her stead."

"Well, of course. But I wouldn't want to stand in any other lady's way," Mrs. Abbott said with some pointedness.

How well did she know Amy Ferguson?

"What about Mrs. Minor, perhaps?" Mrs. Abbott nodded toward Annah. "It is not uncommon that the minister's wife likes to step into the breach."

"Oh, I . . ." Annah's face reddened. "The baby," she said, unthinkingly resting her hand on the smallest of curvings. "You may not know yet," she offered, "but we are expecting a family."

"I'm sure, Mrs. Abbott, you'll forgive Annah for speaking so candidly." Charles turned quickly to his guest. "But the fact of the matter is, we are expecting a family. And since it is Annah's first child, she and I felt that she should not take on the responsibility of the church's largest lay organization at this time."

"We do," Annah pointed out apologetically, "hold the Pilgrim Fellowship meetings here in the parsonage on Sunday nights and often they don't leave until midnight."

"Well, that is the extraordinary case," Charles hurried in. "Holiday time, so forth."

Mrs. Abbott looked at both of their faces and sipped her tea. "It's a pity," she finally said, "that Mrs. Bowen feels it imperative to step down."

"Yes," Annah said.

"It is," Charles finished.

He saw Annah raise her napkin to her lips, and when Mrs. Abbott next bent her head to sip, Annah tongued the remains of a cookie into folds of flowered linen.

"Mrs. Ferguson out by the lake indicated a certain interest in the opportunity." Charles decided it imperative to note this for his protection later. "But she concluded that, in the long run, the distance was too great for her to be traveling."

"Amy Ferguson?" Mrs. Abbott's forehead wrinkled into unknowable speculation.

"Excuse me," Annah said politely, and left the room. "I'll just refill the cookie plate," she called over her shoulder. But she had failed to remove the empty plate from the table.

"Is your wife feeling quite herself?" Mrs. Abbott inquired.

"Oh, quite," Charles replied. "I do so hope you will let us call you President Abbott before the day is out," he put in on a whim.

In the distance he heard the toilet flush.

Annah returned with a fresh plate of cookies and removed the empty one.

After they had waved good-bye to a still uncommitted Mrs. Abbott, Charles picked up the tray, laughing. "Is this the ministry?" he asked rhetorically of Annah's departing back.

"You seem to like it," he thought she said, but it was so quietly spoken he could not be sure. He must remember to stop in on Papa later; Fred said he was much worse.

"Lunch in a few minutes, Papa!" Polly called to Joseph as she came down the stairs. "I'll bring mine in and eat with you."

Joseph smoothed out the blanket that covered his knees; Mama would be coming soon with the food. He would tell her he had made his final choice: a cast-bronze Eternacrypt sunk in an iron ingot vault. Very funny, but she probably would not laugh. Actually, he had told Sam to tell them at Peach's the plainest mahogany and the cheapest vault, just enough to keep the earth from caving in when the box and its contents had vanished. But what would he do about the minister? If he should spare Sam putting him under, he ought to spare Arley getting him up. And spare himself the indignity of his son's attempt. She probably wouldn't laugh at that either; what was the matter with her lately?

Breathe on me breath of God, fill me with life anew. The Estey foot-propelled organ was decaying faster than Charles could persuade Mrs. Lamb to give an electric replacement. Heat from the furnace was finally rising from the fire he and the janitor had laid at dawn. Outside the clear Congregational window panes, thick snow managed a cautious descent. Things ascended and descended, things hung without birth or death.

"He's moving!" Annah had said yesterday, pressing a hand to her abdomen as she felt the child for the first time. "He's alive!"

Why a boy?

The music ended. "From time to time I halt my usual preaching and go out into the world to bring back reports. Last year, if you recall, I listened to the radio for a full week and gave you my impression of radio as Jesus would have wanted us to hear it. And this week I had been watching reel after reel of bedroom sensu . . . sensuality in the theaters of Chester. But we can have clean movies. I have contracted for a series of films. As soon as we can lay a hardwood floor in the social room and paint the walls, we will see locusts over the African plains, we will see Byrd at the Pole. . . ."

He was their son, he ran before them upward. Toward what did he run? It shone. It wrapped him in grace. Eyes, perhaps. A smile. Unnamable. Existing before words as God had in the void before the world. It could not be taken from him, not even if they locked him in a dungeon or raised him on the gallows. But his joy was to give it away. And his labor was to prepare the ground.

Could he be a father, too?

To a daughter, perhaps.

"Trouble," he said to Annah when she stirred. "With one of my people. I'll be back in an hour." He couldn't tell her, not this suddenly.

"What if the baby comes . . . ?" She was only half awake. Last Monday she had finished the question. Who did he put first: wife and baby, or parish? My parish, he had said. We have family to help us out.

"The baby's not due for two months." He kissed her good-bye. "And if it comes, you'll deliver it and have a couple of cups of tea ready, if I know you." He was learning to let his parishioners know he trusted the good in them, expected well of them. In emergencies, he dealt with Annah the same way.

He parked under the elm tree that in daytime shaded Shiloh's Johnson Funeral Home but which was now only an impalpable darkness. This was his first real death, why her? Nobody had died in East Meadow. Mrs. Bowen's invalid father down from Hartford for the last two months had passed away last year in Shiloh, but Charles had hardly known him. He had been sure to call at the funeral home that time in careful black, like Papa. He hadn't known what to say to Mrs. Bowen and had found himself repeating what the Reverend Mr. Tiding used to say in Judea: "I feel they're happy in heaven tonight, he's on his way up." Charles had meant it, had felt it timely for the old man to die. But Mrs. Bowen, a former Congregationalist, had looked away, embarrassed. Methodists would have understood.

A Federated?

Why you? He tried to shut the car door quietly. You cannot, Augusta. He started to talk to her. It was not as if she were gone but as if she had arrived. "If Christians believe what they say, why are they sad at death?" The voice of his sister Maud, her questions.

"Arley?" It was Walter Johnson holding the door open.

They shook hands.

"A pity, someone like that." Walter's lips twitched.

Not the others? Augusta would want everyone who died to be equally mourned. There wasn't any light on in Walter's viewing room tonight. Of course not, car accidents took longer down in the preparation room. Waxy Tissue Builder. Pyramid Blush Powder. Why bother, Walter? he wanted to say. The body doesn't matter. The spirit has already been set free, even received. There is abundance, she is all around us. But he didn't.

"Time of death?" he asked as Walter let him in.

On Thursday it looked like Easter, there were so many lilies and the church was packed. "On this beautiful spring day we gather together to bid farewell to the body of Augusta Stiles, taken from the living before the fullness of her days, and to welcome the presence of her spirit here among us. . . ."

As the funeral service progressed Charles had the sensation that he was reaching under the mahogany casket with hands grown disconcertingly giant. If he should bend in the knees for counterbalance could he not wrest the box from other hands and raise it out of the hole which yawned for it? Is that what you would have me do today, Augusta?

Jesus had done it. He had shooed away the watchers and gone into Lazarus alone, leaning over, calling into the ear, "Lazarus, collect yourself." The self that was scattered into fingertips and earlobes, the self run down into kneecaps and toenails—Lazarus, don't go outward anymore; come inward, come back into yourself, into your place of knowing; be.

You Federateds know the old stories so well. The body already wound in strips of Egyptian linen, already given the cheap man's burial—no salt, no drying out, no evisceration. We in Judea know a thing or two ourselves. Well, they hadn't done that for years, actually, the little cut in the thigh to be later plated with copper, the reaching in with the hooked tool. Centuries. And lucky for him, for Lazarus. The breath of the watchers beyond the door: hurry; no, the healer must never feel any hurry.

"Come back, Lazarus, there is time." And then he needed no more words. Only the power that preceded words, knowing, wishing, causing to be.

Be, Lazarus. Lazarus was a tall man, thin. The wrapped toes were the highest point on the body. Quiet, stillness, at the point of balance; yes, something had happened: the going out had ceased. There was now a waiting. Which way would the power flow? These are the things I meant to study, these are the things I meant to know.

A donkey passing in the street. Walk. Sun shining just beyond the slit of a window. Be warm. He found it again, the place where things could be caused; now he must stay with it, with, within and not think. . . .

The room enclosing them. The bands tightening before release. The heart swelling. Break out. Tears in the outer room. Wild laughter greeting him.

Come forth.

And Lazarus came forth stumbling in the wrappings.

But you cannot trust John.

And there is no account of it in Mark.

So, Augusta, I cannot do it for you. I did not learn it at the seminary. When I lay my hands upon the sick, they do not recover. Nor the dead. But I will take you with me where I go.

"It was *my* mother's people got into Judea first. Before hers." Joseph crooked a thumb toward the kitchen, where Polly was working. "Came upriver in 'seventy-two and hers didn't get here 'til seventeen hundred."

"Hers the ones bought Hammerville from the Indians?" Charles asked. "I've got a Negro woman out there who . . ."

"Bought the whole of western Connecticut," Joseph interrupted his son. "Now, the Minors, close as I can find it, came west from Farmington two years after. . . ."

All Charles's stories paled before his father's. Only Jesus'—the central, the unique, the most important story in the history of man and the mind of God—was equal to those of Joseph Minor, and that only sometimes.

Charles drove Annah to the railroad station in Chester. Her mother would not come to Shiloh and Charles would not go to Pennsylvania. So Annah was boarding the train alone a month before the baby was due.

"Are you frightened?" he asked.

"A bit." Annah wore a green linen maternity dress with a white hat and gloves. "Sad, too. I'll miss having him inside, we've been together so long now." She took off the hat. "Well, I won't be a minister's wife for a couple of weeks!"

"You'll be a minister's wife," he corrected her, as they turned up Long Hill. "You'll just be on vacation."

"Of course." She laid the white gloves flat on the seat between them and ceased talking. She folded her hands, a silver bracelet at each wrist.

She looked like a working girl again, like Annah Trevellack who had gone and gotten herself into trouble.

"She should call me the minute she can," he reminded her.

"Yes," she answered.

Mrs. Trevellack had turned against Charles since the marriage. "He's selfish," she had told her daughter. "He only cares about being a minister." But Mrs. Trevellack did not like many people. Charles had decided it would be best always to treat her like a parishioner. "You tell her I'll be waiting, not to think at the last minute or in the middle of the night that I am not waiting." It was a week and a half before he got any letters from Annah. Three more weeks until the phone rang at two a.m.

A son! May God be praised! May we remember the less fortunate in the midst of our joy! It had long been dark when he parked the Ford at the small house in western Pennsylvania where Annah's mother took in sewing, college boys and her own daughters. Excited and impatient over the hundreds of miles, Charles suddenly felt that he could drive another fifty.

"Hello, Grandma!" After all, it was her first.

"I told Annah to sleep, Arley. Thomas will be awake later and she has to save her strength." Annah's mother led Charles down the hallway from which the light only dimly reached a double bed where he saw Annah resting, beside a wicker basket.

She opened her eyes as he entered the room and she put her hand on the basket. Charles couldn't breathe. He felt enormous. A white flannel blanket was around a baby hardly larger than his two hands. The eyes in the tiny face were shut and the fingers curved into soft nails. Charles put his hand on the white chest and felt the breath of life going up and down. I am with you, he said to himself. You're here. The son he had expected went out of his mind—a lean, red-haired boy of large size and age, maybe five. In his place lay this unknown boy come from Annah, heaved up out of clay. He took his hand away.

"Tell me everything!" He sat beside her and judged her tired and nervous.

"Did you see his hands?" They both looked into the basket.

"Want me to show you his feet?"

He turned from his son. "How are you, Annah?" he asked. But

it was too late. He was sorry he had sent her off alone. How could he ever return to her as she had been?

"Come along." Mrs. Trevellack pulled at his arm and led him out to the couch. "Men never appreciate how hard it is to take care of a baby," she said. Test of fatherhood? Willingness to sleep on a couch? That night in a dream he saw Jesus calling him, motioning, slowly, in slow motion, "Come." And Charles rose and walked along the shores of Galilee, the yellow shores of rounding hills that lead above the land, above Capernaum: woe, woe. "Come with me," the soft voice spoke, the long curls of the beard waving in the breeze from the lake. "Come be a fisher, come grow in the sonship, come unto me and I will. I. The son."

First thing in the morning, he telephoned home with the boy's name.

"Bring me the Bible, Polly." If only Joseph could get his hands on the great book wherein were inscribed all the births, all the deaths. "William Minor!" he would say to it. "You, William, born in Stratford in 'oh-nine, are you the one sailed for Massachusetts in May of 'thirty-five? Walked over to open Farmington, becoming the first of us Judea Minors? Or did you go to New Haven in 'forty-two?" A William Minor from Warwickshire had appeared, disturbingly, on the proprietors' roll at New Haven. If he had stayed in New Haven, he could not have come to Farmington, and wasn't, therefore, his ancestor. But the New Haven William was the only Connecticut Minor who had been traced to an English town. Perhaps you are the same William, going both to New Haven and on to Farmington? Marrying one Frances? Unlikely. There must be two Williams from two different towns in England, marrying different Franceses and dying different deaths. All deaths being different, all deaths the same. *Thomas Percy Minor*, Joseph inscribed in the Minor family Bible, *born May 25, 1931. Son of Charles Percy and Annah Trevellack Minor.* He left just enough space at the right-hand margin for the future date of his fifteenth grandchild's death. Only the past could be inscribed, made permanent.

. . .

The baby opened his eyes and looked at Charles, who slipped an outsized, clumsy hand under the small of his back, another under his wobbly neck. Raising the baby to his chest, Charles walked slowly to the rocker and lowered himself into it.

"There, there now. You'll see."

He sat and rocked. "She's gone shopping. She's gone to buy some shoes. Shoes. Feet." He smiled at the baby. The baby looked into his face with a searching motion of the eyes. Charles tried to radiate assurance. "She'll be back. I'm here." He rocked, continually impressed with the smallness of the baby. Did he seem like a giant to the baby? His arm was as big as the baby's whole body. Did the baby even connect that arm with the face that looked down? Charles smiled at his son. "I'm your dad." The baby's eyes opened wider and his neck muscles tensed. *I looked over Jordan and what did I see-ee, coming for to carry me home?* How reassuring would a face four times bigger than one's own appear? The baby seemed to want to move its fingers, to reach toward Charles, but he could not make his hands go, so he reached with his eyes and touched Charles with those, staring helpless and full of trust. Then he screwed up his mouth and yowled.

Hunger?

Fear?

"TIME FOR TEA!" Annah called from the bottom of the stairs.

At his desk, which had been moved out of the baby's room to the upstairs hallway, Charles finished writing *joy in the work, in our son, and some wife!* and shut the notebook: "Lies flat, turns free, always in alignment." More than he could say of himself in 1931. He had a good record here, why had no city church beckoned him? Should he go back to Union for a Ph.D.? Too late: he had a family. He rolled the paper out of his typewriter. "A lot of those 'twenty-eight values were mythical, each year we can appreciate more fully the simple goodness of milk, the simple pleasures of home."

"Aren't you coming, Arley?"

It was a lovely sight, Annah in a red Christmas dress and the baby rocking on his knees at a sane distance from the fire-screen.

"I thought we might have high tea for ourselves!" Annah announced, pleased with the tray of whipped cream and biscuits, tea in a china pot.

"Happy New Year!" Charles said as Annah poured tea and handed him the cup. "And to a larger parish this year!" He raised his cup. "I wrote to Hartford this afternoon to put my name in at the Congregational Office. And I asked about New Haven, as you wanted."

"To your health!" she said, resting on ritual.

Here they stood at the starting line of 1932. He would be thirty this spring. He took Annah's hand, but when Tommy reached to pull himself up on the fire-screen she let it go and ran for the baby. Were they no better at marriage than the people of East Meadow or of Shiloh?

"This is the year," Annah said, "Tommy will learn to walk, won't you?" She sat with the baby in her lap and gave him jam on a spoon.

"What do you say, fella?" Charles circled a fat ankle with his thumb and middle finger and squeezed. Who suspects until he has a child that he can no longer be one?

Footsteps on the doorstep; the door-knocker.

"Can't they leave us alone?" Annah held the baby closer.

"Come on in." Charles swung the door wide to his third tramp of the month. Why not send him on to Chester jail, where he could spend the night and be fed? HUNGRY AND YE FED ME. "Sir," he added, getting right to work.

"Having trouble finding work, then?" Charles sat with the man who fingered a cigarette lighter and reiterated the ten-dollar total he would need to get to his sister in Damariscotta. He smelled of whiskey and ate little of the ham sandwich Annah brought him. An hour later Charles had relieved himself of ten dollars and offered to make a few phone calls to inquire about odd jobs. He handed the man blankets so he might sleep on the cot in the basement of the church but the tramp had refused them. Who was he kidding about Damariscotta? By morning Charles's ten dollars would be drunk up in whiskey. What exactly was the wisdom that snakes had? Still, you had to trust, expect the good.

The door-knocker again. Two tramps? Two brown circles in the snow where they would dump their unwanted cocoa? This was the ministry? But the man who stood on the step was well-dressed, with a car parked, its motor running.

"Good evening, Reverend Minor." The man put out his hand. "I'm Harvey Cohen from the lake and I wanted to give you this." He handed Charles a check for fifty dollars.

"What's this?" Didn't he remember that face from the barber shop last summer?

"Times are hard and I thought you would know better who needs a helping hand at the New Year." The man stood in light snow illuminated by the street lamps.

"Come in!" Charles opened the door wider.

"No thank you, my car is waiting." He tipped his hat with a leather-gloved hand.

"I'm grateful! We're grateful!" Charles called after him. God had seen his need and sent him a man. A true Christian. Except he was a Jew. Pride of the lawyers of Deuteronomy, he gave alms because the law said give alms. Maybe law wasn't a bad idea. Amanda Lamb had certainly not given him an electric organ yet out of simple uncalendared joy. If only he had given the tramp money from the church funds as Annah had urged. He could have paid it back from Cohen's fifty. But the tramp's money had come from Charles's pocket, out of joy. Hah! He could not repay himself from Cohen's gift. But there must be some good to come out of this. Perhaps he would start off an organ fund with Cohen's fifty. How about that? It was, perhaps, all there was to the wisdom of snakes.

The First Congregational Church of Burlington, Vermont, had asked him up to preach before their people. A city! Not large, but a much more important place than Shiloh. He was still a young man on his way up. They would vote on him right after the morning worship next Sunday.

"Hi, friend!" He stooped to shake the hands of his Sunday School children as they filed out of church. Enrollment had doubled; he must point that out in Burlington. The children liked his monthly sermons to them. He had convinced some of his young people in the Pilgrim Fellowship to teach Sunday School classes. "I hope you're going to have ice cream for dessert this noon!"

"Let's start with hopes tonight," he told the Fellowship that evening. "Each of you name a hope. That's the first step in getting there." No parishioners had taught him that, he had always known it. It was the other side of fear. "Go ahead, Trudy." He motioned to a girl sitting on a pillow by the piano. "What's your hope?" His was to be called to Burlington. Trudy's was to be a nurse.

"I'm sure you told her the right thing, though I can't imagine what it was!" Charles leaned forward Monday night to see through the windshield of the Ford. He was taking Annah to the movies in Chester. She was reporting a story from her sewing circle of a young mother nursing her baby. Her three-year-old daughter stripped off her clothes and ran screaming and giggling into her father's lap. "I told her to switch to bottles." Annah braced herself against the dashboard. "Nobody nurses anymore." At least it took his mind off Burlington.

"Each patrol into its corner now!" he called out Tuesday night. Through rimless glasses Charles examined a Scout diagram. "Now this hitch is for tent ropes," he began, suddenly smelling the bread his Bison Patrol had baked on a camping trip to South-lee Falls: burnt black on the outside, soft and still doughy within. Could it be fifteen years ago already?

"Nathaniel Hawthorne and I share something that I hope some of you other men share with us." He spoke in a voice still rushed if he forgot to slow it. Have to watch that in Burlington. "We both love our wives with a great devotion." The eight women and two men of the Wednesday Night Book Club chuckled appropriately, turning toward Annah, who blushed. Men always turned to look at Annah. But him? Not unless he was opening the meeting or standing in the pulpit. Tommy mustn't get sick, Annah must come to Burlington.

"Wonderful! Beautiful! Just as you always do it!" On Thursday night, he put his arm around a couple of women in the church kitchen. They were as old as his mother; the flesh on their upper arms swung just like hers. They giggled. "Now, next Thursday I hope one of your covered dishes will be Yorkshire pudding." Oh, no! He'd forgotten that the week when he had asked for apple pie, seven had arrived. The women shrieked. He was loved here. He must remember that Sunday. A man had to succeed in the world before thirty; he had only a month left. Friday morning they drove north.

Joseph adjusted his new glasses and wrote to the Boston *Transcript*, whose genealogical column he had read for years as a probate judge. "William Minor"—he paused to control his fingers—"who emigrated from Stratford in Warwickshire in 1635, was he the William who settled as a proprietor in Farmington? And also in New Haven? Are these two settlers the same man?" He signed himself J.M., then whimsically added a third initial, J., for Judea. He was of his town and would last in some form so long as his firm, middle-sized handwriting remained in its town hall. Three hundred years? With the extra J, no one would know that Judge J. M. was now engaged in the old man's game of genealogy. His answer was published a few weeks later, in mid-November—a bad sign, since knowledgeable people seldom responded quickly. Joseph secured his glasses: "The two Williams are not the same man," the answer ran. "William of New Haven never actually emigrated but stayed home in Stratford, Warwickshire, to tend his estates. The origin of the Farmington William is not known, but his descendants live around Judea, Connecticut. W. N. B."

Winifred North Brewster, secretary of the Judea library he had helped endow! He knew more about anything in the world than Winifred Brewster. Who was she to take away his link with his homeland? How could he give his children their true fathers?

Seven fathers stretching back to English soil, seven fathers fixed upon the pages of incorruptible books, fathers to last a man a lifetime and beyond? Fie on you, W. N. B.!

"They'll be here soon, Papa," Polly called, taking off her coat. "Shall I help you to the table now?"

"Did Mama tell you what I ordered her for our fiftieth anniversary?" Joseph sat on a pillow at Sunday dinner.

"No," Charles replied, quieting Tommy in the highchair.

"A diamond ring," Joseph looked pleased. "From the jeweler in Chester, but she doesn't like it much."

"Oh, Joseph," Polly said. "It's just that my hands are so old now."

Charles tied Tommy's napkin around his neck. Well, why had Joseph waited so long?

"Nat?"

"Napkin," Annah mouthed for Tommy.

"How was your service, Charles?" Polly smoothed out the tablecloth in front of her.

"Oh, they liked my joke," he replied. "A man rushed up to his minister after a service and begged to join the church. The minister asked what morsel of his sermon had so impressed the visitor. 'Oh, it wasn't anything *you* said,' the visitor explained. 'It's that my washerwoman is such a happy person and she keeps urging me to join.' "

Joseph and Polly chuckled but Annah did not. Simon came through the swinging door with a platter of roasted chicken, which he set down before Charles.

"Thanks," Charles nodded, as he picked up the carving knife.

"And how are things going at your establishment?" Joseph inquired as his son carved.

"Pretty good," Charles replied. "We got our social room painted. Our richest woman, Mrs. Lamb, painted the top half of a door and our poorest woman, Daisy Thompson, painted the bottom. Mrs. Lamb did not drop much paint on Daisy, I am happy to report."

Joseph did not laugh at that one.

"What about the man with the sick wife whose neighbors took him in?" Polly kept her running account. Henry Ward Beecher: "The mother's heart is the child's schoolroom."

"Doing fine, both families." Charles gave his father a slice of white meat. "Wonderful spirit."

"And what about that salary of yours?" Joseph clearly wanted to begin eating and found waiting for the others to be served difficult.

"Oh, that stays the same!" Charles sliced Tommy's meat into small chunks.

"He even offered to take a cut." Annah's voice had an edge. "To lower the church's expenses."

"Any word from the church in Kent?" Polly inquired.

"They hired someone else." Annah helped him out on that one. "It was better than at Burlington. At least they let us know. Or at. . . ."

"This is Tommy's." Charles interrupted her with the boy's plate.

"You really set on a city church, Charles?" Polly said.

"If I can get one," he answered, lining up fork and knife on the carving platter and sitting down to his plate. He did not make a good first impression, Annah had explained. Get Ping-Pong ball for Pilgrim Fellowship Sunday night. Get paddle. Just what did he do wrong? Pay fireman two dollars. Get notice to Chester paper. You seem too eager to please. Call on phone Henry, Pinkham, Stillwell. Two o'clock Mrs. Trigham. Unsure of yourself. Eleven School Street. The Ideal of Jesus. Nervous. Fix electric light bulb. Get another Ping-Pong paddle.

Tommy knocked over his glass of milk.

"Come on!" Charles said, sharply, uprighting the glass.

Joseph went back to bed before they left, and after napping ate his supper from a tray. Then the dock scene swam before his eyes; its colors merged out of blacks into grays and dark reds, and, as in the portraits by old masters, the rims of all their hats were touched with gold. First, John Percy bent to shoulder a suitcase carved from a tree trunk. He embraced several male and female figures and the smaller figures of children, then he walked up the gangplank of the *John and Mary* in the March cold of the port of Plymouth, not far from his native Taunton three hundred years ago.

Had it been raining? Joseph's eyes traveled to the bedside table. No. He did not feel strong enough to lift the heavy atlas and look up rain statistics. John Percy gained the deck and the noise of farewell ebbed. Joseph squeezed his eyelids to redden the colors and waited. But nobody came. The twenty-two-year-old John Bullman, who had brought his mother's line to the New World, had boarded at Plymouth in that year. How often did the ships set sail? Could John Percy and John Bullman have been aboard the same ship? Was everyone named John then? His eyes turned to the bookcase for a list of ships and their passengers, but a trip across that uneven floor was assuredly impossible.

"Polly?" he called.

She came to the door.

"Are you hungry again, Papa?" she asked him. "We just ate supper!" She smiled at him.

"No," he said, "thirsty," as if the thought of hunger had not occurred to him. "Tomorrow have Sam move that bookcase over nearer the bed. I can't reach anything."

"All right," she promised, returning soon to fill his pitcher with ice water for the night. She tucked him in and kissed him and turned out the light. In the darkness he no longer needed to shut his eyes to see them. He blinked quickly to catch a face shaded by a hat. No luck. A woman with an equally obscured face appeared. Is that you, Frances? He looked carefully but she turned to wave to an older woman on shore. The picture faltered and dimmed. Among his fathers he would go, but he needed time to find them. He needed to write to a genealogist in New Haven. England, New England. Was there a Haven? His eyes shut, he slept.

Charles averaged his church attendance for the first half of 1933 and taped the resulting *96* over his desk on top of 1932's *84*. He smoothed out the nearby quote from St. Francis: *The possession of any property however small is hostile to the Christian eye.* He reread his report on his week at the Methodist Spring Retreat. "We had eleven lads and one of them a Negro lad. We did not think of him as Negro; we lived as followers of Jesus. Now don't get the idea those boys were sissified! We played a full component of sports! This is the Kingdom itself, I thought, in the glow of the last night's campfire. Our Prince is in and among us and we in him, the light of his peace is in our eyes—and our banners would strike terror in the hearts of our enemies!"

He picked up Ted's typed letter and skipped again to the end: "And so I am leaving Methodism as there appears to be little room even within a Methodist college for social change. The church like the slow-witted husband is the last to know. Your brother in Christ, Ted. Or Another Radical Unemployed."

"We're living on the front lines out here," Maud had added in her strong, thick script. "We're installing our seminar on race relations at the Seattle Y, but from now on, no affiliations."

Wasn't Ted ashamed of getting fired? Now Charles could not send Ted the clipping he had cut from the *Star* in which Shiloh's reporter had called him "Beloved pastor." He was ashamed at not finding a new pulpit, but at least he was successful at home in Shiloh and had not been fired. He resumed his sermon draft: "Our Negro friends should be equal before the law, not only respected for the tedious work they do, but loved. The next time someone tells me Negroes are underhanded, sneaky, dirty, lazy or dumb, I'll tell them I plan to reach down to that Negro and raise him up. The Negro has a wonderful capacity to accept the hard truths of life. Why, one time I went fishing with a boyhood friend and when I felt bad for the fish we pulled in on the line, he dropped it in the bucket easily enough. 'Oh good land, boy!' he said and he was laughing, laughing all over his body the way they do. 'That's what the Good Lord made them for.' "

It would probably be the last grandchild Joseph would live to see, and such a solid, squared number: sixteen. Joseph was surprised at how glad he was to have a girl. She made a link of some kind that he could not quite explain. Beyond that was her birthdate.

"Do you realize what that is?" he inquired of Polly.

"What what is, Joseph?" Polly asked, white-skinned, winter-bound.

"One-two-three-four." He wrote it down for her to see. "The first month, the second day, of the year nineteen thirty-four. That won't happen again for a hundred years!"

"Why, yes," Polly said, holding the paper off where she could read it.

"Not until the second of January, two thousand thirty-four!" Didn't that birthdate put dying on your birthday in the shade? A bit, just a bit. But he could only hope for the latter.

"I'll put her name down now." He indicated that Polly should bring him the Bible. "What did you say it was?"

"Sara," Polly replied. "Without the *h*. Sara Trevellack Minor."

"Dear Fellow Members of Union's Class of 1929. Five years have passed since . . ." How was Barclay doing in Atlanta? Was he a bishop yet? Barclay should have been along yesterday in the car as he chased a couple he had married in order to add some celebration to what had been a rather pathetic great event. Halfway to Chester the groom pulled over and tried to give Charles five dollars, thinking he had been tailing them for his forgotten fee. *I may be in Shiloh some time*, Charles wrote in his diary at the desk above the stairs. *These are the people of Nazareth, and Jesus learned to change them.* Not by pork-and-bean suppers, not by thousands of deeds. How? Augusta would have known. He didn't. He must persevere with what he did know: industry. He set the alarm for five a.m., so he could watch the sunrise for a children's sermon.

"He's right there! Isn't he there?" Annah's scream woke him.

"Who?"

"My father! In the doorway! See?"

"No, there's nobody there." He put his arms around her.

Later, he snuffed out the alarm and shuffled to the dark kitchen to put water on for coffee. "Five years I have been with you—the green years, they called them at Union Seminary." Lately, anywhere that enough quiet gathered, Charles could hear a voice inside him that seemed to be always talking.

He carried the coffee into the back yard and hunched into his sweater. Two birds were singing. A dog barked. The judge would not be a ghost to mess with such frivolities as haunting the doorways of his children's bedrooms. He was a strong man. That's why it was taking him so long to die. A low ridge of light-struck cloud cleared over Percyville. The judge's shadow, his soul: where would it go? Of what is the celestial body made: Maud endorsed cremation. How could she?

"Easter tomorrow!" The neighbor's boy was only twice as old as Tommy and had already greeted Charles a couple of months back with a smile of secret understanding. He owed the mothers here something for preparing the hearts of the children; like him, the mothers eked out their slow miracle from endless chores.

Cobwebs sparkled on the ground. A cow mooed. He should run around the yard. Hadn't gotten enough physical exercise lately. A young man on his way up. Five years: the green years, they used to . . .

A red globe burned through clouds, just as it had the morning Tommy was born. His round Trevellack face. Had Annah's father meant to stand at Tom's threshold? Grandchildren are our immortality, everyone said. It wasn't true. We each have our own. Of what is the celestial body made? Groggy; it was too early in the morning. Sara's narrow face with the wide Minor mouth; she looked like Maud. It pleased and frightened him. The great globe hung naked over Percyville.

At noon the sun warmed the top of his head where the bald spot had begun. He stood on the doorstep at the Abbott place. Mrs. Abbott pressed a bill into his hand. "This is for the Aid to give Daisy," she said. "We hear she's laid up." Mrs. Abbott had become his steward, after all. But no one had replaced his saint Augusta Stiles. He had been holding up her end of the table. Nor had Daisy revealed her secret. Perhaps today?

"Hi, friend," he said, entering Daisy's cabin, with the bag. "Need anything today?" Daisy was sitting in her rocker, dressed. He was glad of that, though it was the other way around—black man and undressed white woman—when they hung you. "I brought you some flour and some milk." He set the bag of groceries down on the wooden table where he had first found her working, singing *Sow good seeds and you shall reap what you have sown.*

"I'm laid up," she said, her voice farther inside her than usual. She cleared her throat.

"I know. You need a doctor?" He checked the woodbox.

"Nope, just laid up." She fingered an empty pipe.

He reached into his breast pocket. "You need more wood?" he asked as he handed her the extra little packet he had finally located.

"Not when I got tobacco!" A grin of thanks crossed her face. He knew no more than before.

THERE WAS STILL SNOW on the ground. Joseph raised himself in the front of the Pontiac side-service hearse to get a better view of the road. Simon had come to clean his room today and Joseph had jumped at the chance to join Sam's oldest son on a ride to Greenhill for an Episcopalian interment. A ride got him away from his bedroom's perpetual tenant, the long slow death with ups and downs. Not more than a handful of good days left, among them not the holidays. He always ate too much. Again he had sunk down in the hearse and had to push himself up for vision above the dashboard. Undertaking had always boomed at holidays, a combination of suicide and overeating. He remembered not to chuckle midway through, but the pain that laughing produced came to his stomach anyway. By Christmas supper the turkey was always cold and the pie reheated. This year he had leaned on a grandson's arm to walk over his threshold to the dining room, where his three sons and his pretty daughter and all their children sat. His oldest son was fifty and his pretty daughter was paling toward forty. His smart daughter was absent, as usual. Still in Seattle; she got around. His two daughters were the soft inside of the family, the mothers of other men's children, buttressed chronologically on either side of time by the harder bones of men, their brothers, their descendants and their ancestors.

"A good year!" Polly had said, pouring coffee into a long row of cups. "No deaths and one baby!" Joseph accepted a wavering but filled plate from Justine's smart daughter Martha and sat down next to her pretty daughter Hildegard; funny names. He stuck his fork into cranberry mold—red, quivering. He ate.

The next day, the new wills had come, stating that the undertaking business would go to Sam on the first day of January, 1935. Joseph initialed it. The next week Charlotte Webber died at forty-eight and Sam at forty-nine handled his first job as owner of the business. Joseph slept off and on until February. His vision was darkening, blacking out from poor circulation which the glasses could not help.

To make King George's speech of peace available to American audiences, a C.B.C. worker grasped a broken wire and held it together. The leaking voltage shook his arms and burned his hands, but he held on while the king's voice passed through him to the people.

So may I Lord, burned, shaken. Even though the Springfield pulpit committee would not hire him to pass along the Lord's words. Charles shut the diary and cupped a hand over each eye. Had he gotten the Shiloh pulpit only because Ted had recommended him? Only because he was a local boy? He was a hit here, in this year alone he had laid linoleum in the Methodist kitchen and torn down the horse sheds behind the Congregationalist building. Was his failure to get a new job punishment for pride at having become Shiloh's captain? A road spun out from either eye, parallel; they never joined.

On the night before his thirty-third birthday, when he was becoming as old as Christ crucified, he saw his dream twice, once for each eye. A grim Jesus with blackened face strained to lift a cross and turned to Charles for help; his mouth pulled down at one side and Charles could not make out the words. In a hand-carried chair Charles waved from behind yellow silk curtains. No thanks, not today. All without words, silently because he would never speak to his beloved with such disdain, not even in a dream; no, especially not there. He must wake and climb out of the car, must keep on walking in the footsteps set before him. Perhaps power would come to him through those prints left on the ground.

On the morning of his birthday, Daisy Thompson turned from living into dead, quite by herself. Walter telephoned Charles and when he found that Walter had lugged her into town without her pipe, he drove out to look for it. Perhaps he would find a message, too. Her door was banging in the March wind and Charles took a last look over his shoulder at the evergreens before he entered the dark cabin. Inside he was alone beneath a low ceiling. He saw no pipe on the wooden table near the window, nor on the stone mantelpiece cold to his palm. It had not fallen near his feet on the lumpy braided rug. Nor into the hollows of the pillowed rocking chair where he would not have sat down for ten thousand dollars. He walked behind the chimney toward the bedstead. It was even lower and darker there and when Charles stooped to avoid bumping his head, he saw the pipe lying on the floor near her bed. Dragged off when they took her? He snatched it up; it was as cold as the mantel. Empty, still, the house. Did no one in earth or heaven watch the inside of Daisy Thompson's house? Did God not hover over the dark of the earth? But that did not feel like the message she had left. What he felt was someone watching though it wasn't God. He warmed the pipe in his hands and delivered it to Walter, instructing him to lay it in the box with Daisy. Her secret surrounded him but he might have to hold up her end of the table forever without knowing what to call it.

"I'm scared!" Tommy cried out that afternoon.

"What of?"

"Ghosts!" Charles sat down on his son's bed and leaned against its huge headboard. This room was so much larger than the winter bedroom into which he had been put with a nurse thirty-three years ago.

"Don't go!"

Justine had picked up Annah and the baby to prepare for the birthday party, and, knowing he was stuck, Charles took off his glasses and pushed them under the bed. Then his shoes and socks.

His eye is on the sparrow. That was a restful tune. He hummed; *and I know He watches me.* Might as well be comfortable. He shut his eyes and felt the pressure of air against his soles. That is where his body ended, at the soles. But his soul did not end. It filled the world and could go anywhere, do anything. If he opened his eyes, the world would come back; if he called out his thirst wordlessly, it would be satisfied. There was so much of mystery in everything. Tommy leaned against him and Charles remembered himself as the small one leaning against a larger one. Had that large shape been his mother? Or her, the other one, his nurse? Funny, he would not know Aunt Gracie if he ran smack into her, but she had hardly let him out of her sight from the day of his birth to his second birthday. He slept.

"Tell me how you liked Stratford, Annah." Polly spoke to Annah like a child.

"Oh, it's not much larger than Shiloh," Annah answered obediently. "But I'll go anywhere. We're not getting excited this time unless they call us."

Charles carved a crusty-skinned chicken, careful of Simon's elbow as he placed a last serving dish on the table. Stratford was another hill-town. Back to Bethlehem to start again. He was not judged fit for the city yet, apparently. Still too conscious of the eyes of the crowd upon him. "Say," he said as soon as Simon had vanished, "I've been meaning to ask for almost a year now, whatever happened to Aunt Gracie?"

"Still working, I guess." Polly ladled out sliced beets.

"She must be pretty old by now." Charles severed a leg and landed it on Tommy's plate. He handed Sara's meat to Annah to be minced.

"No! No!" Sara tugged indignantly at the napkin Annah was wrapping around her neck.

"No, Gracie's only sixty," Polly replied. "Younger than I am. You were the first baby she took care of."

"She's sixty-five!" Joseph called out from his bedroom. "Probably still *having* babies. With them they never stop!" They could hear him chuckling.

After dinner Polly handed Charles a baby-book that had been

made by hand. He didn't look at it until he got back to Shiloh. Someone had folded colored paper, run a ribbon through holes and decorated the front with gilded cherubs. On the first page appeared his mother's familiar round handwriting: *A frail baby.* Then he saw the other handwriting, larger, paler, with a distinctive pointed quality. Gracie's? There are those who, unknown, watch us: THEN SHALL WE KNOW, EVEN AS ALSO WE ARE KNOWN. Is that what you meant to tell me, Daisy?

The Estey foot-organ stopped short and Charles rose to announce his call to the pastorate of the First and only Congregational Church of Stratford, New Hampshire, effective after Easter. His people were saddened. In the vestibule they said, "We watched you grow up. But it's time our young man was moving up and on!" They looked down and confessed to each other: "It takes a while to know him, but we'll never get another here like Arley Minor." They launched a string of send-off parties designed to provide Charles and Annah with gifts of household belongings for the empty parsonage to which they were going. Congregationalists did not provide furniture. He would escape the ragged rugs and faded chairs Deacon and Mrs. Bowen had shown him on his first visit up from seminary. "This is the dining room," they had said and continued in a more confidential tone: "upstairs are two bedrooms. It will be a bit lonely for an unmarried man."

"I," he had replied without a hope in his heart, "may marry soon." Polly and Joseph added a living-room set and an oriental rug to the presents. He had property now. He had heirs. He had to die now; they could roll him in the rug. Daisy Thompson had possessed no heirs. Her house stood exactly as she had left it two years ago. Can you still be a saint if you have children?

Thirty-five, half his life was gone. "They say he never eats at the casserole suppers," Justine reported to his birthday guests at home in Judea. "He just gets a slice of meat cut and ready when some old lady comes in and he jumps up to talk. Millie in the kitchen says they lay bets on his not finishing."

"You never did stay as long as we wanted." Millie had hugged him when he resigned. But you couldn't go around believing everything nice that people said about you.

"Do we have to go to your mother's again this Sunday?" Annah asked, as she pulled up the quilt. "Can't we have a picnic by ourselves?" She was glad to be leaving Shiloh; she had lived here longer than any other place in her life.

"All right," he said. "Let's." He kissed Annah goodnight and pulled the quilt over his shoulders. Jesus had owned no property. Left no heirs. Never married. Charles moved closer to Annah. Jesus had yearned for something more than marriage. For a more total union, submersion into something bigger. Jesus had not been held by the bonds of death because the pull to be rejoined with his Father was a stronger bond. He had become unified with the spirit by gradually moving all of himself from the earthly to the spiritual man. He had become boundless. He had lived forever. It wasn't so easy when you had property. Heirs.

"Faster, Daddy!" Charles trotted uphill with Sara on his neck. His farewell sermon had gone well. "Not everything is brought low, felled," he told them from the pulpit. "Our souls rise. I feel them today, the watchers from our past. From the deacons who were the founders of our Congregational church some two hundred and fifty years ago, to those who founded our Methodist church some one hundred and fifty years ago, right up to our recently departed. They are surely gathered here, watching us, cheering us on at this point in our history: Augusta Stiles, Daisy Thompson. . . ." He struggled to keep pace with Tommy, who was leading the way over rocks past a spring brook. At the top, Annah spread out an old blanket and Charles thought he heard blow into hearing the sound of Southlee Falls, where he had walked as a child on Sunday afternoons.

"We used to go on lots of picnics." Annah laid out the pickles. "When my father showed up. And sometimes, if we had already packed the basket, when he didn't. But all in all," she pointed out, "I saw more of him than the children do of you. In the evenings he would sing with us, remember?"

"It was a good idea to come here, Annah," Charles said, waving a drumstick at Shiloh, on which they looked from a gentle height. He was going to escape the valley's heavy, hungry ground. Though his father wasn't. The air was free and empty over his head; he was, after all, a young man on his way up in the world.

Feeling agile, he stood and ran after Tommy, catching him in the air and swinging him overhead.

"Daddy! Daddy!" the boy shrieked, surprised at this attention. Charles promised himself that in his new far-off parish he would become a father.

"He insisted on dressing," Polly told them as they waited by the car.

"Shall I go help him?" Annah inquired.

"No, he wouldn't like it, but let's not be staring at him when he comes out." So they all turned from the house to the lawn, except Sara.

"Sidewalk looks good." Charles surveyed the long band of cement that had been newly grouted.

"I think he's coming." Annah picked up Sara and faced her away from the house.

They all pointed to fresh grass under the lilac bush way off at the top of the lawn.

The screen door shut.

"Grandpa!" Tommy broke and ran toward Joseph. They all turned back again.

"A safe trip," Joseph said, reaching for the Model A with one hand and putting his other out to Charles.

"Thank you." Charles grasped his father's hand, shaking it as firmly as he had been taught.

You, too. On your long trip.

"Drive carefully." Joseph made his way through the liturgy.

"I certainly will." Charles was not able to alter the accepted formula.

"Give it all you've got, there, boy!" Joseph instructed Tommy in the art of the handshake.

"Oh, he knows how to shake a hand!" Charles did alter the formula but nobody noticed; he stood on both feet, balanced, not pulled apart, poised.

"And where is it that you are going, girlie?" Joseph inquired of Sara in Annah's arms.

"For a ride," she said. "I won't throw up."

"Well, don't eat too many ice cream cones, then!" Joseph slipped a twenty-five-cent piece into each of the children's hands. The breath of his mouth smelled bad.

The old man, plump but withered on one side of him; the boy not long out of baby fat on the other; and Charles the lean, full-grown man between them. He felt power and a sudden inexplicable cruelty.

This time it was a hundred miles through the Berkshires with Fred. They had got almost to Vermont before Fred turned the Buick back. All Polly's idea, something to cheer Joseph up: springtime.

Back to his own ridges, Joseph rode now through dark folds of hills, through high land with slanting fields. Dark folds, like those of—what did they call it—Mendip? In that chalky English range had lain the bones of the oldest father he had yet found: one Henry Bullman of his mother's family. A fourteenth-century farmer who had helped his king to cross the English Channel. Joseph had looked up Edward the Third among pages of kings. A thin, long face in effigy. A man carved from a log: no wonder he looked thin.

"That's the Connecticut line." Fred pointed and honked the horn as they passed the sign.

Joseph had read that Edward's effigy was one of the earliest. Before that the crowd had insisted on viewing a dead king himself, embalmed. But Edward's death mask nailed on an effigy was so real they had not needed to parade him. The mask even showed how the left side of his mouth had twisted downward since the stroke. After a stroke, men need not bother to visit their wives. Nor Joseph, living in a downstairs bedroom by himself. Instead, when spring came, she sent him out for rides. The rolling of the hills flattened gradually as they moved south.

"One of the highest points in the state." Fred pointed out the window.

Numbers! They were not enough. Joseph wanted his fingers to touch the face of Henry Bullman as the Englishman straightened in his field to acknowledge the presence of his king. The hills

edged toward Joseph and his fingers flexed to reach out: Henry
Bullman? Is it you? Show me your face! He turned from the
window to the blank profile of his son, a handsome, middle-aged
man so much like himself. Joseph's own close-set blue eyes and
white hair, his own nose that cut through the face with a strong
curve, and his own wide mouth, the Minor mouth. That is, it was
called Minor these days. Joseph knew this to be wrong. He remembered his father's mother; the Minor mouth was hers. And
from whom did she have it? Her mother? He did not even know
the name for his own mouth or Fred's. Nor did he know the
mouth that went with the name Henry Bullman. Words were not
enough either. But what would he know of Henry Bullman if the
man should walk off this very hillside to welcome him, hand
extended? No more than he knew of his own son Fred, who had
driven him a hundred and seventy-five miles on an endless Sunday across the landscape of New England. What did it matter?
What did any of it matter? It was spring. Joseph was angry,
tired, unwilling either to die or to live in such a weakened state.

"Papa is blue," Polly was forever whispering to visitors before
she escorted them into his room. "He had a horrid night." He
must tell her to stop that.

"Red light," he pointed out to Fred. He must not relinquish all
his powers at once.

VIII

Christmas Eve, Around 1940

CHRISTIANITY WAS PEELING OFF STRATFORD, it had been a graft that had not taken. In the spring, I plant, the farmers seemed to say as they eyed his uncallused hands. Then I just hope for rain. I don't pray. Were they expecting him to wind up his story of Jesus with TAKE NO THOUGHT FOR THE MORROW, don't fight when they come to get you, God will help out? Dairy men didn't expect help from God and acted as if they lived before Jesus, following an earlier calendar. It was called Generations and had two seasons. The first was Poking, when you thumbed the seeds into the earth or got the bull to stick his seeds into the cow. The second was Bloom, when young things were produced out of old. There was scarcely any male or female in it. True, you did not fight, but it was not men who came to get you. It was something they imagined as larger than God and less friendly. The calf dies. "What can you do?" they said. Sometimes, "Christ! What can you do?" Charles winced at that, beginning to wonder if it was as close as they would ever get to the name he brought them. Prayer would be silly, yes indeed, like a boy praying for a motorized sled. Red, please, with gold letters on it spelling A*R*L*E*Y. Nobody knew his name here, his past mistakes. Pray for strength in case it doesn't rain.

"Morning the new man in town." The woman had pink cheeks, yellow teeth and long tangled gray hair.

"Good morning, Sunny." He doffed his derby, a hat that was the sign of the double trade of Minor men. But she was gone off, giggling. The closest thing he'd found to sainthood in this high narrow town, she had fallen a few too many steps outward from that grace, to become the village fool, who lived on cookies and the quick-bidden terror of schoolchildren.

Most of the other women here had trouble talking. He called on them in chinkless houses on Main, in farmhouses at the end of tarred roads near barns crusted by rust-protective paint, in shacks beside a faultlessly smooth river that returned only glare to the eye. They opened their doors, surprised to find a vortex hovering on their landscape, a listener for their unvoiced stories.

It took a while. Charles pushed against the door of what had been a fine Federal building and walked through a maze of boards that led to an apartment on one side. A blond girl sat in a dirty stuffed chair, giving a bottle to a newborn baby.

"Hi there, my girl." Charles stood at the doorway of the living room.

"Oh," the mother said, "hello."

Another baby of little more than a year stood at the bars of a crib placed against one wall of the parlor. A Montgomery Ward catalogue lay hopefully open on the footstool near the stuffed chair. Its pages offered the lavender and yellow treasures of spring.

"I guess those won't be for you this season, Susannah, will they?"

"I guess not," she said. The fine hair on her forehead was no thicker than that of a grade-school girl.

"You love your baby," he assured her.

"I guess I do," Susannah said, a blush of pink rising to her forehead, high and smooth as a Flemish Madonna's.

"Hi there, fella." Charles held out his derby to the boy in the crib and encouraged him to grab it. The odor of the boy's dirty diaper mixed with the smell of gas being pumped at the garage next door.

"You must get pretty tired," he said. "Do you get any help from your mother?"

"No." She removed the bottle to burp the baby. "My sister's getting married in June."

Of course. Months of preparation in Montgomery Ward's, school's dragging on to June until suddenly the sober bride would be walking down an aisle lined with eyes that turn to stare her passage from father to husband. Not a breath of air between. Next thing you knew, she's sitting with a white rag on her shoulder, burping a baby. Her own life as a child over. He knew these weddings.

"I see a lot of people at work," he said. "There's no harder job than yours. But it's the best." He never stayed long; he did come often. He got right along to the next person.

Frances McCleod Granopes had taught English before she married. After the ceremony she had danced in a line of women hitched to a line of men and all held together by the red handkerchiefs of farmers or the white ones of restaurant owners. "The Greeks feed half the state," Franny's mother had warned her. "And marry the other."

"Nick put in that window for me," Franny said, pointing over her kitchen sink. "I sway when I look out of it at the cows swaying in the pasture. I get milked, too, every day." She pointed toward the carriage out on the porch where her fourth child slept.

It was a town of women and babies.

"Lately, I've been getting up at five to write down the poems that go through my head all day," Franny continued.

"Just like Kagawa!" Charles said. "He's a Japanese saint who gets up at three for an hour's prayer. Says he couldn't be a Christian without it."

"Well, I couldn't be a mother," Franny laughed.

"I didn't know you wrote poems," he said. "Tell me one."

"Not the whole thing," she said. "I can't remember every word." She sat forward over the kitchen linoleum, her plain face taking on a formal quality which made it at once more distant and more close. "It's about Eve, she's waking up in the garden and doesn't know who she is at first. She goes around under the trees until it gets to be evening. I guess my name is Eve, it's life I give. I'll be the woman of all things that live."

She sat back over the oilcloth covering her table. "We only become the things we know," she explained.

"So you couldn't have written the poem without being a mother, could you?" Charles pointed out.

He took their stories back to Annah, who was finding it hard to like Stratford. "I don't remember the poem," he said, "but it made me think of how when we got married I thought of myself as Adam. All the old stories, they give us things to look for."

"Susannah Hill's lucky," Annah replied. "She doesn't have church work on top of her two babies. And Franny Granopes should be happy she has a talent. I wish I did." In raising her children, Annah was learning to speak out, if only to Charles.

The men in town were accustomed to making pronouncements. Charles stood in the barn at High Dairy while the town's biggest farmer adjusted pressurized spigots onto the dugs of cows.

"I know what she does in there," the farmer said of his twelve-year-old daughter who went to the movies on Saturday nights and returned too fevered and too late.

"How do you know?" Charles scuffed his feet in the sawdust, watching a bent-backed man throw feed on the floor.

"I just know," the father said, reaching for the lamp on its long thick snake of a cord, moving with it farther back into the barn. He had beat his daughter with his belt, commanding her first to lie bare-bottomed across his bed. His wife had screamed in the doorway while the other children had remained soundless and distantly spaced throughout the house.

"She ought to obey you," Charles said, following him past the swishing tails of cows. "But you ought to trust her, too, you know." Startled, Charles said nothing when he noticed a human face staring from a cow stall; it was the face of a girl of four or five, with her mouth open and her eyes fastened on him.

"Trust her!" The farmer laughed. "Not any more than I'd trust myself in Paris France!" He jerked the black snake and skittered it past the stall, where the child retreated out of sight into darkness.

"Men like darkness, Reverend Charley." Nick Granopes rubbed a damp rag over his restaurant counter. A swinging door opened and from the steamy kitchen came the sounds of Nick's relatives. Every week one bunch left by mountain bus and another came to help the Stratford branch of the family rise into the propertied class.

"Three years ago I got the booths. Last year, the bathroom. Next year I want a sign that lights up. And if we pass beer, Reverend, I'll turn one end of the counter into a bar dark enough for the men, you see?" Nick returned to washing glasses. "Men like it dark."

"Well, now Nick, I admire your industry," Charles began. "But beer, why its effect is just exactly opposite that of industry. . . ." He had to go slow. From men there seemed to be so much more their pastor could take.

He walked from Nick's restaurant on Main up to the church. Its steeple needed paint; what steeple didn't? He walked up to the choir room and opened the trap door. He climbed up a splintered ladder hanging from the inner wall of the steeple. If he lived in Ur, the old stories would be suggesting different things. He would be climbing these stairs to a secret room. She of the golden robes would be waiting for him. Somewhere above he heard the slow plodding of feet, heavy, dusty, like the beating of a heart, the opening of a gigantic, creaking bud. He reached the clock room, where the thumping loudened, and he pushed at a tiny window which swung out so quickly he almost lost his balance. Far below he could see the top of the church's cutleaf maple. The summer of his thirty-fifth year was impeccable. He looked down and signaled to the tops of the blossoming trees: "Well done." How animate they had seemed years ago in Riverside Park when he had walked alone and turned his face up to them to be blessed. Lady spring of Ur, Lady bloom of Stratford, New Hampshire, they should not bring the baby to this town. He should.

By mid-summer the townspeople had begun to talk about him. "He walks in the front door, through the kitchen and out the back. He don't stay long." It was his talent to walk about, he explained to them from one of the town's two pulpits. Why should he dig a hole to bury his single silver talent only to have the master return and grow angry that he had not invested it? Charles invested; he pushed himself up from thirty to forty to fifty calls per week. He would witness his people at their sinks and by the glint of their iron tools; for, when they grew out of the gaze of their mothers, someone must pass through and watch them there. Cows can't always do that for you.

He knew it wasn't his talent to be witnessed, not at the beginning. He was hardly surprised that no one noticed on Hallowe'en, after the cold had lowered in the air and the jack-o'-lanterns had opened their orange mouths behind taut glass on Main, that a fat black mammy strode through town. She wore a white apron around her jelly belly and, completing her, under bare, moon-branched trees, was a child at either hand: a skinny Tom Sawyer with glasses and a skinnier Miss Statue of Liberty who tossed her head, with its red, white, and blue crepe-paper streamers that riffled like a bride's veil. When these three reached the high-school auditorium, they sat together on sticky tan leather seats where so many thoughts of love and glory lay, until lo and behold Best Costume was called.

"Mammy!"

And when she got up to the platform and yanked off her red bandana and her black curls and pulled out the feather pillows, everybody could see the sandy-haired bespectacled fellow who usually wore a business suit and derby hat. They weren't confused by the light-colored circles left free of burnt cork around his eyes. Applause. Oh, wild applause that warms the heart and brings rain out of the sky. Even in Bethlehem there were certain forewarnings.

"Dead? Already dead?"

It was Fred's voice telling him.

"What time?"

"About two a.m. He was on dope the last week, didn't talk at all yesterday."

My father died.

A neighbor came to stay with the children; Annah had brought tea in a Thermos onto the train.

He does not walk before me.

She poured some tea for him. He rested it on the shiny black sill and watched the jerking of the train lap the hot liquid just to the edge of the cup but never over.

The eyes of the judge are shut.

"What else did Fred say?" Annah ministered to him, pouring, wiping, talking.

"That he'd been very depressed."

"How's your mother?"

"Doing fine." He reached for his tea, spilling some on his left thigh, just where they come to cut out the circle of fabric on the morning of your electrocution.

The voice of the judge is never stilled.

Listen, I did some good things, too.

In fact, if you'd only . . .

"I told Mrs. Pratt we'd be back Friday, what do you think?" Annah offered him a napkin, indicating his left thigh.

Who would dig the grave? Simon? Peach's son? Or did they use machines for everything now, as in the movie he'd shown on farm implements? He hadn't been keeping up on the family business.

Charles did not touch the neat folder of carefully penned genealogical notes on the table by the bed downstairs. The special blue bedspread that matched the wallpaper had been returned wrinkleless after years of absence.

"Two-oh-eight!" Sam stated his father's parting weight but no one quite dared smile.

"That gave him a kick!" Polly laughed so they could. "When he finally gave up on making it around again to his birthday, he started to weigh himself every day!"

The house was not so empty as Charles expected; it had been his mother's house before and had simply become so again.

"Don't let the ball lightning scare you, Charles!" she called as he and Annah climbed the stairs. She sounded a little too much like Papa, though.

"Justine gave us sleeping pills," Annah said as she undressed.

He turned with surprise. "What for?"

"In case we can't get to sleep." She stepped into a nightgown.

"Not for me!" He watched her settle into the bed. "Twice a week" was what they had both suggested to Susannah Hill and her husband. And this was a special night, after all. He must be careful. Annah was not sure she wanted another child, not unless she could be released from church work. That, of course, was impossible.

Charles backed his father's Buick out onto Stratford's main street. "You take it, Charles," his mother had said. "You need it most." You cannot bring the baby to a town where only stewards wait. Saints are necessary to recognize it. There were no saints in Stratford and scarcely any stewards, though his most promising young man might soon become one. "Only a steward!" The voice of Joseph Minor. "You try it!" Holton Linfield still had little interest in the church, but he was friendly.

"I hated banking!" Holton fiddled with a bulb in the chicken house, where the stench hurt Charles's nose. "You know how it is. My father said I had to learn a profession."

"I know," Charles said. "When do you quit the bank?"

"Another year, another two and a half thousand. That'll give me what I need for the rest of the down payment on the lodge." Holton ran a hand through thick, dark hair.

French ancestors? Charles buttoned his suit jacket over the gold chain of Joseph's watch: he worked for two thousand a year.

"Holton!" His wife called from the house. "You got that bird?"

"Come on, boss," Holton motioned. "Since she got pregnant, there's no waiting for anything."

"What'll you call it?" Charles asked of the abandoned lodge and cabins farther along the road.

"Got any ideas?" Holton reached for one chicken among hundreds. Will it be you? You? Then for the axe. Carrying each in a hand, he led Charles outside to a tree stump. Holding the chicken on the stump by its head, Holton brought the axe down fast and tossed the severed head on the grass.

"Watch this!" He scooped up the bleeding body and set it on its legs at the top of the driveway. It walked crookedly down the dirt drive some twenty feet before it fell into the grass.

Charles liked Holton; he had the swagger of Minor men.

"These people know nothing." Annah's voice was choked. Ever since the doctor had let Tom's cold turn to pneumonia, she had begun to voice her assessment of the town within the privacy of their house. They were in the closet cleaning; it was safe to accuse.

"Satin, she called him. Why not Rayon? Why not Silk?" Annah handed Charles a box of old shoe-polish cans. She had inspected the Sunday School for him yesterday while he preached. "The superintendent standing there wiping a runny nose on the sleeve of her sweater and telling the children someone named Satin would get them if they weren't nice."

"I'll tell her it's Satan," Charles promised. Annah would not criticize in public, should not.

"All those little faces, looking up at her. And me, I knew it was no cold, but I looked up to him. It's lucky the children in this town survive at all!" She did like Stratford's mountain views and its band concerts; she had enjoyed its strawberries and she did look forward to Wednesday nights, when they struggled to keep afloat a play-acting group they had launched.

They heard a car in the driveway, doors slamming, laughter. Downstairs on the doorstep Charles found a middle-aged man with a red nose and a woman Annah's age whose curls were caught in the collar of her suit jacket.

"You the Reverend?" They wanted to get married.

"Have you a license?"

"Sure thing." The man handed Charles the paper, his suit

jacket sending off the smell of stale beer. Annah had once asked him to refuse to marry any couple where the man was drunk.

"Come on in, then." Charles led them to the front sitting room and excused himself. He met Annah on the stairway and they went up to change into better clothes, the least they could do.

"You stand over here." Annah placed the woman near the fireplace and left to return with what Charles recognized as the best of the chrysanthemums from a weekend funeral. She placed the flowers in the hands of the bride, who looked immediately coarsened by them.

"Dearly beloved," Charles began, with his knees backed up against the fire-screen. "We are gathered together . . ."

Sara banged through the side door but hushed herself immediately, familiar with the demands of this potent scene. Her puppy Skippy barked outside. The knot was tied.

"There you go, Reverend." The groom pressed a dollar bill into Charles's hand and smiled. "It's all I've got."

What are you going to buy the gas with? Charles handed the dollar to Annah. What was he going to buy his own gas with? He had given himself a salary cut from two thousand to eighteen hundred.

Annah took the money without enthusiasm.

"He wasn't that drunk," Charles said. "And they would have gone down the street to Jenkins if I hadn't."

"She could have done better than that; she had a pretty face!" Annah took the flowers back to the kitchen. "But what do these people know?"

"We do what we can for them." Charles followed after her, unbuttoning his vest. "It was nice how you brought the flowers. I bet you could civilize the whole mountainside."

She was already rearranging the flowers in their funeral container.

It would not be from that couple the baby would be delivered to Stratford. Nor from Annah and himself, who seemed to have taken to card playing in the late evenings after the various meetings. Why did he keep thinking of it as a real baby? Would it survive? He swallowed and found his throat sore.

. . .

The next day he was sick and Annah put him in the twin bed next to Tom's. There she could bring them twin meals and take twin temperatures. Friday morning he made it up out of bed on will power alone; he was due at the primary school at nine. At eleven he would join the Methodist minister Jenkins at the high school. Their white churches stood almost opposite each other on Main, Charles's with the town's few college graduates and Jenkins's with its singers. On the two men alone rested the bringing of the nativity message here to Upper Galatia, to Outer Thrace. He left Tom in bed and went off to first grade himself. Girls with Dutch haircuts bent their heads over books, exposing their vulnerable necks to his, the ministerial, gaze. The boys were all in some form of knickers and looked twice as sturdy as Tom. It was taking a while for the sophistication of rural Connecticut to wear off his son. "Now listen," the teacher was saying. "Isn't this exciting?"

"The do-or o-pens." A boy looked up with surprise that he could read.

"Some doors open on forlornness," Charles said at the high school at eleven. "One night when I was about your age I went to visit a colored boy in jail and when the jailer unlocked his iron door I saw a boy who was forlorn. You boys and girls are lucky that your town keeps some doors locked for you. Only this November we again voted down the sale of beer. Now, once there was born a child who was himself a door." Charles nodded conspiratorially toward Jenkins at the other end of the platform. "We see him on a hillside saying, 'BLESSED ARE THE PURE.' We see him on the cross, where the door finally opens, hear him say: 'I AM THE WAY, IF ANY MAN ENTER, HE SHALL BE SAVED.' " Afterward, Jenkins took his arm and passed on a field report. "Just saw your Mrs. Linfield coming home with the baby."

Charles drove rapidly up the hill.

Holton pulled back the white blanket to show a black-haired baby girl whose breathing was an event of great proportion and enormous satisfaction.

"That's something, eh?" Holton's whisper was more penetrating than his voice. The two of them stood above the crib.

"She is beautiful," Charles said. He felt better. It was the first birth since his father's death. Time was reinstated, generation. You had to start from there. Perhaps they were not so backward in Stratford. But of course it was only a beginning. And it was hardly the baby he meant.

"I'm going out to get the table set so we can eat quickly tomorrow morning." Annah tied a bow on Sara's wicker doll-carriage. "It feels good having Christmas alone, don't you think, Arley? I like being the grown-ups!" She clumped off in the ski boots she maintained were the only thing that kept her feet warm in the icy ell of the kitchen.

Charles wished Annah's mother and sister were still coming, but blizzard forecasts in Pennsylvania had turned them back at the last minute. Holidays should be noisy. There should be children rolling marbles over the Persian rug. Justine should be opening her present, the pink lipstick she had shown him at the drug store. He pushed the button and Tom's electric train finally gathered steam enough to make it around its intricate oval. His own big present was going to be a black ministerial robe Annah's mother had made.

"You know what?" Annah returned, resting her hand on his shoulder. "You work too hard. It's snowing! Come and see!"

It was the first good snow. Charles stood on the stone step with his arm around Annah, looking up at the stars in the eastern sky. Later that night he stood on his mother's doorstep at home under the roof of the front verandah, waiting for entry. But his father came to the door from the inside looking pale and white. Stepping out over the threshold, he stumbled into Charles's arms and then sank heavily and slowly to the floor of the porch. There he lay, covering gradually with snow; at dawn a newsboy came and tossed a folded Chester *Star* across his mounded face.

Something touched Charles on the cheek.

"Daddy?" Tom was saying as he leaned over the bed. "I heard Santa on the roof."

Out on the road, the chains of a car were slapping in the driving snow. On Christmas day, God opened the door to start again. So shortly removed from dream, Charles peered back to catch a last glimpse of his father's face behind the closing door. He wasn't so angry at him anymore.

"I LIKE THAT LOOK of brightness on the snow," Ruth Linfield said, standing on her couch to trace the line where she had run sunlight through a winter field in one of her oil paintings.

Charles watched her from where he sat on the floor next to the dress pattern she had been cutting when he came to call. She stepped off the couch and her long braid swung. Hers was not the usual hair style for the women of Stratford. That took a kind of courage different from the saints'.

"I don't trust words so much, Charlie," she said, returning to the floor and picking up the shears. "When Nancy lies in her cradle by the window and stares up, I lie there on the rug beside her and stare up. She moves her head to one side, I move mine. I try to see what she sees. The light comes in. But even that is too much of words. There is light. *Light.* Sometimes I get beneath even that one word to the world she knows. Then she makes a little sound—it's all vowels, you know, their little sounds, have you listened?—and I come to stand above her. I'll do anything she wants, I'm her slave, her agent. She asks me in her heart to pick her up and give her something to drink. And so I do." Ruth cut through the marked cloth.

For someone who distrusted words, she talked enough.

"She's like God, Charlie. Her wish is the world's command. She brings the whole world into being just by opening her eyes. Let there be light, she thinks. And there is light. She has so much power. And yet she has none."

"Well." Charles leaned forward over his crossed legs. "I wouldn't go so far as to say she's like God. We're only human. We're quite a lot smaller than God. But I could say it sounds like Adam before he gave the things of the world their names." This woman was different from Franny Granopes, but they were both artists. Artists stood aside from sainthood somehow, and could not be drafted. You had to be careful.

"You mean he can't fix a hinge?" the handyman observed loudly outside Charles's closed study door. The judge's love had been conditional. That's good. But it's not enough.

"He can read a page in a book." Annah's voice took on an edge. "And tell you exactly what it means."

"Well my, my," the man said, turning to hammer at the hinge of the guest room, where Annah's mother would be staying when she came to visit. "What we men up here know is cows and nails."

Charles's talent was to swallow anger. His mother had taught him. How could he work that into his Mother's Day sermon: A Good Start Toward the Next Nativity?

"I want the white one!" Charles passed Sara and Annah on the lawn the next morning, having run back from church to pick up a lost announcement.

"No, you don't want the white one. White is if your mother is dead." Annah struggled to pin a red tulip to Sara's coat. "And I'm not."

"But I *want* the white kind!" Sara wiggled out.

"Nana is wearing white today," Annah continued. "Her mother is dead. But you and I, we both *have* our mothers." She managed to attach the tulip and, straightening, took Sarah's hand firmly. "And our mothers have us."

"God's love is like a mother's, Isaiah says: unconditional." In the new robe that hung wide like a skirt over his shoes, Charles looked out over the guaranteed audience Mother's Day provided. "One day, while Eugene Debs the socialist was in prison, an old Negro murderer was calling for his mother. Debs asked to visit that dying man and put his hand on the prisoner's face. The old man looked up at him with a wonderful smile: 'Ah, Mammy,' he said. 'I knew you would come.' Debs took the man into his arms and sang as he died: *Coming for to carry me home*."

"Why can't you fix a hinge anyway, Arley?" Annah said that evening. "All the other men up here do."

"God bless Mommy and Daddy and Tom and Skippy wherever he is."

"Nobody else?" Charles stood at Sara's doorway as she said her prayers.

"Me." She knelt by her bed in spring's evening light.

"Nobody"—Charles puffed on his pipe—"outside the family?"

"No," she said, wary.

The next day, when Annah asked him to get Sara away from the preparations for Tom's birthday party, he decided to take her to the Rogerses', where eight children lived in a patched-up hen house. As a father he would teach her to love beyond herself. He spotted the bend on the leafy mountain road and pulled in, scattering a handful of children who had been standing in the dust.

"They aren't wearing any shoes!" Sara sounded shocked at their poor taste.

"They don't have any," he said. She refused to leave the car and he chatted alone with Mrs. Rogers as she shredded cabbage for soup.

"You don't like me," Sara said when he started the car. "You just like other people."

"No!" he said, shifting into second for the steep return. "I love you. I love everybody. That's the whole point. I wish you loved more people."

"I love myself and my dog." She fell silent.

"I had to bury Skippy," he explained again. "He was dead." Hit by a speeding car a few weeks ago, her puppy had been found lolling on the road with its tongue in the dirt. He had wrapped it in burlap and set it beside the woodpile until after lunch.

"Sara will be napping soon," Annah had said that day, cutting cucumbers for sandwiches. "And I can take Tommy to the drug store to look for birthday presents."

"Oh." Charles had watched her spread mayonnaise. "I was thinking Tom could help me."

"Dig a grave?" She had stopped spreading.

That's what a father taught his son.

"I guess not," he had said.

"We're late for the party!" Sara complained as they pulled into their driveway. "They're already playing hide and seek!"

Later, when Charles was It, he found Tom huddled low on top of the grave of the dog, hiding.

"Run!" he whispered. "I'll let you In Free." He seldom let the boy win at games. But on a birthday, did he have to be such an instructive father? Couldn't he ease up and be a mother at home as well as abroad?

"Ho, Tinkerbell. Ho, Sally." The dairy owner had pulled his wool hat low on his forehead. The barn at High Dairy was lit by flames from the burning house. Charles stood at the door of the barn and looked in at cattle swaying, their bellies made larger and darker by the odd orange light.

"Hi there! Kids all right? Wife?"

The owner moved too slowly. Was he dazed?

"It's Charlie!" A stream of water hit the roof over Charles's head; they must be wetting it down.

The owner reached the doorway and stared past Charles at the flames eating his house. "Pretty, ain't she?"

Shouting firemen dragged a hose across Charles's feet. He caught a glimpse of the rest of the family in a truck nearby.

"You're a strong man," Charles said. "That's the best rock there is to build on." His father's lessons had had their good parts. Why waste them?

The owner looked at Charles and pushed his cap higher on his forehead. For the first time, things were all right between them.

"Who was your nigger last year?" Annah had asked, after promising she would head the Ladies' Aid the year Sara began school.

"Negro," he had started to correct her. But "Who was your Negro last year" had limitations he could not quite pin down. "You can do it," he said instead. "You're a good administrator and the women will like you." Annah got a headache. He took the children for a Sunday walk.

Holton Linfield turned off the radio when they came in. A broadcaster somewhere in England kept on analyzing the Munich Pact.

"Unzip your jackets," Charles told the children as they sat obediently on the sofa. A cuckoo clock sounded and, guilty, his children sat up straighter.

"Here she is, boss." Holton lifted the baby from Ruth's arms and brought her over. "Miss Nancy Linfield."

The girl smiled at him and he smiled back. "Sara wants to hold her," he explained to Holton.

"Put your arms right around her, Sara." Holton deposited her in Sara's lap, where Nancy whimpered from the too tight grasp.

"Now watch this!" Holton said in his big voice, setting Nancy on her feet, which thrilled the baby and caused her to stiffen her knees in pleasure. Ruth came in with hot chocolate and Holton showed him the latest figures on the purchase of the lodge. Things would work out well for Holton: he had enthusiasm. And he had promised to become church treasurer next year when the job was vacated. Holton would be his steward, a younger brother such as Charles had never had, to bring him sandwiches and sweaters on the job. Not Ruth. "God sent his Son out to die before him, Charlie," she had remarked on his last call. "You expect me to worship somebody like that?"

"Zip up now," Charles said. He and the children left for their walk in the woods. They wanted to find the acre of trees still down from the hurricane. The children missed the ones that had been lying across their own yard on the morning after the storm, when they had woken to the sound of axes. Wood chips were flying; the townsmen were up and at them. Exhilarated, the whole town had run off to the polls a few weeks later and voted in beer.

"Daddy, do I have my baby inside of me now?" Sara ran back from her first approach to the maze of tree trunks.

"Oh, no," he said. "You don't."

"You can't get a baby without a husband, dummy." Tom ran for the fallen trees.

"Now, let's not call each other names." Charles stood and

watched them go along the branches. The first jealousy is that of brothers.

"Will Nancy be one on her birthday?" Sara called from the maze of trunks.

"Yes," Charles said.

"Then is she zero now?"

"Not exactly. She's eleven months."

"I will be four, five, six, twenty, and grow through the ceiling!" Sara said of her favorite topic, birthdays.

"Grandpa was seventy-seven when he went through the ceiling," Tom pointed out from a perch in a fallen pine.

Indeed. Charles saw a line of fathers breaking the bonds of heaven for their sons by swelling through the ceiling of sky. What more could one do for a son? Except one Father had sent his Son to go first! In the woods, Charles laughed, wondering if he sounded hysterical. Thank you, Papa, for going before me.

"Dear Barclay," he had written. "Will you be attending our 10th reunion?" The post card in his box at the back of the drug store was unsigned. "Rev. B. Smith," it said, "is in Palestine. When he returns his new address will be St. Peter's Downtown, San Francisco, California." So Barclay had left him behind. Charles walked back home from the drug store and overtook Tom on the sidewalk, walking rapidly.

"What's the matter?"

"Nothing."

"Hey, stand right here!" They reached their sapling and Charles held Tom to it and laid his arm level across Tom's head and the top of the tree. "Right on the button!"

Tom didn't seem to care.

"Remember how you carried the burlap bag? How you watered it?"

"You know what?"

"What?" Charles dropped his arm.

"They keep calling me a sissy."

"Oh, they called me that, too. And for the same reason, our

glasses. Want to throw a few?" Charles went for the ball and pitched to Tom.

"I hate them," Tom said, connecting with the bat.

"Oh, you can't do that." Charles chased the ball. "You have to rise above anger. Love your enemies. It makes you the winner."

Tom stopped talking.

"Chocolate?" Charles tried again in the kitchen as he set out two bowls of ice cream on the enamel table where Annah always rolled her pie dough. A fly buzzed, spring's first. Time to put up the screens. Charles opened the window and shooed out the fly.

"Hey, Dad?" Tom stirred his ice cream into a brown soup. "Chester gets a penny for every ten flies he kills. He's got to prove it by bringing the dead bodies to his father. Can I?"

"Chester lives on a farm where thirty or forty flies come in the kitchen every time you open the screen door. But we don't have so many here. You can have a penny for watering the sapling."

"But he gets a penny for every ten flies, Dad. First he kills them with a newspaper and then he puts them in an envelope 'til he's got ten. Why can't I?"

"Flies want to live, too," Charles explained, hearing Annah rise from her nap upstairs. She was worried that Tom was too obedient, would wait until January on the back porch if she told him to.

"Now next time they call you sissy, forget what I said about not fighting. Put up your fists like this and hit hard." Charles demonstrated, remembering Sam Percy's broad expanse and the punches he had registered on him. "Don't forget to take off your glasses."

Perhaps it hadn't been wise to start at the point where Joseph's lessons had left off. You don't build the kingdom in a day. You graft it onto something earlier. And the dead are next year's soil.

Franny Granopes would understand, perhaps, what Ruth Linfield refused to know. God did send his son to die, though they were the same substance. By the time Charles arrived at the hillside farmhouse the mother and father were sitting in green rockers like two stone statues, unmoving. They looked straight ahead over their porch railing at the pond below, where the men had been grappling since noon. Charles walked up the porch steps quietly with his hat in his hand; he turned midway to study the boat in the water, the men leaning too far over. He heard a shrill call from the woods behind the house. Couldn't make it out. *Ee-er! Ee-er!*

He remembered the older son, then, a retarded boy with a tuft of yellow hair straight up on his head. He had been roaming the woods since the accident, the fire chief had reported to Charles, calling for Peter. The chief had noted with relish that he had a rubber body-bag ready in his car. The drowned boy had been under the water now for several hours. Charles turned to the blank faces made of wood, made of stone, no longer living, stilled, waiting in their green chairs that did not move a fraction or a hair.

The father. Thin, bare feet stuck into untied shoes.

The mother. In her apron, a dishtowel clutched in her stopped hand.

Charles walked behind them as he crossed the porch over boards that creaked. Surely they heard him? He sat soundlessly in a straight chair on the far side of the mother. They all stared over the railing onto the surface of the pond, where the afternoon sun glinted and the ghosts of life slid noiselessly, waiting for the moment when the water would split open and the body of the son would rise.

FLAT OUT AND ALREADY Easter morning. Sunny Stone stared at him as if she suspected something wrong. Perhaps they would only understand resurrection if it were of the corn. But Jesus had come only once. God had taken on flesh and come down to earth only once. The corn is every year.

"IF A MAN DIE, WILL HE LIVE AGAIN?" he began from behind the pulpit. At breakfast Sara had asked if he had handled the resurrection himself. "No," he had explained, "God and Jesus did that together, by becoming one again. I just tell the story so people don't forget." He had buttered his toast. "But what about Mother Nature?" she had responded, her gray eyes steady.

"What did Jesus say about it? He said, 'I AM THE RESURREC- TION.' "

Stirring.

"What did his followers say? They said, 'THE LORD IS RISEN.' "

Hovering.

"Paul? He said, 'IT IS NO LONGER I THAT LIVE BUT CHRIST IN ME.' "

He motioned to the ushers to proceed to the Communion table. As they walked toward him he wondered if the whole thing might not be in his mind: the lilies, the singing, the whole of Western civilization. Their calendar had beat out his for the second year. Score: 0 to 2. He had nine months from Easter to the next nativity, but who could be gotten ready in that short time?

"Take, eat." Charles said and placed a tiny white cube of bread on his tongue.

Rising. My friends, my brothers. Call it Bloom, if you must, just for today.

A muddy shortcut through woods to Quick River, West Road was the street of the poorest. Would he make it by six o'clock to join his friend Littlefield before the county's ministerial forum? He drove past Estelle Emerson's without stopping, even though she was probably home from school.

"Nobody in this town believes I was really married." Estelle had unrolled her wedding license to prove it. "They laugh at my poor boys."

"I'm glad you have them." He had looked around her dark, shabby house.

"Should a man die before he sees his children grow?" Angry, narrow voice.

"I had a woman in my first pastorate whose mother died the same day her son got polio." Charles noticed the even rows of hooks for the boys' jackets. "She stayed with him instead of going to the funeral." Alan must be thirty-three now? Each other's stories, he was gradually realizing, that was how you changed people. Not by argument.

He passed the turn-off to the Rogerses' chicken coop, where he had driven yesterday to pick up the children for Sunday School. The Rogerses had probably conceived a ninth child while they were gone. In some cases you could change only the children.

He heard thunder as he passed the shack of the four retarded but oddly self-sufficient brothers, each of whom smelled worse than Sunny Stone. "Don't you get cold out here, Sunny?" he had asked her in the child's playhouse where she lived on the large lawn of her dead parents' estate.

She had moved her head from side to side, meaning no.

"I could get a man over to fire the furnace in the big house," Charles suggested, noting her false teeth in the glass of water on the orange crate.

But Sunny had not been listening. She was pulling out a collar from the many layers of clothes she wore.

"Now I've got you!" she said, locking the plywood door and turning toward him with a toothless smile, nodding her head up and down. The parables were simply the stories of people.

Thunder again, a few drops of rain on the windshield of the Buick. Past the Barlow place on his left and a mile more and he would be out of the mud and onto a real road. He didn't even turn to look at Barlows'; the little girl there made him sad.

"Hi! Hi!" She always called to him when he visited. Her mother's lassitude and her father's violence had not yet crippled her. What could he give that child? Whose story would suffice?

What good could come out of West Road? Estelle Emerson's boys would do fine. His own father had grown up in a house like theirs, and he was still financing his son from the grave. Mortgage checks, continuing the kind of usury Charles had vowed never to endorse, could hardly be got out of their envelopes fast enough. Maybe Joseph was right: money first, then grace. Maybe Maud and Ted were right. Social revolution first, then the flowering . . .

His wheels spun in the mud and refused to take him forward. He opened the car door and jumped to the edge of the road. The sky was dark and hardly anybody drove along here. He turned and began to walk back toward the houses he had passed. Then he saw the four dull-witted brothers in single file along the road, each waving a single raised hand. They had come to push him out.

He had been sent a parable. What did it mean?

"It was in a town like Stratford, a small town with a central street high in the mountains, that the baby was born." He remembered Sara giggling last night in the pageant as she tried to sing *O little town of Bethlehem.* No doubt wondering, as she continually asked, "Is my baby inside of me *now?*" He had felt embarrassed, betrayed by her, and then he had grown red-faced with his own desperation not to laugh. "But when I go downstreet and see men buying beer who ought to be buying bread, or young men emerging drunken from a well-known restaurant, or when I hear loose talk and see carnal ideas in the faces of our girls I am tented . . . tempted to believe that there is little hope in Stratford beyond the desires of the flesh." Down the street he heard the Methodist bells ring; Jenkins must be winding up early.

"For what good can come out of a little no-account town like Bethlehem or Nazareth or Stratford? Can we expect radiance here? Let me tell you, you are the saints of Stratford. You are a woman in a barren home who labors to be both mother and father. You are a man whose one promising son was taken from him but who rejoices with his remaining son in the humbleness of that boy's heart. You are a man who has lost the labor of twenty years but who builds strong and fresh. Others may yet bear in their bodies the marks. We are ready for the birth of the child."

That night, Annah hung a second flannel sheet on the screen in front of the fireplace in their bedroom.

"The singing was fun, don't you think?" She had delivered the first warmed sheet to her sister Hope and husband in the next room. "I guess my father wasn't so bad; he knew how to have fun. A minister and his wife don't have many friends, I see."

"People are scared of a minister." Charles reached over the screen to move a half-burnt log farther back.

"They write to us from Shiloh, especially the kids." Annah pulled the warmed sheet off the screen. "They liked us there, I guess. But maybe we'll only have friends after we leave a place."

Charles helped Annah spread the flannel on the bed. Was it really fear? The people paid him to keep alive the drama they remembered from their parents. And he needed them to bring his story to. They needed him not to drink, smoke or disobey God. A hired child. Was it contempt?

"It is not just fear," he said to Annah, turning out the light.

"What is it, then?" She removed her silver bracelets and placed them on the bedside table.

"I don't know." But he did. A pastor was not a man in their eyes; that was the price he had to pay to take care of them.

Was that the trouble with her, too? That he did not seem a man? Well, he would try again. Night after night was going by. How many people in Stratford used their twice-a-week option? The houses of the town were filled with men and women who had searched each other out, had found each other from surrounding towns, selected carefully the one perfect face: you. Locked into life at close range, they turned on each other and saw only the tiny thousand daily blemishes: war. Perhaps the Barlows were drunkenly in bed. Perhaps the Rogerses, if there was any room in the chicken coop.

"I only want to please you, Arley." But he could see in the curve of the eyelid and lip the darkness of the other, always the other, side.

It was New Year's Eve then and she did not join him. He looked over the empty field in the light of night through which he could see. She wasn't there. He began to wake.

She came, remember? You got married after all.

Yes. Yes, I did. I got married. But to whom?

Annah. To Annah.

You didn't take Nancy!

Charles put his hands on Ruth's. "Tell me again what the doctor said."

"If she were younger"—Ruth spoke by rote—"he would call it crib death. Cause unknown." Her hair was unbraided and she twisted and pulled at bits of it. "Just don't ever tell me it's a blessing."

"It isn't." Charles noticed Nancy's shoes beside the couch. Holton came down from the bedrooms and Charles stood up.

"God needed her," Holton was saying even before he entered the living room. "So he called her up there. He knew she was the best there was so he called her right up there to be with him. She was a good girl, Charlie. She was too good to live. She was good." His echoing voice ended in sobs and he dropped his face into his hands and leaned on Charles, who held him in his arms.

The sound of wheels, brakes. The doorbell rang.

"They're here," Ruth said and stood to answer the door.

The town's undertaker came in with an ambulance cot four times the size needed.

How could you betray us all?

Though I could not stop the war in Europe, or in Asia, or in the human heart, I have painted the church and brought the attendance to an average of one hundred and forty-two. I have delivered your baby every Christmas and raised your man at Easter. I have not envied Littlefield his reputation as the preacher of the county and I have forgiven you for taking Nancy, though it was a shock. Yet I believe that I have shown myself resistant to the temptations of the world during my time up here in Stratford. Now will you send me to Jerusalem? The city?

Charles tried to press the irreverent but recurring prayer from his mind as he drove south.

"It looks beautiful." Annah peered out of the car at the towers of Hartford. Charles saw the glint of sun on the capitol dome.

"I have a good feeling about it," Annah said; but when he did not reply she did not elaborate on his appointment Tuesday with the pastoral committee of a Hartford church.

"That's where your mother lived, children," Charles said later as he leaned into the bend on Red Rock Road. "And here's where I started running when I heard the church bell start to strike ten."

"And there's where I cut across the back." He proceeded to the intersection.

"We know," Tom said. "To get home by the last bell."

Charles turned silently at the steep drive.

"Hello there, Miss Annah." Simon opened her door.

Charles opened his door fast. "Good to see you." He shook Simon's hand.

"I'll do that," Simon said and took the trunk keys from Charles. "Your mother just this minute drove over to Miss Justine's."

Simon opened the trunk and set the suitcases on the driveway. Charles picked up two and Simon two and they walked toward the house. The children were already running on the long lawn.

"How're things?" Charles asked.

"Okay," Simon said. "Esther's having her teeth out this week."

Esther smiling at the skating pond. No more.

At dinner Tom and Sara behaved well, though they were the youngest ones. Later Charles sat with Sara in his lap on the verandah in the unseasonable April weather.

"Holding over one hundred and forty or so." Charles answered Fred's question on church attendance. He was the father now, Sara the one who listened while grown-ups talked.

"We start remodeling the Sunday School rooms next."

"You do a good job, Arley." Fred nodded his distinguished head, capped with the kind of white hair that wealthy men seemed to grow.

"I still can't preach," Charles confessed. "But I keep working at it."

"Seems to me," Fred offered, "you're getting smoother as a preacher."

"Oh?" said Charles. How bad did Fred think he had been? He pushed back his thinning hair.

The screen door opened. "How are those taxes going?" Sam swung through. "You going to claim those wedding fees again this year?"

"They're part of my income," Charles explained.

"Nobody else claims them!" Sam pulled at his suspenders.

"Say, I like the lettering on your new funeral parlor," Charles said.

"Minor Funeral Home, Seventy-four Main Street; you like my choice of words?" Sam's hair was gray. His brothers were old men.

"You're in the prime of life," he said suddenly to Sam.

"Hah!" Sam replied. "You don't say! And you, boy, are you your usual ten?"

Charles could not think of a rejoinder.

Sam rattled the screen. "Come on, Catherine," he called. "It was you wanted to hear Jack Benny."

Catherine was gray, too.

"Did Fred tell you he's shipping out guns to the Germans?" Sam kicked at Fred's rocker as he passed.

"What's that?" Charles leaned forward.

"Hah! Thought that would get a rise out of the little fellow!" Sam waved and went off with Catherine. "Come around tomorrow, Arley. I'll show you my new selection room, it's all stocked," Sam called over his shoulder. "Maybe my Liftmaster will be delivered, too."

Fortunately, Sara had fallen asleep.

"It isn't guns," Fred pointed out.

"We have to fight for peace, not war." Charles was careful not to wake her.

"I told the board that," Fred answered without apology. "But I got voted down. And if we don't send them, somebody else will." He rocked.

"It isn't guns?"

"You know the snaps that keep the umbrellas shut?" Fred leaned forward in his chair. "We adjusted the machines to make snaps for ammunition belts."

"But you're making money off the war!"

"I figured you'd say that," Fred replied, leaning back, untroubled.

"Now boys." Polly came through the screen with Annah behind her. "You sound awfully serious!"

Sara shifted position in Charles's lap. He wasn't a grown-up here at all. Would never be. How had his mother become one, living in the same house where she grew up?

"Sam's getting a lot like Papa," Charles said. "Funny how that happens."

I am only a poor follower whom Paul called to the provinces to bear witness to something not seen but hoped for: "Come on over here to Macedonia and help me!" So I came up here and I spoke, as Paul had spoken, with a smaller draw. Still, the schoolteacher confides in me.

I have not allowed Sunny Stone to feel ashamed.

It was I who got Ruth Linfield to direct the Wednesday Club in a nice light comedy.

Paul and the Jews were locked in jail. But an earthquake opened up the door. Paul held up his hand. "Don't anybody leave. Send to the governor. Tell him the jail door is open." Voluntary imprisonment. I understand that.

I will refuse to enlist in the army, if they come. That will cost me a great deal. I want to be like other men.

So why did you let them turn me down in Hartford?

The war in Europe was finally lifting the Depression even that far north in America. They were planting extra land at High Dairy. Charles stood in a field and remembered his brother Sam as a young man outlined in sun-blackness, walking farther off with his canvas seed-pouch, scattering. Growing smaller, back into seed? Jesus knew sons. A CERTAIN MAN HAD TWO SONS. The younger son shook farm dust from his feet. The older son stayed home. The lost son returns. The older brother hangs back by the gate. The father runs to meet the lost son. The world needs such a father. But where is he now? Jealousy, the parable of brothers. Downstreet Charles opened the door to Nick Granopes's restaurant.

"Hello, Reverend Charlie." Nick was jovial. Did he think his minister had come in for a highball now that liquor was passed?

"Hello there, Nick, how's business?" Charles sat in the booth nearest the door so that his brother-in-the-trade Littlefield could spot him the minute he entered.

"Doing fine, Reverend," Nick smiled. The neon light from outside blinked on and off.

"How's Franny?"

"Okay," he said, a dark look coming into his eyes. He settled a small bowl of nuts on the table and left for the kitchen.

Charles bit into a nut, carefully. Lately it was not uncommon that he nicked off a bit of tooth if he set jaw upon jaw with any deviance from the regular position. He ran his tongue over his teeth, over the sharp points of the molars that could so suddenly break. They were made of material that did not stand up well, of himself. Now, his new gold tooth he had come to respect; it was smooth and really solid. It was made of superior material and would last forever.

So long as he was not a European Jew. The Germans were taking the gold right out of their teeth. The latest letter from the Lutheran pastor Martin Neimoller had not mentioned that, but Charles had read it in *Life*. Neimoller had preached brotherhood in Europe and gone to prison for it. In a darkened world, where the Father seemed to be looking elsewhere, it was good to have brothers on whom you could count.

"Minor!" A hearty Littlefield arrived, pushing open the restaurant door. How did he manage to appear more a soldier of God than a parson?

"Littlefield!" The exchange of last names pleased Charles. It gave him the sense that he belonged to a far-flung team brought together, as teams are, to win.

They clapped shoulders and sat across from each other in the booth, ordering the same coffee and grilled cheese sandwiches Annah would have made for them at home if the children hadn't been in bed with measles.

"Oh, those nuns at St. Mary's," Littlefield began, having been south to the hospital. "They disarm a man in twenty minutes. I never quite know whether they're joshing me with those long skirts!" He laughed and lit his pipe, tossing the still-burning match into an ashtray.

"It's the priests," Charles said, lighting his pipe and blowing out the match, "that make me wonder."

"So, Minor, how are the calls?" If Littlefield was famous for sermons, Minor was known for his pastoral calls.

"Two thousand and eight with five more weeks to go. What about yours?" Charles inquired of Littlefield's calls instead of his sermons. Was he even capable of brotherhood? He seemed little better at it than at marriage.

"Oh, upward of seventy, if I'm lucky. Say, we heard Monday there may be a Catholic church going up in Dunville." Littlefield sucked on his pipe.

"The Canadians moving down?" Dunville was only two towns off.

"And signs of the times!" Littlefield nodded to his question. "They gave me a raise for next year, must be getting worried."

"Me, too," Charles responded. "I'm back up to two thousand, just what Connecticut was giving me when I left!" Perhaps he could only swing things as a son, while he studied brotherhood.

Littlefield laughed. "Folks up here'd be surprised to know they do anything like Connecticut. They don't believe they belong to the rest of the country."

"The war in Europe will show them. Since Paris, I have felt it myself."

"Yes," Littlefield stuck the last of his grilled cheese into his mouth. "That's what I preached on last week. You know Hitler said that conscience is a Jewish invention? Forget it, wipe out Christianity and rely on instincts?"

"Yes." Charles read the newspapers, too. "I preached about the thirty-eight Chinese shot at from airplanes while they huddled in their boat on the river."

"Another good one." Littlefield picked up the menu. "You read the new Neimoller letter?"

"GIVE NO PLACE TO WEARINESS? Yes." Charles selected cherry pie. "I bet Neimoller's not getting any cherry pie this noon."

"Bread and water. And half of that he probably gives away." Littlefield looked up at the waitress who was waiting for his order.

. . .

The poverty and beauty of the town showed each other off. Snowflakes fell into the sunken river fringed with glistening ice. Another Christmas, another pass at the golden ring. Singing "Bethlehem" this year, Sara had gotten through without giggles. Charles was proud of her, if only she would not begrudge him his love of the people, nor shut her heart against them. The snowflakes fell on bare branches above West Road, where he had left the Barlow girls standing in a crib she had long outgrown. Her parents were drunkenly asleep in the living room, having left signs of minor violence in the kitchen. They were the poor in spirit. How shall the kingdom be hers?

There was a car in his driveway. He tried to edge by it, too much snow. He parked behind and went in.

"Well, if it isn't the old boss come back from the fields!" Holton boomed at him, extending a hand, the other filled with a mug of cocoa Annah had brought him.

Of course. He was missing Nancy.

"Holton, you're looking prosperous there." He jabbed him about his expanding paunch. "A regular bowl full of jelly!"

Annah brought Charles a cocoa and left them alone.

"Boss, I'll come to the point," Holton began, looking serious and sitting forward on the couch. The point silenced him.

"This is a hard time of year for you." Charles waited.

"I don't want to sit around sad." Holton held the cocoa cup in both hands. "I want to do something, something extra. You follow me?"

Charles nodded, waited.

"What?" Holton drained off his cocoa. "Nothing I thought of gave me much hope."

"You free tomorrow night?"

"Sure, after supper."

"You think you could dress up like Santa Claus? Ruth could make something? Pick out a few of Nancy's toys?"

Holton nodded, turned his face away.

"I'll send some of Sara's."

Holton nodded again, rubbing his hands together.

"Now let me tell you about this little girl. . . ."

The next evening, when Holton arrived he managed to fool both the children. Neither Sara nor Tom recognized Mr. Linfield by the fireplace from which he claimed to have emerged.

"You don't have any cinder on you, Santa," Sara pointed out wickedly, but that was the best she could do.

On the road, starlight brought the snow alive. The shepherds must have seen stars like that, with long points like sparklers.

"How are you doing?" Charles asked Holton, who was silent on the icy road.

"I'm doing my best. The best I can do. When I see the girl, and . . . well, when I see her, I'll be better."

Snow had drifted on the road.

"Hey, look up ahead!" In his headlights Charles saw drifts high enough to block their passage.

"Are you carrying a shovel?" Holton was brightening.

"Ever since you warned me to."

"Well, gun it and go as far as you can."

"Okay, Santa." With a sense of exhilaration Charles plowed into the drift.

"All out!" Holton dropped the toy bag on the front seat and they met at the trunk.

They took turns shoveling.

It's a long way to Tipperary and that's where. . . .

"You hear the one about the bald eagle on the cliff?" Holton dug and tossed. It took half an hour to put the drift that had been in the middle of the road to the side. But then they were under way.

Charles parked out of sight at the Barlow place and they crept up to the house. One light on in the kitchen. Charles stationed himself by the wall of the house and Holton stood on the kitchen doorstep and cleared his throat.

"Ho, ho, ho!" he called, pounding on the door. "Is there a Miss . . . a Miss Barlow about?"

Lank-haired Mrs. Barlow opened the door and stared at Holton.

"It's okay," Holton said to her under his breath. "I'm Holton Linfield from town. The Reverend Mr. Minor sent me out. See?"

He pointed toward Charles, who stepped temporarily into the light and waved.

The woman vanished and came back holding the little girl in her arms. The girl stared at Santa Claus, and Charles, watching, pressed himself again into the darkness that clothed the side of the house.

"Ho, ho, ho!" Holton was doing beautifully, opening the sack full of presents.

Charles could not stop looking at the girl's eyes. They made a star's announcement: see! He never would have guessed the price would be so high.

"THERE IS SUCH A THING AS CONTRACEPTION," he pointed out to Susannah Hill, pregnant for the fourth time.

"I have to love somebody," she said. "And it's not him." She jerked a thumb toward the gas station where her husband worked. "I'll take a baby any day."

"Next week, I want you to tell me some of the good things about him." Charles stood outside, ready to leave.

"I could count them on this!" She raised her thumb again.

"Then, you can tell me the good things about you," he said. "We'll start there."

At the drug store he noticed a look of prosperity about himself in the mirror behind the soda fountain. Approaching his forties, he dressed as if each day was life itself, not just preparation for it.

"Day," a new assistant said. "Sir."

It must be his hairline. "It's not bad," Annah assured him. But what did she say to her mother? Through Jesus he was managing death, but aging was so much more subtle. It could sap your strength.

"You from around here?" he asked the boy, who turned out to be the owner's nephew from Quick River. He got his tobacco and, as the Buick was being overhauled by Timmy Hall at the garage, walked home. He passed through the empty barn; his second away from Egyptian Supreme. He opened the pantry door and then the kitchen door into the smell of apple pie.

"Time for the news?" he asked Annah, who stood by the slate sink. His lips were cold, hers were warm but indifferent.

"Ten minutes," she said. He crossed through the dining room, where the table was set for four, and into the living room, where he turned on the radio that the Ladies' Aid had given them on their tenth anniversary. Paris? London? Berlin? Tokyo? Tom ran to the radio. He was learning the names of the cities as if they had existed forever and would continue to do so.

"It will be four years that we've been here," Annah said later as she sat in his study.

"There was Hartford," he reminded her. "And, after that, Worcester."

"They were a year ago. This is nineteen forty-one." She put down the Stratford library's *Rebecca* and flexed her toes.

"I guess I'm afraid. I remember how hard it was last time."

"You can do it, Arley," she assured him. "You are always loved. It just takes a while." But she did not get up off her chair.

"They don't love me until after four years of hard labor; why is that?"

"I don't know. Me they love right off, and four years later we are decidedly distant." She laughed.

"I still love you, Annah," he said. But he did not get up either.

"If we don't move soon, we will have to get the north bedroom remodeled into a bath. It's hard to raise two children without any bathroom on the second floor."

"I'll put my name in again," he said.

A month later, two short rings of the telephone. He left the radio and brought the receiver down to his ear.

"Telegram from Brooklyn, New York, Charlie." Minnie the operator wasted no time. "You ready?"

"Sure thing."

"Request your candidacy at our six-hundred-member church Sunday the nineteenth, letter follows. Signed, Brooklyn Congregational Church. Oh, don't go, Charlie; there aren't many left like you!"

"Thanks, Minnie. Keep it under your hat, will you?" Brooklyn! That was Lyman Beecher's church, wasn't it?

Six hundred members plus a duplex apartment with heat included, as it turned out in the next mail. A hard job, Protestants moving out. He was ready! The next day he worked on his sermon of the history of the Stratford Congregational church and concluded it with a list of its ministers, to which he added his own name; he already felt historical. He made seven calls on icy roads. At High Farm he took a turn coasting on the sled of one of the daughters. "Excelsior!" he called out as he whizzed past her. That evening he took Tom to a basketball game and shouted descriptions of tactics over the noise. Later he took Annah up to Holton and Ruth's for a party celebrating their purchase of the lodge. Sparkling wine; but, as usual, he didn't drink any. He had always refused drugs.

The next day he made ten calls. Ruth Linfield telephoned to apologize for keeping him so long. She hadn't known he was short on time until she saw him running to his car. At the hospital again he sat quietly beside the bed of an old man for half an hour; the man did not wake up, and Charles left. The oldest daughter up at High Farm was pregnant at sixteen and her father wanted to throw her out. "Franny, you ever plan a surprise dinner for Nick at home, after the kids are in bed?" The whole parish was down with either grippe or chicken pox. Tommy got grippe. Annah would not be able to go to Brooklyn.

Brooklyn! A really important church; God must be recognizing his work up here. He'd go alone, stop off at Judea on the way home, make a gala occasion out of it. On the eighteenth they were up at six and Annah drove him to the train station. He had made some thirty trips over these tracks and knew how the small iced towns by the river lined with glazed trees grew larger in Massachusetts and moved closer together in Connecticut. He passed Hartford, then New Haven and finally reached Grand Central Station, where he stepped off the train bad-breathed, high-voiced and perspiring, with his face frozen into an expression he recognized from the inside as fear.

Mr. Carson's greetings were adequate though not exuberant.

Charles urged himself not to pursue false jollity. He waited for the security of the car toward which they were walking. His suitcase banged against his leg. He had to push himself to keep pace with Mr. Carson, a tall man. He himself was not forty yet, a former tennis star; Carson must be seventy. It was the subway they had been walking toward. It was not the best place to launch his queries. The passengers carried paper bags and boxes on which were written the names of the stores of Manhattan. I have come back among you; no, not yet. Speeding through the tunnel below the river, he did not worry it would collapse. Surely a sign of maturity.

"You enjoy the rural life?" They walked along a wide avenue from which there was no view of The Battery.

"I have enjoyed it," Charles replied. "My hope is to soon contrast it with an . . . with that of an . . . urban parish."

"I see." Mr. Carson's walk picked up a notch.

"Do you walk a great deal, sir?" Charles inquired against his instinct.

"Four miles a day," the old man answered. They reached a brownstone with an arched doorway. It was the domicile of Mr. Carson, abode of his wife and final resting place of a well-done roast of beef and a few beets sprinkled with vinegar. After dinner came the account of a church facing the prospect of being abandoned.

"Those who can afford it," explained Mrs. Carson, "move out."

Next morning at eleven, he looked down upon a lovely sanctuary containing at most forty people past middle age.

"Reboaham . . . Rehoboam was not the man his father was. No, his father Solomon had ruled a prosperous people and could afford to deck out his soldiers with shields of gold. At least his son Rehoboam knew the secret of making the most of what you've got. When time drew near for the military pre . . . procession, he ordered shields to be made of brass, that they might glint in the sun. Now, our downtown Protestant churches do not live with the golden dreams of yesteryear. They must adjust. . . ." His voice echoed.

Afterward Mr. Carson looked no more committal than before.

It was time for the lemon meringue pie. Time to visit the Young People's meeting. Only twelve young people. There had been only twelve disciples! Too much, Charles Minor; you are jovial. You lack a certain rich texture of dignity.

He did not stop off at Judea on the way home. Annah had the grippe and had sent the taxi to meet him.

"Dear Charley," Barclay wrote from San Francisco. "I hear through the grapevine that Brooklyn Congregational thought you a rabid social actionist. Whatever did you tell them? Our old friend J from Jersey would have loved that! Regards to Annah."

Social action? A few rummage sales! Ted and Maud would greet him like a brother. "At least the Methodists assign their men around the countryside," Ted had said when Charles complained last time of the Congregational system of candidating.

"I'll go with you next time," Annah promised.

He bought a new topcoat for the trip to Bridgeport. But it was so warm he ended up carrying it over his arm around that unimpressive city.

"What is the growth in the Sunday School?" Annah asked, sipping tea and not crossing her pretty legs, as it wasn't proper. Was she dying for a cigarette?

The sermon went smoothly. They were a hit. He would take any city.

Thirty-seven days and nights before the letter. Politics in the church. There had been two committees. The other had put their man through. "We are sorry to lose so sweet and meek a man as you." Two years ago Hartford had found him forward and overly critical. Lost a lot of ground since then.

"Some summer I'll manage for you while you go off on vacation," Charles proposed as he kicked at things lying around the floor of Holton's lodge.

Maybe he would have made a good innkeeper?

"Dear Stanton, I was saddened to hear of the death of your mother last month. I can see her clearly at the head of your table, reaching to press the bell for the maid and speaking to her son's friend with grace and liveliness. I think I thought her old then,

Stanton. She must have been all of forty. Isn't it surprising how those old faces in photographs suddenly look young? How we can imagine for the first time Great Uncle So and So as a bounder? My thoughts are with you, Stanton. I still bet my life there is a God and I feel your mother and the others have only been carried over an unknowable line. Someday the veil will be lifted and we will come to know. Meanwhile and until the greater then, joy. Arley." Charles stamped the envelope. He picked up his diary: *Now in mid-passage. Next week I will be forty years of age. May I be pure light.* He set the book in its place and went to run a bath in the new bathroom.

The water lapped around his abdomen. The fish falls into the bucket. "Oh good land, Arley, that's what the Lord made them for!" Simon's teeth white in the darkness above the boat. Was the world still clothed in light for Simon? Out, Jew! Down, Negro! My country! Only Jesus' flag said Break Down the Walls! Holton had driven up to Dunville for his physical, couldn't wait for the sweet camaraderie of war. Ruth had gone for her physical, too. Pregnant again. Who among the men would stay home while the whole ball team was off for Paris?

"You'll go, won't you, boss?" Holton had asked him as they broke up rotten kitchen chairs at the lodge.

"No," he said. "I've got to fight as Jesus would."

"You're kidding." Holton paused and looked up at him.

"He trusted in not fighting." Charles collected the splintered rungs for Holton. "We'll never know if we don't give it a try, will we?"

Holton looked down.

"Well, take care of her for me, will you?"

"Ruth?"

"No, the baby."

It was hard. He was growing bitter. Last Sunday he had gotten angry when the Sunday School children brought in to hear his sermon could not afterward name its four points. "If that's the case," he had said, "I might as well preach the same sermon Sunday after Sunday." He had soured since Brooklyn. Their lacks were not all his fault, though he usually acted as if they were. That way he could hope to change them. But he could not manage eight years here, five was enough.

Dried and in pajamas, he sat with Annah in his unlighted study. Who would want to bomb Stratford? Who was out in the radio shack checking the sky tonight for planes?

"It's your decision," she said.

He could not make out her expression, as the room was lit only by the glow of his pipe and her cigarette.

"It's taking a chance. I might never get another church."

"But you just said it would give you a better chance. Making contacts from a base in Connecticut."

"Well, that's the idea, proximity to the state office. I'll be on the doorstep of any vacancy." Why it's Minor, again. Doddering. Senile. A lifetime of unemployment in the work of the Lord.

"You'll find something by summer. I'll be fine up here. Just the children and me. No Ladies' Aid. No . . ." She stopped, and the excitement in her voice went underground, as if she were covering it with the entire contents of a hope chest, unfolded.

"Would you rather come home to Judea with me?"

"Oh, no," she said, smoothing her bathrobe. "The children should finish out the school year. And four of us would be too much for your mother."

"You feel like double solitaire?"

After cards, he grew too excited to sleep. Annah went to bed but Charles pulled on his coat and boots over his pajamas and stuck his pipe in his pocket. Outside, he walked back and forth across his snowy lawn. There were certainly no enemy planes in this sky. The stars were brilliant in the blackness, like pinpricks in a hard sheath behind which shone the glory. He used to think that about the sky above his own lawn in Judea—the center of the world. Was this lawn the center of the world for his son? He turned in a circle and surveyed the house, the wooded area, the tree in the yard, the black emptiness that fell away to meadows. The sky has two eyes, sun and moon. Why had he ever thought that? You never saw the sun and moon together. Or rarely, and if you counted the evening moonrise the effect would be that of walleyes. A bunch of youngsters passed in a car, full of song. For the first time he felt a generation older than they, a full generation out of the seed pod. But as they passed him in the dark he felt momentarily re-bound with them in the kernel from which the woods, the rocks and the distant sky were constantly being born, and when he pulled on his pipe, the stars glowed brighter. Far away, far off. The skin of the night breathed in and out when he did; the stars enlarged and shrank with each pull on his pipe. Within the seed, he could dance or play tennis or run all night. Incorporeal, he was tireless and free.

Just before summer Charles returned from his mother's for a weekend with Annah. He had no job in Connecticut but, ironically, there was a possibility at Providence in Rhode Island and another in Massachusetts. "I can see you never leave a parish, Arley," Mrs. Abbott from Shiloh had told him when he recounted Stratford stories to her. "You just take on another."

It happened to be the first Sunday that Stratford's new minister was to preach from Charles's old pulpit and the Minors were going to Quick River to hear Littlefield instead. Charles made Annah drive through town with the children up front while he crouched on the floor of the back seat. He didn't want, he said, to interfere with the popularity of the new man.

They drove past farms before West Road, where the men were probably talking about the new dam that would cover their topsoil.

What can you do?

Christ, what can you do?

"Where are we?" Charles asked.

"High Dairy," Annah replied.

Here the farmer had told his neighbor he had never had so much fun as the day Charlie Minor drove his tractor down the hill while he stood on the back, waving his hat. With Charles nearby, did he pause a minute to enjoy the sun, holding his scythe up high, before he swung down through the early hay and saw before him only the beautiful smoothness of his daughter's thighs?

Charles felt the turn onto West Road and sat up in his seat. The fields behind him were radiant and dumb. Did Jesus walk them? The four dull-witted brothers were sitting on the stoop of their shack and failed to respond to the honking of the car that passed.

IX

Brotherhood Week, 1940s

THE GATES of the city finally shut behind Charles and everything slanted toward Golgotha. The earth tilted and said Here; sunrays glancing off the corners of sheets flapping in back yards converged on a day when the gathered light had suddenly gone out and thunder ripped the veil of the holy of holies. Charles walked the concrete testingly, seeking the slightest changes in level that would betray the solid rock Golgotha wherever it might lie beneath the pavement of the city in Massachusetts to which he had been delivered. Who killed Jesus? We did. I did. Whenever I fell short of God's desires.

"You have been running the Christian race with another leader and I with another people; now our paths coincide." He would open with that on Sunday, and it would be enough for these people. They would not become his until he had walked from door to door. The wind was strong in Seaburn, blowing dirt and scuds of newspapers against his trousers. A girl on roller skates sped past and Charles jumped onto the grass. A boy with a green book-bag walked by. On his hair he wore a Jewish skullcap. Not all the people of the city were available. What did they call those hats? Have to remember! The boy was fat. Why were Jews fat? A generalization. Avoid generalizations. And don't forget the thin ones who play the violin! Jesus? Thin. Paul? Fat. Bow-legged, bald. Bald! Now you're talking. It was wonderful to be back at work.

Roller skates and a second girl flying by. Braids, blond hair, green eyes, freckles; she must be Irish. And Catholic. The wall

238

did not run only around the city, enclosing its inhabitants; it ran kitty-corner and in whorls within, separating the people into the Jews of, say, Flower Street and the Catholics of Ben Franklin Avenue. The Protestants were too few to bunch; they were draining off on the other side of Boston. City etiquette: on meeting say first, "Of what brotherhood are you, stranger?" Further conversation depends upon the answer. "Am I Protestant, Catholic or Jewish?" Sara had run home from her first day of school to ask. Choice of playmates depended on the answer and all welcome held itself suspended until she could identify herself. Congregationalist she knew, Methodist. But those other big words? "Boy? Are you a Christian?" His neighbor Mrs. Golden had called after Tom and offered him twenty-five cents to turn on her gas stove every Saturday, such are the ways of the law. Tom felt himself a success in the world: his week's allowance had miraculously doubled and the strangers had approached him before they had his father. Where, and what, was brotherhood? Charles rang the bell at the Orion Home for the Aged.

"Howdy do?" An emaciated man answered the bell.

"I'm Mr. Minor from the Apple Hill Congregational Church, come to call." Charles removed his aging derby hat.

"Howdy do?"

Upstairs on the third floor under the eaves Charles found a sunny glassed-in porch and several thin old men in wicker chairs.

"Mr. Burgess about?" Charles inquired of the room at large.

"Yup." The voice squeezed itself from a chest.

"I'm Mr. Minor from the church." Charles stuck out his hand.

"I'm Mr. Burgess," the man replied, half rising.

The other men pretended to read as they strained to catch the words of this messenger from their youth.

"I'd need someone to drive me," Mr. Burgess explained, and Charles jotted down a note to find a volunteer. He had promised Annah not to drive people to church anymore.

"It's different here, don't you think?" Mr. Burgess said; he had come from Maine.

"The city?" Charles gave the old man knots around which to wind the talk that nobody had elicited for months.

"Them," he said. "They're not like us. They won't have a howdy do with you." Mr. Burgess fetched a cigarette with shaking hand.

"In the country, we know each other's histories; in the city, we . . ."

"I mean, there's us and there's them." The old man circled the crown of his head.

"The Jewish people?"

A modest beginning.

Charles himself began, as had become his custom, with Paul and the race. First an Old Testament selection from Isaiah: HEARKEN TO ME, YE THAT SEEK THE LORD: LOOK UNTO THE ROCK WHENCE YE ARE HEWN, AND TO THE HOLE OF THE PIT WHENCE YE ARE DIGGED. LOOK UNTO ABRAHAM YOUR FATHER, AND UNTO SARAH THAT BARE YOU. . . ." Then on to his New Testament selection from Hebrews: NOW FAITH IS THE SUBSTANCE OF THINGS HOPED FOR, THE EVIDENCE OF THINGS NOT SEEN. . . . THROUGH FAITH WE UNDERSTAND THAT THE WORLD WAS FRAMED BY THE WORD OF GOD, SO THAT THINGS WHICH ARE SEEN WERE NOT MADE OF THINGS WHICH DO APPEAR. BY FAITH ABEL OFFERED TO GOD . . . BY FAITH NOAH PREPARED AN ARK . . . BY FAITH ABRAHAM SOJOURNED . . . SARAH CONCEIVED . . . MOSES FORSOOK . . . AND THE PROPHETS STOPPED THE MOUTHS OF LIONS, WERE STONED, SAWN ASUNDER AND SLAIN BY SWORDS. . . . WHEREFORE SEEING WE ARE COMPASSED ABOUT WITH SO GREAT A CLOUD OF WITNESSES, LET US LAY ASIDE EVERY WEIGHT, AND THE SIN WHICH DOTH SO EASILY BESET US, AND LET US RUN WITH PATIENCE THE RACE THAT IS SET BEFORE US, LOOKING UNTO JESUS, THE AUTHOR AND FINISHER OF OUR FAITH; WHO FOR THE JOY THAT WAS SET BEFORE HIM ENDURED THE CROSS, DESPISING THE SHAME, AND IS SET DOWN AT THE RIGHT HAND OF THE THRONE OF GOD. He closed the book and looked about him in the dark, rounded sanctuary.

He knew the congregation had called a deep-voiced, distinguished-looking fellow with a shock of white hair. But they returned from their summer vacations to hear he had gone to Shaker Heights instead. Did they find Charles, in that man's place, a short, balding fellow with a country voice? Did they wonder why he told them of a race which an Augusta Someone from another church was watching, which a Nancy Someone leaned over their balcony to cheer? If he urged them to shuck off the weight of self-love that made them hate their enemies in Seaburn as well as in Germany and Japan, would they feel vaguely cheated? Had he sinned enough for these suspicious faces? If not, how could he know them?

Charles set aside items from the first few weeks for Annah's new scrapbook:

A typewritten note. "There are several milk companies in this vicinity: Hoods, Whiting, Deerfoot and MacAllister. Mr. Mac-Allister has been a regular attendant at our Men's Bible Class. We have three M.D.'s. Dr. Norris is a man in his sixties whose daughter Miss Norris teaches in our Sunday School. Dr. Pratt is in his thirties and grew up in our church, he used to play our chimes. But he has married into the other faith and we see little of him now. Dr. Bellingham is in his forties and his two children attend our Sunday School. Respectfully yours, S. I. Galabian, Clerk of the Church."

A mimeographed sheet. "Quite a lot of adjectives could be used to describe the unique address given last night at the Rotary Club. It was delivered by the new minister in town, the Reverend Charles P. Minor who spoke with many humorous highlights which delighted the men. His talk was built around a village green in the center of his home town Judea, Connecticut. First among the buildings on the green was the Home, representing love, discipline and work. Then came the Town Hall where types irrespective of race, religion, or . . ." There seemed no end to his innocence, when he saw it in print. But what else did he have to give?

"Only five more minutes," Annah said as they sat in the living room listening to the radio.

"Check," he said. "Pilot to bombardier."

"Are you going to do this for Lent next year?" Annah asked, folding her magazine in half.

"I haven't decided," Charles said. "It's good discipline."

"Don't you ever wonder if it's any different from obeying the letter of the law, like Mrs. Golden on Saturdays?"

"I never thought of it that way," Charles replied.

"At least we get to spend a little time together," Annah said. "Staying up to midnight by ourselves."

"Yes." Charles put down his magazine.

"Are you still thinking about your mother?"

"Yes."

"Only two more minutes," Annah pointed out.

"Maybe I won't do it next year." Charles got out his pipe and tamped down the tobacco. "Well, there are only five more weeks of Lent. And that means four more Sundays we can smoke."

"Only one more minute," she said.

"I'll feel better after I see Mother." Charles got the match ready.

"There it is!" Annah held the cigarette to her lips. "Twelve o'clock!"

Charles struck the match and lit her cigarette and his pipe. " 'Til next Sunday morning!" He toasted her, and puffed.

Fred would meet him at the railroad station in Chester. In his two-year-old Pontiac. As a minister Charles was entitled to extra gas rationing stamps but the Buick had become too expensive to maintain. At first the daily dying of soldiers had never left his mind and had made him want to sacrifice something. Now his total number of calls was plummeting and nobody could sell him a car cheaper than Fred, which was what made it so hard to ask.

Will she be thin and yellowed?

Charles opened the Boston paper. The sky at least should be neutral, bombs should not come out of it. Charles could usually sense the bombs right through the metal of his white air raid warden helmet. Their threats held the groups of the city together by day, though in their dreams the citizens raised forty thousand separate pairs of hands against fire from the sky.

Perhaps his mother wouldn't know him? Her half of the parting already accomplished?

He read.

He dined in the swaying car and poured milk into his tea from a thick silver pitcher. Tea with milk. His mother had served him that most of the month last summer when she and he had waited in the big house alone for a pulpit call from somewhere. At the end of the long dining table she had raised the milk pitcher. Colorless hair, colorless skin, dull eyes. In his mind he saw her with red hair unpinned and bright green eyes. Had he ever actually seen her that way? Never. The first clear picture he had of her was standing at the sink on the morning of his fourth birthday, her waist pinched in by apron strings. The red hair that had come loose from its pins was already beginning to gray. "Don't worry," she had said at the long dining table, pouring milk into tea. "Remember what the newspaper said when you got engaged: 'The most popular boy in the history of Judea High'?"

Popularity did not count at Golgotha.

The train slowed outside Chester and whistled. He saw Fred rapidly scanning windows as the train came to a stop.

Then they were shaking each other's hands.

"How is she?" They walked side by side at a fast clip.

"The same." Fred's voice was somber. "Can't eat much of anything. Only a few sparks of her old self."

"Doctors say anything?"

"Months, maybe weeks."

"Years?"

"No."

They reached the Pontiac.

"Car looks good." Charles went on to admire its polish.

"Drives well, too." Fred started it up and over the hills toward Judea.

"Will she know me?" Charles asked.

"Oh sure, she gets muddled but she still knows us."

Charles settled himself against the door. "How's the umbrella business?"

"Booming." Fred's pale eyes intensified. "Canteen loops."

Charles stiffened against the door.

"The soldiers have to drink." Fred stepped on the gas.

May I please have your car cheap that you got from getting rich on killing?

They were silent.

"Justine's been coming by every day." Fred slowed before the crest of a hill.

"That's good," Charles said. *I would come, too, if I were nearer.* "She's steady, like Mama."

"More than Maud!" Fred laughed.

"You can say that again!" Charles joined his laughing.

Charles looked out at the edges of Judea to watch for the moment when it would jump back forty years and resume the larger, higher dimensions it had had for him as a child. Seaburn had no town center but a Woolworth's and that was not even aligned with the cardinal points.

"How's the work going?"

"My people are practically moribund." Charles did not turn from the window to answer Fred. "Even our Christmas party was dull, but we're trying."

Up the last stretch toward the town hall, remnant of a time when people had felt the power and the responsibility. "You can pretend you twisted it on the job," his parishioners advised each other. "The insurance company will never know." Birdbath. His throat tightened. Lawn looked good. A few doors down, the marquee on Sam's funeral home still looked brand new.

Justine's station wagon was in the driveway and they pulled parallel to it. The kitchen door opened and Simon walked out.

"Hello there, Arley," he said. "Your mother's waiting for you."

So it was that bad.

"Thank you, Simon," he said, meeting his eyes.

Inside he saw Justine standing in the doorway of the downstairs bedroom. Was his mother already in the dying room ensconced among possessions? Mostly memories. He put down his grip and strode toward the room out of which his mother would not walk. He and Justine nodded and his sister stepped aside.

"Hello there, Mother," he said, not saying *Mama*.

"Well . . . Charles. . . ." She spoke carefully. "It's . . . you."

He leaned down to embrace her and was surprised to see that she was blushing.

"How're you feeling?" He pulled a chair near the bed.

"Not . . . bad. The . . . children?" Her nose was larger, but her chin smaller.

"Fine. Tom's playing baseball and Sara pretends she's a Marine."

"Your . . . wife?" Her hands were very quiet.

"She's fine, too. Enjoys being near her sister in Boston."

"Good . . . trip?" She did not smile or change her expression much at all.

"Yes, came on the train. Does it hurt to talk?"

"Not . . . much."

Charles gave her a rest and surveyed the room: its bookcases piled high, its sewing machine, its bedside table. He tried to see his father on the bed beside his mother, clutching the notes on genealogy and weighing out at two hundred and eight pounds. Next to that specter, Polly looked further withered, not the least plump.

"Ma-other," he began. "You've had new wallpaper put on?"

"Cost . . . too . . . much." Her face had settled in yet another way. The space between her lips and the tip of her nose was deeper, slanted inward—you could imagine the skeleton.

"What was it before?" he asked. "Smaller flowers and more blue than pink, wasn't it?"

"Yes." She nodded but stopped midway. Did it hurt to nod?

"Father . . . mad." She smiled slightly then.

"About the wallpaper?" It was feminine and Joseph would have wanted his wife to die beneath feminine wallpaper. "It's pretty," he said. "Why would he be mad?"

"Work . . . man . . . ship." She shut her eyes and opened them. "Hear anything from Providence?" she asked suddenly without pausing to shape her words.

"Providence?"

"Don't . . . worry," she said. "They'll . . . call."

"Oh Mama." He rose and touched her lightly on the hair. "They've already called me. I'm in Massachusetts. It's all right now." He cleared his throat and Justine came to the threshold.

"Come on into the living room," Justine said. "She'll sleep an hour or two." She led him forward, with features and gestures already Polly's: ankles, wrists, the movements of her hands. Sam at least had not taken on Joseph's image until he was decently dead.

"So." Justine settled herself into an easy chair. "What did you think of her?"

"Not so bad," he said, lowering himself to the sofa. "Not so good." He looked around at the roomful of furniture held there for a last few weeks by invisible threads and presences, by words written down at the town hall.

"Is she in pain?"

"She says no," Justine replied. "But the nurse says yes."

"How's the nurse?"

"Mother hates her but she's afraid to let her go."

"Can't we do something?" Charles's eye paused at the large photographic portrait of Judge Joseph Minor at sixty. He looked like a president. Cleveland? Arthur? Who could tell them apart anymore?

"Fred's been working on it." Justine plumped up her curly brown hair.

Of course, Fred takes care of everything for us children. Charles's eye rested on the cluttered mantelpiece, where some twenty or thirty photographs of grandchildren were scattered at contradictory angles as if seeking privacy.

"Paul's working late tonight, but Hildegard should be here any minute." The light from the sewing lamp fell on Justine's hair. Mama's seat; why wasn't Justine sitting on the sofa waiting for Paul?

"How do you do, Uncle Charles." Hildegard's dark-red lipstick reminded him of the things Mama had said when Justine had first worn her barely discernible pink.

"Hello there, Hildegard!" He would help mold her in the correct Minor family greeting. He could be of no help to Justine in what bothered her about her older daughter. Martha was off to college where, Justine complained, she befriended no one but Jews.

More noise on the porch, commotion in the living room, greetings, footsteps across the dining room.

"Supper is ready," Simon announced with a polite nod in Justine's direction. Charles noted with surprise that Simon was developing dewlaps. Who thinks to prepare for dewlaps?

"Come along everybody." Justine is the mama now. The lamplight leaves her hair, her shoulders, her breasts, her widened waistline. It shines on the expensive skirt Annah would appreciate, on the stockinged legs, on the good leather shoes. A scattered march toward the dining room table and a struggle for places: to have or not to have the significantly located seats. Who will sit in Father's chair? Who will sit in Mother's?

"Where's Sam?" Charles inquired. Sam should sit in Father's chair—indeed, had.

"He's got a funeral," Justine explained. "Probably off in the rain dressed up like a priest, reading at the grave of some old lady so poor the fathers won't go if the weather's bad. I don't know why he does that."

"Somebody's got to," Fred said.

Charles shunned his childhood seat to his mother's right and his young man's seat to his father's left and chose a chair down at the end of the table. Below the salt but safe.

Then Simon was among them holding a steaming silver platter to everybody's left elbow. Charles remembered the time at Stanton Goode's when he'd taken too many slices of lamb. *Let us gather at the river, the wonderful river of life.*

A week later Charles was back standing at the graveside as the minister quoted Polly's last public words: "Say this to them: life was good to me and thank you, thank you." Her words on the air rose above the damp spring earth. Back at the house there was laughter over her last private words, to Fred: "A woman my age! I expected to be decently interred by now!" Her words hovered about the furniture which was now to be parsed by rounds. As the youngest, Charles went first and took, in turn: her diaries, her picture in the gold frame, the afghan she had been crocheting. Finally, Maud made him stop and, before everything was gone,

take something big: the mahogany bedroom set, the secretary
where Polly had paid her bills the instant they arrived, a cherry
drop-leaf table, the Persian rug from Papa's alcove. He sat on the
blue velvet sofa holding her leather diary titled *1878, Phoebe
Percy. May our love, Joseph, grow stronger through the year.* A
charm written on the inside cover to a boy who hadn't married
her yet and of whom her mother disapproved. Smaller than
Charles remembered, the diary fit easily into the palm of his
hand, where he stared at it. She was fifteen with life before her,
young enough to be his child. To whom would he now return
from the road that led out beyond home, bearing the world in his
eyes?

"Dear Fred, Sam, Maud, and Justine, in order of birth! Mother
and Father were always interested in statistics, so let's see. Christmas Sunday service, 380 present. Our average Sunday attendance
for 1943 was 109 and we'll come out around 139 this year. We
have put in new oil burners and are lucky not to have a steeple on
this one!

"It was wonderful to see you here last month, Fred, and bar-
ring the unforeseen, we accept with a great deal of joy the invitation to your 60th birthday party this spring. Maud, I got Ted's
letter today and I know both of you are anxious I vote for
Roosevelt. All I can tell you is that I am still undecided. I prefer a
more local feeling of government than his, but I do want the
country to pull as one behind its chief in war. By the way, last
Friday the treasurer of the church handed me a check of $500
from an unrevealed donor in appreciation of my work among the
Protestants of Seaburn. Yours, Charles."

TOM SHOULDERED HIS BOOK-BAG for the long walk to the junior
high school in the center of Seaburn.

"Wait for Sara," Annah said. "You can go by way of her
school."

"She'll have to walk ten paces behind me," Tom informed his
mother.

"I don't want to walk with you, anyway!" Sara picked up her jacket.

Germany and Poland. Charles put on his heavy coat. Last night Sara had asked Annah why God allowed the war. "I couldn't think of an answer," Annah confessed in the large mahogany bed they had barely managed to fit into their small bedroom. Charles picked up his derby and set off to walk to his nine o'clock appointment at juvenile court. Sam had quit wearing a derby. Maybe he should too, but he couldn't afford to buy a new hat. Even though he could afford gas, he still shunned his Buick as his part in the war effort.

At court, where he was one in an informal trio of fates, he took his seat between Rabbi Rothstein and Father MacCloughlin. Did all three brothers believe the same? Last week he had debated whether to take off his hat to the Pope. That is, to an approaching nun. Fumbling, he had dropped a glove and the nun stooped immediately to pick it up.

"She'll be twelve next month." Alicia Kincaid took Charles's hand to thank him for his testimony on behalf of her foster daughter. "And her teen years won't be easy, either!" Alicia smiled proudly at the girl's record of window breaking and couch shredding. Now she had set fire to the kitchen curtains. "But I see a change, don't you, Charlie?" Alicia leaned toward him, her brown hair capping the plain face of a woman who had yearned for children.

"Last week she actually opened the door for me instead of holding it shut." Charles thought of the one good report.

"You see!" They smiled in their knowledge of the slowness of change.

China, before the revolution.

"I believe you love her, too, Charlie." Alicia let go of his hand. "Or maybe you just love everybody!"

Charles pleaded innocent. "There's something about your daughter Betty that makes you want to help!" As there was about all the children in the court. They weren't much like the busload of Rhodes boys he'd seen before Fred's party in Judea. Those had been self-expectant boys riding off to homes with parents who valued work and learning. These dull-faced Seaburn runts went home to families so poor and large no child got enough of anything. Did such Saladinos and Webbers and Abramses really have a chance to become Abraham Lincoln, as he had once told his high school class they did? The flower of Athens was not blossoming at Seaburn High. Whose fault was it? Mine? Have I created Seaburn? It still frightened him to accuse.

Could you blame their parents, who drank too much? And theirs before them? The city? The war? The human heart? "Four pounds of sirloin." He could hear the men whispering before the adult Bible class began. "I know where you can pick up a case of coffee!" The war should be bringing them together with their soldiers at least! How could they buy on the black market when a soldier like Bud Massey was missing?

"Bud must be alive," Anita had said over the box of letters in schoolboy longhand dated France, 1917. "Because his father never got home from France. Never saw Bud. God wouldn't let that happen twice, would he Mr. Minor?" She was nineteen, her hair turned under in a neat roll.

"You phone me, Anita," Charles had answered, opening the storm door onto Bud and Anita's porch. "If the baby comes, I'll get to the hospital any time of night." It was a little thing he did, walking in a snowstorm while other men died—for him.

"They knew from the movies what I was going to say," Marietta Hudson had told him, "as soon as I lined them up on the couch." Their father had been blown apart, shot by a Japanese gunner at a distance of four feet. Marietta had gone to work at the naval yard a week later. With those wages she would be able to save to return to California in a few years. For whom should Charles mourn? Hudson? The Japanese gunner Hudson had shot and killed as he fell? For their sons and grandsons sitting on couches? You couldn't blame any of them.

The wind subsided as Charles turned toward the Termine house on Apple Hill. Their boy was eighteen days unlocated on the Indian Ocean. So young he still had acne, or appeared to in the photograph. "Here he is in his sailor suit!" The pride was gone now. The atlas was kept open by the radio. Were there sharks in that ocean? Would the blue star hanging in their window turn to gold?

Should Charles blame himself for not enlisting? For not shoving Termine aside? "Cambridge, Mass. An oil truck bore down on Robert Glebus, two and a half years old, when he ran into a street today but his twenty-nine-year-old mother Wanda thrust him out of harm's way and was killed." The Glebus boy was innocent, so was Termine, so was Hudson.

"I'm innocent!" Henry Ziegler had grabbed Charles's jacket. Mrs. Ziegler, in the background, had mouthed knowingly at Charles: "Guilty!" Had Ziegler in his window actually pulled open his bathrobe to the girls across the street in theirs?

Legless Mrs. Berry, had she sinned? "Oh please don't talk about Mrs. Berry at supper!" Sara would beg. "All I see is her sitting on those stumps of thighs and I can't swallow my Jello!" The girl still had no compassion. It was hard to keep new people straight, sometimes. At first he had tended to remember Seaburn people by the extent of their various guilts, but war, worse than disease, confused the issue. Talk about Henry Ziegler at supper, instead? It was lunch to which he returned and to Annah crying.

"So I'd been standing there for twenty minutes." Annah stopped to blow her nose. "And the clerk said *of course* we don't have day-old bread."

Charles saw his wife peacefully in line: Switzerland.

"Now, if I'd known they didn't have day-old bread, I wouldn't have asked her for it, would I?"

"Then what?" He sat across from her at the enamel table, on which lay a lunch of soup and crackers.

"I said I'm sorry," she answered. "That's what makes me so mad. *She* should have apologized. *She* was the one who was rude. I was innocent."

"Well, people in Seaburn don't have the country manners we remember." Charles picked up his spoon.

"But I followed the golden rule and she didn't! If the other person isn't following it, that rule isn't so golden! You could get run down at an intersection, you could get killed!" Annah crushed crackers above her soup.

"That's why we have to try so hard to get everyone to follow it," Charles explained.

"Charlie, old man, I thought that was you!" Galabian pulled his car to a halt and motioned Charles in. "Where're you going?"

"In town." Charles had the Turks to thank for Galabian's stewardship. Turkish soldiers had sent a boy into the fields instead of shooting him and the boy had made it to America and produced a son who felt gratitude toward democracy.

"I go right past the elevated. Anything new on Ziegler?"

"Couldn't raise his bail."

"Whew," Galabian whistled. "He wasn't an embezzler, anyway, Charlie. His treasury books are neat as a pin."

"You've been over his books already?"

"Sure. We're fine in the short run. We can recarpet the sanctuary easy. But you're right. We've got trouble in the long run. Only three hundred and fifty members when a generation ago there were seven hundred. But at least we're in Apple Hill, not downtown."

"We are nevertheless laboring against the tide." Charles prepared to open the door as Galabian slowed.

"What's doing in town?"

"I'm going to sit in the railroad station. After Easter I like to preach on things I see around me."

"Say hello to the missus, now!"

"I will!" Annah especially liked Galabian; he had a good baritone. Could Charles enlist the Turkish army to get his people into shape? He would have thought the German army would have sufficed.

He chose a bench and watched the fraternity of gatemen and flagmen, oilmen and baggagemen. He looked for signs of the war in the faces of the well-dressed Americans but saw few. Behind them he could not help but see the refugees of Europe. *We're trying to meet force with force*, he had written last night. *Dare we try another way? Or is it foolishness?*

Next to Charles a pretty girl sat down. She was scarfed, like Annah on the road to Hanley when the spring sun had shone hard enough to strike life out of the buckling tar. Under the camel's-hair coat her breasts rounded and she crossed her leg and pumped it nervously back and forth. In front of them a skinny soldier paced back and forth. Had he swung his duffel bag onto a bus somewhere in Maine early this morning, kissed his mother and, shyly, maybe even his father? Both wondering if it were quite manly? Did he ride now to seared foxholes? Would he come back?

Thomas Pomeroy was enlisting. Charles's Pilgrim Fellowship would be ruined; the boys came to admire him and the girls just to be near. Both the boy and his mother, Frances, had told Charles.

"I know," Charles said to Frances. "I tried to get him to wait until his brother is safely home but he wouldn't."

"Everybody always loved Thos," his mother said. "Maybe because he's so impatient." She was knitting argyle socks for both her sons.

Charles had found the boy, whose nickname was surely worse than his had been, in his church study a few Sundays back. He was troubled by the war and by his friendship with a Catholic girl. How should a man live? "I try to do one good deed every day," Charles had replied. The boy's expression was earnest and his hands were quiet on the arms of the chair. "For something larger than and beyond myself. I call it for the glory of God. It has a lot of names."

"Everybody loves him, Frances, because he's the best," Charles had explained.

"May I sit down?" the skinny soldier asked, his voice dry. The girl on the waiting room bench promptly moved over to make room.

"When a girl's Catholic, Charlie," Frances had said, "they make you sign a paper. That's why I tell him to stay clear of her."

"I know," Charles said. "I told him you have to promise the children."

What?

Everything.

"Attleborough," the girl in the scarf told the boy. "At noon. But I could take the one-oh-four." She had stopped pumping her knee up and down; her expectancy had entered another stage and she was quiet. The boy reached for her hand.

Talk about your hurried war romance!

Thirty-two of his men had gone to war and six women. Talk about giving the children away. Who was to blame? Perhaps if MacCloughlin, Rothstein and Minor could get along, Japan and Germany and the U.S.A. could, too. "It was a relief," the Protestant publisher of the *Seaburn Forum* had written him after Mac-Cloughlin's banquet, "to hear a minister speak eloquently, for once, amidst their rhetoric!" It's hard not to cheer for your own team. If only the team were bigger and included everyone. "I am happy," Charles had begun as Rothstein's guest one Friday night, "to be a Christian, a follower of your man Jesus, and I am only sorry that you, too . . ."

The three of them worked smoothly on the ration board and in juvenile court but when it came time to talk to their boys and girls, Charles suspected, everything fell apart. MacCloughlin whispered to his "the Pope." Rothstein reminded his of "God's chosen tribe." And Minor said, "Follow only Jesus." Despite their affability, none of them would budge an inch. Mac-Cloughlin would insist that Thos Pomeroy give any future children to Rome. Rothstein would explain to Charles that obviously the parents of Sara's only friend had forbidden the girl to play with Sara because they were Orthodox. But what does that explain? And he, Minor, had only two simple requests: one, that the Jews follow Jesus and two, that the Catholics give up the Pope. How could they expect the war to end?

Break down the walls!

Whose first?

The girl stared at the boy's lips as he bent toward her. They kissed. Would this boy dangle from a parachute caught in a tree? Why didn't Charles thrust him out of harm's way? But he had already tried to volunteer. As a chaplain. No guns; he had resisted that. "Take off your glasses!" The recruiters had laughed at him as he walked toward the eye chart. "Hah! You should try the cavalry for a seeing-eye horse!" I was a terrific right guard.

Could you point the finger at God for not watching while Hudson got blown apart? For making men brothers who fight the minute the father leaves the room? No; back home at Judea Methodist they would point the finger at the human heart.

The announcement of a train broke up the soldier's kiss and, when the young man rose with his arm around the girl, she clung to him. After the horizontal bar dropped into place and separated them, they kissed above it. And after the guard had separated them, they waved as the soldier walked backward toward the train. Then the girl returned to the bench and pulled the scarf from her head. She pressed her face into the scarf and sobbed. Anything was possible. These two had broken down the wall. Why, see in how short a time this tow-haired child had chosen the one face among thousands that could now start or stop these tears.

"Dear Fred, the Pontiac is running nicely on these city streets. Have you any wisdom as to investing $2000? One of the issues I bought with Mama's money has been called in. More later, Charles." For the first time, Charles's church study was not a drafty niche at the back of organ pipes. It was a carpeted room with a door of its own and a window from which he could look out upon the dissolution of the Congregational, if not the Christian, Church. Beyond the hollow, where the roofs of downtown Seaburn rose, he could make out a distant spire. There English colonists had built their first Congregational building and asked Cotton Mather to install their pastor. It was a Masonic hall now. In the hollow, Central Congregational's stubby tower bore the flag of the American Legion.

Time to go home for supper. Would Annah meet him with the grain of the couch pressed into her cheek, drowsy from the afternoon nap taken by so many women in his congregation? Only sleep, they all claimed, cured headaches. Increasingly, he had entered Annah's private realm, where she was not afraid to condemn. When he was upset, she made him public again and gave him polite encouragement. Or when she was upset. Headaches. The grain of the couch. Commonly among the parish, those women with the grain would shortly complain of their husbands. How could he help Annah with that? He helped the Bellingham girl instead.

He had kept her from marriage. He straightened the pile of white wedding manuals she had knocked askew. Tomorrow he must tell her parents she was pregnant and that their round-shouldered girl and her pallid boy friend had easily agreed to put the baby out for adoption and let the girl resume her normal life. "Both of you children," Charles had told them, "as well as the unborn baby, deserve more than this." He reached up to the tall oak rack and picked his coat off. The phone rang.

"Charlie old man, you see the *Forum* yet?"

"What's the matter?" Charles slipped into his coat one-handed.

"You're Squire of the Week, Charlie. How about that!"

"The new hat?" Charles felt a wave of blood warming his cheeks.

Charles smiled as he set his old derby on his head and walked through the study door and up the aisle of the darkened church. Outside, the brisk air chilled his nose and he began to run. Too bad his mother and father wouldn't hear of it! He neared the phone booth in front of MacCloughlin's huge complex, Rose of the Sea. He stepped in and drew the door shut, depositing a nickel and picking up the receiver. He asked the operator for Mrs. Paul Hathaway in Judea, Connecticut. But the line was busy. Ethiopia telephoning the League of Nations. He hung up and the nickel fell into the slot. No, two nickels. He took back only his own. "But who will get the other nickel, if you don't, Father?" Tom would be so annoyed.

MacCloughlin's lawn was raked clean of leaves and his bulletin board was crammed with announcements. Without children, the priests must have more trouble staying humble. MacCloughlin had probably been Squire once per decade since 1900. Had Rothstein ever been Squire? Charles couldn't remember. The *Forum* was still a Protestant paper but the Squire Shop was a Jewish store.

Charles stood at the red light in front of the Chinese laundry and raised his fading derby to the nuns who drew to a stop at his side.

They smiled. Did they know?

He waved to the Sungs inside their store, half their ten children at work over ironing boards; one of their boys was a friend of Tom's. America, wonderful. The sky was dark blue and small lights were going on inside the stores but not outside, for fear of the bombs. The Saladino boy from juvenile court leaned against the brick wall of the drug store with one leg up behind him, smoking. Charles crossed the street, but before he could greet the boy Frances Pomeroy came out of the drug store carrying a package of airmail envelopes.

"Congratulations, Charlie," she said, reknotting her scarf. "It's time we got a Squire of our own!"

"Any word from the boys?" He could not acknowledge her congratulations, phrased as they were.

"Thos gets a leave after his basic training!" She went off, and when Charles reached the door to the drug store Saladino was gone.

"So! The Squire! How are you tonight, Reverend?" Bernie Abrams was a fat man with thick glasses who wore his tie-tip tucked into the space between two shirt buttons.

"I'm the last to know," Charles said, reaching for a folded *Forum*. He handed Bernie the nickel and Bernie handed him back the two pennies. Their hands met over a little blue box, into which Charles had noticed customers dropping pennies.

"What's this box for, anyway, Bernie?" he asked, effusive with ordinary conversation.

"That's to buy land in Palestine." Bernie pushed the tie-tip further into his shirt. "For the Jews."

"Well, here's to you, Bernie." Charles dropped his pennies into the box. It embarrassed him to hear Bernie say the word *Jews*, since he himself was always very careful to say *the Jewish people*. Who owned Palestine now, anyway? Not the Jews, apparently. Most of them were here in Seaburn with the Catholics, taking the land away from the Congregationalists who had settled it. It hurt to see your own hills occupied by other people. But

that's what the Indians had said in their odd guttural language
when his English forebears had tricked them into signatures.

Well, this was America. That's what it was for. People came to
it. All kinds of people. We understand each other. We break
down the walls. When he left the store, the Seaburn wind was up
and Charles felt the grit blowing against him. But why didn't the
Jewish people clean up their streets and doorways? They were
careful enough about the insides of their houses. Thick carpets
and fruit in bowls, Tom said approvingly of the house where he
turned on the gas. But outside? No civic pride. Well, they've
been wandering without a homeland. They've had to worry
about fleeing. They've been pushed around. No wonder they're
pushy when they get a minute. We have to forgive them. We're
all Americans. What did they want to go and buy Palestine for?
Weren't they happy here?

He opened the paper and folded it to page five, pausing in
front of the bakery, where light came through the glass: "For his
two years of service to the Apple Hill Congregational church and
the city of Seaburn, as a member of the Ration Board, chaplain of
the Juvenile Court, member of the Red Cross and Salvation
Army Boards, active in brotherhood work with Catholics and
Jews, the Squire Hat Shop nominates the Reverend Charles P.
Minor as Squire of the Week and invites him to drop in and
select a new hat, courtesy of the management. (We hear he's
partial to the derby and we've a new stock in this season!)" His
usual newspaper photo accompanied the tribute. He started from
the beginning and read it all over again. Then he walked on.

Mrs. Berry was reading it with the paper lying flat on the bed
in front of her legless body; Mr. Burgess was pronouncing it in
the darkened sun room at the Orion Home; Frances Pomeroy
was mailing it to Thos; Mrs. Golden was adjusting her reading
glasses and peering past the silver fruit bowl at Charles's dotted
face; his Orthodox neighbors who had forbidden their daughter
to play with Sara anymore were reading it. They would eat their
hats, the little round ones. When he entered the house, Tom
would rise from the overstuffed chair by the radio where he
normally fell into an evening coma and Annah would . . . There
was no end to the rewards of fame.

Until you reached Termine's bones finally confirmed among diatoms, the dismembered Hudson, or Neimoller at his cold crust of bread. This was as self-indulgent as buying black-market gas. He folded the paper into its original shape and rolled it under his arm. All the way up the last stretch to the farther rise of Apple Hill, Charles debated whether he should even show his family the newspaper. When he did show it, Annah kissed him. "You deserve something after all these years!" she said and left immediately to call her sister in Boston about it. Sara shrugged and Tom pulled the report from his hands and declaimed it aloud in his favorite Nazi accent. Charles didn't call home about it, after all. It was only a hat, for Pete's sake. Nothing big. To be inside the city's wall acclaimed in even the smallest way is dangerous. Even for a follower.

I am Jesus, man who hunts for God in the narrow streets of Jerusalem. I am he no more so than the others. Fred's old Pontiac plowed slowly through the slush. The more friction you caused, the greater the resistance. Jesus must have noticed that, searching for allies in the faces in the crowd, for those who understood. One thousand Polish Jews snuffed out in gas chambers by order of Himmler. Jesus knew his search would lead him to death; death is the only thing that reaches people.

Charles pulled up in front of the Apple Hill church, late from his call on Anita Massey and the baby boy she would not let out of her arms. The nurses had waited for her to fall asleep before they removed him. A special case, a boy born without a father. Late for the pot-luck supper. Downstairs in the social rooms, noise, warmth, moist smells of scalloped potatoes. He had not believed in the devil at seminary, only lately, as the red face bubbled up from the war.

"Charlie!" He had grown used to his adult nickname; perhaps Thos Pomeroy would one day get a new name, too. Charles expected to see the boy soon on furlough and carried his latest letter in his breast pocket, above his heart.

"Charlie old man." Galabian was the official host at these pot-luck suppers. Charles walked about in the crowded room, greeting, giving a hand, an ear, a nod. Gradually he became preoc-

cupied by his sense of the presence of a great cross rising above
the wooden sawhorses where the women were unrolling paper on
the long boards. There was only a handful of men to set up the
tables, so many had gone to war.

"Oh, Charlie! You can't get him to sit down!" Hands upon his
shoulder, at his jacket.

There had been soldiers at the cross, sent out from Rome. As
we send ours to the Pacific. Or to Europe, where Bud Massey lay
in the earth. Or to the Indian Ocean. What if this boy Termine
or this man Hudson had been given a prisoner and told to join the
other soldiers hitting him with a leather lash knotted to hold
heavy bits of lead and sharp fragments of iron?

He says he's king of the Solomon Islands! Look at his funny
crown made out of thorns.

"Hail, king!" Would it be so terrible if Termine mocked the
king, hit him with a stick, spit in his face? Surely a boy who had
shot off a rifle into the face of another boy would be capable of
that?

And would have to do it, too, or become an outsider among
soldiers, and that's so very dangerous.

Charles made his way among the wooden boards: some standing on their sides, some already lying atop their horses, some
already spread with the long rolls of white paper and laid with
dishes. The Bellingham girl was dutifully placing a heavy white
plate at slated intervals, her dark hair reaching the neck of her
sweater, her abdomen betraying nothing. Her parents had taken
the news hard but finally agreed to give their daughter a second
chance. Mary of Magdala, you are young. Charles patted the
girl's dandruffed shoulder and asked how she was feeling. He
shook hands and chatted as he walked from social room to
kitchen and back to social room.

Hudson is yanking off the purple robe. The weakened prisoner
who stares off into space hoists the six-foot crossbar onto his
shoulder and tries to carry it up the steep, dusty hill. He stumbles. Gets up. Stumbles again. Annoyed, Hudson hails a traveler.
"Hey, Buster, help a fella out." The Filipino is afraid not to obey
the American soldier. His gun looks convincing and his ammuni-

tion belt—complete with Judson Umbrella grommets—unbeatable.

"Hello, Charlie! Evening, Reverend! Sit down! Sit down!" They take from him, he gives, takes. The paper cloths covered all ten tables, and the silverware and napkins were rapidly joining the plates. He must remember to applaud the Ladies' Aid in his after-dinner speech.

The traveler drops the crossbar hurriedly at the top of the hill. Dr. Bellingham, perhaps? No star in the Apple Hill All-County Passion Play. Draftable, but quite unable to volunteer. The other two victims, Saladino from juvenile court and an anonymous ration-stamp chiseler, drop their crossbars and sit exhausted.

"Off with your clothes!" Hudson orders the other two men to strip. The emaciated victim's arms are pulled out along the crossbar.

"Where?" The rookie Massey from Ben Franklin Avenue selects a nail, large size, from the Street of Nails.

"Between the tendons," Hudson explains. "But if he struggles, just hammer anywhere."

Apple Hill's forty-nine soldiers advance en masse to carry out the order.

"Now what?" the rookie Massey inquires.

"Hoist up the crossbar and fit it in up there." Hudson points to the notched groove in the eight-foot upright. "But take it easy getting him up," he adds. "What they want these guys to die of is the pain."

Massey motions to Termine and Thos Pomeroy and others in the front line and they move in to hoist and settle. The feet hang down too far, even when the crotch is jammed over the peg. One foot is only inches from the dust.

"Nail those feet!" Hudson is worried; sometimes the victims kicked and tore free. Then you had to nail them over again.

"This one doesn't kick," Thos Pomeroy observes.

He just bleeds, all over your hands as you hammer. The screams are not even coming from this one, but from the kid and the gas chiseler it's deafening.

"Hey, king! Drink this." It is Hudson shouting. "Kills the pain." No.

All three up, three heaps of clothes. Hudson and Termine and Massey and the Apple Hill Battalion look them over. Terrific sandals. But you need sandals on the Solomons like you need snakebite.

Hudson examines the quality of the leather and tries not to see the bleeding feet near his own ankles. The victim, who did not scream or kick, tries now to catch Hudson's eye. To say something to him.

"What's the matter, fella, change your mind about the pain-killer?"

No. The man shakes his head. "You're forgiven."

Forgiven!

Hudson, winner of the Purple Heart, could now take out the nails. If he did so, he would be hanging here himself tomorrow. Though he isn't running across the Solomon Islands with a gun aimed at somebody's eyes, it's still the same question. If I don't kill him, will he kill me?

The young man's eyes seek those of Thos Pomeroy and motion to him, bringing him nearer.

"Thirst," he says.

Thos sops a rag with water from his own canteen, and holds it out to the sweating head. The lips suck at the rag. Sweat mixed with blood runs onto it, but Thos stands silently and steady.

Charles checked his pocket to make sure he had Thos's letter to read aloud after the scalloped potatoes. We're not all soldiers, but we are all guilty; and if we're all guilty, we are also all innocent. There's a little good and a little bad in each of us. We each act every part.

We are all the Saladino boy. We stole a battery on Orion Street. Grand larceny. In the pit we heard advice on when to take the painkiller. As late as possible: you die faster. Hoisted, our feet. Sweat and blood over our eyes, the screams of the gas chiseler in our ears. Our own screams.

"Some king!" We are the chiseler. We spit out the words with blood.

Saladino has also heard the talk about this king, and with muscles that seem of stone on fire he turns his unturnable head and half jesting, perhaps only to hear a voice speaking to him—for Saladino has never expected much:

"If you are a king, don't forget about me, okay?"

It is hard to make out the reply; there is noisy cheering as the priests MacCloughlin, Rothstein and Minor troop through to witness.

"You and I"—the man's words come to Saladino—"will be with God."

"You can take me, too?" Saladino suddenly remembers that there was once something he expected, trusted, once, but what? Hands, was it? A bright face?

"Yes. Follow me. We are almost there."

Charles said a short prayer over the assembled guests and bade them eat. Bring on the women.

Anita Massey, the Bellingham girl, Frances Pomeroy, fur-coated Mrs. Termine make their way up. They turn to wave to other women at a safer distance: Ruth Linfield, Augusta Stiles, Susannah Hill, Daisy Thompson and the mothers of the forty-nine soldiers from Apple Hill. The four from Seaburn walk holding their skirts, fingernails pressed into their palms. Three of them know and one imagines the newborn child placed on the breast, his eyes shut in the peace that follows birth. The first child, he who opens the womb.

For whom the doors of the tomb stand wide. She was never surprised by her son, a boy who had gathered crowds to him. A son who had never married. Her other son did not dare come up the hill. Galabian the steward came in his place.

"Take her off," the dying man begs Galabian as the women encircle him, their wet cheeks wet against the wetness that engulfs him. Their arms are too close, their breasts; he cannot breathe. It is not these arms he waits for, nor this face.

Hudson hears the man cry out then, hears the rumble of the thunder, feels the earth shake. Could it be that this man really was a king, a son of God? Could it be that I did nothing?

Charles would have to speak soon, and he picked up his spoon. The coffee sat steaming in two hundred round white cups decorated with single green lines circling their tops. Charles struck his cup with the dull stainless steel and began: "Before we start our meeting tonight, I want to read from a letter Thos Pomeroy sent me." He found it necessary to clear his throat. "Just a few minutes ago, my buddy died in my arms. All he asked for was a cigarette and a shot of morphine. I called out to the medic to bring a shot. And I got a cigarette to my lips to light it for him. But he never got either, Mr. Minor. Everything has changed for me."

"WHOSO LOVES A CHILD, LOVES GOD." A framed motto hung over the lonely dining table of Miss Salisbury's upstairs apartment on Flower Street. Forty-three years a teacher, as long as Charles had lived.

"I like that," he said of the motto, buttoning his coat after a five-minute visit.

"I need it," the plump, gray-haired English teacher said. "With these new children we're getting every year!" She laughed and stood up energetically from the chintz-covered rocker. "Seaburn just isn't what it used to be! If you want your boy to go on to college, better get him into Boston Latin!" She walked him to the door.

He entered juvenile court past a man who was saying, "We need a full-scale social revolution. Throw out cars, throw out money, make life hard again; these kids have it too easy."

In his seat he examined his cards for the morning: Truancy, Larceny in the Daytime, Seduction and Display, Being A Neglected Child. In two hours the court did little to help the children. Alicia Kincaid's fostering of Betty had been a rare high point.

Outside, two passing children dropped their candy wrappers on the sidewalk. Charles picked up the papers. "This is your city," he said to the children. They shouldn't feel themselves alien under a native power. "You should throw the wrappings in a waste basket."

They giggled and walked on. Known, he was loved. A stranger, and he was scorned. The children must feel the same way. Seaburn was a city of strangers.

"You call from in here, okay?" Annah whispered to Charles in the bedroom, where he was working at his desk. "She listens from the couch when I call downstairs. She hears me say incurable."

"All right." Charles took the list of hospitals from Annah. After Hope in Boston and George in California, Annah's mother had come to Seaburn to die. Since they had told her she was dying, all the old accusations vanished. She had become generous overnight; not uncommon. Like storms that bring everyone together. Not like war.

"She wants a place with nuns," Annah reminded him. "They're better for dying."

"All right," he said. She was their last parent, last of the four corners that had contained them. When she died, they would no longer be anyone's children.

He heard an odd noise as he drove the Pontiac into his driveway. Sara and the neighborhood's other Protestant girl were dancing and screaming wildly in the yard.

"What's going on?"

"Hitler's dead!" Sara called. "Didn't you hear!"

He stood on the cement driveway silently. They stopped.

"We do not," he said, "rejoice at the death of any man."

Charles sat next to Annah in the balcony of the junior high's auditorium. Tom was graduating from eighth grade, one of the two Protestants in the college preparatory class. The rest were in general, or worse, business. There were four more Catholics than Protestants in "college," but that was only because there were so many more Catholics than Protestants in Seaburn. *Greenglass, Griffith, Gropetti. Minor, Murton, Obrasky.* Tom walked up on stage, a good build but as sturdy as he would have been if he'd grown up in the country? *Ziegler, Zussman.*

"And now," said the principal, Mr. Shannon, his fingers metallic-sounding on the microphone, "we turn to our two top awards, Outstanding Boy and Outstanding Girl. And I am sure that it will come as no surprise that the Outstanding Boy award this year goes to Thomas Percy Minor. Come on up, Tom!" The applause welled up.

"I bet Shannon just made darn sure it went to a Catholic or a Protestant," Annah whispered to him.

"Come on," Charles said. "Thos Pomeroy got it. And he's outstanding, isn't he?"

"Hey Reverend, you're on my beans!"

Charles looked down and stepped off the patch of newly turned earth. Even though victory in Europe was secured, they were again planting corn in the small lot behind the church. Alicia Kincaid had started the Victory garden last year and for the second season a dozen of them were meeting at twilight to hoe and to plant the seeds that came out of little colored packages.

"Betty!" Alicia called, breaking the rhythmic silence of people at work. "It's time to put in the seeds." Betty shuffled from the grass to the opened earth, a girl with wide cheekbones and light-brown suspicious eyes, strong in her defiance but not without grace. She accepted the proffered seeds and, ignoring the instructions, bent to scatter them onto the soil willy-nilly.

Still, some land on good soil and bear fruit.

Sunday: *Preached the 145th Anniversary sermon at Stratford on the way up here. Wonderful to see the old faces. Got groceries even though it was Sunday and moved into cottage. It looks as if the war will soon be over.*

Monday: *Telephone call from Galabian. Margaret Ziegler put her head in the gas oven but was saved by a neighbor.*

A few evenings later Charles hit his tennis ball long and low with an easy *thwong* straight into the back of Tom's court. The boy stood too long with his racquet cupped in his hands.

"Keep your racquet up! Be ready for the kill!" Charles hit another. His body was quick to run. His eye was on the ball.

"It's good you waited for evening, Arley," Annah called from a garden chair. "Even now your head is getting red!"

"Shall we begin?" Charles inquired of Tom, who already hung poised above his kneecaps for his father's onslaught.

"Sure," the boy called. "If you're sure you're not too old for this."

"Fifteen love," Charles called, after sending his deadliest serve over the net. He must write to Littlefield and thank him again for getting Tom into Dunville Academy so late in the season.

"You better watch out!" Tom called. "I'm going to take tennis at Dunville."

Charles served and won the first game. Tom served. Every so often they could hear a wave breaking on the shore. The world turned slowly up in Baptist Maine. Boston's Jews and Montreal's Catholics cavorting at nearby beaches were out of earshot. Charles had brought Annah to this restricted town quite by mistake, hurrying to give her the shore vacation she longed for after her mother's death. But he had found it felt good to be among Yankees and to show his children the old ways. The people here exchanged village greetings, they returned the change when he gave them too much and they rolled out automatically every Sunday morning to the Baptist church. "I wish we could hear preaching like that every week!" Annah had said before she realized what she was doing. But the comfort and familiarity of his own people was not his life's work. And already it grew late; the sea that washed forty yards from their cottage was this week carrying millions of particles of the atom that had broken over Hiroshima.

Tom spun a fast one over the net and Charles missed it.

"Nice one!" he called. The boy had yet to win a game of tennis from him.

A vacationer passing in a convertible gave a discreet wave and called: "It's over."

"We won!" Tom flung down his racquet and jumped in the air.

Swift uncontrollable joy of victory: Charles kept trying to brush it away lest it contaminate him like a broken atom. Half an

hour later he had prevailed upon a reluctant custodian to open
the Baptist belfry and he stood with Tom to pull the bell rope.
With the first note the smaller joy fled him entirely and the
larger joy replaced it. He celebrated only the end of all the
killing.

"But when you don't wear your glasses, you don't recognize
anyone and they say you're stuck up," Annah complained to Sara
at supper, their first without Tom. "You're hurting your father's
career."

"He can't have made them too Christian if they care so much
about a pair of glasses!" Sara looked unused to so much attention
at the table.

"I know you want to look pretty," Charles said, reaching for
the chocolate syrup. "You don't have to wear them on my account." Her desire to be pretty had coincided with her recent
idealism: she now shed world government pamphlets wherever
she walked in the living room.

"President Truman sent me a thank you note today, for my
service on the ration board." Charles changed the subject.

"Maybe you would just wear them for the first Sunday back,"
Annah continued.

"This ice cream is almost as good as the kind we used to
make," Charles said. " 'He who does not turn the dasher, doesn't
get to lick it,' my mother used to say."

"What's a dasher?" Sara asked.

The phone rang. Sara answered it.

"It's Mrs. Pomeroy," she said.

Frances did not hear the doorbell as Charles sat with her. He
answered it and saw an army truck with a blessedly small square
crate—only the boy's belongings. He watched as Frances knelt
beside it and took out each thing: the argyle socks, a red sweat
shirt, a high school boy's corduroy pants. She pressed the pants to
her face for a short time and then folded them. "Next week," she
said in a whisper, touching the crate with a single finger, "they're
even sending me him."

"Walter Termine. Robert Hudson." He gave their names slowly to his people, "Bud Massey. And this week after the hosp . . . hostilities had ended, in a freak plane accident, Thomas Wilson Pomeroy." Charles spoke to a quieted sanctuary. "A child has died for us, my people. That should change everything for us. For the long Lent of our lives, we should labor at his dream."

He took the baby out of Anita's arms. He held it carefully in his left arm. He dipped his right hand into the water that lay limply in the silver font.

"Bertram Reynolds Massey, I baptize thee in the name of the Father, and of the Son and of the Holy Ghost." He touched a few drops of water to the head. The baby screamed and stiffened its back. The congregation bent forward, stretching out their own backbones, and smiled.

"Here you go, Anita," he said, placing the baby back in her arms. Her cheek was twitching. Charles lifted the red rose from the silver vase but when he spotted a buttonhole in the lapel of Anita's suit, he stuck the stem through there instead of placing it in the baby's hand. She was only twenty years old herself.

"It doesn't look like other years," Annah reported, standing in the doorway of the living room.

"Fewer things?" Charles asked as he struggled to plug in the Christmas tree lights.

"They're growing up," she explained, coming into the room to rearrange Sara's pink angora sweater on the chair where her other unwrapped presents were displayed.

"Clothes," she elaborated. "This is the first year we've given Sara clothes." She took the gold bracelet out of its box and arranged it near the sweater, changed her mind and returned it to the box.

"Did they come in from Boston to pick up the train?" Charles asked of Annah's sister and husband.

"Yes, Hope came for it. I bet they're putting it up tonight for Bobby."

The holidays would bring Annah's family, as usual, rather than his. He liked her brother and sister and their families but he wished his own brother Sam and his own sister Justine would visit him. Neither had ever come to Seaburn, though he visited them in Connecticut whenever he could. Fred came twice a year and Charles did not expect the distant Maud. At least he had his son back home, arriving with a laundry case of dirty clothes and his own plans for New Year's Eve.

"He grew so much at Dunville"—Annah smoothed down the woolen pants in Tom's chair—"I hope these will fit. Maybe he'll wear them New Year's Eve on his date."

"Seems to have been a good idea," Charles said. "Sending him to Dunville." He had finally gotten the cord plugged in but now the lights did not go on. A bulb? He began unscrewing the string, bulb by bulb.

"It's all right for a boy," Annah said, "but I don't want to send Sara away."

"But she already wants to go." Sara had begun to talk happily of the prep school campus in New Hampshire.

"She could go to Girls' Latin in Boston." Annah laid out the copy of the Funk and Wagnalls dictionary on Tom's chair.

"Not unless we lie about where she lives." Charles had unscrewed ten bulbs.

"Everybody does. You can be simon-pure for yourself but not for the children." Annah settled *Girl of the Limberlost* near the sweater for Sara. "Come on, let's grow up. Who's taking care of us?"

"Well, you know what I think about that kind of reasoning." Charles was surprised to hear Annah keep at it so long. It was for the children, that was why.

"My parents moved to Pennsylvania so we could go to college. And you know she can't stay at Seaburn High." Annah went out for the vacuum cleaner, to sweep up the pine needles.

"I forgot to tell you Hope says we could give *her* address." Annah returned and plugged in the vacuum.

"But Sara doesn't live in Boston, she lives at home." Charles finally lit up the chain of bulbs. Eureka. Run about the streets. Tell them Christ is born.

"She can't stay in Seaburn." Annah pressed the button and the machine drowned out the trail of words between them, leaving a connecting chain of gesture: Annah sweeping in wider and wider circles from Charles, who scattered pine needles wherever he moved. Each looking away from the other.

"Why not?" Charles finally called above the noise.

"You know," Annah called back. "Who would she date?"

Date?

"Isn't she a little young for that?" Charles tossed the broken bulb in the trash carton.

He had forgotten to put the water in a pan under the tree stump, just like last year.

"She'll be twelve in a few weeks." Annah snapped off the button. "They start younger now."

"She could date the oldest Hudson boy." Charles wondered where the Christmas-tree pan was.

"Donald Hudson is fat," Annah replied. "And wants to be a minister."

That took care of him.

"There's the Bellingham boy," Charles said. "He's thin."

"The Bellingham boy is a sophomore at Boys' Latin, using his aunt's address in Boston. He is already going steady with a Jewish girl. Didn't Harold Bellingham call you over for a talk about that just last week?" Annah wrapped the cord around the vacuum cleaner.

"Oh, yes." Charles put off confessing about the water. "Well, if we don't send her away and we don't lie to get her into Girls' Latin, what can we do?"

"We could think about moving to a better environment for the children," Annah suggested. She picked up the vacuum. "You yourself were just saying the other day you wished Tom were still at home and that you could give him a Yankee childhood like yours."

"Annah," he said then, wiping the light-bulb grease off his fingers, "I forgot to put the water under the tree again."

It went against everything he stood for, growing up. For the first time he envied the priests.

. . .

"What did you think of the chat . . . chaplains you met?"
Charles cleared his throat and began to read from his list of
questions on the script entitled "A Minister Talks to Three Ser-
vicemen."

"Most were content not to intrude, just to be around." The
major leaned toward the radio microphone to answer.

"Did the creed of a chaplain make any difference?"

"No." Three voices over the plain table scarred with cigarette
burns.

"Were most of the men morally sound?"

"When people get away from home," the major interrupted
the sergeant, "they have a tendency to get away from home
influence."

"Did the labor troubles back home bother you?"

"I wanted to come home and break things up." The private got
in his word.

"Did you find racial discrimination?"

"They had to eat separately." The private got in another.

"When fear came upon you, what helped the most?" Charles
looked up from his list of questions to witness their expressions.
Their faces were blank, embarrassed. Silence over the microphone. Charles looked down at his paper.

"How was the food?"

*A 14-year program to finance the education of the children:
Tom graduates Dunville 1949 and college 1953. Sara graduates
high school 1952 and college 1956. Savings of $500 a year from
salary of $3,100 from 1946 to 1956 = $5,000. Interest from mother's money = $1,500. Total $8,000 to educate both. Borrow $1,500.
Pay back at $375 a year from 1956 to 1960.* That was only the
financial program. Then there was moving out. He was finally
compromised, had sinned. There were limits to his brotherhood.
The children were only an excuse.

Charles pressed his hand to his lips and couldn't help smiling.

"I thought you'd get a kick out of it," Galabian laughed.

The gas in Ziegler's oven had been off two days—unpaid bill— when Mrs. Ziegler had put her head in. Now it was really time to go. He had not known he wanted them to show themselves poorly.

"You can smell the sea." Annah was happy anywhere near the ocean and the streets of Portland all led to the water. There was a spring buzz in the streets and the faces were so Yankee Mr. Burgess of the Orion Home would have leaned out the window chanting, "There's a Yankee for you, and there!" In the drug store Charles heard the drawl of country folk. It was a city but still lovely and peaceful. And after all, the war was over. He could afford to loosen up a little. There were bigger churches than Apple Hill in better cities than Seaburn. He could have his son home to go to high school, ride a bike, drive the car, spend long evenings on the porch. He could have a church he would be proud to write to Union about. Except that he had come up here like a rock thrown from Seaburn only to find himself turning into a pebble. He must not try too hard to impress them. He was what he was, let them find that out. Why should he perform like a circus dog? Why yelp when they said yelp? Bark when they said bark? Lie down. Roll over, Mr. Parson, that we may examine your backside as well.

I come to bear witness to the testimony of the son of the living God.

What was that again?

Five thousand; I must have at least five as I have two children to send to college and my parents' bequests split five ways are my only principal. My carburetor sounds bad again.

Speak up sonny, your voice is wavering.

I used to be a basketball captain. Sort of. At any rate, I was a very good guard and I managed the team. We only lost to Charlottesburg. And I handled my paper route very responsibly. You can ask my dad, he always said that. Though my mother will tell you I cared too much for the game.

Boy?

I have to get my children back among their own kind.

I have been off laboring in a rocky vineyard. I'm tired. I want to come home to a nicer place. I have always been afraid of the dark.

"I don't care if he never comes home." Mrs. Ziegler wore her bedroom slippers clear up to five in the afternoon. When he left her house, Charles saw a peculiar pink light waiting for him. His Pontiac was encased in it, a spring nimbus. But he felt heaviness around his shoulders, and darkness. When he moved through the elastic air like a slug it bounced off him haughtily as if to prove he weighed a ton. When evening fell *kerplunk*, when evening came, he longed to telephone someone he loved, someone who knew him when. How is your life? Mine stinks. They don't want me in Portland. It's too nice. They only want me when they're beaten, abandoned. Then I go, feeling safe. But whom should he call? The old friends? The dear friends? Hello, Barclay, how are things out in San Francisco in your big successful church? Jessica, hello? Ellen? Conley, old fella! Fred? Yes, everything is fine. Heard from Sam? Sam, hello there. Hello, boy! Maud, why do you never speak? Justine? *Cain't no grave hold my body down.* I'll pass the hat, you just keep on playing the piano. Simon, sometimes I want to talk with someone about who we became. Who we didn't become. Look, people shove each other at bus stops here in this city: a small fact, Simon, but so indicative. I'm tired of working at that level of the human condition; I don't know enough parables. I expect certain givens. Is that so terrible? I just wanted to go home to my own kind; you know our kind, Simon, where certain rules are understood? And about the presence, Simon, why the presence isn't always there now. Is that age? Is it the same with you? And Mama, without you is neither victory nor pain. Just to tell you what I've seen. Only nights and days and when I fall into either of those, I am lost.

Charles pulled into his driveway; he did not know how to eat or how to pass out the bread grown stale in his hands.

"Hi," Annah said, sizzling french fries in deep fat.

"Hi," Sara replied as she set his mother's cherry table with his mother's crystal water glasses. This is my body shined up for you, my blood drawn into a fine tubular line and blown into crystal.

Upstairs he changed his clothes and avoided the mirror, where the opaqueness of his flesh repelled him. Downstairs, he carried the *Seaburn Forum* through the pantry to the back stoop and sat outside to read it. His name was in three times. Once in the listing of services. Once in the juvenile court report, when he had spoken for Betty Kincaid before she was given a year at Beverly Detention. "Will you visit her every week, Charlie? Mothers can only visit once a month." And once as one of the members on a new committee to censor comic books. Though he was not unsuccessful in Seaburn, he had sold his right to stay. Man for hire. Man seeks new master.

Not all men worked for masters. Einstein didn't. How else could he have changed all the laws? Newton, Darwin, Galileo. How had they made themselves their own fathers? Marx? Ecclesiastes? Such ways were not for him. He had sinned in wanting to leave this miserable city. So sorrow, punishment. He had fallen from God but it was better to live a vassal and repent. He got up to stuff the newspaper into the garbage can and to walk about the tiny yard.

It was strewn with guns. He stood on the grassless patch where he had found Sara scratching, stamping and pouring steaming water above an ant hill, incoherent. Is this you, Sara, passionate for world peace? Whatever it was had passed over into guns. Guns seemed to have replaced baseball for all the kids here in Seaburn. They slid into foxholes instead of bases. No more high flies over the outfield, no more timeless balls falling into timeless hands. Hands waiting for time. Come time and turn me. Charles examined his hands: the veins protruded more each year, darker, higher; hair grew on the backs of his fingers.

For whom do you mourn, my child?

For me, the child.

"It's ready now," Annah called. "We can come to the table." The three sat together and ate and drank but Charles had little appetite. After supper he chose Tom's vacated chair by the radio and turned the pages of a *Reader's Digest*, his eyes unfocused.

"Goodnight," Sara said, her gray eyes weighing him and finding him wanting. Tom's gaze had always hidden something, too. That same conclusion?

"Goodnight," he said and consumed a few more pages of the *Digest*. Tomorrow there was the Couples Club and Saturday he would be writing his sermon. Sunday there was Pilgrim Fellowship, but come Monday night and he would have to do something with Annah. Cards? Movies?

"I'm going up," Annah said. "I'm tired."

When she had gone, he put his magazine down and walked into the kitchen for milk and cake.

Upstairs, Annah had turned out the bedroom light, and so he undressed in Tom's abandoned bedroom. He slid into the mahogany bed beside Annah, flat, straight out.

"Goodnight," she said, her head turned the other way.

"Goodnight," he said. His days were like dreams in which he propelled himself toward death, flailing rapidly in a running motion, his hands grasping upward for what he only remembered as happiness, all in the past. Shouting sometimes, with yelps of manufactured joy, while something very strong pulled at his feet. The water-level fluctuated from his eyes to his chin, to his open, contorted mouth. The earth moved farther from the sun, toward aphelion. Actually there were no nights or days, only years and years in the water. He laid his hand against his heart to feel the blood rushing out with a tide that seemed to be carrying him slowly beyond the vision of the bathers.

"Next Sunday when I am away from my pulpit"—Charles spoke with the pipes of the organ glistening behind him—"you will have the privilege of listening to one of the most eloquent preachers in New England, my friend and colleague Maxwell Littlefield. Now, I want to point out to the cooks among you that it would be folly to select an oven dish that must be removed from the heat by twelve-thirty sharp—such is the zeal and the bounty of our brother's wish to hail the coming kingdom." Then he was off to Lenox. Maybe they would take him, get him out of here. Though it hardly mattered anymore where he was. Annah told him he should try to use contacts. What's good for the children ought to be good for the adults, she reasoned. And they had used Littlefield to get Tom to Dunville. But there he drew the line.

Resurrection body, does it shine? With the evil radiance of Madame Curie's pitchblende? One hundred and eleven men dead in a coal mine in Illinois. A big job for the Blickens elbow positioner Sam had shown him on his last trip. Scratched on the rocks above them: *Look in everybody's pockets. We all have notes.* Simple notes, impersonal. "Dear Wife, God bless you and the baby." Charles unlaced his fingers; the gesture of prayer was a completed circuit that closed him to the world.

"Arley!" Annah called from the roadside table where she was wrapped in her new fur coat against the wind. He was glad she had it. Even if he hadn't managed it by her fortieth birthday.

"Don't you think it's funny," Annah called. "That last March in Portland you were too liberal and this March in Lenox you're too conservative?" She lit a cigarette. No one knew them on a road in western Massachusetts. "Does it remind you of anything?"

"Annah, I've just decided not to preach to another congregation without first meeting with the committee and getting a guarantee. No more general votes. And wherever I go, it will be only for five years. I can't stay six years in one place. I get angry." He got back in the car. "Not angry at them," he added. "Just angry at myself."

Though congregations could live without Charles, they appeared unable to die, and he and Annah were on their way to the funeral of Amanda Lamb's nephew in Judea. Just over the Connecticut line they had a flat which made them late. Catherine had been waiting for him at the house and sent him immediately to the downstairs bedroom, where he washed his hands with a dry, unused bar of soap. Who was the soap waiting for now? He unpacked his wrinkled black robe and ran across the lawn and up to the Congregational church. The new parking lot was half filled and the Minor hearse had been pulled to the door. The blackness

of it returned a reflection of his face. M*I*N*O*R; the chrome
letters were large enough to read easily, but not too large, not
indiscreet, not cheap. It gave him a thrill. He walked past its
gaping door. Sam and his son Joe and their pallbearers would
meet no hitch in their effort to appear effortless. The extension
casket table would slide out soundlessly. They would not have to
bend or stoop. Smooth, professional, competent. The Minor men.
They knew how to do it. Give them your dead, they will lay
them gently down. Charles felt tired against such men. Their
strength was close to the earth, and surer. His own had been
buoyant but now his black robe was wrinkled. No one wants to
be laid out by a shabby outfit. "We are gathered to bid farewell . . ." he began. When would they come to get him, his
brothers?

"Please don't run into my party and ask us how the boys are,"
Sara said as she washed her hair at the kitchen sink. "It's going to
be all girls. We don't care about boys, yet. Understand?"

"All right," he said. But he forgot, bursting into the small
gathering of the Misses Minor, Hamilton and Ward. "How are
the boys?" It was out before he remembered. "Oh," he said. "I
forgot. I wasn't supposed to ask that." Worse. Unforgivable. He
stared back at the shampooed hair and pink lipsticks. They certainly looked as if they cared.

New Haven was leafy, like Hartford. Its little overgrown streets
were linked by shadowing trees whose leaves were beginning to
turn yellow.

"Turn left now!" Annah was navigating. Concerned about
bleeding through her white linen suit, Annah had worn a brown
print which he didn't like. It made her look old, an old woman's
print. She didn't feel well but the committee would think it
strange if Annah did not join him.

"It's pretty nice!" Annah said cheerfully. She was happy to
leave, to start fresh.

"We're not in our part of town yet." He dreaded it this time,
the work of building. But it was his work and he would do it

where he could; there are no better cities. And do it for as long as he could last at a stand, five years. He rehearsed his yearly rise in attendance at Apple Hill: 109, 139, 154, 176, 205, and 226 for the first half of 1947. He had to get out, no one could maintain that kind of growth. They drove deeper into the heart of the city. "It is a very difficult parish," the letter had added. "Your speciality, as we understand it."

"Now take a right over the railroad bridge!"

The streets began to deteriorate as they drove deeper, but not so much as he had expected. Passable little houses—pleasant, really. Then he saw a lovely white steeple that rose at the end of the street and gave him sudden hope.

"That must be the house!" Annah pointed. "Number Twenty-six Maxton Street. It's not too bad, a nice tree in the yard and a porch."

He glanced at it. A passable house on a passable street; a man could die here, passably. And the man of Nazareth could pass by unnoticed. Did he, by the way, mention me when he came through? Jessica, whatever has become of you? Do you wear a brown print to hide the blood? He would be fifty when he left this new parish.

If they called him.

"We're so happy to see you," the committee chairman said. For the first time, he was a man younger than Charles. "And how was the long trip down?"

Charles opened the window in his study. Annah had gone out to spread a blanket on the snowy ground to catch the magazines he would throw down. She wasn't yet visible through his open window and he set aside a last clipping for her scrapbook.

"Popular Pastor Leaves for New Haven. December 27, The Reverend Charles P. Minor expressed tonight the wish that his parents could have lived to be present at his farewell reception at the Apple Hill Congregational Church. Extra chairs had to be set up in the aisles. Rabbi Saul Rothstein brought the greetings of the Jewish community and compared the departure of Mr. Minor to Abraham of old in accepting a call to other parts of the world.

The Right Reverend Harold MacCloughlin brought the greetings of the Catholic community and commented that Seaburn had lost a real shepherd, one of God's own. 'Jesus walks with Mr. Charles,' he concluded. The clerk of the church, S. I. Galabian, mentioned Mr. Minor's 10,000 pastoral calls and said, 'We came to depend upon his stewardship as we do the daylight.' " A good thing they had not asked the organist to speak. She would have been hard-pressed to credit his musicology.

Perhaps nobody sees beyond himself. Perhaps brotherhood can't be. Call it original sin. Would Germany have listened to brotherhood if America had tried it? How much larger than Hartford was New Haven, anyway? He could point the finger at himself for asking that, for leaving.

"I'm ready, Arley!" Annah called, and Charles started with a handful of his hoarded *Christian Centurys*. He leaned from the window and tossed them out. It was simpler than carrying them down, and they lay against the air like birds, some falling flat, some plummeting at an angle, some opening and flapping as they flew.

X

Midcentury

"I JUST HOPE they have a halfway decent Young People's group," Sara said from the back seat. Charles caught sight of her in the rear-view mirror and pressed harder on the gas. It was his job to get her to proper fields; he could not afford to let her blossom here on the highway through Massachusetts. For the second time he passed the red moving van that was carrying Polly Percy's mahogany and Annah Minor's maple southward over ice. When had it passed him?

"The Pilgrim Fellowship in Seaburn was awful." Sara fixed her lips in the new sultry expression she had been perfecting for months and that now hung fully realized above Charles in the rear-view mirror.

Why didn't you roll up your sleeves and pitch in? Why didn't you knock on the door and say "Daddy, here is a wonderful Young People's group which I have built for you?" But he drove, silent.

"Sara," said Annah, "you could help Daddy out in New Haven by pitching in and building up the Pilgrim Fellowship."

Yes, Annah voiced accusations for him, allowing him to retain a public innocence. And he spoke for her the affirmations she dared not risk. Fair enough. But no answer from his daughter.

"Father," Tom said from his right, "you could go over fifty without getting arrested, you know."

"I know," Charles said. "But can I do it without getting killed?" He had slowed down past Meriden, where Sara and Annah fought over whether Sara should become a nurse (and meet nice doctors) or a doctor. "I never feel right about women doctors," Annah had said to support her own choice in the matter. Pace was critical, not just on icy roads. He must cut down from fifty calls a week to forty once he got to New Haven. Must begin strong but not overshoot. There was a steeple again, decaying this time, not just peeling. Six months 'til it fell down? Two years 'til the paint streaked completely off? Best to open with a single fund-drive to both undergird and paint it; nobody noticed when you had fixed your rotten understructure.

"I hope my bedroom is as big as Tom's." Sara took up her refrain. "Last time he got the big one. And if it's papered pink and blue again, I'll just die."

"Who cares? I'll be back at school in a week, anyway. I don't even live here anymore." Tom slumped against the window.

Where?

The highway arrived at flat land that spread out and ran into sand beside the unimaginably heavy waters of the ocean that were pushing with more trouble than joy into the inlet between Connecticut and Long Island. Charles stepped on the accelerator; far in the distance he saw the red van again. Should he race it? Or hold steady?

Sara's room was pink and blue, after all, and she retired to it in a stunned rage. "It's smaller than I remembered." Annah stood in the living room while empires shrank around her. An orange glow from globe lights lit the dark woodwork and brought twilight indoors to mix with a lost, faint smell of winter coats. Snow united the back yards between Maxton and Trebor streets and restored them to the field they once had been. Indoors they unpacked and laid out their two Persian rugs, which filled the living room and dining room. Other people lived for furniture, homes, amusement. Their own house began to take shape, to look nice. But bare trees scratched at the side of the house as they moved furniture experimentally about. My house, Charles stated to himself, is in the belly of a whale. And I am Jonah come here against my better judgment. Come to fight a battle I can never win.

Down the street the church was white and soaring and four times the size of Judea Congregational. Its steeple rose over the roofs of corset shops and drug stores and above a nervous coastal people, dark with amulets, who skittered about the winter streets. He made a few calls by car the next morning but after lunch left the Pontiac in the small parking lot behind the church. By foot he would explore the foreign city that lay before him like the Nineveh Jonah had tried so hard to avoid. No Plymouth of the Anglo-Saxons, no Runnymede. God had chased him out of there. He turned onto Station Street and, without opening his address book for help, he tried to smell out his own sheep. Which were they? Brick apartments at a corner, no lawns and a well-dressed woman: Jewish. Attached two-family houses with freezing bedspreads hanging out on front porches: Italian Catholics? Slovaks? No, a girl with dirty knees and no socks opening a door, pale-faced and brown-haired: English, Protestant. His own kind. She waved at Charles and he waved back.

Charles turned off Station onto Holbrook. Toward him walked Negroes with hats pulled over their ears. They wore their jackets directly over their undershirts, producing a white triangle between their lapels. Liquor stores doubled and tripled along the street. "I'd feel hard-pressed," he'd told them in Seaburn, "to turn away a Negro family who wanted to join our church." But there hadn't been any in Seaburn. Would a Negro come up to him now, grasp him by his lapels, hold him pressed against a fig tree and stare with him at brown-skinned Nineveh, begging to join the Banner Avenue Congregational Church?

Called Banner because its great crusading minister of half a century past had hung the banner "Free Seats" across a street. He had raised a choir and preached to the hundreds of men who thronged in for the warmth and singing and who then thronged out to buy shirts and go off booze. The crusader had finally moved from his tenement downtown and gone off to Southside, Chicago, for another springtime in the kingdom of God. A real saint, penniless. But Charles wanted more Persian rugs and pretty dresses for Annah, roast beef on Sunday; Justine might come to visit in her expensive woolens. How to get through the eye of the needle? Oh, don't send me to Nineveh, Boss! I been there! I seen it!

Simon had left the Minor homestead in Judea and gone to a suburb of Chicago, too. The letter had surprised Charles, both the letters. The irritated one from Catherine at the old house, describing how Simon had just up and left them after all those years as a family fixture, and the happy one from Simon. "My new people are very rich which means there are more in help and the work is easier. No oak, either. Esther will come out in a few months and I am sure she'll love the lake, it's beautiful. Stop by if you ever come west." It was the first letter Simon had ever written Charles. An apology?

On Station, Charles passed the Bide-A-Wee Bar, above which the Filmores lived. He had been there that morning: four small girls sitting in step-stool order at the kitchen table waiting for the youngest's birthday cake. Bill Filmore was going to get out. He had cut his budget in half for the next ten years to save for the down payment on a house outside the city. Should Banner Avenue Congregational do the same? I WENT INTO THE HOUSE OF THE LORD, to carry it away.

Before he could decide, Charles had to get the church into shape. Forty-eight new members for 1948. That sort of slogan got people going. He needed young men to launch it, maybe Junior Metcalf? "Is that you, Doctor Livingstone?" Junior whispered it now and then to his white colleagues when the bells rang in the high school and the corridors darkened with half-grown Negroes. At least Junior stayed in the city to work. The eye of the needle expands to hold the universe; it spins, it twists, it hovers over the city. Any city. Nagasaki? "Thousands seared to death," the newspaper, damp with ocean spray, had said that summer at the shore. Plymouth? He could have rested there. It was Jesus who broke down dividing walls, not Charles P. Minor. He left, he fled to his own kind. Or tried to. It hadn't worked. He felt very far from home; though he was actually much nearer than in his last two parishes.

Within whose safe gaze did he walk, known just as the sparrow is? His steps were circling him back to the church corner and he saw lights on inside the parish house. It must be the Yale student who served as the church's assistant minister. The young man had endured hours of struggle today to write a sermon he wouldn't deliver until next month. It was flattering to have an apprentice, but expensive. Charles had already listed the assistant's salary as one of the first cuts from next year's budget. The second was to reduce the aged custodian's hours from full- to part-time. Already the soggy winter lawn looked inferior to that of the Flannagan Funeral Home across the street. Charles stopped for a traffic light in front of Walter's Drugs and studied the sidewalks littered with gum wrappers and beer cans. Should he install trash baskets on the church lawn? Too ugly? Would it take a year to train people to pick up trash? So rudimentary, the lessons needed!

It was not the ends of the earth. A mile downtown and he could stand at Church and Chapel on the site of the trolley platform where he had changed every August from the Chester to the Lighthouse Point trolley. The thing was, neither of his parents knew he was here. He crossed the street to the church parking lot and drove the short way down Maxton Street to Annah, who was ripping dirty linoleum from the pantry floor.

"You would think," she said, "they'd take care of their own dirt. They didn't have to cart us down from Massachusetts to do it!"

"Yes," he agreed. "They ought to have provided clean linoleum."

"What?" Annah stopped ripping. "I never heard you find fault before!"

"Fresh linoleum is not too much to ask." He stooped to help her rip. *Since leaving Seaburn for my own selfish reasons and knowing I was guilty,* he wrote in his diary that night, *I can more easily see when I'm not. And when others are.* He did not add that the more accurately he could accuse others, the easier it was to forgive them. Though not himself.

"No, WE'LL NEVER MOVE OUT," Rosamond Wilfred assured Charles in a spacious living room quieted with half an acre of Persian rugs and fitted at random stations with marble-topped tables. "The fact is, the superintendent of schools can't move out, it's written into city law. We have to live in town."

"Oh," Charles replied, sipping tea from the delicate China cup, amazed at his continued innocence. Still not for you the wisdom of snakes, boy? But even the school superintendent?

"So," she smiled. "We live out here on Bellevue Avenue as near the city line as possible. Roger goes to grade school, though I must say, the element is already moving along the avenue. His best friend is named Ronald Rothenberg, I believe. And we send the girls out to the Nottingham School." She picked up a sugar wafer from a plate brought in by a Scottish girl.

I have come here on an errand of the Lord.

"Will you have another cookie, Charles?" Her smile was sweet, her blonded hair carefully arranged, her dress generally understated. In Seaburn it had been cheap cuts and flashy colors, Annah pointed out, whereas in New Haven it was all tweeds and pastel suggestion. Quite beyond her clever purse. A pastor must meet with women but not come to know these things. He must know nothing among them but Christ and him crucified. How to begin such knowledge over a cup of tea? Over tinned biscuits imported from England? Over such assumptions as Rosamond's? As his?

"And where are you sending your daughter?" Rosamond raised the teapot in collusion.

"She'll be attending Thatcher in the fall," Charles answered, convicted and found guilty. The tuition-free school, the one you had to be smart to get into.

"A lovely school," Rosamond allowed. "The Thatcher girls, of course, are—one might say—all too smart, though, perhaps, there's no being *too* smart?" She smiled, twisted into a protective posture and was wrapped in nets and caught in a thousand minor misdemeanors that did not add up to sin. She was his congregant, a woman whom he had come to save. If only he were a priest they would not have to look at one another but could co-exist in a dark corner where she might bring the secrets he had no desire to elicit here. Not over Persian rugs, over spilled milk. *There is a green hill far away without a city wall*: would that do the trick? Would that turn Rosamond Wilfred toward him, seeking? For without that turning on her part, he had no power. *What a friend we have in Jesus:* how about that?

"And your son?" Rosamond suspended her chewing to hear his reply.

"A junior," Charles confessed. "At a school in New Hampshire."

Charles noticed tea leaves in the bottom of the cup; they arranged themselves in a swirl that he, accustomed to tea bags, had not seen for a long time. Dear Simon, it is seven years now since I have seen tea leaves in the bottom of my cup.

Along Bellevue the cars ran at a good clip and there was no traffic light. Charles waited several minutes before starting toward his humble Pontiac on the far side. He had a sudden premonition that with his next footstep he would start the second, the downhill part of his life, closing the circle. But that could not be. There is no diminishment. There is only progress, only going forward. Alicia Kincaid kept him posted on it: "Betty writes me she is learning to sew and eat a lot of different kinds of vegetables. She misses your visits but she says she has learned from her additional six-month detention at Beverly that it is time she learn to obey the laws." Didn't that prove it?

The houses on Findlay Street were closely spaced two-family affairs hugged by concrete paths leading to concrete back yards where garbage pails stood ready for anything. A good thing, as they were due to fill up: the Negroes had already bought at the south end of the street. Sally Metcalf led Charles through beaded curtains into her dark living room, where the baby stood clutching the chintz of a chair cover. Charles stooped to hold out his finger but the boy shied away.

"He's just this week become afraid of strangers," Sally explained, pointing to the couch, where Charles might sit. "Right on the button, too. The book says to expect fear of strangers at nine months."

Does it say when it will end?

Charles set his Squire Shop fedora on the couch. "How is the night shift working out?"

"Okay so far." Sally sat down. "Junior feeds him and drops

him off with a woman down the street. I sleep 'til noon and pick him up."

"Do you get enough sleep?" Charles held his hand out toward the baby, who was examining him cautiously. A young mother needs strength.

"More than I did the other way!" Sally bent to tie her saddle shoes.

"How about the baby?" Charles held out his hat to the baby, who advanced circuitously. A baby needs its mother.

"Fine!" Sally said. "He sees a lot more of his father, and his mother is twice as good-humored as she used to be."

"And Junior?" A man needs his wife. Should women work?

"He's glad I'm working, if that's what you mean." Sally's voice took on annoyance. "My salary will be our down payment for a house in Bellingburn."

Oh. The hat, which Charles had pushed to the edge of the couch, fell over and the baby screeched and reached for it, drooling.

"Bellingburn? I was just going to ask Junior if he'd become a deacon!"

"Oh, we'll keep coming back to Banner," Sally said. "But we can't raise a baby here, not with the element that's moving in!"

"I do hope you'll keep on at Banner," Charles said. "Though Bellingburn will probably build its own Congregational church some day and you'll want to attend in your own neighborhood." He retrieved his hat and brushed the dampness of drool off it with his coat sleeve. The element. Sally was the youngest person he had heard use that word. A changeable item meaning "stranger"? Element ninety-seven on the periodic table, somewhere past uranium and twice as deadly?

Pete Allenby's half-timbered Elizabethan place stood out past the Wilfreds' on Bellevue Avenue. Charles drove up its semicircle of pebbles and came to a stop. An Irish setter greeted him; there had been no grandeur like this in Seaburn. But he missed his old parishioners, people who already trusted him. You could get to work faster that way.

Allenby opened the door to lead Charles through the house to a glassed-in porch that looked upon a tennis court and over a darkening lawn to tall trees at its distant rim. On the porch Allenby paused by a flower cart that served as a summer bar.

"Can I get you something, Charlie?" His tone could mean either a) I know you don't but it's polite to ask or b) of course you do because all the ministers do now. Very smooth; no wonder Allenby had made a killing in finance.

"No thank you, Pete," Charles said. "I took the pledge when I was six."

Pete raised his eyebrows but pointed to a chair for Charles before lowering himself onto bent iron and crossing one leg over the other.

"You play tennis, Charlie?" Allenby tried again.

"Not so much as I used to, but my boy does." Charles settled into a wicker chair.

"Bring him around anytime, by all means." Pete eyed the bar but did not fill a glass for himself.

"Pete, I came to get your informal opinion. Do you think we could raise a hundred thousand dollars, pay off our debt in one lump and invest the rest to get interest enough to cover our annual deficit?"

"Hold on! Why pay off the debt so fast?" Pete cleared his throat.

"When many more of our people have moved out to the suburbs, we're going to have to do something. Maybe we'll sell and move out to Bellingburn, too. But we can't sell with holes in our pockets."

"Center Church is doing fine despite the element." Pete fingered the pack of cigarettes resting on the arm of his chair.

Which one did he mean? Was there a third?

"Center Church has long ties with the university," Charles countered. "It'll be the last Congregational church to go." He felt thirsty. "First Church could drop out in five or ten years. And Banner even before that. Right now, we've got the people but First has got the money. It's neck and neck. Now"—Charles sat forward in his chair—"how much capital do you think we would need if we were to clean ourselves up and merge with First?" He already knew the answer, had the total written in cramped careful numbers on a piece of paper right in his pocket.

"Say, before we go over it"—he interrupted Allenby's response of silence—"have you got a ginger ale over there?"

UPSTAIRS IN HIS PARSONAGE STUDY Charles turned the wire recorder back on reluctantly. It embarrassed him to listen to his pinched voice, where the accusations he did not make seemed to have gathered. Moving carefully so as not to erase himself, he picked up the notebook, whose endpapers daily advised "test of death, hold mirror to mouth; for mad dog or snake bites . . ." He opened to his notes and read aloud: "A visitor to New Haven asks on a Sunday morning where are all the people. 'Why, the Jews are in their shops,' he is told. 'The Roman Catholics are at church and the Negroes are out at Lighthouse Point. The Protestants? Oh, they're asleep.' " Trying to take a quick breath, Charles discovered he had no more room for breath and rushed on. "We cannot sleep. The acids of paganism are upon us. When God goes, we turn to cheap, physical thrills." His voice had risen so high and small that Charles switched off the machine again. Could he do nothing right? No, it was his lot to work hard for little reward.

After a vanishing squeal, he heard himself speaking from another season. "Faith begins with discipline." His voice over the wire was disembodied and incorruptible. He must have pushed "replay" instead of "off." Was "incorruptible" simply a synonym for "invisible"? "My father milked cows every morning and evening; he had a great faith in the discipline of work. He made surprise visits on me at the centu . . . cemetery to see if I were truly earning the twelve and a half cents he paid me. And though he may not have had a firm conviction in the resurrection, he knew you had to set the ground for any miracle. Once, when our church was without a pastor, he bade me raid its vestry for the metal letters needed so he might set up 'He Is Risen' on the bulletin board. He had a dignity that seems to have passed from the world with his generation." The wire reached the end of its spool and spun raggedly, its sharp wild end flailing the air.

Annah's footsteps up the stairs, her knuckles knocking on his door.

"Arley? It's the mail. You busy?"

"Come on in," he said, switching off the machine. "I've just finished."

"Have you got a few minutes?" Annah sat on the ottoman and tucked up the scarf she wrapped around her hair for the morning's housework. Her shoulders had acquired a slight roundness.

"Shoot." He gathered papers into stacks.

"I've been working on a plan. Why don't I go to work? Tom's never home more than a few weeks a year and Sara's gone off the whole day at Thatcher. Pretty soon she'll start summer jobs, too. Nobody needs me to be at home all day."

"I always need you at home, Annah. And at church. Hey! You could be my secretary! We'll never have room for a real secretary in the Banner budget!"

"But it's money I want, Arley. We can bank it for . . ."

"Maybe I could arrange a *little* from next year's."

"Would that look right?"

Charles arranged the stacks of papers side by side.

"The thing is, Arley, I get frightened when I look ahead. Don't you?" She folded her hands and looked up at him. "When you come down to it, we don't own a thing, do we? Who could take care of us if need be? Not the children. I don't want to have to do what my mother did."

"I've always thought we could build a little house on the old farm in Judea." He swept pipe tobacco off his cleaned desk. "I know how to build cellar walls myself."

"How could we build? We don't pay off their college until nineteen sixty. That's twelve years. And if we retire in 'sixty-seven, that would only give us seven years to save."

With walls built, with dirt heaped up around him to protect his borders from the comer, was that not the perfect way to start a burial mound? Best to remain without worldly goods. Unencumbered, disembodied as you can get. "I need you at home," he said. "It doesn't look right for the minister's wife to work. We have to be respected."

"Who respects you if you don't have a house?" she answered. "My father would be surprised to see me living in this place." She pointed beyond the walls to the street. "He expected me to end up in one of those big places on Hathaway."

"What?" he turned to her. "You never liked those big houses we had in Shiloh and Stratford!"

"Well, they were hard to clean." She stood up and walked toward the bookcase. "My first choice would be one of those nice ranch houses they build in Bellingburn. Arley"—her tone changed and she walked toward him—"we could end up renting somebody's upstairs bedroom. They would put in a kitchen in the corner of it. I've seen it. I know. Aren't you afraid to grow old without any walls around you?"

Yes. But it's worse with. Still, he could hardly keep from nodding.

"Please don't get a job, Annah. I need at least one full-time supporter."

Forty-nine new members for 'forty-nine! It had worked one year, why not again? Charles kept his calls down to forty a week. He drove about the city, looking at it from the high floors of downtown stores, from the rocks of West Haven, from the water's edge. It would have been wrong to transplant Tom to New Haven; last time they had visited him in Dunville, they found him on an enormous green ballfield. "Hey Minor!" Charles had turned, startled. But of course the call had been for Tom. After that, how could Charles order him here?

"Dear Dad," Tom wrote from school. "How does it feel to be forty-seven? They say that life begins at forty. But I bet the guy that wrote that was twenty. We skied against Stratford High this weekend and I stayed over at the Linfields' lodge. They have a dining room that seats a hundred now and ninety acres of land. Happy Birthday and see you at Easter."

· · ·

"Forty to thirty!" Tom served hard into Charles's side of Allen-by's court. The blood pounded in Charles's head as he ran to return it.

"Game!" Tom's call was a bark of triumph.

The first game lost to his son, and only after Tom had spent the summer teaching tennis in a camp. But good he had done it now; in two weeks he was going off to start college at Wilby. He needed fortification.

"Well, you had to win sometime, didn't you?" Annah sounded pleased as she served Tom at a family picnic in their cramped back yard.

"And you had to lose, didn't you?" She handed him a plate.

"Where's Sara?" Charles asked, in a hurry to get at the sliced chicken before the flies overcame it.

"She's finishing up her last wall; didn't you see it? All green, the walls pale and the floor dark-green. Maybe I'll build a grill out here for hamburg and steak." She surveyed their rectangular segment of the former field.

You do what you can.

Creamed for shaving, bitten by a mad dog, foaming, Charles looked into the mirror. The test of death? That's when you don't foam at the mouth anymore. Not bitten. Still.

Still, still with Thee, fast falls.

The dream last night falling, thrown against the corrugated cat's-mouth dune of the sea and the water too high, waves dashing him against a neck of sand. Going down, going under. He had woken thinking of Jessica. Indeed he found himself of late turning to examine tall, slender, gray-blond women. Is that Jessica, here in New Haven; is that what she came to? A worn cloth coat, hair parted severely in the middle, plastic glasses before her eyes? The star-shaped hands stuffed into bulging pockets? But it was not. Someone else, ruined.

A knock on the bathroom door.

"Okay," he said to Sara as he dried his neck. Why did she and her Thatcher friends spend so much time at the mirror? They were all beautiful. Why had the boys' faces he had scanned at

Wilby last week driving Tom up all possessed sky-blue untroubled eyes? Even Tom's. Would the call come? The letter full of fear? The Wilby boys had not had eyes like that when he was young! Not all of them handsome; no! Even the runty and the vain?

"I'm out," he called to Sara as he retreated into the bedroom, where his dream still hovered under the wrinkled blankets.

Fifty in 'fifty was too much; his feet were wearing out. He must perfect his voice. "On this third Sunday in Lent, we find ourselves at a narrow river where a bunch of people are listening to the words of a cousin of Jesus, one John." Charles raised his head to look at the congregation that filled a surprising number of seats in the overlarge structure. Every Sunday in the church, time stopped and he took them to the story that was always going on.

" 'REPENT! You will be judged on your own actions, not on those of your family before you!'

" 'Wash me, then!' a voice in the crowd calls shyly. 'And me!' another mocks. Then Jesus steps into the water and feels the touch of his cousin's hand upon his head and the shallow river deepening as John presses him under. He stoops at John's feet. Rising, he feels the sky opening and he hears a voice: 'THIS IS MY BELOVED SON IN WHOM I AM WELL PLEASED.' " Charles looked up again into the white sanctuary.

"Now, why did Jesus allow himself to be cleansed? Had the Sinless One any sins? No, it was as Eugene Debs once said: 'While there is a lower class, I am of it; while there is a criminal class, I am of it.' And, as Father Damien showed us when he lived among lepers until he became one, we are only as strong as the weakest among us."

"You didn't sound quite so nasal," Annah said at the cherry table in the dining room. "But you shouldn't keep looking up and down."

"After his baptism, Jesus parts from John and walks south, thinking." Charles followed the words with his finger, keeping part of his gaze down and part up: tricky.

"Should he give up sensual desires? Selfish wants? Could he trust the spirit to sustain him?" Charles took his finger off the page.

"Palestine and Connecticut, my friends, are not so different in size. And if we have Jesus being baptized up in the river at North Haven and then walking to the wilderness of brushland that still surrounds parts of Bellingburn, we are in scale. He fasts and grows hungry until, walking one morning on a road by the shore, he sees large stones and hears a voice saying, 'Look at all those stones! What good bread they would make! Why not turn them into fresh-baked loaves?'

" 'No,' he says. 'It isn't just by bread I want to live.'

"He walks along the highway to New Haven and climbs to the sixth floor of Malleys, into the ladies' hat department, say, and looks out through the venetian blinds at the people below who are coming and going. He hears the voice again. 'Why not make a big show? Jump out and then the second you're about to crash, while the crowd is gaping in horror, call the angels to help you land serenely on your feet. Wonderful! You'll be famous. You'll be written up in the *Register* and reported over WNHN, maybe you'll even make it onto television. Mind over Matter, Man Who Defied Gravity. How about it?'

"No, it isn't dramatics that last. It's patient nurturing.

"He walks to the hills of West Haven and climbs up to survey Yale's stately quadrangle, the towers of the churches on the green and the busy harbor. 'Listen.' The troublesome voice reappears. 'Are you sure you want to give up the flesh and the world? How about a nice professorship at Yale?'

"No, he says. For I never forget them. 'Who?' the voice asks. The sorrowful, the kind, the frightened."

"You're not supposed to use clichés," Sara answered over the ice cream with hot chocolate sauce. " 'Busy harbor,' that sort of thing. And my mind wandered in the middle of it."

Life is. Avoid.

"John is in prison and his men come to Jesus with a whispered question: 'Are you the one to take over?' John's voice is silenced by the executioner. Jesus' voice rises over the lake. 'Good news

for the poor! Good news for the sick! Good news for the imprisoned! The Kingdom is already here—it's within you!' And he
proved it with his healing." Charles kept his place on the paper
with a finger and leaned over the pulpit to confide.

"Now, when I started my ministry, some of these healings
struck me as the per . . . preposterous inventions of excited
minds. But I no longer hesitate to speak upon the healing done by
a man so in tune with God's power that he could focus it like
sunlight through a magnifying glass. Though," Charles added
before returning to his paper, "I am still somewhat troubled by
the healing of Lazarus.

" 'Who do people think I am?' Jesus asks his men.

" 'God's son Messiah,' his friend Peter replies. 'He who will save
us.'

" 'By suffering. They will kill me.'

" 'But everybody loves you!'

"The voice of the tempter. It has to be by the self made low.
The only power strong enough to bring the kingdom in is voluntary. It is when a fellow takes his foot off your neck because you
have made him want to, long to. Now, one evening on a mountain Jesus became white and radiant, a mist enveloped him."
Again Charles stopped reading and spoke directly. "Now, in my
parishes I have seen these transfigured faces, too. They appear on
men and women who see suffering ahead and chose not to flee
but to stand." He returned to his spot on the paper.

"This Easter morning we stand in a garden of olive trees. To
one side there is a limestone cave with a millstone that has been
rolled outward. There is a dark hole into which we gaze and our
feet are on holy ground. We know God walked in this garden
earlier and it was not his son who died this morning, but death."

"It was pretty good, Dad," Tom said as he received his plate of
roast beef.

Charles nodded, eager.

"Say, will it be okay if I take the car tonight?"

Before the oval mirror which had hung until a few years past on
the sunny wall of his parents' bedroom in Judea, Annah sat and

brushed her short hair. Charles lay propped to read in his parents' mahogany fourposter.

"He says he likes it well enough at Wilby but that he really wanted to go to the University of Pennsylvania."

"Why didn't he say so?" Charles's eyes stung. "He could have gone there!"

"*He* didn't think so," Annah said significantly, as she pulled a hairnet over her head.

"Why not?" Charles's chest felt heavy.

"He said you wanted him to go to Wilby so much he didn't know how to tell you he didn't want to." Annah's face was not visible, only the image of it in the mirror. "He was afraid it would make you too sad."

"Me, sad?" Charles spoke with a rasp. "Not at all!"

"Well, Arley, you did talk a lot about what fun you had at Wilby, how you'd love to be going back, love to think of him up there. You did." Annah picked up a jar and dipped her fingers into it; her neck wrinkled as she turned.

"I wouldn't for anything in the world want him to go to Wilby just on my account." Charles moved his unread book to the table. "Does he want to transfer to Pennsylvania now?"

"No, we've moved around so much, he says, he'd like to stay in one place now that he's there." In the mirror Annah's body rose and, when she reached up to pull the chains that hung from miniature lamps on either side of the mirror, vanished. "It just shows you," she said, "that you sometimes do better to speak out." Vanished into the mirror to replace the image of his mother?

It had been such a relief to see Tom move through his first year of college without the letter home, the call for help. Without Charles standing on his threshold to smell him out and bring him home. "He's already been away to school at Dunville," Annah had kept pointing out. How could he have worried so pointlessly? Only to find something worse? A boy afraid to displease his father not because of that father's strength but because of his fragility. Terrible. Oh, forgive me, he said over and over to himself; make me strong, or at least to appear strong. Had he been a son too long ever to become a real father? A distant face nodded him toward dawn.

WHETHER THE CROWD WAS TURNED toward him in mockery or praise or turned at all, Charles no longer cared. At Seaburn he had slipped from Golgotha and begun walking again on its lower reaches. But he was accompanied—as he had been since Hanley— by the sense that the spirit was within. "Look at this!" Charles would say to the presence whom he rather absently imagined noticing or nodding at whatever bit of hope Charles had uncovered. Walking to the Trebor Cinema one Monday night with Annah, Charles searched the faces of the people on the street. Did each set of eyes have such a secret landscape within? With faces and voices that echoed there? A barrel-chested youth, a shuffling old woman: he could tell nothing from the outside. Though he always knew when he crossed gazes with the saints.

"Hello there, John! Hello there, Maybelle!" Charles held the door wide.

"Just a little visit," John Raphael said. "We were driving by."

"Annah should be back soon. She'll make tea."

They were through the door then, the wheelchair carrying the young woman over the threshold.

"Annah out shopping?" Maybelle inquired, pulling the blanket higher over her knees.

"No, she's gone to her art class down at the university." Annah was not a saint, therefore Charles could forgive her everything. "How's it going, John?"

"Pretty good, Charlie." He indicated his wife's withered body. "We got her up six hours a day now. You remember when they gave her a month?"

"That's when he started to work on me," Maybelle answered in Charles's place. "Two hours a day, massage of the whole body." It was a litany recited on each visit.

"I weighed eighty-two pounds then," Maybelle said, flashing a smile.

"Tell him what you weigh today, Maybelle."

"One-oh-four, on the button." She readjusted a troubling knee. "That's only ten less than I weighed on Broadway." She moved into the second part of the recitation.

"That was in nineteen forty-one, when we danced as a team for the first year," John joined in.

John gave more than required. John went the second mile, all right. Had Charles done anything like that for Annah lately? No, he told himself, he would first have to give Annah the pride that he refused to give himself. He would not do that. It could kill. Why didn't it kill John? As father, he would not point the finger at anyone; he would crook it and beckon to the saints, be beckoned by them.

His people began to say that nothing was too shocking for Charles's ears. He wiped away sins like crumbs off your Thanksgiving table and started fresh with the one good thing about you. Except for those, they did not add, whom he considered to be on the same team; these could neither slip nor slumber. There weren't many of them, though, and there appeared no pattern in selection: his daughter, for instance, but not his son.

Sara wasn't home at two o'clock on a Saturday night.

"Why can't she think enough of you to telephone?" Annah lay in bed.

Did that boy look as if he drank? Were they at the side of a road, crashed? Not crashed? At 2:30 Charles heard the front door and he stood at the top of the stairs in his pajamas, holding out his gold watch.

"Is that you, Daddy?" She walked up as if it were 10:00 p.m.

"Young lady, I am very disappointed in you." Old Faithful, the rage of years, though cooled into disdain, was reserved for those on the team.

She didn't look the least bit interested.

Abroad in the world, he never lost hope. Not for those brushed by the wing of fire, stamped with the mark of ash, burned into peace.

. . .

Above the Trebor Tavern lived the Amorcos with their daughters. Thank God there were only two. Phyllis Amorco supported them from her salary as a clerk at Malley's and Charles visited her on Mondays, her day off as well as his. She also supported Amorco's drinking, and in return her husband walked a couple of blocks down the street to Bide-A-Wee instead of stopping at Trebor Tavern's ground floor. Phyllis Amorco was ironing at a board set on chair-backs near the stove and Charles sat down at the kitchen table and watched her. She did not look well. She must be about thirty-five but looked his own age.

"She does very well at school," Phyllis said of her older daughter. "But this year she goes to Second Quarter High and I'm scared." She sprinkled water from an old soda bottle onto the collar of her husband's shirt. The gesture was that of Aunt Hay, the washerwoman who had brought Charles the Sunday "Katzen-jammer Kids" every Monday morning when she came. First she would stand by the stove with her long wooden fork, stirring the wash that boiled in the brass kettle and singing: *Enoch walked with God, God said walk a little farther you look tired, come and visit me in my house for a while.* Then she cooled and wrung and hung and sprinkled.

"My younger one, she's not so smart," Phyllis said, raising wisps of steam, the iron making a sizzling noise. "But she's got strength. She believes in herself, you know what I mean?" Phyllis turned from collar to cuffs. "Not the older one, she'll do anything to be loved. Drink, smoke, boys, you name it."

"How's everything else?" Charles asked of her husband.

"The same," Phyllis said. "He hasn't hit the girls, though, not since Christmas. That's something. And he's making a little money. Funny, he's both drinking more and making a little money; doesn't make sense, does it?" Phyllis placed the shirt onto a hanger which hung from a knob on a kitchen cupboard. She buttoned it all the way up and pushed the collar neatly into place.

"It's easy money now," Charles explained. The water rising up off the river condenses into mist. Who was he to comment upon the life of this woman? Only to witness, though, wasn't enough. "They have a new Alcoholics Anonymous group at St. Theresa's Episcopal," he told her as she started on another shirt.

"I tried that," she said. "He won't go. He's really very sweet, you know." She tucked the point of the iron in and out between buttons. "When he's not drinking. Maybe I should leave him, for the sake of the girls, but I'm too tired. Too tired to sit down and think about it, know what I mean? I guess it's that I'm too tired for anything much else but Paul Amorco."

On his way home, Charles stopped at Walter's Drugs and picked out a Mounds bar.

"Hey Arley!" Walter had played on Chester High's first string. They had discovered each other with disbelief. "A fellow came by today who hadn't been around in a couple of years. He said your paint job is the one good thing that has happened to the neighborhood."

"Didn't he mention your new sign?" Charles said, but Walter laughed.

"Hey, keep 'em working, will you? I made over ten bucks last Thursday night from your Repair Group."

"We're doing the parish hall now," Charles said. "Putting in a better kitchen."

"What for? We'll be the only ones left in the city."

He dropped in at the parish house to look over the afternoon mail. In a manila envelope from Seaburn there was something wrapped in tissue paper and a note: "My sister Theodora Salisbury left a note to the effect that this embroidered sentiment be sent to you on the occasion of her death. Hugh Salisbury." Charles took off the tissue paper. "Whoso loves a child, loves God." Augusta Stiles in Shiloh had promised him that the bread he cast upon the waters would come back, if slowly. But she hadn't mentioned that the cost was often death. Other people's deaths engulfed him; he could not keep pace before them. As his father had not been able to during the time of the flu. He drove home.

Through the door he saw that the globe cast its orange light on the piano, making a mellow scene. A big tray with tea things stood on a stand before the fireplace and the logs splattered sparks against the screen. The voices of visitors were low and there was laughter.

"Charlie old man!" The Galabians had driven down from Seaburn on a whim.

"I didn't call to tell you, Arley! I thought you'd like to be surprised," Annah said.

He hurried out of his hat and coat and joined them. They gave him news of the former parish. Marietta Hudson had died.

"She never got to California?" Annah's voice was small.

He must write Marietta's three sons.

The Bellingham girl was getting married to a Harvard graduate. Onward and upward with education. Annah prepared dinner. Sara came home from Thatcher. The phone rang several times. He felt happy. Annah brought out a dinner of southern-fried chicken. How did she do it? A hundred chance meals like this, teas for various events, receptions here and there, birthday parties, holidays. Everything always in place, the table always ready, the dishes always tasty, her welcome warm. She sat at the other end of his table and graced his life with life. "Oh God," he said to himself, "make her happier. For I cannot." Tuesday: *Life goes too fast.*

Nodding at the nurse's desk, Charles made his way down to the front of the sanatorium and Burt's room. He swallowed, cleared his throat; the sanatorium always made him want to spit. Just to check up. Not today. It was his job to speak the news.

"Burt! Hello there!" He did not try to sound cheerful, just forceful. He noticed, against his will, the location of the color photograph of Burt's little boy. Burt's wife had said at the other hospital that the undertaker needed it to work from. Burt's bed was strewn with sections of a model airplane. Here was a young man who was keeping busy and making slow progress toward health, but was he able to take this unexpected news?

"Margo asked me to come over, Burt."

"Oh?" Burt's expression clouded just slightly. "What for?"

"Your little boy." Charles waited, to bring Burt in slowly, to be interrupted.

"Bobby?" The brown eyes changed but not enough.

"It's very bad news, Burt. The tonsillectomy; somehow they . . ." He reached for Burt's pajamaed arm.

"What's the matter?" Burt jerked at his touch.

"They lost him. He died."

"What are you talking about!"

Charles remained silent.

"It was a tonsillectomy, for God's sake! You must be crazy!"

Someone appeared at the door but Charles motioned her away.

"Bobby?" Burt started through it again.

A good sign. Charles felt his lips trembling.

"Bobby is dead?" Burt's cheeks were bright red.

Next time a nurse came to the door, he should motion her in to check on Burt. He would ask her to get the color photograph later, too. He had wanted to bring life eternal and everlasting; he had become a messenger of death. Better he should do it. Experience and all, the family business. *Hardest call I ever made.*

"You'll be fifty in the spring," Annah said. "We have to think of the future."

Charles pressed his Edgar yard-clippers over a knot in the grapevine and cut through easily. A good company, Edgar Clippers. Charles's father had known old Mr. Reinhold Edgar, a gentleman with a walrus mustache.

"So," Annah continued. She was kneeling by the pile of bricks that she was finally turning into an outdoor grill such as the other women who hung their wash between Maxton and Trebor possessed. "We ought to talk about money, don't you think?"

Charles sliced through another knot. Darkness was coming into the narrow green strip where on weekends wisps of smoke ascended from the neighborhood grills. Each grill was a copy of the larger grills on Bellevue Avenue. The wisps met in an air-draft in the corner where Charles's grape arbor stood. The arbor was a copy of one left at home in Italy by the parsonage's original tenant. The heart is seldom satisfied. "Do you mean I shouldn't ask for a salary cut?" He dropped the clippers and pulled off his yard gloves, beginning to pick the few grapes that were left on the vine.

"Does it make sense to cut two hundred dollars off our five thousand when Tom has two more years of college and Sara starts next year?" Annah laid mortar and put her first brick in place.

"What else can we do? Banner has to learn to keep current. We've dropped the assistant. We've reduced the janitor to part-time. We could give up the house, I suppose, and move upstairs in the parish house. Would you like that better?" He picked ripe purple globes and pressed them into his mouth, tossing the skins on the grass; they would be good later under the snow; they would help the ground.

"We have to keep current, too," Annah said, settling the second brick in careful alignment. "And that is one of the reasons I am planning to go to work."

"What?" Charles picked up his gloves and walked toward her. The neighbors should not hear her talking this way.

"The other reason is that twenty years of petty little fights about rummage-sale chairmen is enough for me. You have more faith than I, Arley, but I think it's just pearls before bald old ladies leaning on canes." She splattered mortar on the second brick, avoided Charles's face and ran the white glue sloppily over an edge.

Pyramids of Egypt.

"I have to get out before I become one of those old ladies myself. One more evening of picture-slides showing the Old Faithful geyser and my hair will go totally white." She plunked on the third brick and with a paper towel removed the glue that had oozed out.

Charles studied her face, the lines at the edges of her eyes and the vertical marks between her eyebrows. Her voice was not shaking and she did not look as if she would cry. Was she finally abandoning him?

"Where will you work?" he asked. He felt himself removed from her, though his feet stayed in the same spot of grass. Was it rather Mr. Reinhold Waybury who had had the walrus mustache?

"For one of the doctors," she answered, finally looking up. "Are you angry?"

"No," he said, slapping the gloves in his hand. "Disappointed." She blinked her eyes then, and returned to the bricks.

"I worked at it twenty years," she repeated, head down; but he would not answer.

"Maybe we're not all saints, Arley," she said, and he could hear the tears gathering behind Annah Trevellack's voice as she walked over snow, carrying her books.

"Annah," he said, stooping and taking the mortar blade from her hand, so that he could hold her hand in his. "I'm sorry. You did work very hard all those years and I thank you. It meant everything to me. You deserve a rest. I'll talk to Doctor Walters about a job. And I won't ask for a salary cut. What's a measly two hundred bucks when Banner needs radical surgery?"

She started to cry and put her forehead on his shoulder.

"Not out here," he said, standing and pulling her to her feet.

"Daddy," Sara said by the stove, where grease spattered from the frying pan as she cooked supper. It was Annah's late night at Dr. Walters's. "When we go to the school party after the hockey game next Saturday, please don't do what you did last time, okay?"

"What was that?" Charles folded napkins to add to the sparse settings at the kitchen table.

"Run in and say in a loud voice, 'I'll take tomato juice. I don't need liquor to raise my spirits.' Before you've even been asked what you want to drink."

"I'll try to remember." He stuck a napkin under a fork. They sat down.

"How was school?"

"I got ninety-eight in algebra. I'm on the student council again.

How was your day?" Sara rushed on; she did not take congratulations any more easily than he.

"Well, congratulations," he said. "That's wonderful; a position of responsibility and trust."

"How was your day?" She poured catsup on her hamburg.

"I made my calls and ended up in the mayor's office, where I was asked to speak on television next month." The hamburg was greasy all the way through, but Charles chewed dutifully.

"*You're* going on television?"

"Young lady, your father is a big gun in this town." Charles spoke without having finished chewing.

Sabbath afternoon, Annah working overtime, Sara riding in cars with boys; but Charles dared not nap. Waking from naps frightened him. To come back after having been stilled and reunited with slower forms of life—with currents of air moving in giant eddies or with moss waiting on forest floors for the light that would strike them only once in a thousand years? That startled him. To be swept to the bosom of the Lord and sheltered in the everlasting arms as they rose as one over the Atlantic, then to wake? Eerie.

Don't nap. Drive. Past the mental hospital, where a poor old man signed in by his daughter feared he was mad. "My grandfather took ten years to die," the daughter had told Charles, "right in the back bedroom, and I'm not putting my children through that." Drive back-country over roads strewn with red and yellow leaves that swirled in gusts across his path, mid-century. The world had turned fifty almost two years ago; and now it would happen to him in the spring. He was weltered, mired, stuck in the years of his century. There were so many on either side of 1950 that he could not imagine living out to its edge. He set his blinker and veered off the Judea road to the Southlee turn, where Justine had bought and restored a Colonial house and filled it with her soft blue velvet furniture. He pulled over the pebbles of Justine's drive. Her station wagon and Paul's Chrysler were both parked in the garage. Charles extinguished his throbbing Pontiac. He walked across a back lawn that stretched far off to shade trees.

"Is that you, Charles?" A voice just like his mother's came from a second-story window. Since his mother had died, Justine had called him Charles, as if to replace the lost intonation.

"It's Charles," she confirmed at the kitchen door. She was imposing, and that she had been her father's favorite was easily told by her carriage. When he kissed her, he smelled the beauty parlor in her hair. They sat on the back verandah over paved stones, with dogs and cats, near tables, shaded by a seventeenth-century overhang; all of which was supported by the boat business from whose rigors Paul Hathaway was napping.

"Have you heard from Maud?" she asked, her forward lean his mother's.

"About Ted?" he sighed. "Yes. Tests don't say benign, don't say malignant."

"He's lost forty pounds." Justine supplied the missing information. "And Fred says he walks like an old man."

"Oh?" Charles could not think of Ted's round face gone thin. "What about Catherine? Sam didn't have the results when I called."

"Malignant but operable."

"When does she go in?"

"November, week of Thanksgiving."

He nodded.

"He's giving his body to Harvard."

"What?"

"Ted. It's part of his will: *send body to Harvard*."

They laughed.

"What are we laughing for?" Justine wiped tears from her eyes with a chance paper napkin and the colors in it ran onto her fingers.

"Maud will want hers at Radcliffe!" Charles couldn't stop himself.

"No," Justine said, laughing and crying. "Cremation; she's already decided. Ashes to Father's cemetery."

"Cremation! In Father's cemetery?" Charles attempted to rise to the defense of many people in conflict.

"She says he would have come round to it: better for the soil, doesn't take up so much space."

Maud, nobody's favorite.

They laughed again. Oh Maud! Oh Ted! What will they think of next? Yet it was Maud who had gone into the world and come to know more than they.

"How serious is it, really, with both of them?" Justine's porch was several times more luxurious than Pete Allenby's.

"Ted's prospects are nil. It's a matter of how long and how painful. Catherine's are good. The thing is small as a lemon; she'll be her old self." Justine crumpled the stained napkin and placed it on a wrought-iron table.

"Maud?" he asked. "How is she doing?"

"She's as rational as you would expect, but Fred said he had never seen her look so sad." Justine placed a hand on her short neck. They were all past fifty now but him.

"And you?" Charles inquired. Leaning ever so slightly toward her.

"The girls don't marry, Charles. Why not?"

"They date a lot of boys, don't they?"

"Oh, yes, but Martha's twenty-six and Hildegard's twenty-three."

"They will," he said. "They're both very pretty, even Martha."

"I don't know," Justine said.

"Hi there, Arley." Paul came out the door, well-dressed.

The men talked of fishing, Justine displayed her newest wall-paper samples. Soon Charles was being seen off in his Pontiac that didn't kick over. He pretended patience, and when the motor finally caught Paul directed him as patiently away from the rose bushes. "Good-bye," Charles waved to them. They stood arm in arm protectively, as parents stand when the child leaves home.

Charles proceeded through Southlee to Judea. It wasn't only his memory of them as a boy: these were beautiful towns. Judea's stores still had modest fronts, as if they suspected they did not occupy eminence in the imaginations of the housewives. Even the new supermarket was modest; what did a bride know now of packing fresh sausage? An old man's thoughts. What had his parents known of atomic fission? Of radio waves bouncing off the moon? Of television? He pulled up in front of Fred and Georgia's, a house built for a bride who had known the art of hanging sausages but never practiced it. Though the three-story house no longer smelled fresh-cut, it had just been painted. He let himself in and found Fred sitting in a rocker reading; Georgia was upstairs napping. There was a sense of quiet and stillness. Fred had begun in the other century; he need not feel pressed about getting out of this one.

"Sam? Oh, he's quite hopeful of Catherine's quick recovery." Fred remained the handsomest of Minor men, his mother's favorite. He expected things to go well. "And how is your family?"

"They all like what they're doing; Annah's at work, she's glad to be out of the ministry, says it sometimes struck her as the blind leading the blind." He smiled. "Sara likes school. Tom likes college."

"He playing any sports?"

"Track, skiing; the individual sports."

"Not like his dad?" Fred smiled. His rockers were soundless on the pale-blue rug.

"Basketball?" Charles acknowledged his former self. "No."

"Maybe it's good I never had a son," Fred said. "I would have ridden him too hard."

"Like Father?" Charles asked. Nobody called him Papa anymore. It had gone out of style.

"Ha! I guess so!" It was as if Fred hadn't thought of it 'til now. "By the way," he continued. "You'll be fifty soon and Sam thinks you ought to have your big sixtieth birthday party on your fiftieth. He wonders who'll be left when you're sixty!"

"Hard to think of that," Charles said. "I'll see." Would he never grow as big as they? When he got up to go, Fred decided to walk him over to the old house and they scuffed through fallen leaves along the short street past Sam's first house and onto Hathaway.

"There's my tree!" Fred pointed out the maple that grew over Charles's sleeping porch.

But it's my tree! Charles smiled to himself. So, Solomon said, cut that tree in half. No! Are you, perhaps, the true boy who owns this tree?

"Funny, I always looked on it as mine," Charles said. "It grew right over my sleeping porch."

"They'd probably award it to you," Fred replied. "You were always their favorite. You ran the family."

Me?

They were through the door then before the entry could be savored, calling, "Catherine?"

"I'm in here!" Her voice answered from too near. She lay propped next to the dead Joseph and the dead Polly in the downstairs bedroom.

"Hello there!" Catherine's blue eyes were brilliant and reassuring. Her scalp showed a touch of pink along the part in her white hair, but her hand was warm and she was not yet surrounded by the pictures of her grandchildren.

"There's ice cream." Catherine indicated the direction of the kitchen. "Sam brought it this noon from Howard Johnson's."

Charles crossed the wide oak boards past the dining table into the kitchen. He should not come to this house alone again; he would wait a month and bring Sara and her friends to a football game at Rhodes. Maybe the Amorco girls, if Sara would consent. Their mother had it, too. But of the breast. He looked for traces of Simon in the kitchen but found none.

Out the kitchen window he saw a white-haired Sam walking toward him from his funeral parlor.

"Say, you're having a birthday soon, aren't you, boy," Sam announced as he opened the kitchen door.

MOVING OUT DID NOT SOLVE everything. Charles rang the bell at the Nicholses' ranch house for the tenth time, then he pushed open the yellow door on Wandering Lane in Bellingburn. Death of the only child, by his own rage. Even now the boy poses on the car's front fender and throws the rope around the uncased beams. Charles walked into the living room, where no fire burned behind the skirt-front screen. The boy in the red plaid lumber shirt removes his familiar cap worn to everything important in his life: the hunting trip, the wild Hallowe'en rambles, the daily humiliating ride in the school bus where he sat in the back huddled over the warm radiator staring at Her.

"Once he fell out of his stroller," his mother had said frantically to Charles on the phone. "The doctor said he was fine, but after that, it always seemed to me that he was not, not the same child." Indeed, the boy had drifted oddly as he walked, Charles recalled, as if his mind were some eighty feet ahead. Now he arranges the looped rope neatly around and underneath the collar of his lumber shirt and he replaces the much-loved cap.

"He had everything," his father had told Charles. "See the swing I made for him? And downstairs a roomful of records? Did you see the Ping-Pong table?"

He steps off the fender, victorious.

Only a few minutes, too, before his father's daily entry into the garage to rev up the Buick for the drive into the city.

Swings. Is still.

It will never be forgotten, it will always be taking place.

Charles found them downstairs in the rec room, sitting on lawn furniture in a cold corner of the paneled cellar, drinking. The radio sang to them.

"Hello there." Charles walked to the edge of the Ping-Pong table. "Let's go up for a cup of coffee now; they're ready for you at the funeral parlor. Someone from his class called the funeral home, you know. The boys and girls wanted to stop by to see him tomorrow after school. But I told them to come before school instead; we don't want to put the funeral off too long, do we?"

"Now," he nodded suggestively at the father. "You can always get a good cup of coffee at the Nichols's house. And while you're making it"—he nodded at the mother—"your good husband can go upstairs and change into fresher clothes." They did what they could: who could call them or anyone guilty? Such distinctions did not matter anymore. Charles leaned over the mother and offered her his elbow, and together they began the long trip up to the kitchen. "Each minute," Charles said, pausing stair by stair, "leads to another."

"Not for him," the father said.

Ted died age 70. Missionary to Rhodesia. Helped found National Roundtable of Negroes and Whites. As the years went by, Ted left the traditional religion of his youth. No service is planned.

"Work got you down, Rachel?" His incompetent choir director sat head bowed in the loft when she ought to be practicing for the Christmas cantata. "I love everyone in the world," he frequently told Annah. "I just love Rachel a little less."

"It's not the work." Rachel pressed a handkerchief to her wide cheeks. "You must have heard the rumors."

"What's that?" He had heard them, but not from Rachel.

"That I'm making a fool of myself with one of my students."

"Yes?" he said.

"He reminds me of DeWitt." She spoke as if to herself, eyes blinking rapidly.

"Who's that?" Charles tried again. The inventor of the steamboat?

"Oh, DeWitt! Such a wonderful man. He married another girl." Rachel folded her handkerchief into a tight square. "Twenty years ago."

"Where does he live?" Charles asked.

"Boston. He does a program called 'Orchestral Classics' every Wednesday night from WBZ. I listen all night, sometimes I hear him breathing."

"Now." Charles put his hand cautiously on the keyboard; it wouldn't do to undermine the needs of the choir. "Why not take the train up some Wednesday after Christmas, when the cantata's over, and pay him a call? Walk into the broadcasting station. One look at the actual DeWitt and I bet you'll stop carrying the torch!"

"You mean he'll be bald or something?" She looked up interested.

"Well, maybe." Charles felt slapped on the top of his head.

"Whatever it is, I bet you'll be over him by the return trip."

"But then," she said, tucking the lump of a handkerchief into her sleeve, "what would I have?"

"Your work," he explained. "And come spring, who knows? By the time we're singing 'I Know That My Redeemer Liveth'?"

To boost morale millions of pictures of pin-up girls are being sent to soldiers in Korea by Hollywood studios. Down to see arthritic and paralytic swimmers at the Y. Lunch at Burt and Margo Storemont's, their Bobby was a boy who should not have died. Tom home tonight, a fine boy, may he be spared the war. Chicken pie.

Rachel made it through the Christmas Sunday cantata and the Pilgrim Fellowship's surprisingly well-produced Christmas Eve Nativity pageant. Charles wondered how she did today, in the grip of Christmas itself. He should telephone her after dinner.

"What are you reading now, my girl?" Charles handed Sara a dinner plate, on which rested her turkey leg. The children shall have the legs for ever and ever.

" 'Murder in the Cathedral'," she replied dryly.

Charles severed wing from breast while Annah in her bright dress placed sweet potatoes onto passing plates. He felt suddenly lonely in the bosom of his family.

"And you, my boy?" He sliced white meat in flaky slabs.

"Chaucer, the 'Wife of Bath's Tale'," the boy said. "Not your cup of tea, Father."

"Thin slices, please, Arley." Annah commented on his performance.

Charles hadn't really liked any of his presents, either. The doorbell rang and when Tom went to answer it, they all listened.

Scott. Was she drunk again?

He laid down the knife, then picked it up and handed it to Tom. "Teach yourself carving," he said. It was harder to liven up his own dinner table than it was to warm up the Ladies' Aid. Or help people in trouble who came to him. Once they came, it was easy. Charles led a red-faced shaking Scott into the kitchen and shut the door. Charles stood with his hands tucked up under his armpits and waited.

"She left me this morning, Charlie, and I'm going to follow her and I'm going to kill her. You're my witness, Charlie; I'm not trying to get away with anything." Scott's round face and two-toned glasses made him look exactly like what he was, a pharmacist. His enraged voice came out spasmodically.

"Well, I guess you're strong enough to do it." Charles spoke slowly; he must not appear troubled.

"You can say that again." Scott unzipped and zipped his pile-lined jacket and his breathing came a little more naturally.

"I guess you're also strong enough to let her go," Charles said.

"Let her go! I'm going out now to find her!" Scott looked confused, suspicious.

"Why hold her against her will?"

Scott did not answer, eyed Charles in the center of the room.

"You're a generous man. You're a big man. Let her go!"

Still no answer.

"It isn't as if you hadn't been expecting it, now is it?"

"No." Scott smiled a little, looking down.

"Well, now," Charles said, taking his hands out from under his armpits. "Want a little turkey?"

"I couldn't eat today." Scott rezipped his jacket and stopped fiddling with the zipper.

"Tomorrow, then," Charles said. "Come on over for supper."

"I'll see," Scott said. "I've got a lot of things to tend to, I guess, Charlie."

"Now." Charles resumed his position above the turkey platter. "I forgot the stuffing. Who wants some?"

Loyal bunch of trustees, over to synagogue, Sara drawing murals at the Thatcher gym for a dance tonight, starting our men's Bible group tomorrow. Annah going up to Boston to visit Hope soon. Tom wants to buy a car in New Hampshire. Mine needs new brake linings.

. . .

"Are you warm enough here, Selma?" It was cold in the cell where Selma's rage had taken her, but clean. The toilet was free of the yellow stain that had marked those in the basement of Judea's town hall.

"I love children," Selma said, her elbows on her knees, her hands twisting. "I was a good baby nurse."

"I have heard many good things about you, Selma," Charles said, his eyes examining the muscles of her forearms, of her hands. She was, all in all, bigger than he was. To the baby? A giantess! He looked up; he must not appear frail.

"I love babies and they love me." She twisted and turned one hand into the other. "That woman shouldn't say those things about me. How will I ever get another job?"

"We'll see about all that sort of thing later, Selma. Now you must search your heart. You must ask yourself, 'Did I do it?' And if the answer is yes you will work out the best way to tell us and we will help you whatever happens. And if the answer is no we will help you work that out."

"The man is all right. He doesn't say that I did it." With her pudgy, ringless left hand Selma pushed mousy hair from her large forehead. "But that woman says I did do it."

"Only you know the truth, Selma," Charles replied, realizing that perhaps only she did not. He caught himself staring again at her hands. Was she left-handed? Had the police examined the neck of the dead infant to tell if it had been strangled by a right- or left-handed person? Was the baby's mother right- or left-handed? Was Selma's sin so heavy that it held her in balance? Would she teeter and fall once she gave it over?

"Do you think I did it, Reverend?" She looked up now, the green eyes distant, vague.

"Circumstances point in that direction, but circumstances are not always right. I'm no judge, anyway, Selma," Charles said, leaning toward her. "I'm here to help whether you are guilty or innocent and," he added quietly, "I'm here to help even if you don't know which."

. . .

Calls way out to North Bellingburn, good getting into the coun-
try. A rainy day with a walk after supper with Annah. The fair
very successful, friendly spirit. May I keep a growing and a quiet
center. Phyllis Amorco is much worse.

Charles shut his study door behind the young blond woman and
pointed to a chair; outside in the corridor what was left of the
custodian dragged a mop along the hallway of the parish house.
Counseling took so much time; the conscience seemed to have
come unhooked since the war and moved outside, into talk, talk,
talk. He sat down in his high, vaulted study with French windows that presented him with a narrow scene, and he listened.
People came to him here, strangers like this, having heard of him
from his own people.

"But I did not do any of those things she accuses me of." The
woman was about thirty and seemed honest, but who could tell?
"It's a trumped-up charge," she continued, "that the sergeant put
against me because *she's* a lesbian."

"Why would she be against you?" Charles inquired, examining
the outside corner of the eye, where lies register.

"Because she wants her friend to be promoted. Not *me*." The
woman's WAC uniform fit snugly around her breasts and hips;
she had a good figure and was a demure-appearing blonde who
looked Scandinavian, the niece of a parishioner.

"And what is it you want me to do, again?" Charles inquired.
She gave him a foggy feeling. With whom did she hold her inner
dialogue? With whom did she talk in prayer?

"Write me a character reference to file with the court," she
said, her eyes as clear a blue as Catherine's.

"How many of these character references are called for?"
Charles asked.

"Three."

"I want to help," he said, "but tell me, why are you coming to
a total stranger for a character reference at such an important
moment in your life?"

"Well," the young woman said, blinking several times, "my

aunt told me you were the first person she would go to if she were in trouble. She said you always know a person's heart and find it good."

"You are in trouble, young woman," Charles said, filling his pipe afresh. "Now, let's try to think this through again, together." It was true. He seldom got angry at them anymore. Fathers shouldn't.

Sara on a date. Good congregation out. A beautiful day, the sun through clouds. Betty Kincaid has a boyfriend she met at Reform School. Over to the Old Folks Home this afternoon. Saw television at the Allenbys' tonight.

Without her iron and her soda-bottle sprinkler, without the heat of summer scorching her from the bar below, Phyllis Amorco looked much younger dead. She was dressed in a long white gown, at least so far as Charles could see into the half-couch casket; from the waist down she was covered by a gentle wooden curve not unlike that of a baby buggy.

"She's in her wedding dress!" Sara whispered in pianissimo shock. He had insisted that she come, not that she was a friend of the Amorco girls but because she might be. What else could he offer?

Indeed, Sara was right, it was Phyllis's wedding dress. Charles's eye located the pins holding the veil open to the sides of the face and determined that the hands crossed over the cancer-ridden breast were carrying a bride's bouquet. Orange blossoms?

Whose idea was this?

A disturbance at the doorway. Charles turned on his heel, which swung the rows of empty folding chairs before his eyes and brought him Paul Amorco entering the funeral parlor, broadshouldered, black-haired, red-faced but sober. He was carrying a black leather Bible in his hands and after he had placed it near his wife's, he went to sit beside his daughters, whom he pulled into his arms, where they both wept with him.

"He seems very nice," Sara whispered. "Why do you say he's so bad?"

"People always rally round in a crisis. Wait a few weeks."

Two older women came up to the coffin and one pushed the Bible out of sight beneath the buggy cover: "Didn't look so very nice against all that white, now did it?"

"He treated her like dirt," Annah said as they drove back from the cemetery. When Charles had finished the reading at the grave, Annah had taken the two silver bracelets from her wrist and silently put one over the hand of each Amorco girl. "I'll just buy some more now that I'm working again," she had said to Charles as they walked to the car.

"I hope he drinks himself to death in a week and those girls get a chance to get out of that hole." Annah rolled down her window.

"He hasn't had a bed of roses either," Charles pointed out. But half of Charles had already turned to cheer Annah in the old crowd below. The other half stood shading its single eye from the disappointed gaze that rested on it from a few steps up Golgotha.

CHARLES TOOK ANNAH and Sara for a Sunday afternoon drive, the goal of which was to eat supper at the new roadside restaurant in Bellingburn. He drove out by way of Bellevue Avenue. A mistake, as it turned out.

"That one's nice." He pointed out a large brick house on a corner. "I always liked brick. Remember our brick house in New Hampshire?"

Annah in the front seat said nothing. Nor did Sara in the back.

"And that one's not bad," he said, slowing down in front of a three-story frame house with a round tower. Still no response. Were they having another fight?

He turned his head and saw that Annah was pressing a handkerchief to her eyes.

Some joy-ride.

"I don't care," Annah said. "You should have one of these houses!"

"Well, now." He changed the subject at the corner, where he turned up a steep hill to Bellingburn. "This is a bad corner. Lots of accidents here. The police stand around here on graduation night just waiting."

"Why," asked Sara, "do most of those gory accidents you tell about take place on graduation nights or on honeymoons?"

I wonder how Tom is doing, he said, but only to himself. His son sent him clippings from the college newspaper, where he was a sports reporter. Jesus never had become a father, except by rejoining what he had once left.

"Dear Boss, We'd love to join you for your First Annual Couples' Sunday, even though you didn't marry us," Holton Linfield wrote. "But the little beauties herewith enclosed somehow prevent a six-hour drive." Charles picked up the color snapshot by its edges: one of the Linfields' two daughters looked remarkably like the dead Nancy and both smiled as they looked up from buckling their sandals. Would anyone come? The custodian could never groom the lawn of its beer cans and cigarette wrappers in time. Charles hired Tom, who was home for a week between college and his summer tennis job, to work on the lawn. Seventy-five cents an hour. "You're asking me to work on the Sabbath?" Tom drawled, taller than Charles this vacation, broader, deeper-voiced. Charles felt himself an old man who wore a coat that was too large and gloves that could be drawn to the elbows.

Twenty men and twenty women whom Charles had joined together in other parishes returned to him with their children. Little ones wrapped in blankets, bigger ones eagerly balancing on unstable legs, grown ones careful to notice everything in the world through their recent disdain; the harvest of almost a quarter-century.

"Marriage as one of you once told me, is a sixty-sixty affair." He made sure not to focus on Annah, who sat in the congregation now instead of in the choir loft. Dr. Walters's late hours came on the same night as choir practice. "Children are the fruit of it, but not the core." Yet those below him in the pews knew

mainly the love of generations: old to young, young to old. The
ones who were loving as men and women do were far away out
in the garden falling, falling. Or in hotel rooms. Or off at college,
waiting. His pews were the refuge for the great return. Which
often began with all these weddings. Nonetheless he invited the
congregation to the wedding and reception the following Sunday
afternoon of the oldest Allenby girl.

It was the first reception to be catered by a group of younger
women who had rebelled against the Ladies' Aid. The Aid had
too long limited its reception menu, the younger women complained, to squares of bread cut to fit beneath one cucumber slice
and all designed to be eaten standing up. The new Sunshine Circle wanted to serve what they called "sit-down chicken." In the
receiving line Charles noticed that the affronted Aid stood huddled beside the piano, refusing to bend their bodies into chairs.
He should never have endorsed the Sunshiners. The church
would be torn apart. Oh Philippians! Oh Galatians! The strong-
jawed Allenby girl stood near Charles with her waist-cincher
probably adjusted, like Sara's, too tight. She uttered a too high
Ah! as a tea tray bearing a cake on which stood a tiny man and
woman was wheeled to the piano. It was parked smack in front
of the ladies of the Aid, who went pink with mortification. But
what did it matter on the scale of glacial epochs? He must not
grow too tired here; his rage might rise before his time here
was up.

"I can't believe it's happening!" the bride said. Was her shortness of breath due to her waist-whittler? Or to a surfacing dread
that her desire for her husband was fast becoming memory? Did
she already feel the waters of life shake themselves back to their
proper bed? Throw up the dam and round themselves into a
small salty ocean fit for a child? Would the Aids leave early on
bent legs, tapping their canes and smiling wickedly?

"We'll try some dictating today, Myra." Charles spoke to his
new part-time secretary. "I'll go slow. Now this first letter send
to two people, to the presidents of both the Sunshine Circle and
the Ladies' Aid. Okay. Dear Ladies, I am well aware that one

cannot belong to an organization without developing ties of loyalty. . . ."

He paused to let her catch up. "But I want to tell you that thanksgiving filled my heart when I heard of the vote on the part of both your organizations to reunite. This move I feel to be a step toward the gospel. Sincerely yours."

Dictation was not efficient with a volunteer secretary. He read over a short note that had come yesterday. "Dear Brother, Our 25th from Union is coming up in a couple of years. I'd love to get together with you boys to compare what's happened to us all. I have a church of some 2,000 members out here in Des Moines. What do you say? Bob Sommers."

"Now for the second note," Charles said to Myra, who sat with her pencil as ready as it ever would be. "Dear Bob, It's good to hear from someone who cares about the class. I would love to have a reunion. I am at Banner Avenue Congregational Church in New Haven, a fine city in which to live. Is Barclay a bishop yet? I still feel our class prediction of his becoming one will come true!"

"Is there anything you want to ask me before you go off to college?" Charles inquired of Sara as they sat together on the small porch on Maxton Street watching the night come on.

"I'd like to know what we're all doing here." Sara stopped picking at her finger-ends and spoke in a serious voice. "Whether life is chance or not, has any meaning, and what existed before the world."

Oh, you would?

"Those are the great questions," Charles replied, pulling on his pipe, "that you will be considering at college."

"But what do you think, Daddy?"

"I'm undecided, though I do believe we are put here on earth to glorify God." He had to be careful: she could so easily trap and outwit him.

"I see," she said, as she rested her hands in her lap. "Do you think I'll need the typewriter first semester?"

"Yes," he said; he could still answer the small practical questions. "The professors like it when you type your papers—easier for them to read. We'll take the old one up in the car, and then at Christmas you'll get the new one we talked about."

"Okay," she said. They were silent as the darkness shaded the white porch rails, filled up the lawn under the thickly leaved trees arching the street and finally crept up to their ankles and their knees.

"No date tonight?"

"Tomorrow night; the play at Westport."

"Who with?"

"Peter."

The one that was going to Princeton. Last night was the one that was going to Dartmouth. The night before the one that was going to Williams.

"Doesn't anyone go to Wesleyan anymore?"

"Art Peacham is going to Wesleyan."

What did that mean? Charles was afraid to ask. Who was Art Peacham? A mess-up? A creep? A jerk? A no-good? Night had come then and touched his forehead.

Inside the house he had fallen asleep in the stuffed chair. As he had done on the evening of his fiftieth birthday party, when all his brothers and sisters, even Maud, had come and gone. Tom had sent him a cheering telegram from Wilby: *Remember Handel wrote the Messiah at 55.* As he had done on New Year's Eve before he'd written the essay planned for the back of his diary, on how the world so long viewed from a distance now invaded his own corners with his wife working, his daughter drinking and smoking, and his son seeking a life of comfort. As he had done a couple of years ago just after the ball had dropped into 1950, when time wrenched itself turning. With the children off dancing at the palace of the king, he and Annah had slept in an armchair by the new television while Guy Lombardo pumped the music of life through the closing veins of air that circled their living room.

The metal alphabet in the wooden box was heavy. No wonder the custodian had quit. Charles set it down and swung open the glass door of the bulletin board. He picked out last week's rusted letters and tossed them onto the grass. Then he set up this week's: HAVING DONE ALL, STAND FAST. It was Paul's urging to the saints. Get yourself ready and hold steady. It was especially good advice if you couldn't move forward. And despite its doubled membership, its recently burnt mortgage papers, and its new paint, Banner Avenue was not moving. The world was moving in upon it. Should Banner Avenue get up and go to Bellingburn? Leave the steeple here. Sell it to the A.M.E.? Can a synagogue have a steeple? No. Stand fast.

Nine Jews, seven Roman Catholics, three Protestants and one Nothing made up the average twenty residents of the Second Quarter. The quarter lay, said the newly published report, "in the zone of acute deterioration. It is the city's least favorable area for Protestant cultivation. It already has three Protestant churches: St. Theresa's Episcopal, Jones Street Methodist, and Banner Avenue Congregational. They all lie directly in the line of the chief thrust of the Jewish population. It is not likely they will all survive."

Here they come!

Stand fast.

The survey had ignored the fact that Negroes were moving up from their footholds in Bellmont Square. Which army would reach the steepled fortress at Maxton and Trebor first?

Help might yet come from First Congregational. Its ten or twenty widows still bowed their heads in hand-carved pews and paid their coal and electric bills on time. Heat and light would remain to grace their going out. Let him bless you; we are all God's children. I don't want to rush you. But we're under siege.

Just after Easter last, Charles had attended the installation of a new young minister at First. M. M. Molton had looked fresh but unseasoned. Charles decided it would be better to give him a year before arriving on his doorstep with troubled portfolio. He was overdue. He must call on Molton soon and make sure that Banner could stand, though its minister left it soon, as per his arrangement. The dissolution of the Protestant church as we know it in New Haven might not be entirely his fault but he was determined to keep his part of it standing here. No fancy suburbs, no Bellingburn.

It was wrong to leave the city; this corner needed a church, a witness. The head trustee was moving in October and the prima alto in November; one family a month left. So far they all came back to Banner for worship and activities. So far, Charles pointed out to Pete Allenby, who underrated the severity of the situation, as usual. "The church had been going downhill twenty years when you came, Charlie. Now we're prospering; what are you worried about?"

The armies, Pete. Solid phalanxes from opposite directions. You don't see their banners? Hear their trumpets?

He shut the glass door and picked up the scattered letters. Gone to grass were the eleven hundred sermons, the forty-four thousand pastoral calls, the five hundred and eleven new members, the two hundred and twenty-six marriages and the three hundred and sixty-one baptisms of TWENTY-FOUR YEARS IN THE MINISTRY. He picked up the heavy box. He must remember to come back and rake away the cigarette packages. Four and a half of his five years were up. This should be his last autumn at Banner. It was too hard for a man his age. Could he pull off the merger in less than a year? Find a new job? Through Maud, no doubt, Seattle Second had already sent him a letter of inquiry. But Seattle was too far from the children.

"Annah?" he said in December. "Would you give up your office work in the new parish? I don't know if I could really start in all alone."

The rush of flight was upon him by then and he knew he flung himself forward into this last lap at a pace that was too fast. "I'm not afraid to travel," he told himself after Christmas. "I haven't been afraid since Hanley." And he went off eagerly in April, leaving his curtain up in the sleeper as he rolled by moonlight over prairie fields. He did not want to miss anything and he knew his silent companion, his listener, the Holy Spirit, was within him. There were limits to his servitude as there had been to his brotherhood. Perhaps that is why the spirit left him. At any rate, he was startled at the station in Des Moines when he thought for a second that he saw a faceless shadow standing on the platform among the strangers come to welcome him.

XI

Commencement, 1954

IN AN AIR-CONDITIONED OFFICE, with boxes of red, yellow and blue pushpins on his desk, Charles sat and stared at the pine-paneled wall opposite, where he had hung a grid map of Des Moines and the hand-carved wooden cross given him by a former parishioner. Nobody needed the story of the cross; Des Moines knew no sorrow. For fifty years he had felt a presence watching him, in the sky above the long lawn at Judea, in the dark bedroom above the kitchen. After a few days in Des Moines he seemed to have crossed a boundary, to have traveled beyond the eye of God. The colored pins that were sticking in the paper streets summarized the Neighborhood System Charles had been called to Des Moines to effect in his capacity as assistant minister to the Reverend Mr. Bob—Bobby—Sommers. Through this Union classmate, the job had materialized.

"Coffee?" Lena stood inquiringly at his door.

"I guess so, Lena. Thanks." After years of being on the road by nine, calling at homes where he drank only a sip out of each cup, he was getting used to whole cups. They went well with paperwork. The Protestant tide had beached at Pearl Parkway Community Church. It had two thousand members, a budget of sixty-five thousand dollars, investments to a quarter-million, a Sunday School of sixteen hundred, a nursery school, a youth choir, an adult choir, Boy and Girl Scout troops, Brownies and Cubs, a minister of youth, a parish worker, a director of Christian education, one black custodian and two secretaries: Lena, plump, unmarried and jolly; Bernice, more slender with darker lipstick.

It had a young and an old couples' club, Bible-study groups, a Lenten seminar, a woman's guild, a working woman's guild, youth programs, a day camp, retreats, two Sunday-morning services, released-time religious instruction, and a parents' council. No need for Alcoholics Anonymous. Almost the entire membership had graduated from college and there was not a single one poor enough to receive a Christmas basket. People looked like each other: large, blond and under forty. What did they want with a man who died of his own free will to still the wrath of God?

"There you go, Charlie," Lena said, putting the coffee down carefully. "I heard a new one on Bobby, but I know you'd never let me tell it to you." She smiled and returned to the women's office outside his wall. He took some pins from the boxes on his desk and walked to the map. He removed a blue pin and stuck in a red to show that a neighborhood had held its second meeting. He pulled out a yellow pin and pushed in a blue: they'd had their first. So far sixty-six neighborhood meetings had been held, where neighbors sitting in chairs in sun parlors and sunken living rooms had talked about themselves. Fears, disappointments, sorrows. Sickness was unearthed, even death the unknown twice witnessed unto. Hopes crept out of the upholstered sectionals and from behind the television bunny-ears. Ending with hot Swedish nut rolls and Norwegian breads. This well-kept race of grown children seemed not so much to be living as passing through a home movie. Until they heard each other's stories. Charles walked back to his desk to stare at his draft for the annual report.

"Here he comes," Lena whispered. You could hear a whisper through their dividing wall very nicely.

"With the aid of the deaconesses," Charles typed busily, "we have established over a hundred Neighborhood groups and located a Hostess for each." Over a hundred hostesses. "The size of the church overwhelms me, but gradually, there is coming to me a sense of knowing more of the families."

"Good morning, Charlie," Bobby waved as he marched by.

"Good morning, Bob," Charles called out at the space left in his doorway.

"Sermons preached: 7." The only ones Bobby let him do. Those on the down Sundays immediately after big holidays or on holiday weekends, when half the congregation dispersed to lakes. Should he bother to report that he read Bobby's Scriptures for him every Sunday? That, he enjoyed: Holy Writ didn't have to be submitted to Bobby beforehand. Charles's prayers did. "Oh Father God Who gave us our being and was our dwelling place before the earth, before Whose face the generations rise and pass away, grant us a sense of humor, good manners and some dignity." Submitted, the prayer had been returned with *sense of humor* crossed out.

Some job, when you couldn't pray to smile.

"Weddings performed, 7; baptisms, 9; funerals, 8." Those on rainy days.

"Teaching a Bible Class to some thirty-five adults has been an invigorating assignment. Our fall course dealt with the letters of Paul and during our first meeting we began to call ourselves Brother and Sister as Paul would have us." He x-ed that out, too intimate. "The potential at Pearl Parkway Community Church is tremendous. I grow conscious of my limitations in performing the specialized ministry to which you have called me. Charles P. Minor, Minister of Fellowship."

He pulled the paper out and carried it to Lena. A hundred hostesses, fifteen deaconesses and two secretaries; he was a man among women more than ever before. They typed him out, spoon-fed him, amused him, backed him into a corner and patted him. Last summer his open office window had even brought him the shouts of children at their recess directly outside. He waved to the children from time to time. It was hard to keep them straight in his mind; they looked more like each other than their parents did.

"One page?" Lena inquired. "Why, Bobby gave me eight and signed them 'Your Minister.'"

"You're not turning the other cheek so much these days, Lena." Charles buttoned his suit jacket.

"You know you need me to say it," she pointed out.

Like Annah?

No, he wanted to say. In the office I need a partner in not saying it. Not feeling it.

"By the way, Charlie," Lena continued in a lowered voice, "it's clear from the other reports that everyone loves you. Bobby says as little as he can about you in his. He's jealous."

And that.

"I'm not the senior minister," he said, weakened.

"Would that you were!" Lena leaned on her typewriter, parishioner more than a secretary.

"I knew a woman named Millie with arthritis of the spine," he said. "She used to serve weekly suppers for a hundred people. She said the only way to forget the pain was to work harder than it did. We have to work at giving Bobby room, at letting him grow."

"He never will," Lena stated flatly and flicked bits of eraser off the typewriter carriage.

"Now we don't know that, do we?" Charles noticed the paper bag set out on her desk. "I'm off to lunch," he said. "And this afternoon I'll be out calling."

The voice of the tempter is sweetened by Danish sugar buns.

He returned to his desk for his notebook. He had asked two questions of the head of the pastoral committee before he had come from New Haven. One, does the job demand the full talents of a man? Two, could the senior minister handle the situation if the minister of fellowship should draw up the love of the people? Yes, the man had answered.

Wrong on both counts.

Charles would not race Bobby for the love of the people. He reached for his file of personal letters brought from home this morning so he could respond to Alicia Kincaid. Her daughter Betty was getting married and Alicia wanted him east to handle it. But cost was prohibitive and it wasn't good for a former minister to keep going back to the old ground. Yet letters from his old parishioners were becoming his lifeline. He thumbed quickly through his file, looking for Alicia's note. Annah would have lunch on the table. Or maybe not. She had agreed to help him in Des Moines with the church work—and a good thing, too, as she had become exhausted since moving here. Depression common to her age, the doctor had said. But it was more than that. He was being broken here and it was Annah who fell to the ground. The doctor had urged her to take six weeks in a warm climate with Charles. How could he take six weeks off when he had barely started? So he tried to help her in his pulpit prayers: "O God Whose grace runs down from the cross, open to those who are crushed and cannot rise the reservoir of the waters of life." But her improvement, if she were indeed improving, was very slow. Charles's hand overturned a letter in shakily penned ink:

"We here at the New Haven Home for the Aged often speak of you and share any item of news about you and your family. As for Mr. Molton, he has been to call only two times. I had a question on faith healing ready and he took fifteen minutes to say what he could have said in four words. Perhaps his forte is raising money. From an old lady who remembers better days..."

The four words: *I don't believe it?* He kept turning over letters.

From Judea: "Had a fine Christmas, thanks for the book on Iowa. I noticed it is 500,000 years old out there. Was that before Adam and Eve? Fred called up Maud's last night and the report is worse. The course of her illness will probably run as Ted's did. As for myself, don't know just what to say, am feeling better but some of the tests taken last week were not up to those a month ago. Hired a technician at the Home, he'll do the dirty work for Joe. Guess we have to acknowledge that age is creeping up. Had our first deep snow, nine to ten inches, very light and easy to handle. Sam."

Hurriedly, Charles turned to another.

From Seaburn: "Your letter was of great comfort to me and will be in the future when I have time to read it over and over again. I found her the morning of January 12th unconscious from a cerebral hemorrhage. It was a great shock since she had been so full of life...."

From Oklahoma: "Five years ago last night was my ordination service at Banner Avenue. I was just looking over the printed program and thinking of you. The half year I spent with you as a student minister was the grounding of any success I will . . ."

From New Haven: "December ninth fell on icy steps and cracked a vertebra. Have to wear a corset and stay flat on my back in bed. Things are going along nicely though we are having some time selling the old First Church building at Bellmont Square. The A.M.E. thinks we're rich and expects it half price. But we need the money to pay off our new parish house. It was a mess, tearing the old one down. Molton is friendly enough and if we can't have you, he seems like the right man for Banner and First. . . . Pete Allenby."

What had happened to the kitchen sinks and stoves he had labored to install in the old parish house?

From Judea: "I saw Sam yesterday and think he is responding to treatment. He should go home Wednesday but how well he will be is uncertain. I confess I am a bit pessimistic about his future. I am more optimistic about Maud's. But you know Maud! We are pretty well. Yours, Fred."

Had any of them really known Maud?

From Bellingburn: "I stopped in at Walter's drugstore in town today and Walter was thrilled with your little note. He talked about it for ten minutes. Sally and I are relieved we don't have to drive in all the time to superintend the Banner Avenue Sunday School this year, though we both miss Banner. The colored are coming into the church and that is hard for some of the old timers to swallow. I am finishing out my last six months as a deacon and you would have been shocked at the mutinous tone of the last meeting. We could have used a chat with you. . . . Junior Metcalf."

From Hartford: "Charlie, your name is the most widely pronounced here at the Connecticut Center for Congregationalism. . . ."

Then why couldn't you get me a job?

From San Francisco: "Your note on the upcoming 25th reunion was a dandy. You must be happy in your ministry in Des Moines. My regards to Bob. I'm doing an article on the toughness of the career of the assistantship, got any ideas? I am sorry to

hear that your sister Maud is ill. As ever, Barclay." He had pen-
ciled an additional note: "Charlie, I'm sorry to read in this morning's paper that your sister Maud has just passed away in Seattle."

News gets around on the West Coast.

From Judea: "Just to let you know that I finally got out of the
hospital—harder to get out of there than the State Prison and I
told them so. Started back to work three hours a day. A nice
turnout at the memorial service for Maud. The urn came airmail
from Seattle right on time, for once. I'm for earth burial myself.
Your boy Tommy was here and after he'd gone I found out that
his girl friend had been sitting out in the car the whole time.
Didn't get to look at her! But I did meet Hildegard's young
fellow, not bad. I knew what I was saying when I told you you'd
better celebrate your fiftieth birthday instead of your sixtieth,
didn't I? Anyway, we have had many happy family gatherings
and I expect to have some more left. Sam."

From Boston: "Dear Dad, Yes, I think I made the right choice
in coming to journalism school here in Boston. I'm sorry I could
not make it out there at Christmas but . . . Tom."

From Stratford: "Dear Charlie, I guess I can call you that now.
You were right in directing me here; it's a grand place to live,
Stratford. But more and more I am conscious of the incidental
and casual place Christ plays in the lives of the majority here. I
get that feeling whenever I try to preach something other than
the golden rule. T'ain't easy, as you know, to pump up a weekly
sermon that will both sear and comfort. By the way, Minnie
Favor, aged lady who used to be a telephone operator, told me I
was the only Congregational minister to call on her since Mr.
Minor. She was impressed; and so was I, to be in such good
company. Your friend up here among the encroaching padres,
Donald Hudson."

From Framingham: "Charlie, Old Man, Saturday twenty-five
men including yours truly met at Apple Hill and proceeded to
change the time-honored color scheme from a questionable
(1906?) yellow to a modern two-tone green in about six hours.
The new minister does not like green and said so, which makes
for the new paint's popularity! I'm enjoying it out here in the

Framingham countryside and do less and less parish work in Seaburn. . . . S. I. Galabian."

From Wilby: "Dear Daddy and Mother, I wanted to mail this letter from Connecticut when I was there at a Wesleyan weekend. But we stayed up to 4 a.m. every night and . . . Sara."

From Bellingburn: "I have to let you know that things look brighter this month at First and Banner. The Deacons are picking up, your last letter came at just the right time and helped us. Yes, Molton is a good preacher and most everyone likes his sermons. But I'd still vote for your Yankee delivery. I was saddened to read in yesterday's *Register* of the death of your brother Samuel Minor. . . . Junior Metcalf."

From Glasgow: "Dear Mr. Minor, I'm Marion, the Scottish girl who used to work at Mrs. Wilfred's on Bellevue Avenue and . . ."

From New Haven: "Dear Charles, Thanks for your note, it's good to get a vote of confidence. Of course, we do have our little difficulties. Most stem from rivalry between the new and old members of the board of Deacons. But the merger is a huge success. The two groups do begin to merge and distinctions do fade. . . . M. M. Molton."

From Stratford: "It's been a long time since I've heard from you, but there isn't a day goes by I don't think of you. Just yesterday I . . .

From Shiloh: "Do you plan to preach for us again at our anniversary this summer? I hope so. There are few like you, Arley, I am convinced. If unselfishness is the core of religion— and I believe it is—then your whole life expresses it and stands as a testimony to it. You are not a national great man, but you are a very humble person who . . ."

Charles shut the folder. He wouldn't write to Alicia today. It was time for lunch. He grabbed for his other papers and left, giving Lena a wave. He fell awkwardly into the car parked in the gigantic lot.

This afternoon he would call at enormous street addresses: Mrs. Alfred Andrews 14587 Pillsbury Avenue; Mrs. James Stricklan, 43089 Shore Road; Mr. and Mrs. Schubert Ogden, 11574

Grand Avenue. A man! Was he sick? Charles stuck the key into the ignition. His job definitely did not require all the talents of a man. He was almost fifty-two. He had gathered no moss. A second-rater. "Methodism means mission," he had said when speaking one Lenten Thursday at Des Moines Methodist, "and I have the feeling that your mission is to keep your best ministers for your own pulpits and send the second-raters like myself over to sister denominations." The congregation had laughed. Annah had not spoken all the way home.

He backed the car out of the lot. If he wanted the full ministry, who really stood in his way? The vanishing back of the ghost of that other son? Who had not turned his face toward Charles since the first few days in Des Moines? But the vow of obedience in Des Moines was killing him; he could see that in Annah. If he was not a saint, he could still be a soldier and fight a few more years. Tomorrow he would rework the last sentence of his report. Not out loud: Lena would hear him through the wall. "I must say that after my first months I have serious doubts as to whether an assistant man . . . ministry is the best medium to bring forth what little talent I do possess." The Pontiac was actually purring and he turned onto Pearl Parkway. "A man does his best work in a situation of natural ease and I suspect that . . ." Both he and Bobby would always be hired boys, but he did not have to remain the younger. He felt his rage subside; he could rely on himself. That much pride would not kill him.

He turned onto his own neat street with its five hundred modern houses. Somewhere behind him train tracks stretched eastward on a narrow bed toward Albany and, from there, south to Chester. Somewhere Fred waited for him in a Buick or a Chrysler or a Cadillac, at the end of a long red tongue of rug he had ridden via Fred's wired ticket. Oh thank you, Fred, for my first Pullman ride and on the occasion of my brother Samuel's death. You who knew the earth are covered with it, snow has fallen on your head. And Maud my sister lies in a glass case with an apple stuck in her throat. Are these the sleepers of the palace? Have the birds that were their selves taken flight? Resurrection body, is it all wings? Eyes? To know?

Would Jesus have come here? Sixteen hundred people had jammed the church for the Christmas Eve pageant. Three large identical post-Swedish kings had made their way down the aisle booming "We Three Kings of Orient Are." It was beautiful, but empty. Would the baby have been born here, would he have gotten up on the cross if he hadn't even hoped for a nod of approval? Just a gesture? Just something to say, I been watching you boy up there in Nazareth, Capernaum, the Wilderness, Caesarea. For I'm with you, yes, right out to the ends of the earth and that includes across the wide Missouri.

Sure he would! No crying he makes! You can never win against him. Charles laid his forehead on the steering wheel in his own driveway. Father in Heaven, do not strike me out now on the inspector's conveyor belt, a black, withered pea among green giants. Only give me the strength to continue without the nod. Give me the faith of the missionary looking down the barrel of a gun: "Shoot me and I shall soon be with God."

And brace up there. Charles took the key out of the ignition. He was just an early laborer who had set himself to pick grapes at the day wage. He should not be angry at the late laborers, who got equal pay. "You're all getting what you said you'd work for," the paymaster smugly pointed out. Irritating, brilliant. Charles opened the car door and walked along flagstones to the house and into the modern curved kitchen to find his lunch set out on the counter.

"Annah?" he called. Strange. A bad feeling. He ran upstairs.

She was lying on the bed under a quilt. Sleeping, ah. He pulled the quilt over her foot. She had fallen so he wouldn't have to. He turned toward the stairs. He had better get busy acclaiming life for her! First he would let her sleep while he ate. Then he would take her on his afternoon calls and for a ride along the river. He ran downstairs. She liked the largeness of the sky here and the moon's looking bigger. In twilight the low hills of the old road would be rounded by snow and look like home. He would drive her into town and buy her her favorite lobster dinner. Maybe the steakhouse downtown had flown some in from Maine? He felt he could keep running, right down the cellar stairs, but he came to a halt in front of the stove. He heated water for tea and leafed through the mail. Electric bill: these stoves sure cost a lot. Salary five thousand dollars, but you have to pay your own light and heat. Generate it, too.

Wilby College, Office of the President.

Sara? Trouble? What had she done? He reached for the letter.

"Dear Mr. Minor: It is my pleasure to convey to you the unanimous vote of the President and Fellows of Wilby College to confer upon you the honorary degree of Doctor of Divinity in recognition of your twenty-five years of pastoral service. Since honorary degrees cannot be awarded *in absentia*, the one condition is that we shall be honored by your presence at our Commencement ceremonies on Monday, June 14, 1954. We hope very much that you will find it possible to be with us and receive this honor. Sincerely yours. . . ."

"Annah!" he was running up the stairs. "It came!"

He sprinted toward the top.

"Annah! Oh thank you, Annah, for staying with me through Shiloh, Stratford, Seaburn, New Haven, and Des Moines." His heart was pounding as he crossed over into the bedroom, where she woke reluctantly.

XII

Until Lincoln's Birthday, 1963

A HORN HONKED and Annah raised her spade to wave. "It's Wilton and Doris Goode." Her voice carried across the wide lawn and Charles waved at the passing car, too. A convertible screeched at the Southlee intersection in front of the house. Boys, no doubt. It pulled out with a rush. It would probably come to another screeching stop a few miles to his left at the Judea intersection, near the house where his sister-in-law Catherine lay permanently in the downstairs bedroom. A few miles to his right stood his former Federated Church of Shiloh and the white house with the well where he and Annah had lived, where he and his mother had turned the horse on the Wednesday ride to Percyville. Like Prince, Charles was on the homestretch and he, too, had saved something for that final pull on his way home. Because now he ran for himself, or tried to, forgetting the face at the end of the race and the nod. He may have gotten to Southlee through Justine's influence in the church, but this time he trusted the people would accept him soon enough. Acclaim was not the point, it was what you did with their attention once you got it.

"I bet we'll have some of these blooming at a wedding one of these days." Annah patted down the earth over a sunken bulb, where she crouched near the house. Like most of the women here, she did not look as old as his mother had in her early fifties. She was happier now. When Wilton Goode's secretary left to have a baby, Annah was going to take her place at the pediatrics clinic. They had agreed on something of that nature before they left Des Moines.

"Lucy only came for dinner!" Charles had liked the girl whom Tom had brought up last Sunday from the city-room at the New Haven *Register*, where they both worked. Maybe they would get married; Justine's younger daughter Hildegard had married last summer. "You're late-bloomers, you Minors," the dean at Wilby had told Sara on her graduation day. But Sara, riding away from a boy she loved, had not cared.

"Won't it work out?" Charles had asked, remembering how Annah had failed to join him at Wilby.

"No."

"Why not play hard to get?"

"You're kidding." Sara twirled the tassel of her mortarboard around a dial on the dashboard. "Weren't you the one who always talked about the second mile in honesty? I love him. He doesn't love me."

Had he brought her to this? He did not remove the tassel.

"Well, they don't come up for two years!" Annah laughed and straightened up from covering bulbs to dig again.

Faith of the planter. His people came now only with their babies to be baptized or their children to be married, nothing more. The story was nothing to them. The Sabbath had petered out here, after all, and nobody had carried the old stories forward from one generation to the next. Now was not reaping, not here among Princess phones. It was not even sowing. First the soil must be turned again, prepared. He charged his new Southlee congregation to memorize sections of the Gospel and of Paul and he waited. The soil was prepared with death. "Oh Lord," Littlefield had written from White River Junction. "Comfort the afflicted and afflict the comfortable." It would be a long wait. For here there was no death, at least not on Saturday or Sunday, as those days were strictly reserved for recreation. If death should come, it would be apt to show up on a Tuesday night under cover of darkness, never while the children were awake. And when the new highway was finished things would get worse, with New Yorkers here among the already self-interested.

"There are good people in Elmsy, too," Charles reminded them from his eighteenth-century pulpit. "It's not enough to send our children to the dentist regularly; we have to train them in the real stuff of life: that there is suffering, that there is joy." Were they ready for his saints?

"There was once a man," he wished to begin, "whose four-year-old son was to have a tonsillectomy. 'Bye! Bye!,' the boy waved to his mother. 'Have the ice cream ready! I want chocolate!' The doctor picked up the boy and carried him in his long white robe down the corridor, waving." But they weren't ready. Who was ready for that?

"I made it for you," the boy's father had said, as he handed Charles the hand-carved cross, which he had carried everywhere since: hanging it beside his grid map in Des Moines, standing it on top of his file cabinet at Southlee. "See." He must bring it to the pulpit some day and set it up in the place of the gold one, but not yet.

Inside the house the phone rang. "I'll get it!" Annah called, dropping her trowel. "I have to wash my hands anyway."

Was it Sara? She had telephoned about this time last week to say she had found a job doing what she called paste-ups for a magazine and had seen Stevenson at a rally. A Democrat! Charles finished raking the last small pile of leaves and pushed them into the basket. It was getting dark. He carried the basket to the churchyard and added it to the others in the incinerator. Above him rose the steeple of Southlee Congregational, right over his shoulder. This was the first time they had lived so close to their church and, though he had been doubtful initially, he liked it now. At first he had worried that it stamped him as a preacher. Just last week he had felt happy when a young hitch-hiker had mistaken him for a businessman. Why should he have felt happy? Everyone should be able to see that everything had changed for him, that he had been with Jesus. And he should want them to see! But had Paul never been glad not to be recognized? In Antioch when he was tired? In Rome, frightened?

Returning from the incinerator, he noticed a narrow line rising smack across the center of his lawn. "Never goes away," his father had always said. "Can't get rid of a mole tunnel for seven generations." Charles was marked, for what?

Annah came back to the screen door and snapped on the kitchen light. The bugs gathered instantly on the outside of the screen.

"Who was it?" He walked toward the house.

"Margery, but please don't go over. She's afraid of Stan again."

"Then I have to go." He stopped and looked over the darkening lawn for left-out equipment.

"Arley, she thinks he's got a gun this time." She spoke quietly.

He picked up Annah's trowel and went back for his two rakes.

"I have to help Margery." He started toward the garage.

"Well, let me go with you, then," Annah said. "I'll run up and change."

"Okay," he called. "I'll put these things away and be right up." He carried the two rakes and the trowel, stopping to pick up a pail and a watering can whose handles he hooked over his arm. He walked toward the garage that must once have been a barn—old, sunken—and switched on its inside light.

He heard a sudden movement on the far wall and turned to see Stan shield his eyes with one hand from the light. In the other hand Stan held something dark. A gun?

"Stan, what are you doing?" Charles stopped midway between dropping the garden implements and clutching them to his chest. It was a gun.

"It's you!" Stan said, moving a bit to the side, his eyes adjusted to the light. "You made her turn against me!"

"No, I didn't, Stan," Charles said. "I'm trying to help make it better for both of you." He could smell the liquor that had enveloped Stan off and on for years.

"I'll kill you for it!" Stan's voice was hoarse.

"Kill me then," Charles said. Slow, steady, hearing his own voice at some distance from his head. "It's all right, Stan. What have I got to live for?" He stood, neither defended by the pail and the watering can nor freed from their encumbrance. It was as they had all said: there was no fear. Time stretched out elasticized and reverberating; he was volunteering. Nor was there any shot. Though later, when Charles was to remember the scene, he sometimes heard a rifle shot: he had, after all, never heard a pistol fired.

"Shit!" Stan spat on the floor. "Shit!" He scraped his spit into the floor like a cat.

There was the sound of the front door shutting in the distance.

"Arley?" The sound of Annah's voice calling over the dark lawn. Stan broke and ran behind the church and onto the back road. Charles heard a car motor start up from an idle: Stan had left it running. Charles put the garden tools in their appropriate places and walked around onto the grass. "Wait a minute, Annah," he called.

"Let's go inside for a minute." He put his arm around her and led her inside the screen door. He had to warn Margery by telephone. She must get away to her sister's immediately. Then he would call the doctor to help him find Stan. Would they need to involve the police? Possibly. It was, after all, an armed man they were after.

STAN HAD BEEN AT THE COUNTY HOSPITAL for months, starting in the "worst" building, where his wife was allowed to visit him once a month and his minister twice. Charles checked in first at the "best" building, where Winnie Baker was scheduled for the morning's midlife shock treatments, but she was already drugged. He continued on to the last lobby with Margery's brownies and his old copies of the *National Geographic*. With such, we ward off insanity.

"Good morning, Doctor Minor!" A gray-haired volunteer he did not fully recognize called out. He was well-known around the loony bin.

"Hello there!" He listened for intonations, looked for gestures of the hands that might bring back this woman, but he could not place her. He would ask about her at the desk coming out.

The box of brownies Margery had wanted him to deliver was slippery atop the *Geographic*s. Margery was good. Charles waited for the elevator. More and more it was the good things people did that stopped him in his tracks. The extra things—the second mile, with which he had started. The ten-year-old Hannon girl, with her earnest eyes assuring him that chlorophyll was more powerful than atomic fission. The Prentice boy's operation finished. "We didn't have to take out the eye." These fogged his throat more than their opposites. He had felt little watching the sheriff remove the stiffened body of the girl Jeannette from the car in her parents' garage. A month earlier Jeannette had answered his sermon's plea for a young person to pick up the cross and volunteer for foreign missions. "Sixty out of every thousand is American, but we have half the money. A hundred are Protestant, but four hundred and fifty are Communistic. Half the world can read, but two thirds is hungry. Who will go?" he had wound up rhetorically. "I come! I come!" Jeannette had come staggering up the aisle. Tranquilizers, old *National Geographics*, brownies: there were missions closer to home. He had not helped Jeannette at all; but you can't do everything.

The elevator door opened and Charles stepped out along the route to Stan's room. Empty. The bed rumpled. But standing on the window sill was Burt Storemont's wooden cross that Charles had brought to Stan several months back. For the first time since he had given it to Stan, it wasn't hidden away in a drawer. It stood on view, its sandpapered surface smooth and its stain deeply engrained. It announced: I am made on the occasion of the death of an only begotten son. Charles turned and left. Stan did not need him anymore.

"Stan's gone up to the gym," an orderly said.

You cannot help people by doing for them the things they can do themselves: courtesy A. Lincoln, country boy. In his Judea High valedictory, Charles had set Lincoln against Napoleon, bidding his classmates choose. He smiled at himself. So innocent! As if there were such a choice. Shall I be king of England? Or king of France? We do what we can in lesser and lesser circumstances. We go down the elevator.

"The woman with the braided gray hair, in a peach-colored uniform?"

"You must mean Trudy Grey. Yes, that's Trudy."

Trudy Bowen Grey from his Pilgrim Fellowship in Shiloh; her hope had been to become a nurse. Of course! Next time they would talk. We become volunteer aides. We go out to the parking lot.

The new lot at his church had cost four thousand dollars, just for tar! This was five or six times as big, but the insane are assembled by county. He climbed into his own new Ford, to which he had transferred Sara's graduation tassel. This was the first brand-new car he had ever been able to buy. He picked up his notebook to check his calls, typed out as Lena had done in Des Moines. But order was nothing new. He'd never, after all, driven willy-nilly from one part of town to the other. Lena's last letter: to know you is to know Jesus. Okay Lena, but you take it from there. She never would. Simply remaining unmarried did not make you a saint.

And Sara? Was she bound off on the hard road of the saints? She certainly found something wrong with all her suitors. Passing the county line, Charles decided to take the new highway home. It would be longer but this was the first time he'd been down here since the road opened. He ascended onto the wide new highway by a slow curve and found himself rolling along at sixty miles an hour in no time. The hills were beautiful. Truly, this was one of the most beautiful parts of the world. Maud herself had said so, and she had seen more of the world than the whole population of Judea and Southlee and Shiloh put together. Why had she been the one on whom the seed landed, who went out to the world? "Once a seed was cast onto a congregation of a solitary boy in a Scottish kirk and that boy went out to become a missionary whose name you . . ." No, Jeannette Peterson stumbling, foaming. Bitten by a mad dog, volunteering. Have to avoid bringing up that memory. Exit fifty-nine, is that where he should get out? No. Try sixty. "A certain man made a great supper and sent for his guests who one by one made excuses. He got angry and called in strangers and the poor to eat. We of this beautiful valley are so busy with the secular, we don't often answer the invitation to Christ's banquet. If we don't, his kingdom will be offered to the others: Porta Ricans, Negroes, folks in Elmsy."

Snow was gone from the hills and the branches of the trees on either side of the highway had that reddish color his father had considered peculiar to January thaw. The lay of the land was familiar, yet unfamiliar. He saw it for the first time from this angle, and it was changed in form and plane as land is in the paintings of those Frenchmen. His speed was part of it; there was no time to know Shiloh's fields individually before they were upon him in a string, eerie in being both known and unknown. This was not his own former foggy parish running south to north but a new land he cut across obliquely, suddenly finding spread about him on either side what looked like the hilltop of his Grandmother Percy's farm. Now he remembered what Fred had reported: "Lies right under exit sixty for Percyville. The structures are all obliterated, but the pastures recognizable." Or almost so. Charles signaled wildly and pulled to the right. Nobody behind him, road deserted. He descended carefully on his expensive tires and turned right and right again and then left onto the old road. All so odd. Such echoes. He found he hadn't been breathing regularly and he rolled down his window. The air fresh, comforting. He proceeded a few more yards, and yes. He knew where he was.

This was the corner of his grandmother's north pasture; a right angle of stone wall had been left standing. It ran a few yards either way before tumbling into piles of loose stones. An apple tree stood in the corner, cold, slender and small, as old people are—less than they once were. He parked the car and got out. "Over there." He imagined he spoke to a visitor whom he guided. "Those two, yes, those two elms, see them? They shaded the house. And there, that's the rock split by a tree. It shows you that you've got to keep on trying. Only the tree is gone now, see? And look, the house is plowed right over, as if it were never there, covered right over with dirt and grass as if the ground had been there from the beginning of time, creation grass, God-made grass. But such, such, my dear friend, is not the case." He searched the man-made hills for other traces that corresponded with his own inward landscape. But there was little—the general lay of the land only, particulars smoothed out by plastic surgery, as are the burned faces of war veterans. A car sped by overhead and whistled down the hillside to exit sixty-one. Charles walked hurriedly toward the familiar corner; old apples lay half pressed into the ground beneath the tree. He climbed over the stones and sank to his heels at the base of the tree and leaned his hand and then his face upon the stones.

The gun and the birds, the hired man and Fred never shooting again: the spirits of the field speaking one hot noon to his wild great-uncle Win: his mother reining in the horses and his grandmother making her slow way down the stairs: It's Phoebe. These presences he could understand, but not Simon's.

Why you, Simon? Tears came over his eyes as he pressed his cheek to the stones, no sobbing: he would not allow himself to sob. Esther's voice on the phone, speaking long-distance. Can you come to do the service? Thursday? Chicago. The long ride on the bus—only way he could afford to go—voices of the people around him and, to meet him, Esther with the children. The Negro cemetery on the poor side of town, he the only white, as Simon's rich employers had not seen fit to watch their steward into the earth. Esther, the children and himself. The caretaker of the Negro church and its minister to stand by, but Charles Arley Minor to give the words. The cold November day, with gusts of rain-forbidding wind—from where, the Great Lakes? The hillside bleak, the hole the color of all holes, the box going down into it. "Good land, boy; that's what the Lord made 'em for!" The smile on the dark lake and then good-bye.

The stones were wet with tears. The more he tried to wipe the tears from his face, the faster they came on. The others had laughed at him when he returned from Chicago. Catherine, Justine, Paul, Fred, Georgia, even Annah and Tom. Only Sara hadn't. At the Chicago Greyhound station he had lost the key to his suitcase and had been forced to arrive unshaven at Chester and still in his black suit. Annah had found him cradling a hand infected from a cut he'd gotten trying to bang open the lock at a rest stop in Cleveland.

Charles hunched in the corner of the wall as a car passed slowly on the old road. It was okay, he had not been seen weeping. He staunched the flow of tears with his shirtcuffs. He turned, still crouching, and, finding his eye drawn to a certain slant of the fields, he stood up and walked a few feet to his right. Yes, perfectly sighted, as in a rifle: the tree against which his great-uncle Win had sat and prophesied Charles's death come summer. It was, Charles reminded himself, Win who had died that terribly hot August when the war began.

SOUNDS OF HAMMERING DISTRACTED Charles from his memorandum: "If I get the promise of twelve of you, I'll arrange a breakfast for our thirtieth reunion from U. T. S. We can set our sights for coming years. We aren't through yet! Some of us have our best years in the future!" The hammering was too loud. Charles stood up from the modern chair and desk in the study of his brand new parish house. Going up in the third year of his Southlee ministry, this brick building was the first structure Charles had raised in Christendom. It was built not by volunteers but with time and a half for overtime. The once-in-a-century review of Protestantism in America had just listed M. M. Molton as Banner and First's minister of the century, because he had unified the two congregations and built a huge new parish house. No mention of Charles. And no doubt 2059's review would not find newsworthy his then one-hundred-year-old contribution at Southlee. Ah well, he had a new Persian rug left him by a parishioner, and his Ford.

"Hi Hank," he waved to the overtime plumber in the corridor. "How's Winnie?" Home from the county hospital long ago, but still teary.

"She's feeling a little better, Doc."

The folks who used to call him Rev now called him Doc.

"We got a letter from Maureen in Boston. She's living at the Y."

"A letter should help." Sara hadn't written in a month; she was drawing cartoons, last they had heard. Maureen and Sara were both girls from whom one expected mixed news. Charles walked over to the old church; it smelled of paper tired of being sung from, of worn velvet cushions containing the quiet during-sermon wind of young children, of summers long past. Its squared-off balconies hung quietly, no longer expecting to be vibrated by a shrill call to prayer and emptied forever of Negroes or of prisoners brought weekly from the county prison. Some prisoners had carved their names on the backs of pews; no free seating here, no wild-eyed Banner Avenue crusader, no Teds who lost their jobs because they had been born ahead of their time. Had he himself perhaps been born a bit behind his?

Lately he had trouble defending himself against his intense assistant minister, a former Jew that Yale Divinity sent him bi-weekly. Martin Hirsch did not believe that the Negroes could pull themselves up by their bootstraps. They needed Martin Hirsch and half of young America's time and money. Charles had allowed as how the boys in Seaburn's juvenile court had lacked an equal start, but did money help? Could you subtract courage from the formula?

"Doesn't welfare demoralize people?" he had wound up his objections as they sat in the old study behind the choir loft.

"Charlie, are you going to take dependent children off their milk allowance?" Martin sounded shocked, as he and all men his age usually did.

Had he grown old? Well, he could still give them Christ cruci-fied, and as for complaints, he would validate those only from any man who had exhausted that message. Such a man did not exist.

He liked Martin, though. He had trouble keeping his mind on Martin's heavy sermons delivered in a style old-fashioned enough to have become Yale's latest thing: delving into context, seeing the then and not the now. Whereas Charles at Union had learned to take the light of the Gospel and focus it on today's enduring fears: jealousy, aging, frustration. Not bad, ought to write it down.

Up past the pulpit and Charles crossed the choir loft into his vacated study, where he dragged out his screw-seated desk chair and sat down. His eye went automatically to the top of the battered file cabinet where he had once kept Burt's cross: Stan was moving up through the middle-behavior houses. After settling his gold watch with the long chain and the jackknife on the oak desk, he pulled a piece of stationery from a drawer and a ball-point pen from his pocket and wrote in small, careful letters that conveyed thoughts under control: *Aging.* He would be fifty-seven, qualified to talk. Where was the clipping about the woman doctor who learned to drive a car at seventy-five and slept out at Boulder Dam at eighty? *Keep growing; wear out, don't rust out.* He drew a careful line under the last phrase.

Justine: he had promised to stop by at half past two. Why had Paul called to invite him over when he knew he stopped by every day? "Let's have a talk before you go up." Had someone told Justine? Or would he be appointed this afternoon to do it? *Death,* he wrote. *King Philip of Macedon's slave instructed to shout outside his tent each morning, "Remember, King, thou must die!" Trust God, he will not annihilate the innermost being, resurrection body!* Charles's script grew larger and he provided an exuberant exclamation point.

The bells shook the wood of his study wall. Two o'clock, have to hurry. *Loneliness: Jesus abandoned.* The plumber Hank Baker and his wife Winnie lonely after the last child had left home. Abandoned lovers, unrequited love the great leveler. Annah, himself, Sara. *Loneliness of the ones who are different*—himself refusing alcohol and the eyes upon him. *Loneliness of the rusher-about* —Jane Wakefield, the young Ladies' Aid president always with people and never physically alone, had confessed to him that in the recesses of her heart there was a distinct void. That was himself, too; why call it Jane Wakefield?

The vibration in the wood again. Quarter after two. *Frustration.* He bore down on the ball point. *Thwarted people. Blocked hopes. Poisoned dreams. Once I lost a basketball captaincy and thought it was the end of me, but looking back, it was the keystone of my later accomplishments.* How much he still had to tell them! By the sufferings of others he had brought himself from the dungeon, if not to light, at least to where, standing, he could glimpse it. Now he would give it all back. *Sickness:* Justine. He folded the paper and put it in his pocket.

Outside, he dashed across the parking lot to his car and drove through the handsomest end of Southlee, turning onto a low road that led by the Goode place. His childhood tennis partner, Doris Cobb of Percyville, had married Dr. Wilton Goode of the Judea Goodes. Annah and he saw even more of the Goodes now that Annah was working for Wilton. They had been over there last Saturday night for Italian food. "Town is growing up too fast, Charlie," Wilton had said. "We've got to get some zoning through." The Goodes' children were all grown, too, except for the fourth, Jennifer, who seemed a straight-shooter like her mother. He waved at no one on the Goode lawn and pulled into the next circular drive. Paul motioned to him from the door and made the request Charles had suspected.

Justine lay in her neatly tucked sheets in a lovely old room between dormer windows, as a girl lies in an attic room the year before she marries, wondering.

"It's Charles, come in." Justine motioned him to sit in the visitor's chair by her bed. Her violet eyes seemed designed for her handsome head; a woman of grace and property.

"Any more news on the wedding?" Justine asked. "Tom getting cold feet yet?"

"No." Charles found it difficult to speak.

"By the way, tell Annah that we did find my French wedding veil upstairs and she's free to offer it to Lucy." Justine talked on about her favorite topic, weddings.

Who, indeed, would be left when Charles reached sixty? He tried to focus his attention on Justine's room but it was sprayed with cologne that brought back the lilac bush at the end of their long lawn where they had often hidden together. This was no time for memories. Still, what but memory can we call our own? Justine's wedding picture stood on the bureau watching Charles from another generation: she had blossomed, borne fruit, and now she withered. As the grass. Could he do it?

"Justine," he began. Help me, sister, for I bring you death.

"What is it, Charles?" She looked up sharply and the reading-glasses that hung from a gold chain upon her lace-covered breasts swung uneasily to one side.

"I have bad news." He did not sit on the guest chair, but remained standing between bureau and bed.

She gave him a long look; the violet eyes glimmered but her lips did not move.

"Nobody else could tell me?" She spoke huskily. "Is that it?"

Yes. He nodded wordlessly. He dared not open his lips to speak, for separated from each other he would not be able to control them.

"Well." She cleared her throat and sat back a bit. "How long?" Her hands were plump still, not at all the bony claws of their sister Elizabeth she used to imitate for him beneath the lilac bush.

"Months," he said, stretching it, his voice coming through only a narrow passage in his throat.

"Thank you, Arley." She smiled at him before her face stiffened.

"Very well, Charles," she resumed steadily. "I have two requests: please bring me the Kleenex"—she motioned to a box on the top of the bureau. "And then leave me alone." He laid his hand upon her hair—it felt soft—and pressed the Kleenex into her lap before he turned and left the room. He did not look back from the door but ran down the stairs to report to Paul on the terrace.

Papa would have been proud of her, as usual. He slowed as he crossed the long living room toward Paul. He saw Justine and Paul on their wedding day, tall, larger than life, dark-haired and pink-lipped, driving off together in the front seat of an open car, laughing, waving, calling good-bye, moving toward this moment and toward the next. Justine, you were so beautiful; he leaned toward the spectral bride, in veiled white, and reached out a hand. Paul stood to greet him and they clasped extended palms.

The dream of the swimmer seeing he is too far from shore, waving to her on the beach as she stands among the pebbles gazing at her feet. She is not watching him, not seeing the dazzling circles of light in the green waters off the shore, where he can no longer swim. He is suddenly pulled farther out into the darker waters, beyond the breakwater, as far even as the black broken trunks that lie beneath and the sky ready for rain. I'm here! Here! But she will not look up. The four-a.m. bells had awakened him.

All is well, he reiterated silently as he lay in a twin bed next to Annah in the bedroom of the seasoned, settling house. Justine was gone; only he was left, and Fred. "None of us alone can replace you," the letter yesterday from the minister of youth in Des Moines had begun. "But perhaps together we . . ." Reverend Bobby had left last month and the committee had wired Charles to come back as senior minister but it was too late, he had told them. Now that he was home. He kept his eyes on the dark-blue rectangle of window which the steeple almost filled. All is well, you are safe; but the dream of the water contained him for much of the day.

"How's sin doing, Father?" Tom asked at dinner. Was Lucy blushing? For the way a son addressed his father? Or was it the pink cheeks of pregnancy?

"Holding its own," he answered. He remembered standing, marrying them the day between Justine's death and her funeral. "Let's postpone it!" everyone said. "No," Charles insisted. "My sister always loved a good wedding." His son's face, like other sons', not yet settled, earnest, expectant; Lucy's a flower petaled in all that frothy veil. Not Justine's lace, fortunately. He would have found that impossible. After dinner he took them into the church to show them the mahogany Communion table Paul had given in memory of Justine.

"Your cousin Hildegard and her husband are moving in with your Uncle Paul in a few weeks," he said. "July, that's going to be a hot time to move."

Life swelled and flourished, was fruitful and multiplied itself, though tonight they gathered in the hand-carved pews for the ceremony of a young woman who went forth alone and not to marriage. The congregation fanned itself with paper calendars and waited for the threatening summer thunder to break and cool them. Sweat ran down Charles's back under the heavy black robe decorated on this special occasion with his doctorate's red hood. Indeed, all was well. Not much actually changed in the world, did it? Most of the Goodes and Minors stayed where they were. It was not all that important why people were the way they were, only that they were. Only that they managed in each generation to send forth one or two to take on the work of the called. He rose to speak.

"And the church inquired as to who among them would go forth to spread the good news and a strong, sure voice answered, saying: 'Here I am. Send me.' Jennifer Goode"—he nodded toward her as agreed—"will you come forward to the podium." Jennifer stood from the middle of the congregation and walked down the center aisle toward him; he remembered her mother's rocking walk on the tennis court. The girl climbed the steps up the podium and he left the pulpit to stand facing her.

"We invest you, Jennifer Goode, with our tidings to the people of Ghana. May you bring them the spirit of the risen Lord in the healing of your hands which are trained in the skills of modern medicine and in the healing of your heart which is reared in the faith that over us reigns one who gave his son that all the children of the world might live." He handed Jennifer the rose. She had freckles, just as her mother had had.

He raised his hand above her head in benediction.

"We thank the Lord that he has chosen to set among us one such as this young woman who answers the call to service, who speaks in a sure reply steadfastly and without tremble: 'Here I am. Send me. For I will go.'" They shook hands and Jennifer walked back to her seat within the congregation. How like a child she seemed, but she was as old as Justine had been as a bride, older than Mama.

IT WAS A WONDERFUL DAY. He was reprieved. Not just that it was Easter, Him up again, hope up again, no. Charles had changed his mind about announcing his retirement effective in one year.

"But you promised!" Annah had been piqued last night when, down to the wire, he had finally confessed.

"I can't do it." He watched as she stopped serving ice cream at the kitchen counter.

"So that's what you want? To run yourself into the grave?"

She set the two bowls down and the vertical lines between her eyebrows deepened.

"I wouldn't know what to do with myself if I retired." He poured chocolate sauce onto the ice cream.

"That's why I have been working and saving, Arley. So we could have a few years out of the church in our own house. You could learn to relax." She sat down on the stool across from him.

"I know." He spooned up the ice cream that he loved under almost all circumstances, even these. It wasn't the only reason she'd been working, either.

"Don't you ever want to get away from the church?" She didn't eat.

"No, I guess not," he said. "I lived in the harness, I can die in it." How could he leave the service of the one who had given him life?

"All right then, Arley." Annah gave up. "But next Easter after you turn sixty, will you announce it then?"

He nodded. He ate. Surely he would never be as old as sixty.

"Annah," he said. "Thank you."

But she was already changing the subject to the only one on which they could talk freely, the children. "Tom called again, he isn't sure they'll make it up to church tomorrow."

As Charles looked out upon his Easter congregation, he was pleased to see it spread through the sanctuary and up into both balconies. A year from now would he be standing here announcing retirement? And a year from then would he truly be gone? They would build a little house in Judea somewhere and clear out of Southlee to make room for the new pastor. If only Catherine hadn't gone and sold his father's farm to a developer, he would have built there. But they would find land somewhere, grandchildren would come to it.

If.

Tom and Lucy were not in the congregation. A miscarriage isn't easy the first time around. Not even for the would-be grandparents. Yesterday he had run into Wilton Goode in the shoestore buying a pair of those shiny black shoes little girls wear.

Wilton could afford one daughter a saint in Africa. He had three children married already. Charles longed to buy a pair of those shoes for a granddaughter of his own. But would he live long enough to do that? He was slowing down. Things were changing. How soon would Lucy dare to try again? How soon would Sara marry? Each man she brought home seemed wilder than the last. "But when she marries, what will we have to talk about?" Annah had said, jokingly. It wasn't so funny. Justine's older daughter had never married.

Martin Hirsch rose to read the Scriptures; it was his third and last year at seminary and Charles smiled to himself, remembering his mistake at trying to get Martin and Sara together at Christmas. The four of them in the small dining room among silverware from the people of Shiloh, plates from Seaburn and crystal from Stratford far, far away. In the hazy hills where I gave up my youth, Sara. Don't wait too long. Annah and himself, Sara and Martin Hirsch. It was all right. Yahweh, God, they were pretty close. More important, Martin had accepted Jesus and didn't drink. But he had succeeded in bringing the two young people together only to have it end in Sara's pitting the men against each other over the racial issue. Charles preferred it to her other cause. "Did you march for the amendment to let women vote, Mother? Well, was Grandma Minor a suffragette?" But alas, Martin had gone South to picket Woolworth's and Charles could not keep from saying it wasn't right for northerners to go a thousand miles away to mess in other peoples' property rights; a man worked a long time for a Woolworth franchise and one had to consider the owner's rights, too. "Why not do it in the north, if it has to be done that way?" he had added conciliatorily.

"It's only organized in the South and we need the pressure of numbers to start it." Martin had brought his own girl friend up the following week. At the side pulpit Martin now announced the Easter hymn, and at the main pulpit Charles stood to sing.

> *Christ the Lord is Risen to-day-ay*
> *Ah-ah-ah-ah-ah-lay-ee-loo-lee-yah.*

Odd, the vowels, first voiced of the newborn's sounds, as Ruth Linfield had told him; the infant born with the holy name within its throat. I am: ah, yah, I am.

The earth at Southlee Falls was softened and warmed by the late spring sun; light filtered through the leaves of its woods. Charles longed to stretch out on the ground close to the earth, as a woman preacher had done after her welcome to a Maine town: "Everyone they send us is worse than the last and now they've sent a woman." She had gone to the woods and lain down on the earth to sleep and be healed. She had woken with a leaf clutched in her hand. When Charles had told the story to Patty last fall on her first visit up from Yale Divinity as Southlee's new assistant minister, she had given him a funny look. It was too damp, anyway, to stretch out. And the pull of the earth was not the one he wished to answer.

Charles had walked here through fields from Justine's, getting directions from Hildegard when he stopped by the house, as he did almost daily.

"I used to go there Sundays as a boy," he explained to Hildegard, who stood at Justine's kitchen door as if she had always been the woman of that kitchen, holding the baby in her arms. Matthew Hathaway Stevens, a stranger by name, but his own great-nephew and born with a few strands of red hair. "So I only know how to get there from Judea." He laid his palm against the baby's sole.

One field out, under a dome of sky that circled to enclose him, he felt the other pull and nodded: "Soon." Shutting his eyes, he turned his face toward the sky. There seemed to be two suns behind his eyelids, eyes of heaven summoning him. "But not quite yet." Perhaps it was good he had never quite become a father to his people, else how rise? To whom join himself? In the second field he asked permission to trespass from a chunky Polish farmer in a checkered shirt. He made his way to an unfamiliar entrance through the woods of Southlee Falls. As soon as he entered the small stand of pine and fir, he was drawn inward by the sound of water in the cool darkness and easily reached the ravine with its sweet-smelling banks. Now he sat on a sun-dried rock.

Women crying. The woman preacher. Alicia Kincaid desolate long ago after a doctor said she would never bear a child. Maureen Baker home from Boston but not wanting to give her unborn child away. His own daughter-in-law Lucy tactlessly placed in the maternity wing after her second miscarriage. Perhaps he was a man who would never have a grandchild. Funny, he could almost feel their souls waiting to be released to flesh so they could be wrapped in white flannel and set in his arms. Hello, my boy! Hello, my girl! Grown a bit, they would sit on his knees and later walk beside him on these paths where he had rambled on Sabbath afternoons when the world stood still, when the beginning and the ending of it were bound silently in the minute, looking out.

Lately, he was not so much afraid to die as curious. Perhaps the face of God would appear, the old hope? Better than the old fear of no one watching. What fear had come back to his father in the downstairs bedroom: "Papa is blue." His father had gone manfully before him and Charles would go before his children, too. Except he wanted to see their children first and not leave Tom and Sara fatherless and childless at once. But here he was, turning on death again when, with the stream tinkling and swelling beside him, he should begin to hear the heartbeat of life.

"Arley! What's the matter? That isn't like you!" He remembered Annah leaning over the small table in the new skyroom of the Chester Hotel just before his sixtieth birthday party had begun.

"I'll wait for another Easter and announce an August retirement. It's breaking my promise again but it's only for six months. Half a year, Annah?" Fred and Georgia and Paul had come in then and interrupted the talk. Later, Annah had agreed. Then, since he had twice given round-ups of the Gospels in anticipation of leaving, he had nothing to preach on. So he had decided to spend the spring of his next-to-last year reporting from the world. He had already done the supermarket where young couples took their night out with the baby in a food cart. Did they make as regular Sunday trips to God for the living bread and the water of life? "You could preach on anything," his people said. "Report from the Dump: the body dies but . . ." No, today the report from Southlee Falls.

He listened to the birds by the rock above the falls, where an intractable Indian had warned against selling the land to an insistent Mr. Bullman. Then, intoning his own requiem, the Indian had jumped to his death. The falls did not look a big enough drop to kill a man. We can't all be Niagara. He could start it there.

Charles took off his shoes and socks, rolled up his trouser legs and walked carefully to the edge of the stream, where he stood in the cold water, kicking spray. If he were a political man like Wilton Goode, he would launch a fund to buy the falls for the town. But his territory was the spirit; he had no right to mess in his parishioners' pocketbooks. Far off he heard the noon whistle and then his own church bell. He stepped out of the water and put on his socks, his wet feet dampening them. Once he had been running somewhere and fallen in a brook and Mama had said . . . where had he been running?

He knew that around one more corner and he would understand. Resurrection body: like the kingdom of God, it was already within him, it needed only to be born. He could feel it. And though the presence of the spirit of Jesus had left him at Des Moines, that was only his way of saying Charles could climb alone. Gain strength to rise. Or perhaps he had gone on ahead again? It didn't matter. There was a joy Charles felt within that would be born. He did not want to hurry anymore, but only sit among sweet pines, breathe in. He did have to hurry, though, for Maureen Baker was coming down from Boston to thank them. Thank them? It was Maureen who had borne the child, only to give it away. "Dr. Minor," she had written last month, "they make us keep the baby three days to make sure we don't change our minds. He looks up at me so worshipfully, as if I were God, or something. He's so powerless and his fate is in my hands." Was there anything more difficult than that? God gave away his child, too, he had assured her. Maureen was bringing Annah a present, she had said over the telephone, a rug she had braided for them as she waited in the agency's home patiently spinning a life. We are the ones who should thank you, Maureen.

The ice storm had coated the branches and twigs and the light shattered itself in a thousand directions as Charles went out on his calls. Slippery. Sara driving up from New York with a friend; drive safely. Some nerve! "I sold a cartoon!" And it had turned out to be a scene of a family at the Thanksgiving table with nobody wearing any clothes except the turkey. What was funny about that? Let her get married and keep her ideas to herself. All her suitors had turned to drink. If only the new one wouldn't smell of it when he stepped through the door, that was all he cared about. Sara had too long reminded him of himself at Union, but he had settled down at twenty-seven. She was already twenty-eight and for a woman, that was old. So, Justine, I know how you felt about Martha.

But you ought to see your grandson! I go to see Hildegard's boy every day. He says Ma-ma. Well, once, last week, Hildegard claims. He only says aaaah to me. The Pilgrim Fellowship would be using Matthew tonight as the baby in the manger scene of their pageant. Charles had never before had a real baby in the pageant but it had been suggested by the Hannon girl, who was playing Mary and who happened to be Matthew's babysitter. Hildegard had decided her son wouldn't cry if he were given enough juice in a concealed bottle. All Matthew had to do was lie in some swaddling clothes in a make-believe manger. No crying he makes.

Charles drove down Willow Street past the new high-rise housing for which he had finally signed an open-housing petition several months ago. His name had been published, with the others who had signed, in the *Star*. It had taken him so long to make up his mind. A lifetime? But what if, instead of being lent a twenty-thousand dollar house in Southlee, he owned a fifty-thousand dollar one? Would he want a Negro on one side and a Porta Rican on the other? Risking a property-value drop of ten or twenty thousand dollars? Puerto, Sara was always correcting him. It was his first political act, but these were the last days; he could take a chance on apocalypse.

"I am through trying to fit Christianity into my native prejudice." He had kept his voice steady in the pulpit. "It is very simple. John told us that a light shines in the darkness. Do we shut out the blazing light of Him who came to break down walls? It was foolish to take so long debating. I am signing the petition. Will you?" He posted a copy in the vestibule but only two young people had added their names below his. Most of his congregation had given him clipped good mornings; they preferred "Report from the Supermarket."

At the foot of Willow Street, just before the old houses broke into a field of those slim, new ranches Annah liked so much, he found Margery's garage door open and her car gone. She was probably off collecting Stan. He had been allowed home at Thanksgiving, too, and would be released permanently this spring. Charles turned his Ford around in Margery's driveway and drove back up Willow, past the high-rise, which you could see was already one-quarter Porta Rican. Puerto. They wash their clothes against rocks in their bathtubs, Annah had heard at the clinic.

Tonight would be his last Christmas Eve in the pulpit; next August he must retire, and what church would want a guest next year on this big, this holy night? The candlelight was mellow after the brilliance of the ice storm; he didn't want to leave his people. The smell of pine was heavy and sweet, the carols soft and lulling, and his congregation swayed to the songs as all congregations did each Christmas Eve, waiting for peace. There must be four hundred people below him in the crowded church. He smiled at Annah, who had outdone her usual fine dinner in the parsonage. Sara's friend hadn't smelled of liquor, after all. They sat next to Tom and Lucy. The youngest Wakefield boy came forward to recite his piece.

> *In a manger, meek and mild*
> *There was*

The boy stopped, neither his blue blazer and his bow tie nor his short pants cuffed above the knee were sufficient to bring forth the lost verses.

He started again.

> *In a manger, meek and mild*
> *There was*

And again, the sudden stop. He rocked back and forth on highly polished shoes. Charles left his position behind the pulpit and went forward to the edge of the platform. He took hold of the boy's hand.

"Next year," Charles spoke to the congregation, "William will make his offering again. We thank him for what he has been able to give us tonight. The most treasured offerings are often those that are most difficult to part with." He squeezed the boy's hand and bent down to whisper in his ear: "Now go down the stairs to the left and tell your daddy that I for one was mighty proud of you tonight."

He returned to the pulpit; just one big night of walking back and forth, Sara would say. "Were I given a chance to come into the world again as a baby, I would hope that the grown, as well as the infant Christ, might be magnified in me, that the resurrection and the life be more than words—that I would not hug the shore but dare launch out. The Father dared, in sending us his only Son, and lost. And won. I dare you to take in that Son. For only he can do what we cannot do ourselves." He motioned to the Hannon girl to start the pageant and sat down in his chair behind the pulpit.

The music began and Matthew lay peacefully in his cardboard manger, though he was wide awake, sucking at a nipple that released apple juice to him. The manger walls were high and only Charles and the pageanters were privy to any view of the bottle. When the children began their movements on the podium, the baby looked restlessly from side to side and seemed to be listening to their bits of song.

Charles peered out into the vaulted box of the church, lit by banks of candles. Fire hazard? No, it had worked well in other years. Hildegard sat alerted in the front row, in case Matthew needed her. He didn't want to leave his people yet. The three teen-aged kings were coming down the aisle. He hadn't done quite all he'd meant to do. Matthew stirred in the manger and as Charles looked at him the baby gave his great-uncle a searching examination. Matthew did not look a bit like Justine, though Hildegard grew to resemble her more every day. The Hannon girl picked Matthew out of the manger, without his bottle, and carried him to Egypt. Charles turned to study Hildegard's face, which was visible just over the corner of the polished Communion table Paul had given for Justine. How Justine had wanted to see her grandchild! Open, open world, and let me go.

The Pilgrim Fellowship was crooning to a close; behind them, on a sheet hung against the pipes of the organ, fell the shadow of Mary holding the Baby and of Joseph leading a cardboard donkey out of Egypt. The peaked hills of Bethlehem rose behind them and, above all and taller than any of it, the cross.

In the Hannon girl's arms, Matthew began to wave at Charles and then called wildly, "Aaaaaaah." The congregation tensed, unsure of the correct response. Charles stood up from his pulpit chair and interrupted the Pilgrim Fellowship's slow fade-out by crossing the podium to take the baby from the girl, and then he indicated to the pageanters that they should file off a touch earlier than planned.

Matthew reached for Charles's glasses and the congregation took a nervous breath. The baby felt damp as Charles pressed him close to his black robes and walked to the front of the platform, smiling. The swaddling clothes were beginning to unwind, and when Charles swung the baby up in the air above his head the white cloth peeled off entirely, revealing a bright red velvet suit beneath.

"For God so loved the world," he said, holding the baby high enough so the whole congregation—as well as Justine, from where her spirit was ingrained in the Communion table—could see him, "He gave us all his child!" The congregation breathed out then and smiled at the baby. Charles swung Matthew down and motioned with a nod for Hildegard to come and collect him. "That we might," he continued from the pulpit, leaning out over it with his arms extended toward them, "have light, and hope, and life abundant and everlasting." Announcing the last hymn, he raised his arms and brought the congregation to its feet.

XIII

Founder's Day, 1967

RAIN LANDED ON THE WINDSHIELD in big introductory drops and Annah flipped on the wipers as Sara got settled in the front seat.

"When does it begin?" Sara asked, pulling the belt of her raincoat from where it had stuck in the door.

"Two-thirty," Annah answered, backing her Impala away from the train station. "We've got plenty of time. Look at that! He went right to sleep."

"Yes, as soon as you start the car." Sara sat back and resettled the baby at the same angle he had slept on the train from New York. "I may have to wait outside in the car, you know. Two-thirty is when he usually nurses."

"Outside?" Annah said. "I wonder if it's safe? You won't know the place. It's gone downhill."

They should see where she wheeled Josh in the city. She should see, her mother. Her father had been dead four years now. Dying in the same year as Kennedy. Sara saw it immediately, the huge metallic insect wheeling itself over the cut in the winter earth to deposit its long box. Sometimes she saw it unexpectedly at night when she shut her eyes.

"Who's giving these chairs, anyway?" Sara asked. Better to think of something else. Grandpa Minor had insisted her father take five plots in Judea Cemetery; not four but five, in case another child should be born. The readiness is all.

"Banner's deacons," Annah answered. "They've been remodeling the church or they would have dedicated the chairs in 'sixty-three."

Annah paused politely at a traffic light. "How's Michael?"
"He's worried about the war," Sara said.

"The war?" Annah drove hesitantly through the intersection.
"The one in Israel," Sara explained. "The Jews. The Arabs."
"Oh," Annah answered, carefully.

"Do you think Daddy would have wanted chairs?" Sara helped
her out.

"I hoped someone would give a college scholarship, something living," Annah replied. "But it's nice when people give
anything."

Twenty-pound chairs in memory of a man who hoped to fix
up New Haven by the spirit? Sara looked through a rain-spotted
window at the skyscraper mirage New Haven's mayor had sunk
in the city's freshened concrete. How to clean up Jerusalem?
With guns? Money? Itinerant reformers with their parables? You
never know just where the revolution's coming from. "How's
everything?" she asked her mother.

"All right," Annah said. "We've got trees growing on our
part of Willow Street, you'll see it all later. I get lonely around
suppertime but I still love my work at the clinic."

"That's good," Sara said. Her breathing had slowed to the speed
of Josh's, as if they were one body. If she stared out, the buildings
of the city might take on subtly different shapes and she would
have an idea for a cartoon. Probably not. Things did not come
to her lately as images, but only through the ears. She was already
listening to the fump, fump of the windshield wipers beating
one, two like a metronome. A simple rhythm, steady as a hymn's
and words to match it collected in her ears: *The rain keeps raining,*
fump, fump, *raining on and on.* Doggerel. That usually happened with windshield wipers.

"I just wish I could get his face out of my mind." Her mother
launched the latest chapter of the family liturgy.

The story of the face, Sara knew it almost word for word.
He died on Lincoln's Birthday. He was buried on Valentine's
Day. So formal, her brother Tom would say, so American. He
got out of bed at six a.m., Annah would continue, and he fell
over onto the floor, calling out something I didn't hear. His

fingers moved back and forth on the slanting floorboards. Thank you, Annah, he said, over and over after the doctor had brought his heartbeat back up and called an ambulance. Don't rush, the doctor said, drive over in your own car. He's all right now.

"I'll never forget that look." Annah waited at the next big intersection.

Died in the elevator, the story went on like a song. All alone except for the elevator operator. Your floor, sir? Sara added her own sinister details: the operator turning to find himself suddenly alone behind sliding doors. Sara wouldn't ask about the look. I can't tell you, Annah would say. Because you would never forget it. What could it be but fear? Dying alone with a vacant-faced stranger when you had expected light and transcendence, the shining face, the glorious presence of. Who was it? Whose face had her father run toward all his life, expecting to be greeted, raised up, held?

"That's why I stayed so long at the funeral parlor," Annah went on. "They had taken that look off his face."

"What kind of look was it?" As usual, Sara couldn't help herself.

"I can't tell you." Annah maneuvered onto an avenue. Rain flew at the windshield. "Because you would never forget it."

The song keeps singing, fump, fump, *when we sing the song.* Sara shifted slightly with the words that seemed to have their own will. The baby was warm against her thighs; she and the baby were melting back together. She glanced at the clock on the dashboard: quarter of two. He would wake soon. At the thought, two small circles of dampness appeared on her blouse.

"There it is!" Annah pointed down a leafy street to Banner and First's steeple, surprisingly near, and soon signaled to turn into a paved parking lot unfamiliar to Sara. "You can see the place has gone downhill," Annah assured her as she eased the Impala over a ridge in the tar.

Actually, things looked terrific. The steeple was freshly painted and though Sara missed the dark Gothic parish house, the new one was clean and modern. Would her father walk out its door? "Go and look at him in the funeral home," her mother had advised that other morning, after that other train ride. "Or you'll never believe he's dead. You'll keep expecting him to walk through the kitchen door." Josh opened his eyes and moved his hands toward Sara's face when Annah turned off the motor.

"Hi Josh!" Sara put both hands around his middle. "I'll have to get in the back to change him." She opened her door to step out. No trace of her father's footsteps on this new black tar. Maybe on the grass? She got in and shut the back door and unfolded a diaper. There had been blood on the blue plaid bathrobe that Annah had asked her to take to the cleaner's. "Here," Sara had handed it over the counter to the clerk, a big fellow, six feet tall. His shoulders had shaken as he picked up the bathrobe. "A fine man," he said, through the strain of controlling his voice. "The finest man I ever knew." Should this blood be washed, washed, washed away?

"Come on." Sara closed the pin and picked up Josh. "Let's look inside the church." She held the baby close and stepped out, pulling her raincoat around him. Annah followed her up the stairs of the portico and through the doors into the vestibule. It was too early, nobody there.

"I see the chairs up front," Annah said, her voice muffled as she peered around the black leather door into the sanctuary. "And I think I can see the bronze plaques on them where they put his name."

Sara could not look down the long aisle. Don't run inside the church, he had said almost thirty years before, you might bump into God. Living memorials were certainly better; chairs only confirmed a death. She found herself standing by the table where the guest book lay open and, shifting the baby against her hip, picked up a ball-point pen. *Sara Berger* she wrote as gracefully as she could. And under it *Joshua Charles Berger.* The Charles they would know. The Joshua was so he could blow down walls. He would have to. But her mother had already promised a six-pointed star on the Christmas tree and her in-laws had stopped saying *goy,* at least in Sara's presence.

Annah let go of the leather door and it swung out, expelling the odor of sealed interiors.

"Josh is going to have to eat." Sara wanted to run, just as she had at the funeral parlor, unable to touch the waxed hands or to shut her eyes against them.

"Mrs. Minor! Annah Minor!" A woman Sara recognized as Banner's organist from fifteen years back came through the front door and embraced her mother.

"And Sara, I believe?" The organist looked unsure. "Why look at you!" She gave a finger to Josh.

"Place has really gone downhill, hasn't it?" The organist spoke in collusion to Annah.

"Say," Sara interrupted. "I'd better take Josh out and nurse him. I'll come back in a little while and find you." She got out the front door and stood under the portico. The rain was coming down slanted as it had on the day she had helped Annah sort notes and cards: *the finest man; the best friend I ever had; where-ever he is, he's busy; he is waiting for us all.* The illustrated cards pegged out at a couple of crosses, a few sunsets with rainbows, half a dozen candles, and an overwhelming six hundred pictures of flowers. Mystery of the bud, mother and child, straight out of pre-copper Canaan! Was Christ still hanging on his cross, unnoticed? Someone should go and take the stiffened body down. A woman, that was one of the rare jobs open to ladies of the New Testament. No, tasteless to rehearse her own, her generation's, concerns here. Her father's was another time. His death in the elevator had gone unwitnessed, too, but his funeral had been a sell-out. Both balconies filled and latecomers seated in the parish house beneath loudspeakers. Bigger than Easter. How blasphemous he would find her.

Josh reached for the hair at her collar and when Sara turned to twist the strand from his fingers, her eyes focused on a hot-dog stand at the far edge of the church lawn. A black man was selling hot dogs. A black woman bought one for a black baby in a stroller. They were in Harlem.

We are overrun!

Have overcome!

She herself held the portico of the fort beneath the steeple: for in the last days blacks and women and the rest of the world's *thems* shall forward into the fray with their hot dogs and their babies. Already she stood behind white columns carrying a child of two tribes in her arms. How far would it go? What was the optimal *us*? She would debate complexities at the campfires outside the city when . . .

"Aah! Aah!" Josh's face reddened as he wailed.

Marvelous, the end of days, even though she was suddenly parted from it, hadn't the time. Parents can't afford the revolution. She dashed out from under the portico and ran through rain past a car coming into the parking lot. Opening the back door of the Impala, she laid Josh on the seat while she sat beside him to undo her blouse.

With her hands she gathered him to her breast where he quieted the instant he sucked. He stared up at her, his dark blue eyes wide and fixed on hers, pulling her in. I know who you are, he said, you're you. She stared back, her right eye becoming sun and left his moon forever. I am I, he said, don't let me go. Her face would lie behind his eyelids all his life; I'll never let you go. Another car circled to park nearby, its windshield wipers fluttering louder as it slowed. *The rain keeps raining, raining on and on.* Suck. Fump. *The song keeps singing when we sing the song.* Fump. Suck. *Your face my dear bespeaks enduring charms, as here I hold you in the everlasting arms.*

A Note on the Type

The text of this book was set on the Linotype in Janson, a recutting made directly from type cast from matrices long thought to have been made by the Dutchman Anton Janson, who was a practicing type founder in Leipzig during the years 1668–87. However, it has been conclusively demonstrated that these types are actually the work of Nicholas Kis (1650–1702), a Hungarian, who most probably learned his trade from the master Dutch type founder Dirk Voskens. The type is an excellent example of the influential and sturdy Dutch types that prevailed in England up to the time William Caslon developed his own incomparable designs from them.

This book was composed
by Maryland Linotype Composition Company, Inc.,
Baltimore, Maryland.
Printed and bound by American Book–Stratford Press,
Saddle Brook, New Jersey.
Typography and binding design by Virginia Tan